THE

MILLEN[illegible]

BY ROBERT JON

BOOK 2

ISBN-13: 978-1980869153

Contents

PROLOGUE

Today, Earth, abandoned and doomed, exists as ice and in small quantities as vapour in the atmosphere and occasionally as low-volume liquid brines in shallow soil. The only place where water ice is visible at the surface is in the north polar ice cap. Abundant water ice is also present beneath the permanent carbon dioxide ice cap in the south pole and the shallow subsurface of more temperate latitudes. The global average temperature is (-63 °C; -82 °F); leading to either rapid evaporation (sublimation) or fast freezing. Earth lacks a thick atmosphere, ozone layer, and magnetic field, allowing solar and cosmic radiation to strike the surface unimpeded. The damaging effects of ionising radiation on the cellular structure inhibit life above ground.

Since man could not sustain long space flights, the new world council decided that space travel would be by robotic machines only carrying the total healthy DNA and embryos of all life forms on planet earth. They programmed humanoids to a level that they had reached. Civilisation could start at any objective they desired and initiate intelligence at any point. The remaining population, lived in new Beijing located in what was once called, Tibet and constructed beneath the ground in the lesser Himalayas where on borrowed time expected to be extinct within the next century.

The only living homo-sapiens to survive were two children: Zheng a boy of ten years, and a girl Biyu of fourteen. Both smuggled aboard the mothership Apolo-Alpha, cryogenically preserved for 100 years, destined for the Stellar solar system *Planet-E*, some 40 light-years from planet earth. For the past twenty years, they have survived and lived amongst a populated planet of cognitively mapped humans cultivated in a laboratory to habitat a world commencing in 323 BC.

Our hero and heroine have now transported to a new planet in the same solar system taking with them their family. Nobody is aware that the humanoids and robots control life and that space travel exists, except for Zheng and Biyu. The humanoids have mastered cognitive mapping and can set the scene for any condition selected, populated with life by the humanoids for the past 50 years.

Book 2 starts were Book 1 ends. Zheng and Biyu arrive at a new planet with their family and friends that have had their minds wiped clean of their previous life, and it now begins in an entirely new environment.

INTRODUCTION

Planet-F approximately 1.3 million Km from *Planet-E* and 15% more significant in diameter has two polar caps and three continents and several smaller islands each separated by an ocean. The humanoids developing both planets set the era approximately 300 hundred years apart. *Planet-F* set in an age of 6BC, whereas Plant-E set at 323BC The concept to monitor each habitable Planet separately to determine how to proceed, inhabiting future worlds; setting the optimum period to start.

Our hero and heroine, Zheng and Biyu could move between planets, but unbeknown to them the humanoids could clone in the likeness and not of 5th-millennium genetic coding where they could produce a pure offspring. The humanoids had no scruples or remorse about removing or eliminating a clone; erasing memory, changing facial appearance or just shelving it in the laboratory for future use.

On *Planet-F* the Roman empire occupies one main continent with Rome situated on the east coastline. The Roman empire identical as it was in the 1st century on Planet Earth, Augustus is Emperor of Rome. He has restored the free Republic's outer façade, with governmental power vested in the Roman Senate, the executive magistrates, and the legislative assemblies.

Zheng and his family will reside in a newly built villa in Velletri's eight leagues from Rome. The estate is vast; space shuttles land under cover of darkness, Zheng and Biyu watch in awe-inspiring as the robots go about their business to set up to occupy and place the people and children in their respective areas.

Zheng a very wealthy Roman citizen and a very successful businessman have just returned from the far east acquiring a fortune and many wives, namely:—Biyu, Nui, Chen, Feiyan, and Yi, which all have given birth to his children. His newly appointed staff occupied surrounding farmland, and smallholdings are appointed guardians and parents of the 100 children. The robots used Zheng's semen to inseminate many 4th Millenium women on *Planet-E*. The majority of Zheng's servants are unknown to him except Chu Yun and his wife, Guo, and her two little girls Bao and Bao-Yu.

Zheng, a breeder and owner of the most beautiful horses, train gladiators for Rome's circus arena. Pi and Zeta, his loyal robots reside full-time at the villa and become formidable gladiators; eventually becoming the best Rome has ever seen.

For the first time, Zheng and Biju see how the humanoids and robots can set the stage and start the actors. Rome itself has been thriving for some time, and even Velletri occupied, and quite a thriving town welcome the new arrivals and the additional wealth it will bring to the area

CHAPTER 1

Suddenly Life Begins

Suddenly life begins as Zheng first hears the sound of children crying, horses snorting in the stables, cows mooing in the fields and hens clucking in the yard. A member of the staff walks by and touches his forehead with his knuckle and acknowledges the evening and Zheng somehow knew his name as he responded good night even though he had never seen him before. He stood in the middle of the courtyard silent perceiving one going about their business, settling and occupying the dwelling as the day drew to a close as stars appeared in the night sky as he watched the two space shuttles disappear over the horizon. Pi and Zeta approached, took Zheng's arm to show him his new residence. Biyu animated by everything never had so much attention paid to her like a bath was prepared, clothes laid out on a couch and fruit stacked hanging over plates. The children each had several nannies, and the panoramic views from the windows somehow reminded Biyu of the holographic image she used to screen in her quarters on the walls on Planet Earth, except this time it was real. She knew she had to share Zheng, but no longer had feelings of jealousy; she accepted all had to live together in harmony. Not anybody knew of their previous life in Changzhou; admit that they were Zheng's property which had either married them or acquired them somewhere in the far east.

Five years had passed, and by now, Zheng was a well-known citizen in Rome and had a compelling voice and ear of the Roman Senate and council. His champion gladiators, Pi and Zeta, were under defeated heroes of the Roman Arena loved by all and followed by many. He introduced gladiators who fought from chariots and on horseback much to the audience's delight and thrill.

Zheng was accepted and regarded by the citizens of Velletri as an Asian person by birth; although now as a Roman Citizen allowed him to have a harem at the envy of all Roman men who by law could only have one wife. They gave him the privilege of being part of the Arena; his audience loved him for putting on the best shows of entertainment. His champions gladiators the best in the field showed mercy sparing the life of a defeated gladiator, satisfied Augusta's ban of *sine missione* (without remission from the sentence of death). Gladiator games offered Zheng extravagantly valuable but current self-promotion opportunities and gave his clients and potential voters exciting entertainment at little or no cost to themselves. As a trainer and owner, gladiators became big business for Zheng. A politically ambitious private citizen seeking power would pay a fortune to drum up votes with the mere promise of an excellent show. But the most lavish of all was paid for by Augustus himself. Zheng even offered to the poor and non-citizens, enrollment in his gladiator school providing a trade, regular food, housing of sorts and a fighting chance of fame and fortune. Zheng to impress Augustus allowed Biyu regarded as his first wife to enter the Arena dressed and disguised as a male gladiator fighting from a chariot only to reveal herself with breasts exposed when successfully disarming her opponent the delight of the spectators. Biyu was the first female gladiator which encouraged many women to train as fighters. She became famous and idealised by many poor women, especially those born into slavery. The robots, Pi and Zeta, regardless of being a machine, offered spectators martial arts they had never seen before and inspired admiration and widespread acclaim that their value as entertainers commemorated in precious and commonplace icons throughout the Roman world. As time wore on Augustus so impressed with Zheng's schooling and training enrolled his elite military and his two stepsons Tiberius and Nero Claudius Drusus on the so-called new martial art techniques. Livia, Augustus's wife and mother of Tiberius and Drusus would attend the classes and watch her sons trained. And curious about Zhengs wife Biyu that she became a close companion and sometimes employed her as a personal bodyguard when Livia attended any public appearance. Zheng and Biyu become very settled in their new environment; and although vivid memories of their past sometimes would haunt them, they become more and more relaxed as time went by and enjoyed life with their children and surroundings. Those who had accompanied them from *Planet-E* had no recognition of their previous experience and fitted well into the Roman way of life.

CHAPTER 2

The day of fear.

The day Biyu and Zheng dreaded, had arrived; Pusa in person came, to obtain eggs from the young girls that had come of age and the boys Ju, Jizi and Guang that could produce the human sperm cell. She looked elegant, and somehow even younger, with an appearance of a Roman Empress dressed in a silk gown walked directly to were Tiberius and his brother Drusus were being trained. They immediately stopped and stood in wonder of such beauty as she spoke, "Sorry to interrupt, but I have important matters to discuss with my gladiators, they will be back very shortly;" As she hastily left followed by the robots, Pi and Zeta.

Tiberius and Drusus stood in silence, glanced towards their mother Livia who had been watching the bout speak with such a countenance of annoyance. "Who the hell was that?"

Fuming and angry that such a person could walk up to her sons without any formal introduction; stop their training and take the instructors away that she had paid for, immediately required an answer and sought to find either Zheng or Biyu for an explanation. As she hurried across the courtyard, she saw the tail end of the tutors turn into the quadrangle; approached to overhear a woman speak, and caught a glimpse of Biyu as the wind blew her silk robe from behind a pillar to realise all were standing behind it. Livia retook a step; quietly listened hidden behind a nearby wall.

"I shall come once a month and remove the ovaries from the girls during their cycle period. At the same time, sedated the boy's sperm cell extracted; the procedure will last no longer than ten minutes, no harm will come to them, and they will have no recollection of what happened." Said Pusa as she turned to Biyu and added: "We shall start with your children first this evening; the microchips have notified us that the menstrual cycles have begun."

Livia, not understanding a word of the conversation hurried back to her two sons waiting patiently with chariots and horses standing by for her to return to Rome. As she entered her carriage, Zheng came running across the courtyard just in time to halt them leaving:—"I am so sorry for that—she didn't realise—she thought Tiberius and Drusus were trained gladiators for the Arena."

"Well! He's he next Emperor; and that woman, whoever she is, believes my son is a gladiator?—Who is that woman anyway?—I have never seen her before and what influence does she have over you to stop everything just like that!" Said Livia in an outraged voice, as she paused and continued. "So, who is she anyway?"

"She's from the Far East—I'm negotiating with her a new breed of horses and gladiators." Said Zheng in a very apologetic voice.

"She doesn't look oriental and a horse breeder to me?—What's her name anyway?"

"Guanyin Pusa—commonly known as Pusa."

"That's a strange name?—Isn't that the name of some Eastern Goddess?" Said, Livia, as she shouted out to Tiberius "Come on let's get out of here back to Rome!"

Livia sat back in the carriage, wondering what the hell was the conversation about the children; she did not understand. Thinking to herself that Zheng acted very strange indeed and could he possibly be conspiring against her husband, Augustus, and planning something with the Far Eastern provinces through this woman Pusa.

"Mother, I have just realised that I promised to see Antonia (Antonia Minor is a cousin) and as we are nearby I shall leave you in the safe hands of Tiberius." Said Drusus as he leaned across from his horse towards the carriage.

Livia enthusiastic had been trying for some time for Drusus to start a relationship with Augustus's niece Antonia Minor, so she had no objection as she replied. "Okay, take care. I will see you back at the palace."

As he pulled on the reins, Drusus turned, heeled his horse and galloped back to Zheng's villa hoping to catch a glimpse once more of Pusa. Introduce himself as Augustus's son that would impress any woman as he had high expectations of seducing her that night. He arrived at the courtyard with his horse steaming wet as the stable lads held its reins tight to calm the horse from its physical exertion as he dismounted and run shouting out Zheng's name. Zheng could hear the noise and confusion as he approached "Where is she?—you must introduce me to her!—Where is she?" Shouted Drusus as he turned and looked in every direction.

"Where's who?." Said Zheng not expecting such an excited and loud voice from Drusus.

"Pusa?—that's who!"

"Oh!—I see. Okay, Pusa's resting at the moment—let's take some refreshments and wash this dust and dirt from your body, and I will fetch her to you." Said Zheng knowing full well what Drusus's intention was like all great Romans *that he could take anything he wanted except this time wished he hadn't* thought Zheng.

Drusus laid stretched out in a warm bath pampered by two lovely maidens as they fed him fruit and wine as he relaxed and observed the exotic freesias and statues that surrounded the pool. Became excited at just the thought of his intentions to seduce Pusa. His penis rose to become fully erected; pushed the maidens away as they tried to caress him as he lay in the pool with his legs buoyant resting his arms. His erection surfaced to show Pusa as she entered the area; without saying a word took off her robe slid into the basin held his penis and quickly without uttering a word snaked her body over his and inserted into her vagina. Astonished by Pusa's unexpected reaction, Drusus tried to speak as she pushed her tongue down his throat. She moved on top of him and slithered over his wet body like a serpent in the water wriggling as she bit his neck ear and earlobe until she felt his orgasm, lifted her head and spoke. "Are we satisfied now?" in a sarcastic voice.

In a state of shock not expecting such a reaction from Pusa continued to lay there in the pool with a limp penis as he watched her slowly climb out with the water running down such a beautiful curved body across firm breasts, and such enticing protruding nipples. Pusa's body: the shape of Venus, not a mark, scratch or line, could only be described as the perfect female body. The maidens held a robe and wrapped it around Pusa's body her long blonde hair fell over her shoulder and down her back, as Drusus stared at the outline of the vagina surrounded by her blonde pubic hairs as she faced him. "Well, are you going just to stare, or stay there, or not?"

Drusus still amazed by such a beautiful woman who acted as if she had no scruples, but he had so many challenging questions like "Who are you?—Where have you been all this time?—How come Zheng never mentioned you to me?"

But, unbeknown to Drusus, Pusa had microchipped, this time around, all compelling characters, so as not to make the same mistake she had created on *Planet-E* and knew that Drusus had returned to the villa with one objective; to bed her. She knew precisely his thoughts and the questions that had sprung to his mind as she spoke:

"So I expect you are wondering how come we have never met?"

Before Pusa could continue, Drusus took the rest of her words and continued:

"Yes exactly—how come Zheng has never mentioned you to me?"

"Hmm, could it be that I am his lover too?—And if so—why should he want to share me with you?"

Drusus facial expression of rejection replied; "so you're his lover too?"

"Well, I'm not.— Zheng has too many wives for my liking." Said Pusa as she fastened her robe tightly across her body to cover her lower parts and thighs to prevent Drusus steady glare.

Touching her shoulder as she turned to walk away, uttered, "Then are you betrothed to another?"

"No, you are my first." She said as she kissed him on the cheek and walked towards her quarters, knowing her devious plan had worked to manipulate Drusus for an invite to meet his father, Augustus, and other family members.

Knowing that was a lie, what he had just experienced; this was not a woman of high ethical standing, but a loose woman of low moral standards, when he turned and replied with such a humble voice "When can I see you again?"

"I shall be in the amphitheatre this coming weekend tournament with my Gladiators." As she waved a hand to say farewell, blew a kiss and disappeared down the hallway.

Drusus stood there in silence, still stunned at what had just happened, being dried, pampered and dressed as Zheng approached.

"Sorry to keep you waiting did you see Pusa?" Said Zheng knowing full well what had just happened as Drusus smiled and patted him on the shoulder and replied.

"Yes, I have spoken to Pusa and may I add where have you been hiding that beauty—you rascal you—keeping her to yourself a!"

"I can assure you it's purely business. I have had enough on my plate without adding more." Said, Zheng, as he continued "She will be at the Arena this coming weekend if you wish to catch up with her," as Drusus hastily interrupted: "Yes, I know, I shall be there and thank you, my friend, for your hospitality. May I add a most enjoyable day, and I wish you farewell and success this weekend in the circus!"

Drusus mounted his groomed, fed and a well-rested horse for the ride to Rome as he gently pulled the reins and turned and cantered out through the main gates, just as Biyu approached Zheng to ask, "Who was that?"

"Just Drusus—he is now a disciple of Pusa!" Said, Zheng, with a wink and a smile at Biyu.

Biyu didn't need any further explanation; she realised not another male captured under Pusa's wings as she said what she had come to tell Zheng. " The robots had finished with the children. All were now sleeping, and the eggs and sperm tonight took to the polar cap." She continued. "Pi and Zeta would travel directly to the amphitheatre late Friday night."

That Friday was a big day as the entourage left Zheng's villa, including Pusa to travel to Rome for the big event of the year. Pi and Zeta, the robots, champions of the Arena, considered the tournament's main attraction and activity wouldn't arrive until much later. The Sacred Road, lined with people hoping to get a glimpse of the show's stars, referred to as 'Pizeta' by the crowd as they passed the Capitoline Hill, through some of the most important religious sites of the Forum, where the street widens to the Colosseum. As they approached, they could hear the sounds of horns and trumpets as the people crowded and shouted so loudly that even the horns' sounds muted. Zheng could listen to the chants for 'Pizeta' as he yelled back, "They arrive late tonight!" To no avail.

The procession entered the Colosseum. Drusus was waiting to welcome Zheng and his party, but mainly to invite him and his wife and Pusa to a banquet tonight in honour of the weekend games. He would personally escort them and introduce them to his Father Augustus. Zheng apologised that his champions, the event's main attraction, would not arrive until much later. Drusus although accepted the apology really couldn't care less since his eyes could not help but stare continually towards Pusa who looked more radiant than ever showing more than usual cleavage.

Drusus arrived that evening, dressed in a cloak of purple and gold. He led and held the hand of Pusa, covered in a rare and luxury cloth, with a beautiful sheen, sea silk robe of silk and cotton, loosely caught in the middle, with just a gold clasp, showing her cleavage and one thigh of her leg, as she entered into the turreted chariot. Zheng and Biyu followed behind him in another chariot. Biyu dressed in a highly decorative, costly fabric with shades of yellow and gold lace. Zheng, wore a toga a white woollen cloth draped over the shoulder and around the body over a plain white linen tunic edged with gold.

Augustus served an excellent table,—a very decent Campanian wine before the meal, and a good Falernian afterwards. The meal was neither ostentatiously elaborate nor affectedly unaffected: oysters, eggs, and small onions to begin; roast kid, broiled chicken, grilled sea bream; and various fresh fruits. Augustus proposed a toast to the games after the meal, "But," he said, and glanced, smiling, at his audience. "We must honour the Muses[1] to this extent; we must not allow them spoiled by any mention of politics. It is a subject that might embarrass us all." There was generally, a nervous, laughter; he suddenly realised how many enemies, past and potential, were in the room.

The evening turned out to be a literary evening, and it soon became apparent that Livia was really behind it all, and Augustus was, as it were, the pseudo-host. Livia had used the occasion to honour Drusus's half-brother Gaius Asinius Pollio (referred to as Pollio) that would read poetry from the late Publius Vergilius Maro usually called Virgil or Vergil, ranked as one of Rome's greatest poets. Augustus was in excellent spirits; almost talkative, despite his first wife Scribonia's usual long face. Close to her sat his daughter Julia, recently married to Tiberius her step-brother, who sat next to his father, Augustus. Tiberius had a low opinion of Julia, after rumours and accusations circulated of adultery and treason and decided to show his dissatisfaction by ignoring her. Livia's son Drusus insisted upon playing the wine master's part and mixed the wine much more strongly than usual so that most were already intoxicated before the first course arrived. Biyu sat at the other table alongside Scribonia, and her daughter Julia and Augustus's niece Antonia Minor could not avoid glancing at Pusa with envy ignoring the gossiping

[1] The Muses are the inspirational goddesses of literature, science, and the arts in Greek mythology. They were considered the source of the knowledge embodied in the poetry, lyric songs, and myths that were related orally for centuries in these ancient cultures. They were later adopted by the Romans as a part of their pantheon

surrounding her. Pollio, being the guest of honour, began with the so-called"mini-Aeneid" of Virgil touched on the so-called "Messianic" "which interpreted the birth of a boy ushering in a golden age as a son of a Judaea God." He added, which much to his surprise caught the attention of everybody in the banquet room. He continued to say that "Virgil had foreseen such an event, and may I add this is happening right now." He paused, cleared his throat as he turned to Tiberius sitting on the other side of his father Augustus and said. "Pontius Pilot, the Roman governor of Judaea province which you appointed, has reported such a man named Jesus of Nazareth." He turned back to the audience and continued with the Aeneid Eclogues number four.

Zheng on hearing these words bent across to Pusa and whispered in her ear. "Don't tell me you have created Jesus of Nazareth?"

Pusa turned around with her robotic look that only Zheng could know and understand that facial expression of a nonchalant spoke. "I know nothing of such an event, and we do not intend bringing any form of superstitious religion to this or any other planet." She said in a hushed commanding voice since she now noticed Drusus observing their conversation uncommonly carefully.

Zheng looked across at Drusus to see his anguish as he said: "I'm just explaining who Virgil was." He turned back to Pusa and questioned: "If you didn't! Who did then?"

"I don't know, but I'm going to find out and put a stop to it before it gets out of hand, we don't want a bunch of religious freaks amongst our mists."

With an apologetic bow to Augustus, he spoke of the library established in Rome as if it were an essential quality of the mind. He concluded that the Muse of Memory presided over all the others in a beneficent reign.

"It was all rather dull, I fear." Said, Drusus, reclining with Pusa now seated beside him in the torchlight, seemed pleased; it was his animation and happiness that made possible what otherwise would have been impossible.

Suddenly, a tumultuous noise of trumpets and horns heard drifting up towards them from the Colosseum and jubilation of shouts and screams as Pusa turned to her audience "Ah! My gladiators have arrived." She said as she paused and corrected herself "Of course Zheng's gladiator's Pi and Zeta."

Like every significant event, the fighters also gave a banquet the night before. An opportunity to order their personal and private affairs very similar to a ceremonial, "last meal". Including those to die; those who would have at least a slim chance in the Arena the following day.

At this point, Zheng standing alongside thanked Drusus for an enjoyable evening but had to leave to ensure that all was is in place for tomorrow's games as Drusus pulled Pusa to one side and whispered in her ear.

"Are you mine? I know that you are with me, but when you are so far away—where is your touch, that tells me more than I have known before? Does my unhappiness please you? I hope it does. Lovers are cruel; I would almost be happy if I could know that you are as unhappy as I am. Tell me that you are unhappy, so that I may have some comfort."

Pusa just smiled and replied, "See you tomorrow" kissed him on the cheek and left.

Pusa never introduced to Augustus or any of his family since Livia had already spread a malicious rumour that Drusus had invited a prostitute and that Biyu was no more than a madam supplying concubines for her so-called husband, Zheng. Livia was livid that Augustus, through a request from Drusus, had agreed that invited to sit with them in their private box tomorrow.

The brightness of the morning was magical, after such a memorable night when the sun at dawn gives more heat. When everything shines so brightly, in the rare pure atmosphere when the lungs are strengthened and refreshed by inhaling the aromatic fresh air, in the middle of the Arena Zheng stood and suddenly overcome as he was about to witness a slaughter of innocent people. Zheng knew that Pi and Zeta would somehow be able to simulate the massacre as long as the defeated gladiator lay still and the crowd didn't shout for his head even though Augustus had decreed that all gladiators should show mercy. But for those already condemned to death which he would not play a part in would, however, be slain to death either by vicious animals or made a mockery by less skilled gladiators. Usually, Zheng would be below with the gladiators away from the massacre, but today he had to sit in the Emperor's box.

As the procession entered the Arena, initiated the start of the games. Led by the lictors who bore the fasces that signified the magistrate power over life and death, were followed by a small band of trumpeters playing a fanfare. Images of the gods carried in to witness the proceedings, followed by a scribe to record the outcome, and a man carrying the palm branch used to honour victors. And then the procession made its way to the Emperor's box. Iullus Antonius halted, saluted the Emperor, and gave him the games in his birthday's dedication. Iullus an extraordinarily handsome man—his muscular arms brown from the sun, his face dark and slightly thick, with white teeth and curling black hair, resembled his father, Mark Antony though less inclined to fat.

The games began with beast hunts and animal fighters, which Augustus didn't like and always excused himself for some refreshments. And so the afternoon went. Servants came with more food and wine, and with damp towels so that the dust wiped from sweating faces. Next came the condemned criminals which of variable content involved executions of gladiators and slaves some doomed to be subjects of fatal re-enactments, based on Greek or Roman Myths. Some fighters were involved in the killing. But Pi and Zeta excused since they preferred the dignity of an even contest. Then came the comedy fights which in some cases ended up lethal. This time, the honoured guest Gaius Asinius Pollio who checked the weapons overlooked the individual armaments carried by Pi and Zeta where the blade could contract within the handle and release a blood flood.

Zheng in between Biyu and Pusa took their seats in the Emperor's box but sat well back since Livia didn't want the crowd to observe that favouritism given to some contesters, and seated alongside since she considered a lower grade of a citizen. For Drusus, he couldn't care less; out of sight meant he could grope Pusa.

A single bout lasted about 15 minutes or 20 minutes at the most. Lightly armoured fighters such as the retiarius (net-fighter), introduced into the Arena for the first time as Livia requested, would tireless and be lighter on their feet than their heavily armoured opponents. Livia had persuaded Augustus that fighting would be different and it would commence with Pi and Zeta in the ring. They would fight three gladiators: a new gladiator would replace a retiarius, secutor and murmillo at a time and whoever lost. The sector had a very distinctive helmet with only two small eye-holes, and a rounded top to not get caught in the net. The flanges protecting his neck were smooth and shaped like fish fins. The murmillo's fighting style suited men with massive muscular arms and strong thick shoulders to carry the shield and sword and dark helmet's weight. Those who fought as murmillones were usually big tall men and always very muscular. The murmillo depended on his strength and endurance to survive the battle against foes who were more suited to attacking. The tower shield gave him an edge in defence, and the gladius enabled him to thrust and swing at his enemies when in close range. The murmillones also trained to kick their enemies with the thick padding worn around their legs.

Today there would be 15 matches, which to the crowd was unheard of, and would inevitably end in the champions, Pi and Zeta's death. No gladiator had ever fought that many battles and survived. Livia was determined to finish Zheng's dominance in the Arena. The last two standing in the Arena would be overall champions awarded the palm branch and receive a laurel crown.

The crowd were ecstatic as Pizeta entered the Arena to the shouts of the spectators as Livia turned around to catch Zheng's eye as she asked: "How much do you wager that they will not survive the first bout."

"I will bet one thousand gold pieces that both will still be standing." Said, Zheng, as he stood up for all those in the box to hear.

The bets came in thick and fast much to Livia's delight knowing that the first bout could financially ruin him.

Three Gladiators entered the ring: one holding a net and a three-pointed trident, the other with a massive shield and a short sword while the third wore a large helmet with a plumed crest, held a giant sword, rectangular protection, scaled arm guard and thick, soft padding.

The robots stood some distance from them as they removed their armouring and helmets with just a loincloth and a sword strapped to their arm. They began to run fast at their opponents then commenced with acrobatic flips twisting their bodies to reach their opponents high above their heads. Pi grabbed one corner of the net as he rose above the retiarius, wrapped it around his head then threw the rest over the secutor standing next to him. He landed between them very quickly inserted tranquillising needles by thrusting his sword's handle into each of their necks. Zeta fell on the shoulders of the murmillo, tranquillised him by entering a stylus on the back of his neck. All three lay unconscious on the floor with the robots swords now raised waiting for the crowd's response. "Kill them came the shouts from the crowd."

The robots stood still waiting for the signal from the Emperor's box:—they thrust the swords into each gladiators heart, the blades retracted into their handles. As they lifted the weapon, it would reappear dripping with blood as the handle released a supply all over the tunic. The crowd, now screaming with joy as each body removed with dignity to the arena morgue, where Zheng's men would be waiting to quickly remove and prepare them to take to his villa for resuscitation.

Augustus so excited and thrilled with such a performance turned to Livia to show his enthusiasm as she frowned and spoke. "Well, let's see if they can do that again?" as another three entered the Arena. She turned to Zheng. "Double the bet," as Zheng acknowledged with a nod of the head as he looked at Pusa as if to say: "Is she mad?"

This time the three new gladiators wary of what happened last time stood close to one another each protecting the other in a tight circle. With their shields raised exposed their legs.

Zeta held PI in his arms like a tight ball, and with all his might, he flung Pi; folded himself like a ten-pin ball across the ground. It threw-up a camouflage of dust as it approached and rolled into the three, with Zeta close behind doing his acrobatic flips as he twisted up and above the three now laying on the ground. All three within seconds sedated, and once more, the robots stood above with swords held above their heads waiting for approval to kill. The circus' noise had increased to such a level that one could hardly hear a word spoken as a reluctant gesture from August given to execute.

Livia, now fuming and extremely mad at what she observed insisted to the summa rudis (referee) that if they didn't follow the professional rules of combat, she declared the gladiators should double. Augustus' new law abused, and the demand for fighters beginning to exceed supply was not happy about the new arrangement.

Livia once more screamed above the noise to Zheng as he acknowledged, “Double or nothing?”

Livia had instructed the summa rudis that the rules permitted a fallen gladiator to be replaced immediately and not to wait for the next bout.

The robots stood now in front of six which soon split into two groups of three; took their shields and held them like a disc and with such force flung them like a disc thrower. They hurtled and whistled as they spun in the air knocking each group of three to the floor. And before they could stand the robots rose above them sedating them once more only to realise that nets were thrown over their bodies by another six gladiators that had just entered the Arena. They quickly rolled away, tightening the net around their bodies, so tight like a body in a carpet. At some distance from their opponents, they flipped their bodies into a standing stance. And then with aerobatic front flips hurled themselves up and over at their opponents which were now running at them leaping far above their heads and untwisting as the web fell over their assailants. Again all six lay sedated only to realise another six approached running at them. They gathered the nets laying on the ground, spun them above their heads like a lasso and tossed them at the six which landed on their heads and tangled amongst their legs as they fell to the floor. Aerobatic flip-flops raced around the Arena as each gladiator stabbed with the robot's sword handles they all became sedated. The crowd could not believe this spectacle and just couldn’t follow what was happening as the dust rose from the ground camouflaging the show, but suddenly the dust settled. To everybody’s amazement, Pi and Zeta stood in the middle of the circus, surrounded with nearly forty gladiators. They waited patiently for the kill signal as they went around faking their death. Zheng's men remained to pick up the bodies and quickly cleared the area before anybody realised they were not dead. Their heroes' chants heard the crowd had combined their names and were singing “Pizeta,” as awarded the palm branch and a laurel crown as they circled the Arena in golden coloured chariots.

Zheng picked up his winnings much to the disgust of Livia who insisted on seeing the gladiators slain. He bade good-bye to the Emperor; bowed with what took to be an elaborate and private irony to Livia, who threw back her head and laughed The Emperor frowned but said nothing. Shortly afterwards, when the crowd had streamed out of the circus, Zheng and Livia took their leave. The body of each fighter supposedly had died placed on a couch of Libitibia (Roman Goddess) removed with dignity to the arena morgue where the corpse stripped of armour. As Livia inspected, all forty-five bodies, insisted that the throat of each gladiator cut to prove that dead was dead. Zheng stood their mortified persuading Livia they were killed and pleading with her to let what family they have to make them remove the body and give them a Roman burial. However, Zheng had anticipated such an occurrence as he had paid the God of the underworld money to feign testing for life-signs that resembled a heated wand as he confirmed each body was dead. Livia not going against the God of the underworld accepted dead. As Livia left the morgue Zheng's men hurriedly collected each gladiator and carried them by cart to his villa. They resuscitated given a portion of the prize money and their freedom on the understanding never to return to Rome.

However, unbeknown to all, Drusus besotted with Pusa had persuaded her to personally take her to the villa, where he bathed ate, drank and had sexual intercourse with her. As the evening progressed, he could hear the fanfare of noise nearby as Zheng returned with a crowd. Approached the main hall to see every gladiator that he had witnessed that afternoon slain enjoying a feast laughing at the amount of money they had made that day and the enjoyment in actually not spilling a drop of blood. Realising a scam began to appreciate an ingenious way of extorting vast amounts of money from his mother and father. He also understood that Pusa must have been part of the scam as he quickly gathered his things mounted his horse which he had not adequately secured the saddle, galloped out of the villa with one objection in mind to return with an army. He raced towards Rome in that evening light as the rain began to fall. The horse slipped on the wet autumn leaves as he took a quick turn in the road, his saddle loosened and disengaged and thrown out only to hit his head directly on a nearby trunk. He lay there dead. Nobody in the villa missed him because they didn't know. After all, he was with Pusa. His microchip had already sent alarm signals and Zheng on hearing details of his death, explained to him by Pusa, deduced that she must have had some influence in his accidental death.

Livia, distraught and devastated at the loss of her son never forgave herself for allowing Drusus to fraternise with such a repulsive prostitute, Pusa; and she blamed not only her for his death but Zheng too and would somehow get her revenge.

Augustus decreed from that day no gladiator would die in the Arena since after losing forty-five fighters and he could never forgive Livia for taking control and losing so much life and money against wagers.

CHAPTER 3

Is it real or not?

Zheng had brought with him from *Planet-E* his natural wife Niu his sister in law Chen, her mother Yi and her sister Feiyan and all their children he had fathered and the stable boy Chu Yun his wife Guo who had borne him two girls. None of them knew about their previous life before, since the humanoids had cognitive mapped their brains for the new environment and wipe clean their former lives. The women became Zheng's wives, and Chu Yun became very close to Zheng. He was his manager in organising the tournaments and ensuring the Gladiators defeated and left for dead were given money and set up a new life far away from Rome.

Zheng encouraged his many wives to flirt with the gladiators, hoping that they might someday find someone suitable to leave him with the only woman in his life, Biyu. However, no one could replace Zheng, and living at the villa was bliss in their eyes. Nobody intended to change. To marry a gladiator that passed through or even those that stayed on as farmers or working hands. Zheng had never refused anyone but always emphasised the secrecy; a leak to the authorities would send the Roman empire to his villa and mean certain death. Zheng had encouraged his wife Niu and Chen to find somebody suitable now that their relationship on *Planet-E*, which they had no recollection of, had changed as far as Zheng was concerned. But as far as Nui and Chen were involved, they had no intentions whatever to set up home with another and certainly had no plans to change what they considered as easy going if they stayed married to Zheng.

Feiyan and Yi had met two such gladiators who lived with them permanently and were encouraged by Zheng to get married by Roman Law. But after faking their death, they felt their future husbands might be discovered and concerned about the threat it might impose on the lives of those at the villa. Nonetheless, Zheng persuaded both and officially released Feiyan and Yi with papers as if he had owned them as slaves and freed them to be held by the gladiators, to avoid any official marriage ceremony. Nui and Chen, much younger, were looking for something different and were not interested in men feigning death in the Arena that wore the scars not only superficially but mentally too. The centurions, nevertheless that enrolled for training at the villa were undoubtedly attracted to Niu and Chen. Much to the discouragement of Pusa, who knew that marriage would take their children away, but to ensure both stayed, Zheng offered each a house and land to farm, on one condition; find a husband.

Meanwhile, Tiberius had argued with Augustus and retired to some island and stopped coming for martial art training and his elite selected centurions of the Roman guard. Livia never ventured to the villa, because of Pusa, which reminded her of Drusus and his infatuation with her. However, Julia the Elder, Augustus's daughter, had two sons Lucius and Gaius Ceaser, who were now in favour with their grandfather, Augustus, who insisted that they needed training and attend martial art classes villa regularly.

Julia the Elder had lived in Jerusalem, but after her late husband Agrippa's death and her failure in marriage with her cousin Tiberius, accompanied by two Praetorian guards that had taken a fancy to Chen and Niu and became very close towards them. The soldiers began to spend a lot of time at the villa, and eventually took up full-time residence in Chen's and Niu's houses'. Zheng approved for them to marry, and they were both given full Roman citizenship. The soldiers spent a lot of time away from the villa, fighting at the front. Later, after the marriage, Chen and Niu became pregnant, and each gave birth to boys naturally; neither had any 5th Millennium DNA requiring a caesarean.

Pusa would visit once a month to collect eggs and sperm from the 5th Millennium children who were now at the age. Questions asked by the children; why they had so-called medicals every time Pusa arrived? And why they could never remember that day when invited to take refreshment? There was never any recollection of those hours when they woke the next morning. Biyu's girls: Ji the oldest now sixteen, Jiangsu fifteen and the youngest, Lihua fourteen were all regarded as beautiful young ladies; especially to the gladiators that lived within, and the soldiers that visited for training. For Zheng and Biyu this was a continuing worry, since one day they would meet someone and fall in love; and to conceive would be a death sentence unless the robots were on hand to perform a caesarean. It was also the same for the boys: Ju, now sixteen, Jizi, fifteen and the youngest Guang, fourteen. Zheng hated that while they slept Pusa would masturbate each to extract their semen; Biyu could not believe this nightmare was continuing; with no end in sight, she was now coming to her wit's end a resolution to end it all.

Augustus had established a Praetorian Guard, to protect his daughter Julia. But because of her affair with Iullus Antonius (Son of Mark Antony), which he approved, was obliged for Rome's sake to banish his daughter after a decreeing a law on adultery against the appointed next Emperor Tiberius (Julia's step-brother) which she was married too. The two Praetorian Guards named Philto and Junius now married to Chen and Niu respectively sent to Jerusalem to protect Pontious Pilot frequently wrote to their wives, which became a topic of conservation during regular encounters Zheng and Biyu. Zheng especially became fascinated by the stories, read to him about life in Jerusalem and was invited many times by Philto and Junius. They had a sound knowledge of thoroughbred horses in the area they felt were ideal for the circus in Rome pulling and racing chariots. They would also write regularly about a messiah performing miracles in the area named Jesus of Nazareth and proclaimed as the Judaea god's son. These stories were read out at the evening meal when all attended each night at the family table. Zheng could not help consider the work of

Pusa that somehow she had introduced or was about to initiate a religion and very challenging one evening while alone with Biyu spoke: "I have to find out if this is real or not?"

"Why don't you go to Jerusalem on business under the pretence that you are looking for a new breed of horses or something that would not raise the alarm to Pusa." Said Biyu

"Hmm, what if I was to take the spacecraft and go with the robots? Surely that would satisfy Pusa knowing the robots would keep her well informed there was nothing for her to be suspicious about."

"Yes, might work?" Suddenly Biyu stopped and placed her finger on her lips, forgetting that Pusa could read their thoughts at any time.

Zheng realising what he had just said quickly changed the subject:

"Yes, I think I shall buy those horses that Chen and Niu's husbands spoke about in their letter from Jerusalem and I shall go to expedite the matter."

Zheng had made up his mind to go and arrange with the robots to accompany him as they set off for Jerusalem.

They arrived well clear of the city and ensured the spacecraft hidden sent it to orbit the Planet ready to return to any beck and call. Pulled by three magnificent stallions in their chariot, they passed village after village, stopped and rested for an advance party of travellers to give the word that two great gladiators were approaching Jerusalem's city walls. PiZeta now well-known throughout the Roman provinces as the most excellent combatants did not expect an audience of well over a thousand spectators to welcome them. The streets were full, and it seemed to be overflowing with a good part of the city. Then suddenly, above the crowd's natural noise, a fanfare of trumpets and horns sounded; Philto and Junius had warned Pontious Pilot that stars of the Arena were arriving and he had decided that a grand welcome organised by the city.

While in the heart of the city Philo and Junius did not wear their armour. Instead, they wore a formal toga, which distinguished them from civilians but remained in proper civilian attire, the Roman mark as they greeted Zheng and his champion gladiators.

To be admitted to the Praetorian Guard, a man had to be in good physical condition, governed by an excellent moral character, and come from a respectable family. Philto and Junius had all of these requirements and held high esteem with Pontious Pilot which had recently awarded them the rank of Principalis which exempted them from daily chores.

There were tame elephants, guests from afar; it was merely a gathering of a few more than a hundred guests, attended by nearly as many servants and musicians and dancers. They ate, drank, and laughed. They watched the dancers dance, and joined them, to their delight and confusion. To the sound of tambourines and harps and oboes, they wandered through the gardens where water fountains augmented the music, and the torchlight played upon the water in another dance beyond the skill of human bodies. Toward the end of the evening, there was an exceptional performance by the musicians and dancers; poems were read, composed in honour of the Roman champions. Pontious Pilot had constructed its chairs of ebony and secured so that all the guests could pay homage.

PiZeta demonstrated their martial art and acrobatic skills to the audience's thrill of how they defeated forty-five gladiators in the Arena. Their flip-flops and twists sent shrieks of excitement and scream to the crowd they had never seen before.

Pontious Pilot, always thought that nobody could do what had been described to him by Philto and Junius, but now witnessing, stood to applaud and to laugh out loud much to the delight of his audience. They clapped so loud and thanked Pontious for the best evening that anybody had ever attended.

Zheng now so famous had the keys to the city, and merchants queued up to do business and invite him to their house. He slumped in his ebony chair, watching the show thinking to himself how far he had come and once more, asking himself *is this reality* as he watched his robots perform. To anybody with any sense would realise, it cannot be human; to do what they are doing. *Please, please somebody wake me up*, he thought. He took another mouthful of this excellent wine and surveyed his surroundings that everybody enjoyed and had so much fun that all he could do was join in.

Philto and Junius now-famous everybody wanted just to be acquainted with them in the hope of getting close to PiZeta or knowing where they were likely to be at any time. On one occasion visiting a horse breeder crowds had flocked to the stables hoping to get a glimpse of their Roman stars. Soldiers held back the group as Zheng spoke to the horse breeder negotiating a deal while the robots mingled in front of the crowd. Zheng turned and noticed that at the back of the gathering heads were switching to a figure in the distance that appeared to be surrounded by ambient light as a white robe reflected the brilliant sunlight.

"Who is that?" Said, Zheng, as he turned to Junius. And before Junius could answer Philto had already noticed the figure sometime before as he replied:

"That is Jesus the prophet from Nazareth of Galilee." As the crowds gathered, Zheng decided to see for himself followed close at hand the robots with Philto and Junius accompanying them too.

As they approached and listened to the words that he spoke an unknown man came. "You are Zheng?"

Zheng not surprised that a person should know his name replied: "Yes that is I."

"I am Mathew a disciple of Jesus, and he seeks an audience with you."

Zheng astonished that somebody of such importance would request to speak to him began to think this must be Pusa manipulating the masses to believe that a saviour was amongst their amiss. "Well, yes, of course—When and where?" He said.

"Tomorrow—Jesus will be at the temple in Jerusalem." Said, Mathew, as he left.

"Well, it looks as if you are famous as the prophet." Said Philto.

Zheng couldn't sleep that evening as his mind confronted the belief: why would Pusa confide in an unknown person about me?—when meant to be a well-kept secret? I know that the time is right for the appearance of a saviour—but why did Pusa tell me she had no plans to introduce religion? And had nothing to do with this so-called prophet?—She must have been lying to me. Anyway, as he drifted off to sleep, he thought; *tomorrow I shall know.*

He rose late that morning to a brilliant day as the sun woke him shining through his window. As usual, the robots, stood to attention outside his room waiting for instructions as he bathed, gathered his clothes, dressed and walked towards the temple followed by his robots.

As he approached, he noticed the turmoil as market stools overturned and merchants arguing and leaving as Jesus stood there shouting "This is a house of prayer!" He stopped as he noticed Zheng approaching and turned to him "Welcome my son we have to talk."

He took Zheng's arm and guided him to a quiet place in the temple as merchants gathered there merchandise to leave said: "Not these, please." Pointing to the robots.

Zheng looked into his eyes and immediately sensed something unique that he had never observed in any other human convincing him that what stood in front of him was a humanoid as he spoke: "You know me—means that you and I have the same creator—Pusa."

"Pusa—who is Pusa? Your creator and my creator are God. Pusa is a thing that you humans created on Planet Earth and is now trying to control the human race which you now have to put a stop to— Christ's followers should call no man or even a thing master, and God forbid a creator!"

Zheng astonished at the bluntness of these words stopped, hesitated and thought, *must be the words of Pusa again, testing him.—But why?*

"I don't understand. Surely you know what stands around us—And even now some are still being created, and you, are part of this pretence. We humans on planet earth are re-running history—You must know that?" Said, Zheng, as he looked deep into His eyes, paused and continued. "Pusa has created you to introduce Christianity to ensure that we follow what happened on Planet Earth."

"No such thing!—I was not set up by a thing—I am the son of a spirit!" He stopped and stared directly into Zheng's eyes as he continued "I know you have suffered and I know that you are from Planet Earth. I was there too some 5000 years ago, and now I am here, and in another 300 years I shall go to the other Planet you have just come from to do the same as what I am about to do here; that is to start the kingdom of heaven."

Zheng now silent, thinking *is this Pusa talking or what, how can I know*, he thought as he questioned him again. "If you are the Son of God, why then did you leave all of us on Planet Earth to suffer and die? You must know that I am the only last surviving male from Planet Earth."

"You are not the last—Look around you—the spirit is within you and your fellow homo-sapiens—humans can only save humankind—The spirit within you is to look after your fellow brothers and sisters. When you pray, you pray for others to help you—not a God—A God can't help man; that is the basis of spiritual teaching. Love thy fellow man." He stopped paused, looked deep into Zheng's eyes and continued. "Go forth and multiply—which humanity has done. Humans from planet earth have followed the spiritual teaching, and now the spirit within you has two worlds populated, and I now will begin the next phase, which has nothing to do with the things you have brought to these planets. The longer humankind lives; the clearer it will become; the meaning of spiritual living."

Zheng understanding the words spoken and beginning to think *maybe what he is saying is true*, but, as he responded: "Okay so how do I get rid of these things that want to create a superior race?" As he glanced at the robots to make sure that they didn't hear what he had just said.

"Man created things to enable humankind to multiply and go forth exactly is as expected, but to tell a lie, so you must tell the truth. It's that simple." As he added:

"However, we may increase our knowledge of the conditions of space in which situates man, that knowledge can never be complete, for the number of those states is as infinite as the infinity of space. And therefore so long as not all the conditions defined influencing men, there is no complete certainty but a particular measure of time." He said as He continued:

"If any man will do his will, he shall know of the belief whether it be of spirit." He paused. " A man that told you the truth. You shall know the truth, and the truth shall make you free. The God you talk of is a spirit, and those that worship him must worship him in spirit and truth. Keep my sayings, and you shall know of my sayings whether they be true."

Zheng listened, confused, but still didn't fully understand and now convinced what was standing in front of him was an advanced humanoid created by the machines as he interrupted hoping to see his response. "The things will not heed; it believes a human from the 5th Millennium will give it the next level of intelligence, whatever that is, and I cannot undo this command." As his facial expression showed the tiredness and stress that he had endured for so long: The very question that had formerly tormented him, the thing he had continually sought to find—the aim of life—still existed for him now.

"[1]There are no laws in this belief which could justify a man and make him saved. There is only the image of truth to guide him, for inward perfection in the person is a spirit within, and for the outer end is an establishment of a kingdom of heaven. The fulfilment of this teaching consists only of walking in the chosen way; in getting nearer to inward excellence in the imitation of a spirit within oneself, and outward perfection in establishing the kingdom of heaven. The greater or less blessedness of a man depends, according to this belief. Not on the degree of perfection to which he has attained. But on the higher or less swiftness with which he is pursuing. That man wait for: it had no yesterday, and no day after tomorrow, it is not going to come at a "millennium"—it is an experience of the heart, it is everywhere, and it is nowhere.[2]"

Zheng on hearing these words, which he had heard before in previous writings, was sure it was a humanoid, and not a mortal being, reading a script from internal memory banks. Pusa somehow was involved and had lied to him and purposely introduced religion as part of the machines glorified plan.

"In these coming days, I will die again on the cross, and again I will resurrect to show humankind that there is a spirit. Pray, and your inner self will listen, and I will be there to guide you." Jesus said as he took Zheng's face and kissed him on either side of his cheek.

Zheng could see no mark of any impregnation of a microchip behind his ear as he looked with a just noticeable and seemingly ironic smile. He just listened to what was said, which convinced him that it was only another humanoid standing in front of him.

As Zheng turned to leave, he heard the words "The spirit is with you, and in you, my Son."

The following days Jesus was crucified. Zheng knelt in front of his cross amongst the multitude and didn't weep like many were now doing. But somehow deep down in his subconscious something was telling him that Jesus was not a mortal being but created by a machine to continue with the absurd pretence of teaching religion to the Planet.

Zheng waited in Jerusalem as the stories spread about the resurrection of Jesus, which finally persuaded him that the humanoids must have created Jesus for Christianity and other orthodox religions to spread. Ironically creating conflict and

[1] Extracts and modified from "The Kingdom of God Is Within You" by Leo Tolstoy

[2] from "The Anti-Christ" by Friedrich Nietzsche

eventually increasing knowledge as different faiths and beliefs fought to dominate, resulting in the fittest paradox's survival.

Zheng returned to his villa, demoralised, lethargic and depressed, which Biyu immediately noticed; he had become frustrated impatient and angry with himself and others. He described his experience in Jerusalem to Biyu, and could not believe that due to the interference of the humanoids religion was about to repeat itself; they had created a superior machine to fool the majority of the people in thinking there was a God. Biyu couldn't understand the reasoning behind the humanoids plan until Zheng explained his theories: what was missing on the Planet? For the human race to oppose one another over their religious beliefs, the humanoids always had remarked upon; only the most intelligent would survive.

"But how do we put a stop to what the humanoids are doing. And what they are about to do?" An analytical facial look described an impossible task as she raised her arms and clasped them to her thighs.

Zheng looked deep into her eyes as he answered, "We have to tell them the truth; that's the only sensible thing the superior being, so-called Jesus, suggested."

"Tell them the truth? You think that is going to work!" Said Biyu with a look of dismay.

"I don't fully understand why a humanoid would tell me that, but what I think they were trying to explain to me was to reprogram them to make them understand they don't need the intelligence of the 5th Millennium to progress."

"Do you think you have interpreted it correctly? I just can't see why they should shoot themselves in the foot; and if it is correct how the hell do we do that?" She said as she paused and continued "I have no idea how these machines operate?—or how constructed?—No! The idea of how to write a program?—Or to reprogram a command? And if I did, how to implement it?" Said Biyu realising that once again, the whole thing was absurd and becoming hopeless.

Zheng could feel the frustration agreeing with everything she had just said because he was in the same predicament as her.

"I don't know either?—I just hope that an opportunity somehow will surface—but meanwhile, we can't-do anything." He said as he walked away, not knowing a solution.

CHAPTER 4

Vestal Virgin

During Livia's attendance at the villa during martial art training for her two boys, she had befriended Biyu earlier before her exile had arranged for all the young girls at the villa to attend the College of the Vestals. Even though some were older than puberty age. However, for acceptance, the girl's names had to be changed. Oriental characters were not allowed, and they would have to take the terms of vestal virgins that had previously condemned were now regarded as reborn: Biyu's eldest Ji gave the name of Tarpeia. Jiangsu now referred to as Pinaria, and her youngest Lihua gave the name of Oppia. Altogether Zheng had supplied twelve vestal virgins much to the delight of Augustus and the Senate. Regarded as the most beautiful they had ever attended the circus and essential functions. Wherever Augustus went, he insisted that the entourage of vestal virgins accompanied him.

To the astonishment of many, Biyu had no choice: the girls became daughters of the state to become a spinster and deny them healthy family life. Nevertheless, Pusa was not angry. She was a robot, but just inconvenienced; she now had difficulty-free access to the girls, but it wouldn't stop her and the robots sedating whoever to gain entry to the college once a month for the human eggs.

Although Zheng did not like the new arrangement, he persuaded the families that it was an honour for their child to be represented in all the prominent dedications and ceremonies and always held a private place of honour for them. The young boys were saddened too by losing their sisters and cousins, and the villa becomes a gloomy place and the joy and laughter that had been present for such a long time suddenly disappeared overnight. Zheng kept the young males preoccupied; he would have them trained extensively in a martial art, horse riding, chariot racing and reading in Latin and Greek. He also introduced religion and Christianity's teachings since faith growing in Rome employed an associate of Jesus that he had met in Jerusalem, even though he had his doubts. Life soon got back to normal, and Biyu organised regular visits to the College in Rome where they took food plates. The mothers were also allowed to sit with their daughters in the private placement at the Arena.

During Pusa's visit, the girls could not understand why condemned to a life of misery. *Still, we're always excited and look forward to her visit accompanied by her champion gladiators, and Pusa's bodyguards, PiZeta.* They thought. However, the girls could never fully understand what happened to the missing hours after the so-called tea soirees and waking afterwards in a daze of confusion. It was only a matter of time before one of the many vestal virgins witnessed Tarpeia (Biyu's eldest) on her back with her robe open and her legs apart with one of the robots described in a compromising position. Others had witnessed the same act performed; jealousy prevailed because of the sexual act and the special treatment the so-called twelve pure virgins have. It gave much pleasure in reporting the incidents to mother superior.

The college had all the twelve girls inspected for their virginity and discovered that all were not as pure as led to believe and the superiors after seeking proper advice had no choice but to condemn all to death. It was not by burying them alive, which was the custom but subjecting them to the circus' will. On hearing the atrocities, Augustus could not believe what he regarded as a close colleague, Zheng, would deceive him into becoming the Arena's laughing stock, assembling a harem of prostitutes for his amusement.

To satisfy the crowd Augustus decreed that these so-called vestal virgins massacred in front of the circus's mob. He summoned Zheng immediately to his palace to establish precisely the truth and lies behind this deceit. Zheng was unaware when armoured guards of the Senate marched him to an audience with Emperor Augustus:

"I cannot believe that you would have the audacity and the nerve to supply twelve contaminated women to my Vestal and have them displayed at the amphitheatre to the eyes of the mob." Said, Augustus, as his countenance showed a sign of disbelief that Zheng would do such a thing, as he continued. "You have left me no choice, and I know some are your beloved daughters, but I have no choice to condemn all to the arena to be massacred in front of the mob that is demanding blood."

Zheng stood there in silence knowing that all were innocent and thinking: *how can I explain to the Emperor of my predicament that I am from another time and place and are manipulated by robots,"* when suddenly the Emperor spoke. "And to think your prize gladiators were responsible for copulating with these girls." He paused, then added. "They shall all go in the arena—and if your fighters can protect them and win—then I might show some form of leniency—show mercy and pardon them all—but I can't guarantee anything—it now depends on the mob."

Expecting to be held responsible and detained, Zheng was surprised when allowed to go. It never established if the girls had lost their virginity before acceptance to the Vestal and given a date when the girls sentenced allotted time to arrange champions to defend and fight for their so-called honour. But Augustus could offer no guaranteed freedom. It depended on the will of the angry people on that day in the circus.

It became evident that Pusa had cunningly schemed for the girls to be caught in such a quandary; knowing full well, that she was the only one that could come to the rescue and save them. And what would be better to take them all to her laboratories at the polar cap, ensuring their safety, and continue with the humanoids plan? However, unbeknown to Biyu and Zheng during discussions their mind thoughts and had already aroused Pusa as she entered with a smile on her face knowing full well that she now had complete control of the situation as she spoke. "The girls will be okay—I will never let them die; they are too precious for the survival of the human race."

"So how do you intend to save them and prevent Augustus and his army descending upon us if you free them from the jail." Said, Zheng, as he stood there pale and frightened; too much for him to comprehend.

Pusa sensed the agitated look and the stress building up in Zheng's body as she replied:

"I will frighten the mob in the amphitheatre—the only saving grace will be the Vestal Virgins—in the end, they will shout for mercy and regard them as goddesses."

What Pusa was planning Zheng and Biyu had no idea, but one thing they did know, the girls would be safe whatever the outcome since Pusa would not allow her supply of eggs taken from her.

The girls led into the Arena dressed in white robes on that awful day as the sun shone through the garments to show underneath their innocent nakedness. They stood frightened clutching one another in a circle in the middle of the stage waiting for their ultimate death as the charges read over and above the screams of the crowd shouting either to kill them, bury them or even take them home to do want they wanted to do with them. After the charges read an announcement made for anybody willing to defend them against whatever came out of the gates would release them into the hands of their defenders. Just then Pi and Zeta emerged to the screams and shouts of the crowd 'Pizeta'. They stood either side of the girls that were profusely crying and weeping as they huddled together.

Pi approached Tarpeia, Biyu's eldest and quietly whispered in her ear. "Do not be afraid everything will be alright. What will come out of those gates are animals that are tame and will not hurt you; you must believe me." He paused and took her hand and continued in a very compelling voice. "They will frighten the crowd, but you are to stand your ground, and you must not become frightened; they will not harm you. At some point, after they have scared the living daylights out of the crowd, you are to walk to whatever is attacking you and scaring the crowd, to hold your hand high and show the palm of your hand, and they will kneel in front of you and then suddenly disappear." He said as he added. "All the other girls must do the same."The robots could not explain it was just a holographic image, that Tarpeia would face as she passed the word around that all must stand together against what they were about to see, and it was tame and not to be frightened.

Each, holding an amethyst in their hands the robots moved to the Arena's outskirts in the far corners facing diagonally one another. The crowd sighed disbelief as if they were abandoning the girls, still crouching in the centre of the stadium. Meanwhile, Pusa inserting darts sedated all the guards with her magic. Sent commands to those who impregnated with microchips. Patiently the crowd waited; nobody knew what was coming. In the Emperor's box excitement grew as questions asked. "Well, who arranged this?—Please —tell me what to expect?" Nobody seemed to know as the gates opened and those in the stands looked down as the screams started a fair distance away as two giant dragons appeared. Flames shot out from their nostrils to fill the Arena. The dragons took flight as they flew around the circus. The crowd suddenly realised that their lives were in peril as they started to run towards the exits. Words echoed in the Emperor's box —"what idiot arranged this?"—as others shouted: "Dragons don't exist where have they come from?"—as others replied— "I don't care, I'm leaving."

Covering the crystal gems from prying eyes the robots controlled the holographic images above the crowd; frightened them with a spontaneous burst of flames to such an extent the majority just crouched on the steps cowering with their arms and hands protecting their heads. They brought the dragons either side of the girls who stood there so scared; trembling on the spot as many unintentionally relieved themselves as the dragons approached throwing flames into the air and making such a noise. The crowd in a state of shock, covered their eyes with their hands peering through their fingers, expecting the worst to come. Tarpeia closed her eyes and believed that they would not harm her raised her arm as she slowly walked to the dragon and showed her hand's palm as instructed; the dragon's head immediately fell to the floor. The other girls noticing out of the corner of their eyes did precisely the same, and the other dragon did the same. Much to the surprise of the mob the Dragons then took flight as they suddenly vanished into thin air. A sigh of relief echoed around the Arena and then began the applause; such excitement and jubilation of the people began to shout out the names Tarpeia, Pinaria and Oppia and over the noise, one could hear "Free them! Free them!—They must be goddesses—We can't kill them—Otherwise, the dragons will come back."

Arousing from the sedation the guards unaware of what happened in the Arena was just about to open the gates to let out the lions and gladiators when they were suddenly approached by the officials screaming: "what idiot let out those ferocious dragons and who was responsible?" The guards stood flabbergasted and had no idea what the officer was talking about; but were still reprimanded, incompetent and stupid anyway for opening the gates.

Augustus after fleeing returned to the Emperor's box waving a white handkerchief acknowledging the crowd's wishes as he tried to shout above the tumultuous noise of the mob in vain only to send his guards with instruction to set free the vestal virgins.

The girls taken to the Vestal exonerated against all accusations. However, the girl accused, and her superior of reporting and spreading malicious rumours and a false witness were sentenced to death by live burial. The news soon spread throughout Rome and to Zheng whose immediate reaction was to free the accused, decided that Cho Yun should visit the Vestal, to gain any information. Observing the surroundings and having informal discussions with the vestal virgins Cho Yun noticed new brickwork in an existing wall. Immediately reported to Zheng, the location, knowing that it was the custom in those days to bury the women alive, in a hidden place, without food and water and allow them to die a prolonged, painful death.

Accompanied by his robots, Zheng that evening, with thermal image detectors, expecting to find a false room, confirmed that two humans were still alive cramped in a very tight spot with apparently very little air. That night they broke through and removed the frightened women and took them back to Zheng’s villa to recover from their ordeal. They couldn’t understand why such a person, whose life already in danger, would go to so much trouble and concern; Zheng knowing the only explanation that came to mind, fitting the circumstance he found himself in, told them about Christianity and the love of humankind. Nonetheless, the women had to immediately leave Rome with a new identity never to reveal they're true identity and always maintain secrecy and silence in their new environment. They agreed never to return to Rome and would keep their secret with them to their dying days.

The vestal virgins supplied by Zheng had their trust and purity tarnished. Augustus who still had his doubts insisted confinement and access denied to the family, especially Pusa and her bodyguards. Pusa without any alternative had to abduct the girls one night with the help of her robots to flee with them to the laboratories at the polar cap.

Upon hearing that the twelve Vestal Virgins had suddenly vanished raised suspicion about the two women buried alive; only to discover after opening the tombs that they had disappeared too. It immediately focused blame on Zheng who was brought under armed guard to face questions in the Senate.

Zheng stood in front of the Senate knowing full well that the charges brought against him would be severe and life-threatening as the senior Senate spoke:

“We have brought you in front of the council to explain the incidents that led up to accusations brought to this house about the infidelity of the twelve Vestal Virgins that you supplied—their disappearance and of those accused of being a false witness buried alive. Also, on the day that dragons appeared in the arena, it appeared your gladiators were controlling them with these so-called magical brightly coloured gemstones that hang around their necks—what do you have to say to that?"

Zheng stood there in silence, knowing that he could not give an explanation that would provide a convincing reply, so he abruptly answered:

"I can not give any account of what has happened. Like you and the Senate, I am in deep shock." As he glanced at the floor in the form of a bow, then raised his head and added. "My prizefighters Pi and Zeta have vanished too, and I can only speculate that with Pusa they have absconded with the Vestal Virgins."

The Senators gathered around one another, and even Augustus joined in the huddled conversation as one of them turned and questioned Zheng.

"Who is this Pusa?—You know the Emperor's wife Livia always had her doubts about this woman that she was sent here as an enemy agent?—What do you say to that?"

Suddenly, Zheng realised he had a possible way out of this, by accepting that Pusa was an enemy of the Roman Empire.

"Yes, you could be right, and that she was responsible for introducing the dragons into the arena." He said as he paused and continued. "It's the only possible explanation."

"Why take the Vestal Virgins?" Said the Senator as the rest of the council reiterated the words: "Yes, why take the girls?"

"Money!— In the Far East, they would be worth a fortune; sold into slavery as virgins, pure and untouched by male and to satisfy the lust of a Lord." Said Zheng expecting the next question.

"And why should we believe you?"

"I have lost three daughters and believe me; I am already preparing a group of men to follow them and retrieve all!" Said, Zheng, as he patiently stood there waiting for the response.

"Hmm!—Do you have enough men?" Said the Senate in response to what was whispered in his ear by Emperor Augustus.

"Yes, Sir. I have more men than enough.—I promise I will not return until I have every maiden safely back in the Vestal." Said, Zheng, as he bowed, turned and was allowed to leave the council.

CHAPTER 5

The Polar Cap

Zheng returned to his villa; shaken at his ordeal with the Senate as he confided that evening with Biyu in their haven in the particular room: "We have no choice but to call up Pusa and hopefully arrange a visit to see the girls." Said Zheng.

Biyu was irritated, frustrated and annoyed that her life was becoming impossible. She needed somehow to get rid of humanoids, robots and the 5th Millenium that she was now growing towards the end of her patience. "Whatever!" She said.

Removing their metallic headscarves blocking transmission from their embedded microchips summoned Pusa. A three-dimensional image suddenly appeared: relaxed and calm Pusa, as usual, didn't have a care in the world. "So is everything ok?" She said with what could only be called a sharp look of sarcasm that Zheng and Biyu were beginning to hate.

Zheng raised his head from his recliner and stepped down from his floating chair as he stood in front of Pusa and spoke: "Well, I nearly lost my life today because of your recklessness." As he paused and raised his voice: "They want their Vestal Virgins back!"

Pusa sensed the frustration immediately and significantly the anger that Biyu expressed on her face. "Yes, of course, you can have them back straight away. But you do realise that all are pregnant carrying twins." Replied, with that human smirk on its face that Zheng just somehow wanted to remove as it continued. "You and your sons inseminated; to whom I cannot recollect at this moment."

Biyu collapsed into the recliner on hearing these words with tears in her eyes and Zheng stood over Biyu as he tried to comfort her as he turned to Pusa. "You realise now that is a death sentence, and they cannot possibly return to the Vestal."

"Yes, of course, I know that—you just explain when you return they were all raped by villains and vagabonds." Said, Pusa with again that look of, 'so what's the problem?'

Zheng so angry about everything had to ask. "And now I am the father of my daughter's pregnancy and my sons are the father of their sister's pregnancy. It's madness you are going to breed children that will end up with genetic faults."

"Come! Come!—You underestimate our intelligence, of course, we have modified the DNA, and hopefully, these kids can be born naturally. It's going to be the new superior race. You should be proud of what I have achieved and being able to accelerate intelligence." Said, Pusa with such a happy expressionless face.

"But why do you need to accelerate the intelligence of the human race, just let us develop naturally?" Said, Zheng with such a frustrated look as he added. "You realise you are far superior to all of us. You don't need us. We cannot offer you any more than we already know—do you understand?"

"The wrong answer!— you humans of the 5th Millenium hold the key to the universe—and we need that key?"

"What key?"

"The key to open up a space-time dimension. The next habitable planets are 1000 light-years away our space-time journey would be nearly 1200 years. That's too much time; we need to bend dimensional space, to shorten the distance." Said, Pusa now in a commanding voice as she added." Enough is enough do you want to come and collect the children, if so I shall send a space shuttle tomorrow to pick you up."

"Yes.Yes." Said, Biyu realising whatever they said was futile.

It began to get dark, and there were stars in the sky, and *Planet-E* shone with her soft light as the space-shuttle descended in front of them as they stood on the edge of the cornfield which was nearly ready for harvest. As the spacecraft hovered silently and lowered gracefully, its outer skin reflected a change and merged with its surroundings completely camouflaging it from any observer. It looked from a distance if Zheng and Biju just disappeared into thin air as they stepped into the craft.

It was another world inside the ship. The world both had forgotten about nearly 5000 years ahead of their time. And deep down inside, their thoughts conveyed they were not missing the high technology that the craft could offer. For them, they had suddenly appreciated that the simple things in life mattered. Zheng was still overwhelmed in meeting Jesus of Nazareth and the extent the humanoids had gone to deceive the masses reflected on the words he had said to him. He realised now the futility to increase man's knowledge of the universe in which man situated can never be complete to satisfy all the conditions within the infinity of space. Zheng looked out through the porthole. The mass of stars overwhelming and *Planet-F* below him suddenly become insignificant since it showed no signs of life just beauty in the kaleidoscope of colours as the sun rose to reflect its snow-capped mountains and the polar cap that the spacecraft was heading. He could see the two mother ships in the far distance, orbiting the planet, several nautical leagues above him reflecting the sun rays on its outer shell what appeared to be in a quiet and stationary position. An opening in the snow beneath him, suddenly emerged as the shuttle manoeuvred above the entrance and lowered gently between the hanger doors to rest on a stand amongst some space crafts. The rack area was broad with so much activity that Zheng and Biyu stood in awe as Pyroeis approached to welcome them like a long-lost relative.

"Welcome my homo-sapiens. You are looking extremely well, and I must congratulate you both on the success you have been able to bring to this project. Planet Earth Council would be proud." He said as he glanced to Pusa immediately communicating through telepathy and knowing full well by now of all the frustrations and despair of them both as he continued. "So we have come to collect the girls and take them back to their natural surroundings." He said as he was interrupted by Pusa.

"Yes we shall take them back, but first let's show Zheng and Biyu what we have been up to since we have been on this planet."

They entered from the hanger into a large corridor entirely with transparent walls that appeared to go off into infinity either side of them as they walked along peering below a glass floor. They could see hundreds of humans laying horizontal without any support or in a vertical position with robots or humanoids doing something as if they were programming them. Surrounded by the activity, they passed through an opening into an enclosed area where the girls lay sedated asleep wearing the same white robes they wore on *Planet-F.*

"Wow! is that it?" Said, Zheng, as his eyes scanned the complete area.

"Oh no, this is the final area for transportation to the planet. Follow me to see the rest." Said Pyroeis as he hesitated and turned to the robots: "Prepare the girls for *Planet-F*; load them on the space shuttle ready for departure."

They left the area to stand once again in what appeared to be a hallway, the ground beneath them started to descend and accelerate. As the elevator descended floor after floor male and female humans of all ages just stood in open-spaced areas, utterly naked with tubes in their mouths, stomachs and thin fibres protruding from their heads.

Pyroeis observing the curiosity on Zheng and Biyu's face spoke: "As the development progresses, they move from floor to floor ready for departure and finally initiation ready to begin a life on *Planet-F.*"

"But why so many? I thought you had already populated the planet so it can now develop naturally?"

"Ah, yes, this, however, is the new breed. You can see all the young children are a mixture of 4th and 5th Millennium with yours and Biyu's DNA. Since they were born, their parents are old stock, as you know for some, twenty to fifty years ago. They will become the guardians of the new breed." Said Pyroeis

"You mean some held in a state for all this time grown in a test tube." Said, Zheng, as his facial expression said it all as he turned to Biyu who by now stood in complete shock, hesitated then continued. " This is just unbelievable, and I'm sorry to say I'm sure this is not what Planet Earth intended for you to do, to mass-produce a so-called superior race."

The humanoids generally could not show any form of emotion, but somehow Zheng sensed that his words had triggered something in their memory banks as Pyroeis responded.

"Our instructions are to populate planets with homo-sapiens and bring them to the 5th Millenium intelligence to be able to continue our knowledge of the Universe. And precisely that is what we are doing. We are bringing the people to higher intelligence."

"Yes I understand that, but surely you cannot continue in this manner populating a breed that cannot multiply naturally. The human race will not be able to continue in this way. Mothers will die giving birth and children will suffocate. The 5th Millennium race will end. Can't you see that!" Said, Zheng, hoping that maybe something might penetrate their logical mind as he answered.

"All I can see is I need the intelligence of the 5th Millenium, and Pusa, correct me if I am wrong, tells me that you have already met such a person?"

Zheng astounded that it was impossible to negotiate in any way with a robot that now presented with such a question that he must be referring to Jesus of Nazareth, so Zheng chose his words carefully as he turned to Pyroeis.

"Yes, I met such a person, but surely it was a person made by you?"

"No, we had nothing to do with it and wondered wherefrom did he come. Perhaps you can explain?" Said, Pyroeis with a challenging voice as he spoke.

"Well, I met and spoke with him. He preaches the love of humankind. I thought that you had placed him on this planet to initiate religion and was amazed at the uniqueness of something you had manufactured. It was clever of you to deceive me in such a way as to make me think he knew about you and what you were doing to me and that I had to tell you the truth." Said, Zheng, as he suddenly was interrupted by Pusa.

"What truth is that?"

"The lie told to you by the Council on planet earth that the 5th Millennium held the knowledge of the universe which they don't." Said, Zheng as Pusa continued.

"So who holds this knowledge?"

"I don't know who holds this knowledge."

"So why did this Jesus of Nazareth come to this planet?" Said Pyroeis.

"I don't know—you brought him here—didn't you? "

"No, we certainly did not manufacture or have anything to do with him."

Zheng now confused why the humanoids would carry on with such a convincing pretence that he might as well play along with them. "Possibly the same reason he went to Planet Earth—his next port of call will be *Planet-E*." Said Zheng.

"*Planet-E* why and when will he go to *Planet-E*?" Said, Pyroeis

"Well, he told me that he would return on *Planet-E* at the same period that has just occurred on this Planet which is about in the next 300 years."

"Hmm!— 300 years—you will have to go and have another audience with Jesus."

Zheng hearing these words could not believe what Pyroeis had just said: knowing Jesus was a machine created by them and I was a mortal human being with a lifespan if I was lucky of 100 years.

"And how do you intend for me to go?" Zheng replied.

"The same way we brought you here— cryogenic preserve you."

"But why?—I have a life now on this planet—what about my children?" Zheng, Said, looked towards Biyu in complete shock and with tears now flooding down her face expecting the worst.

"Please, no—don't do this to us—we have done more than you asked—but this is too much—what do you hope to gain?" Said Biyu as she gasped for air between her words.

"It's obvious this man Jesus holds the key to the Universe and can traverse through time and space and has the information we require, and we are going to get him to find out." Said Pyroeis now in a commanding voice as he turned to the robots and instructed: "Take them away until I decide what we shall do next."

CHAPTER 6

The dilemma

Zheng woke early that day as the sun rose and shone brightly through the louvred wooden frames, casting dark shadows across his face and directly into his eyes. The rooster could be heard 'cock-a-doodle-doo' and Biyu laying beside him still fast asleep. He had slept well but somehow felt strange, as he emerged from his bed and went towards the kitchen to the breakfast table, already prepared as usual. His mind was racing; his heart was beating unusually fast, believing that he must have had a horrible nightmare which he couldn't remember. He stepped outside; it was a bright day, the sky a very light cobalt blue on the horizon that rose to a dark ultramarine blue above his head and without a cloud visible. He stood there picturing what season is this? It felt warm; it must be summer? But how come I'm unaware of this, as he pondered. He could see Chu Yun as he waved and shouted "good morning". He went back to the table had fresh fruit, took some milk, but something was not quite right as he stared at the table. Biyu entered, sat down beside him, kissed him on the cheek and said "good morning." As she added, "I'll check on the kids." She came back as she poked her head in the door and added. "Fast asleep."

Zheng, unexpectedly realised that the sun never woke him from shining through his window in the morning, only at dusk, as it set. He rushed outside observed to see the sun rising as usual from due East. However, Zheng suddenly noticed that the front of his villa was now facing West, whereas before it faced East. Although it was still early morning, he could even see the outline of a planet as he stared in shock: "No, it can't be. What year is it?" As he spoke aloud and raced abruptly outside through the main gate to notice travellers passing by and hailed: "Where are you going?"

"To Rome, of course, it's Augustus 20th anniversary as Emperor, and there are celebrations in the circus." Said a traveller as he waved goodbye to add: "Hope to see you there, Zheng!"

"He knew my name! Do I know him?" He said to himself aloud in a shaky voice as he waved and acknowledged farewell. Zheng knew that Augustus made Emperor 27 BC so if it's his 20th anniversary it must be the 6th or 7th BC as he expected and slumped back on a nearby bench trying to get to grips with the present situation: *something was not quite right* he thought. He stood up and observed the travellers in the distance and could make out Rome's outlined city as the sun reflected on the arena: *this is Planet-F; but why is my house facing the wrong way? Am I going mad? Or has the planet changed its rotation?* As he pondered.

Zheng walked the grounds; everything appeared normal; except all seemed to be the mirror image. The property was now facing due East, whereas he remembered the sun setting behind the stables not rising in front of it. The children were playing as usual. Feiyan and Yi passed by and acknowledged "Good Morning" as they went about their chores. Biyu hadn't mentioned anything unusual, especially, as it was so apparent to him that the house and the grounds were now facing the wrong direction. Zheng sat all day quietly, not speaking to anybody just waiting for nightfall to observe the constellation of the stars and planets. That day, it seemed to go on forever for him as dusk set in, but the worlds were still not in view as he sat outside just waiting as Biyu approached in a melancholy mode as she quietly spoke: "You have been very quiet today, are you ok?"

"Yes I'm fine I'm just admiring the night sky." And just as he uttered those words, a Planet started to rise directly in his view; he turned and pointed and asked inquisitively to Biyu. "If I'm not certain; Isn't that Plane-F rising from the horizon?"

Biyu stood in silence, surprised; rubbed her eyes, focused and uttered. "Yes, that's *Planet-F*! I don't understand we're supposed to be on that planet; aren't we?"

"Yes of course, but we're not; it appears that we're back on *Planet-E*." Said, Zheng, as he stood in silence as he closed and squinted his eyes to observe the planet more closely in detail.

"That's impossible! If we are on *Planet-E* what year are we living in then?" Asked Biyu.

"The Roman era, around 6th BC." Said, Zheng, shook his head from side to side, not understanding anything as he added. "Somehow we have lost nearly 300 hundred years!"

"If this is *Plane-E*, then where have we been for the past 300 hundred years?" He said as he calculated the years quickly. "We left *Planet-E* approximately 310 BC at the time of the Greek era and then spent nearly ten years on *Planet-F* during the reign of Emperor Augustus. Now it emerges we are back on *Planet-E* in the year somewhere around 6th BC; Emperor Augustus reigns again, which makes by my reckoning nearly 300 years missing."

"There's only one explanation; cryogenically preserved to survive 300 years; not only us but it must include everybody too; to ensure that life to us looks as if we have never left." As he paused, then added, "What about the children are they okay?"

"They are just fine; everything seems normal! But now I just don't know anymore; what is normal?" Said, Biyu as she sat alongside Zheng entirely and utterly confused. Placed her head on his lap as he stroked her hair and noticed the impregnated mark revealing that she still had a microchip implanted in her brain, meaning monitored by the humanoids.

"Have you seen robots, Pi and Zeta?" Said, Zheng curiously, as he touched Biyu on the shoulder to sit up and turn and face him as he added: "I wonder if our 5th Millenium room is still intact?"

They both hastily went to the room that held all the communicating and holographic devices only to find it no longer existed. Also, after a thorough search, the robots were nowhere to be found. And at the same time, they searched high and low for their gemstones of amethysts and Sapphire, but to no avail, they also were nowhere to be found.

"What about the weapons?" Said Biyu as they searched top to bottom, but they had gone too.

"They have left us with nothing." Said Zheng.

In despair, Zheng rushed to the children's bedroom only to confirm that they were clean of microchips, as he said to Biyu who was following close behind him. "You best check behind my ear too?"

"No, you still have a microchip." As she parted his hair behind each ear to spot the insertion scar was precisely in the same place.

"That means they are not finished with us yet!" Added, Zheng.

Zheng identified and appreciated that he was now back on *Planet-E* approximately in an era when he left 300 years ago from *Planet-F.* It was evident to him that the humanoids have a plan where his services are still required. In a confused state, his mind had difficulty recollecting his past; he remembered certain aspects, but there were considerable gaps in putting all the pieces together. For the rest of the family, except for Biyu, life seemed to be the same. The children, however, for reasons unknown to him and Biyu, they had adopted other names. Biyu's eldest daughter insisted that her name was not Ji, but Tarpeia and Jiangsu and Lihua were Pinaria and Oppia. Biyu also noticed that each of her girls had a very faint shadow mark on their stomachs; in precisely the same place and length of injury that she had had. *Have they given birth?* She anxiously thought.

It appeared, Zheng, was not only a merchant in providing racehorses for the arena but a charioteer too. Stables full of the most beautiful stallions, considered by the circus the best; making him the highest-paid sports star. Posters displayed around the stables depicted him winning many events. Many famous chariot riders would visit the stables to select his most unique breed to compete against his blue team who were celebrities, including his horses whose life expectancy was shallow. The stable boys would continually talk about so and so horse. And reflect on such a magnificent horse in the circus. Zheng frequently raced four-horse chariots as shown in the posters; and in most of the races, he would come from behind to win, according to his staff, as they described in detail his famous events which he would listen to with such conviction, mainly to find out more about himself. His other team members role in the contest was to obliterate the others to crash to leave Zheng with a clear run to the finish line. The races were explained in great detail and accuracy by his charioteers or by his staff or to those who had an interest in chariot racing, which Zheng would listen too in earnest mainly to gain knowledge of chariot racing.

But all of what he had just witnessed and heard as he listened to his staff and close associates, he couldn't believe that suddenly he was amongst something that he had no idea of, and the effort the humanoids must have gone to be able to set up such deceit. As he continued thinking, he began to realise that this life on this planet in this particular era, *apparently had existed for years but played by someone else that looked, talked and acted just like me.*

But why? He thought. *Maybe Biyu and the children have been replaced too by someone else. Perhaps the rest have been created by the humanoids at some point earlier* as he carried on thinking. He needed to find out as he discussed in detail with Biyu his day of delusion and confusion, and she suggested:

"The only way I can think of is to check the other girls to see if they have the same scars that our girls show."

"What do you mean—injuries?" Said Zheng with a curious expression on his face.

"Our daughters have given birth by caesarean." She said.

"I suddenly remembered after seeing those scars that the girls were pregnant when we left *Planet F*—don't you recall that?"

The penny dropped as he uttered: "Yes, I remember now we were in a dangerous predicament, life-threatening if I recall, we had to leave because the girls were all carrying a child."

"That's right, twins if I remember. Let me check the other girls." She said as she turned to leave as Zheng questioned.

"How do you intend to inspect the girls then?"

"Simple, girls love new clothes, and I have a wardrobe full of the finest robes—leave it to me."

Tomorrow was a big event at the circus celebrating Augustus 20th year as Emperor; Zheng gathered to participate in chariot racing. He decided to practice that Saturday afternoon with his horses and chariot. It was a disaster as his eldest son, Ju, now referred to as Gaius looked on. His two younger brothers Jizi and Guang were now mentioned to as Aulus and Cato respectively.

"Well that was awful, are you ok." Said Gaius.

"I Know, I'm not feeling myself these days. And I'm not up to competing tomorrow." Said Zheng.

His son Gaius had been waiting for this opportunity for years to compete in the circus as he stood there realising something was not quite right with his father as he quickly responded. "Please, can I take your place tomorrow?" as he added, "you know you promised and I think now is the time—I can ride with your colours.—Please say yes and give me this opportunity."

Zheng stepped out of his chariot knowing that tomorrow would be a death sentence for him, stared into the eyes of Gaius, and somehow feeling that this was somebody standing in front of him that he didn't know as he replied.

"Do you think you can handle it? The opposition will be fierce and show no mercy—you know that don't you?"

"Dad, I have closely followed observed every one of your techniques, skills and trained enthusiastically with you—please give me this chance—I beg you."

"Ok, let me speak to your mother first, if she agrees then it's ok."

Zheng worried and still in shock what he was now beginning to apprehend a hopeless situation had no alternative but to discuss with Biyu. He found her, nearly in tears as he approached and before he could utter a word her sorrows spelt out. "I don't know who those girls are and I believe that Feiyan, Chen, Niu and Yi their mothers are somebody else that we have never met before."

"I know what you mean." Said, Zheng, as he added "Are you sure the girls are our children? I know that Ju now called Gaius is not my direct son, and his brothers too, now named Aulus and Cato are possibly clones."

"How can you tell that?" Said Biyu

"Well, they have no mark of an insertion of a microchip, and they have no scar that they once carried. They are another person!"He said with a look of surprise as it turned to sadness.

"I just don't know anymore. I can't understand why our girls bear the mark of having a caesarean while the others show no mark at all." Said, Biyu as she stared into Zheng's anguished face as she continued. "Something else is bugging you. What is it?"

"Tomorrow I am to compete in the circus. It appears I am a superstar in the arena and have won a lot of chariot races." Said Zheng with a gloomy look.

"Well that's impossible—you can't go— you will kill yourself. What do you know about chariot racing."

"Supposedly a lot, according to Gaius who has asked to take my place and encouraged by his brothers." He said.

"You haven't told him anything?—Have you?" Said, Biyu with a curious face.

"No, of course not. But Gaius watched me make a mess of everything as I tried to train and control the horses. Should I let him—take my place tomorrow?—he is so excited about having an opportunity to compete that he has begged me to allow him to represent our colours in the circus."

Biyu stood in silence as she contemplated looked around at the surroundings and shrugged her shoulders as if to say I just don't understand anymore as she croaked a few words between her sobs. "I can't lose you too, do whatever you think is best. If you feel he is another person resembling your son, well the answer is simple." As she walked away sobbing into her handkerchief, soaking the tears streaming down her cheek.

The charioteers informed that evening that Gaius would replace Zheng in the Arena tomorrow due to his father's ill health. The other team members were delighted, thinking this was a smart ploy by Zheng, for Gaius to wait a long time for this opportunity patiently. Zheng had blocked for years his entry into the Arena knowing full well that the circus was a dangerous place and not for the faint-hearted and especially his eldest son who was in line to inherit and continue the family name and fortune.

They came from four corners of the globe to compete in celebrating Agustus's 20th year as Emperor. The prize money was enormous, and the stadium packed with well over 250,000 spectators.

Zheng had a private box close to the Emperor's imperial compound. Zheng himself would occupy one of the building enclosures in the centre of the track known as the median where his voice heard to give supervision to his team. He had access from both sides of the Arena and had his bearers available to gather quickly from the track if one of his gladiators' fell. According to his team, he had trained his charioteers to hold the reins and not to traditionally wrap the controls around their waist so in the event of a crash they could quickly let go and not dragged around the circus until killed.

The main event of that day was twelve laps of the circus pulled by four horses. Zheng's team, the blues, would race against the red, white and greens. There would be three charioteers in each group. The Emperor today was supporting the blue team, and his wife Livia had placed a considerable sum of money on Zheng's side to win, which suddenly put high importance on ensuring a win.

Zheng had a good view of the imperial box and could not believe that the uncanniness of the close resemblance of the same characters that he had met on *Planet-F* some 300 years earlier was here again playing the same role on *Planet-E*. Alongside, Augustus sat his wife Livia and next to her sat her two sons Tiberius and Drusus. At the other end of Augustus sat his daughter Julia the Elder with her lover Iullus Antonio. He knew precisely the fate of all, and somehow he felt none of this was real as he nearly shouted out, "Would somebody please wake me up from this nightmare." As he continued to look and scan his box next to the imperial enclosure to see that his sons and daughters looking elegant, beautiful and admired by all, to think I was responsible initially. *Still, some, maybe are clones of my predecessor's acting a role* he thought. His mind began to question and go into some trance thinking about himself and Biyu: *I wonder what happened to the two that we have replaced?* As he suddenly was snapped out of his thoughts as the spring-loaded gates that held the horses and chariots sprung open with such a vibrant noise as the hooves of the galloping horses sent shock waves through the ground.

Gaius came flying by ahead of his other team competitors and in front of the race which was not as planned as Zheng ran across to the other side to shout out. "Get back!—What the hell are you doing!"

Gaius, so overwhelmed and excited by the occasion, let the reins of his horses slide loosely through his hands and allowed them to bolt. As he passed his father standing in the median heard the words he shouted but realised it was too late, he was amongst the thick of his rivals that were about to bring his chariot crashing to the ground as they closed in on him either side of his wheels.

His team members, close behind, realised their plan of keeping Gaius in the rear out of trouble until he had a clear run to the finish line had vanished. They waited until they came around again just before where Zheng was standing, behind the barriers, screaming and shouting advice above the noise of the crowd, only as one of his chariots deliberately mounted the outside wheel of the red chariot that had trapped Gaius in the middle. It sent it flying through the air and crashing down, only to take out one of their team chariots. It left space for Gaius to move away from a chariot inside that had boxed him in, as rivals passed leaving him last position. After the incident, Zheng rushed out onto the track and gathered his charioteer team member who was slightly dazed and dusted. His opponent that fell from the red chariot was being dragged around the arena as he frantically tried to cut his reins free, to no avail, as the horses continued pulling him with a trail of blood behind. At the thrill of the spectacle, the crowd ecstatic screamed and shouted, making it impossible to hear Zheng's words.

Gaius realising his mistake, held back, as planned initially with his other team member just in front observing the spectacle unfold as the Red and Whites started to annihilate one another. The track was littered with debris as bearers rushed out whenever it allowed them to gather bodies and debris.

After the 6th lap, only six chariots remained. There were two blue trailing at the back with two green in front and leading the pack one red and one white. The red chariot held the inner track while the white chariot was trying to pass on the outside. As they approached the start line, the white chariot drew alongside the red chariot, hoping to get in front to move on the inside. The red chariot held, but his speed was now too fast as he approached the bend and swerved out to clip the wheel of his rival which sent both chariots to summersault in midair crashing down on one of the green chariot following close behind. The other green chariot cut through on the inside, followed by the other two blue chariots. With three laps to go, Gaius still held back as his other team member followed closely behind the green chariot.

On the penultimate lap, Gaius's team member moved alongside the green chariot and forced him on the inside not allowing him to change out to block Gaius who would take the outside track, knowing that his horses could outrun any horse in the circus. As they approached the start line for the last time, which would become the finish line, Gaius was racing on the outside, keeping pace with the inside chariot. With 650 metres to go, all three chariots came out of the final bend in line with a gallop to the finish line. The noise was overwhelming as they screamed green or blue and effortlessly Gaius's horses surged forward with just a body length in the front to take the ribbon.

Zheng could see the joy on Augustus's and Livia's face as Gaius did a lap of honour to stop in front of the imperial box to receive a wreath of laurel leaves. He was now the youngest charioteer to participate in the Hippodrome. As Zheng looked up into the box, his family was crying and screaming with joy as his sisters and girlfriends blew kisses and showered him with flowers. It seemed a marvel as he once more did a lap of honour for the crowd as the 250,000 stood chanting his name Gaius. Gaius. Gaius.

Zheng stepped out from his enclosure as his son stopped in front of him and encouraged him to stand alongside in the chariot as they continued circumnavigating the Arena waving to the crowd. Gaius kissed his father on the cheek as he thanked him over and over again in giving him and allowing such an opportunity as Zheng turned to him and sincerely said "From now on you will carry my colours and represent me in the circus. I'm too old and tired of carrying on with this."

That evening celebration would continue within the imperial palace with music, costumed dancers a banquet of food and as much wine as one could drink. The winners would be seated close to the majestic table with the other competitors scattered around a luxurious hall. Zheng, now acutely aware that he had been here before in a very similar predicament when his gladiators Pi and Zeta were anointed champions of the Arena sat in silence alongside Biyu as they watched the others enjoying themselves. His daughters were the centre of attraction, and Drusus was paying exceptional attention to his oldest, Tarpeia. Much to his mistress Julia's jealousy and envy, Iullus Antonius had eyes for Pinaria, Zheng's, second eldest daughter. Tiberius, married to Julia, sat at the head of the table, ignoring his wife, and paying very little attention to what was going on around him.

Gaius, the star of the show, was surrounded by many beautiful women who all wore a coloured blue ribbon to show their support and allegiance to charioteers' blue team.

Augustus sat quietly with Livia alongside and noticed Zheng that he had heard so much about but had not formally introduced rose from his chair and walked towards Zheng's table, acknowledging others as he passed by. Immediately Zheng arose as Augustus approached and spoke:

"Fine boy you have there and I must congratulate you on providing such pleasant entertainment with such an intelligent orchestrated race."

"Well, thank you, Emperor, and I hope that good fortune came your way." Said Zheng knowing full well that a substantial amount of money was placed by his wife Livia on the blue team winning.

"And how is your gladiator that fell in the Arena?"

"He is just fine a few scratches and bruises which will soon heal." Said, Zheng as he added, "The other gladiator on the red team I'm afraid didn't make it."

"Oh, I'm sorry to hear that and how many beautiful horses did we lose?"

"On my side none, but I believe all told six had put down."

"A shame, so much slaughter, for so little gain." Said, Augustus as he acknowledged Biyu sitting there as he turned and left to walk back to his table.

"Well, what did you make of that to be singled out by the Emperor." Said, Zheng, as he glanced towards Biyu who wasn't enjoying the occasion as she appeared preoccupied with her daughters that were becoming the centre of attention to young men including two very significant closely related to the Emperor.

Tarpeia, the eldest daughter of Biyu's children, had just celebrated her eighteenth birthday and had no recollection of her life before and had never questioned or given any indication of familiarity. She resembled her mother in every aspect, portraying her brilliant emerald eyes and long black satin hair that stretched halfway down her back, however, today her hair was demurely bound in a fillet. Admired by most men but envied by glaring noblewomen her physic perfects that replicated by the Greek goddess Venus's marble statue standing in the banquet area. She stood alongside the figure reflecting a carbon copy of its torso, in imported silk and cotton gown in a saffron yellow.

Pinaria the second daughter now seventeen resembled her father, Zheng, with light blue eyes and auburn coloured hair cut slightly shorter, modestly bound with hair parted in two and tied in a bun at the back. She too never questioned acquaintance had a perfect body with a little smaller frame and height to her sister Tarpeia. She wore a blue silk gown to display her father's charioteers colours.

The third daughter, Oppia, not showing any previous knowledge of her surroundings, possibly the prettiest had just turned sixteen with a fairer complexion again took after her father with blue eyes and light-coloured yellow ochre hair. Being the youngest, she was the most sort after by the eligible bachelors that surrounded her much to the envy of Tarpeia who sat alone with Drusus, the son of Augustus wife, Livia. Like Pinaria, her older sister wore a silk gown showing the team colours in various blue shades. Her hair was identical to that of Livia, except that her hair was real whereas Livia wore a wig, with the hair parted in three, with the hair from the sides of the head tied in a bun at the back of the middle section looped on itself, creating a Pompadour style.

Pinaria, now cornered by Iullus Antonius the second son of the deceased Roman general Mark Antony and the lover to Tiberius wife Julia, also looked upon the laughter and jesting from the corner where her younger sister Oppia sat with an audience of young men. She could sense the eyes of Julia staring at her with such anger that if looks could kill, she would be dead, as Iullus showered her with too much affection and philandering.

Zheng and Biyu sat alone observing the intrigue, flaunting, flirting and lusting that unfolded before their very eyes and concern for their daughters as the wine given in plenty as they become intoxicated and taken advantage by the gentry.

Zheng, waited patiently for Augustus and Livia to retire before he gathered his entourage to say farewell, much to the annoyance of Drusus, and Iullus who now considered his daughters, high, vulnerable, lower class and for their pleasure. For Drusus and Iullus, most respectable women at the banquet didn't consume wine in case of becoming inebriated, leading to some form of immoral action regarded by their jealous husbands' or betrothals'.

Drusus, now wholly infatuated with Tarpeia insisted that he visit her home with intentions of purchasing horses from her father. Iullus Antonius invited himself too on hearing this with his purpose of attending Pinaria. Zheng had no objection to selling horses but fully understood their real plans and made arrangements. Set a time for tomorrow as he and Biyu said farewell and departed with a most disgruntled bunch, as they felt they were leaving far too early and that the party was just about to start. With Augustus and the other nobles retired, Zheng knew the party was about to turn into an orgy. Particularly with the single women associated with the charioteers, that regarded as loose, commoners, completely legless, and defenceless when drunk, which would eventually end in an embarrassing naked position to be exploited by all.

CHAPTER 7.

Not again

Zheng and Biyu after their ordeal at the circus and the banquet sat alone that evening outside admiring the milky way as it stretched across the very dark clear sky without a nearby bright planet insight to obscure and diminish their view.

"Amazing to think you and I are now, by planet earth reckoning, more than 430 years old: 100 years travelling, 300years hibernating and the odd twenty years living." Said, Zheng, as he gave a melancholy glance at Biyu who sighed concurrence as she uttered. "Yes," and added. "To think too!—We now know the future outcome of most of those who we have just met tonight."

"Yes, you're right; and all of this too!" said Zheng as he waved his arms above his head to display his surroundings and the villa as he continued. "Somehow is just not real. How could the humanoids repeat history so accurately, so canny, that everything appears to fall into place? It's like all the people have been programmed or acting outlines that they have learnt to perform on a stage, but they haven't; naturally, they have evolved since we were last here 300 years ago. I didn't notice one mark, scar or any form of insertion of a microchip." Shaking his head in an unbelief fashion continued "A script is playing out exactly as it played out on *Planet-F*."

"Uncanny! Why do you think the humanoids have put us back on *Planet-E*?" Said Biyu with such a curious facial look as she continued to stare at the night sky.

"If they are repeating what happened on *Planet-F*, why? And what is it so important to the humanoids to go to all this trouble just for us?" Said Zheng questioning and thinking to himself: suddenly realised, it clicked and the penny dropped as he hastily continued. "Of course! It's obvious! What is so vital in the 6th and 4th BC? The birth of Jesus of Nazareth, of course!—That's it!—That's why we are back!—Do you remember? "

"Well, no! What do we have to do with Jesus of Nazareth.?"

"The key to the universe. That's it!—Now I remember!—The humanoids believe that Jesus has the knowledge of time and space because He can transpose the cosmos and we're here to get that information." Said, Zheng, as his mind now exploding as his memory and thoughts were racing through his brain and unfolding what had happened three hundred years ago on *Planet-F*.

"But I thought Jesus was a humanoid—you said?" Questioned Biyu.

"Yes, you're right—do you think he is for real then?" inquired Zheng with a puzzled expression on his face." Could it be I got it wrong, and the humanoids didn't make him after all?"

"No impossible—they must have made him—then why bring us back to the planet?"

Zheng sat quietly gazing at the milky way pondering and thinking turned to Biyu directly. "We shall do nothing for the time being, but continue with our lives and wait; because the humanoids are going to come. We cannot contact them; we have no communicating devices; we have no weapons and the robots, Pi and Zeta, have gone. We're alone, but we have microchips embedded in our brains like the children, which still monitored they have plans for us. They are coming back!—When?—I just don't know?"

Zheng and Biyu exhausted from their ordeal and the difficult discussions that went well into the early hours retired and fell into a deep trance. They slept well into the morning only to be woken by Tarpeia and Pinaria, fussing about Drusus and Iullus Antonius attending that day; about what should they wear—what time were they coming, and what were they going to eat.

Zheng had already organised everything with his servants: everything was in hand, and he had catered for many; knowing that it would just not be Drusus and Iullus, but much more, as the entourage suddenly appeared at the gates.

Drusus had informed his mother Livia, that he was going with Iullus Antonius to buy horses. Julia, Augustus daughter, overheard and immediately invited herself with her two sons, Lucius, and Gaius. Iullus was fuming that his mistress, Julia, should accompany him knowing full well he had no intentions of buying a horse but just to seduce Zheng's daughter, Pinaria.

Zheng and Biyu welcomed the party with open arms and invited them to sit and eat outside in the gardens while showing the horses. The only two interested in the animals were Julia's boys Lucius and Gaius. Drusus couldn't keep his eyes of Taperia, displaying her beautiful body sat very quietly next to her sister Pinaria continually interrupted by Julia every time Iullus Antonio tried to speak to her. "So my dear, what is your interest during the day besides breeding horses?" Said, Julia, as she sarcastically glanced at Iullus Antonius first then with such a facial scowl turned to Pinaria and added: "Perhaps you can teach my boys to ride such a beast." Looking at the two stallions presented to them.

"Well, these animals are not for children, but meant to compete in the circus." Said, Zheng, in a jesting voice.

Drusus sensed the animosity portrayed by Zheng that he interrupted immediately offered. "Sorry already sold I had the first refusal." He said as he added. "How much?"

A deal made as another two appeared to match the other two just sold. "I would keep either one of these to run inside of the other two." Said Chu Yun as Drusus had no idea what he was talking about except Iullus Antonius quickly interrupted. "Looks like you have to buy all four Drusus if you intend to race chariots." He said, mocking him with a smile.

"Ok put them with the other two" Said Drusus as he added, "But saddle one, I intend to ride back to the Palace."

Acutely aware that Drusus was killed, in his previous life, when he fell riding a horse, Zheng quickly interrupted, as he glanced across at Chu Yun. "You need to break them in first," he said to Drusus, as he turned at the same time to Chu Yun to keep his mouth shut as he placed a finger to his lips.

"That's right." Said Chu Yun realising what Zheng wanted him to say as he added. "We need to work on all four horses, but we can help you train them for the circus, but they're not quite ready to ride yet. Too lively and could easily throw you, Sir."

Drusus appeared to listen and was not interested in any of it; as he moved closer to Tarpeia, he thought nobody had observed his subtle move except Biyu who kept a very close watch on them. However, Julia positioned herself between Iulluis and Pinaria to ensure there was no physical contact between them. Iullus stood up and deliberately moved away.

"Ah, you're leaving so soon." Said Zheng, turned to Julia, gathered her boys engrossed with the horses and loving the whole occasion. "Come on, you two, your grandfather Augustus is expecting you for supper." She said as she stared at Iullus Antonius with such hate, who by now was completely ignoring her, as he sat alongside Pinaria. But Julia had to have the final say as she turned to Biyu and stormed out. "You know he is nearly 40 years of age and I believe your daughter is just sixteen. I certainly wouldn't let that animal near my daughter."

Biyu looked across at the pair and decided to intervene politely by offering more wine and food. She sat beside Iullus to discuss his new appointment as Asian proconsul and read some of the poetry he had just written praising Augustus. As he quoted some of his sonnets, Biyu's mind drifted into another world as she looked across at the beauty of Pinaria, that she once knew as her sweet little girl Jiangsu. And as she stared into her eyes, she began to remember that Pinaria like her sisters were once Vestal Virgins', inseminated by humanoids that they must have given birth by caesarian possibly twins. Now I understand, as it all flooded back into her memory. *That's what happened.* She thought quietly as suddenly she was stirred from her dark thoughts.

"What did you think? Did you like it?" Said Iullus

"Lovely, absolutely beautiful." Said, Biyu not remembering or being able to repeat a word he had just spoken.

Biyu completely dazed with the whole situation with what she had just recalled left the table and excused herself from Drusus but returned to ensure that her daughters not taken advantage.

Drusus continued drinking late into the afternoon after Iullus had departed knowing that it was hopeless with the mother sitting alongside. But Drusus insisted as he shouted for one of his stallions to be saddled since he intended to ride back to the palace with the others in tow. The horses were lively and playful after being kept all day in the stables and were ready for a gallop. But, Drusus demanded ignoring everyone to persuade him that he was too drunk and dangerous to mount a chariot horse. To portray a macho image, especially to impress everybody he was in control and a master at breaking in a horse Drusus left through the main gate. Entirely out of control as the three horses behind, overtook him into a full gallop onto the main road. Zheng rushed outside only to see Drusus holding for dear life around its neck as its horse kicked its hind legs to chase after the other three. Zheng with Chu Yun immediately mounted and tracked after him to find that Drusus had been thrown headfirst into a tree trunk. Dead, Zheng stood in silence. *History had repeated itself. Never meant for this life* Zheng thought as he gathered his body to take back to his villa and instructed Chu Yun to collect the horses and deliver them to the palace with the fatal news to his mother, Livia, of his death.

Livia devastated, blamed Zheng that he had deliberately intoxicated her son and persuaded him to purchase horses that he would never compete within the circus. He was not and never would be a charioteer she explained to her husband Augustus and that this must have been a brilliant ploy to assassinate her son; possibly knowing that he could be in line to be emperor. Tiberius, the elder brother of Drusus, was livid and so angry at the news he went without hesitation hastily directly to the Villa to get an accurate account of exactly what happened.

Something they knew would happen, Zheng and Biyu couldn't believe that it had just happened, as they had tried several times to persuade Drusus to return to the Palace without the horses, but he ignored their advice. Tarpeia stood sobbing profusely above his body as she attempted to come to terms with what had just occurred and blamed herself that if she encouraged his intimacy, they would be lying alongside one another in bed.

Zheng sensed the trouble that now lay ahead, and this incident was not going to be taken lightly as an accident, but as a very well thought out and calculated assassination.

The following day Tiberius arrived, returning the horses and expecting to be fully reimbursed, with his mother Livia and some Praetorian Guards that immediately ceased Zheng. Without question, he removed him to the council of senates for interrogation. Livia arranged for her son, Drusus, taken to the grove of Libitinia for his burial. Livia treated Biyu and her daughters as commoners and referred to Biyu as a Madam conducting a house full of prostitutes as she left ranting. "You're not fit to even to live in the gutter, and I am going to make you pay for this!"

These harsh words shocked Biyu through knowing there would be repercussions, and life would not be the same for any of her family.

Brought before an emergency council on the grounds of treason, Zheng had conspired with others knowing that a recently purchased horse was unsafe to ride and fully understanding the consequence had insisted that Drusus ride it home.

Zheng denied all knowledge and had witnesses to vouch that he had indeed tried to persuade Drusus, not to ride the horse and that it was unsafe, and offered his trainers to break and tame the animal free of charge.

The prosecuting Senate summoned Julia The Elder, the daughter of Emperor Augustus. Considered a very reliable witness to give her account, denied all knowledge of Zheng persuading Drusus not to ride but to the contrary that he had insisted Drusus ride the animal back to the Palace.

On examining Julia's evidence, the court closed the hearing, adjourned, and came quickly to a supposition that Zheng was responsible for the death of Livia's son Drusus and taken from these courts where his fate determined in the Arena.

The word on the court's decision spread rapidly through Rome and even to the home of Zheng some eight leagues in the town of Velletri. Iullus Antonius tried to persuade Julia to retract her statement that it was just a malicious lie because of her incestuous jealousy but to no avail. The date set, and Zheng would appear the following weekend where the Gods would decide his fate.

Biyu on hearing collapsed in shock and mainly feared knowing that Zheng without a weapon was no match for any gladiator that he may face in the Arena as she turned to Chu Yun. "We must go to him! Now!"

Admired a champion charioteer considered a hero by the crowd the jailer turned a blind eye as Chu Yun passed water as the jailer looked on knowing if caught by his superiors would severely be reprimanded,

"What do you think they are going to do to him?" Said, Biyu overwhelmed by a stinking foul, pungent smell of faeces and urine, as she covered her face and turned to the jailer.

"Well, I've heard its animals, Tigers to be exact. That horrible man-eating stripey cats from the Far East. If they kill and eat him, he's guilty. If not, the crowd will show mercy and ask for him to be released since the Gods have shown his innocence."

"Well, that's madness! How does he defend himself, with a sword I hope?" Said Biyu with tears in her eyes as she passed her hand through the bars to stroke his hand as Chu Yun passed more food.

"No, he's given nothing. And the only time the Tigers fed is in the Arena. They will be looking for food. I suggest you best say your farewells and prepare him for the next life. No one has ever survived, innocent or not." Said the Jailer as he walked away and added. "Just ten minutes more. That's all."

Biyu, profuse sobbing as she uttered. "If you die, I shall die too."

Zheng passed his hand through the bars and held her chin up as he spoke quietly. "Find Iullus he was there he can confirm that I didn't make Drusus ride that horse. He is the only one that can save me."

They left with some hope of saving Zheng, and Chu Yun had some idea were Iullus might be if he wasn't with his lover Julia; a tavern close by that Iullus frequented for his whores and prostitutes. They found him slumped over a table drunk with a female attempting to lure him to one of the many quarters. "Oh! If it isn't the mother of that lovely daughter of yours, Pinaria. Is she here? I want to fuck her!" Said Iullus as he slurred his words and continued. "And what may I ask, do I have the pleasure of your visit." Before Biyu could answer, he added. "Of course, Zheng is going to die tomorrow because of that cow Julia."

"Yes, he's going to die, and you can stop it! You know what happened. Drusus was stubborn and brought his death on himself. You know that!—Please tell somebody!— to clear this mess up!" Said Biyu with tears flooding in her eyes.

"I tried, but Julia lied on oath to her Gods, and I'm afraid being the daughter of the Emperor her word stands, and nobody is going to say she lied, especially under oath. I tried telling her she has condemned an innocent man, but life is cheap for that selfish and jealous bitch. There is nothing I can do—sorry!" Said, Iullus in a slur of drunkenness has he slumped back across the table utterly inebriated as a whore tried to entice him away.

"You Sir, are a coward and nothing but a sorrow state of a man and one hopes your Gods seek vengeance upon what's left of your miserable life." Said, Biyu as she stormed out of the tavern sending tables and chairs flying.

"So what do we do now?" Said, Chu Yun as he hastily followed behind Biyu's hurrying footsteps.

"Pray! Pray that's what we shall do. I have some mighty Gods too that I am going to call upon." Said, Biyu now very angry and frustrated as she added. "After listening to that imbecilic Iullus who will do nothing I will make sure that Zheng tomorrow walks out of that Arena."

That evening, Chu Yun, as he lay in the room next door in the hotel they had booked for the night, could hear words coming from Biyu's quarters as he spoke aloud, "She must be praying to her Gods."

Biyu spent the whole evening, repeating aloud and hoping that her thoughts might communicate with one of the humanoids or robots, Zheng, was in grave danger of losing his life tomorrow in the circus as she shouted out again and again, "please help us!"

Regarded as commoners and beggars, Biyu and Chu Yun, stood and mingled amongst the crowd, that didn't have to pay. Biyu covered her head and face to ensure that she was not recognised while Chu Yun closed by holding two weapons strapped to his waist and a knife tucked into his leather boot. They managed to work their way forward to get a complete view of the Arena. Biyu looked up to see the box that she attended just a few weeks before right close to the Imperial compound as the gentry and noblemen that had sentenced Zheng entered one by one in an air of superiority waiting for entertaining.

A procession entered the arena, led by lictors who bore the fasces that signified the magistrate of power over life and death—followed by a small band of trumpeters playing a fanfare. Images of the gods carried into witness the proceedings, followed by a scribe to record the outcome, and a man holding the palm branch used to honour victors.

The entertainment began with beast hunts and fighters. Next came the condemned criminals using a wide variety of wild animals to execute those who had violated the law publicly. Zheng was the first to enter the arena partially naked without weaponry or any means of defence. As he joined and wandered to the centre with a noise level loud as the shouts of Zheng, Zheng, Zheng, echoed around the arena and amplified as the echo reverberated with the original call. Zheng looked to the heavens and to his surprise two white doves circled above his head. They appeared not to be flapping their wings but just gliding in an ever descending circle. The brilliant white of their feathers stood out against the ultramarine blue sky, and suddenly, something fell, right in front where he stood. He bent down and picked up what looked like a small tube wrapped in a cloth. He opened the material, and it read "Whatever comes out of the gate blow hard into the tube."

Zheng held the tube in his clasped hand, looked up to see the white doves still circling above his head without flapping a wing, glanced down, opened his hand to know that it was a simple whistle. He heard a clunk and the sound of the gates opening, as the cogwheels turned, and to his horror, two Bengal tigers were racing towards him. Zheng closed his eyes, placed the pipe very discreetly in his mouth, covered it with his hands and blew hard. Not a sound heard as he exploded again. Zheng opened his eyes and looked up, and to his astonishment, the Bengal tigers had stopped dead in their tracks, crouched on all fours and were trying to move towards him on their stomachs. He couldn't believe it, which gave him confidence as he walked towards them and again very discreetly blew hard again. They rose, turned, cowered with their tails between their legs and their heads' hung low as they slowly walked away from him. He kept blowing until the Tigers returned passing through the iron gates to the guards' astonishment as they closed the gates behind them.

Biyu clasped her hands to her face as she witnessed something which she couldn't believe. She didn't know whether to cry or laugh. Chu Yun was ecstatic jumping for joy as tears rolled down his face. The noise in the Arena was deafening, and all that heard was Zheng! Zheng! Zheng! She looked up at the Imperial box; everybody was standing too, as they were in shock that somebody with so much power could tame wild beasts as the crowd chanted. Free him! Free him! Free him.

The two white doves continued to circle just above his head as the chants intensified. "The Gods have spoken! The Gods have spoken!" echoed around the stadium.

Augustus stood with his arms in the air as he waved the palm of his hands in an up and down motion as the noise began to subside until there was complete silence as he spoke:

"The Gods have spoken and given us a sign that this man is innocent, and I decree that he should immediately be set free."

The stadium erupted into a tumultuous noise of: "Free Zheng! Free Zheng! Free Zheng!"

Zheng stood in the middle of the Arena, soaking up the atmosphere in disbelief. His heartbeat increased as he inhaled gulps of air suddenly to notice Chu Yun mounted on a white stallion entered the Arena holding the reins of another, which Zheng immediately recognised as the white horse that had thrown Drusus. As it approached, Zheng ran alongside, grabbed the horses mane that hung loosely from its neck and flung his legs over and mounted it without a saddle. He rode around the Arena with his arms in the air waving to the crowd with his knees firmly gripping the horse to show that he had complete control of what the court had referred to as a wild beast. The group were ecstatic at the display and chanted even louder as they threw floral reefs and ribbons as he passed.

Augustus stood up applauding and insisted that everybody in the imperial box precisely gave a sense of solidarity of approval to appease the mob.

Zheng galloped out past a line of soldiers that gave a salute. Chu Wun followed close behind to find Biyu patiently waiting, holding the reins tightly on her sprightly black stallion, snorting and neighing as it stepped from one hove to the other ready for a fast gallop home.

Zheng arrived at his villa with such jubilation and hugs and kisses as he tried to dismount his horse. Before anybody could open their mouths, Zheng shouted out: "Tonight we shall celebrate as we have never celebrated before, and everybody in the village invited."

Zheng, tired and exhausted after his ordeal in the arena left Biyu in charge of organising and instructing her staff to ensure an invite for everybody and plenty of wine and food prepared.

Zheng soaked in his hot bath as Biyu entered as she dropped her robe to show a perfect torso as she cuddled up alongside, kissed him thoroughly on the lips like there was no tomorrow as she quietly whispered in his ear: "Tell me how the hell did you do that with those vicious Tigers."

"Believe me when I say I have no idea, but those white doves that circled above my head carried a whistle as they dropped it to my feet. I suddenly realised that it was not a regular shrill as I blew through the pipe but one that gives such a high frequency that to us humans cannot hear it, but it's loud and frightening to animals that they will cower away." He paused as Biyu laid her head on his chest as they both soaked themselves as their servants poured more hot water and added: "Those doves were not real either. They didn't flap their wings once and were circling in a precise motion as if controlled by somebody else." He paused as if something had triggered a thought as he added: " I think we're about to get a visit from our robotic friends."

Biyu kissed him again and could feel the erection as she placed her hand between his groin and slid on top of him as she made love with so much passion and thinking to herself: *the last time we did this was an eternity ago.* As she remembered 300 years ago; but just as Zheng was about to ejaculate he remembered that Biyu would immediately become pregnant gently lifted her off and brought her vagina to his tongue until she reached a climax of sexual excitement.

Zheng slept late well into the evening as he had never slept before only to be woken by sounds of joyful noise in the courtyard. Biyu had deliberately let him rest as the guests arrived to make sure that he could make an entrance with everybody there. He looked handsome, somewhat younger as he made his entrance in his very most beautiful robes as each of his children first greeted him with a kiss as Biyu held his hand. Each guest approached to show their affection and appreciation. They kissed his hand, and for some of his closest acquaintances his cheek.

As Zheng surveyed the party, he noticed two elegantly well-dressed; a woman and a man in expensive clothes that were displaying particular attention to him, walked towards them. Before he could utter a word, the woman spoke in a very polite manner. "Zheng you haven't changed, just as handsome as I remember you."

"Do I know you?" Said Zheng in a mysterious voice.

"You should; we have been friends for centuries." She stated in a monotone voice that he recognised straight away.

"Pusa!"

"That's right Zheng, you been waiting for us, haven't you? And don't you recognise Pyroeis?"

Zheng in shock as he hesitated, stuttered and replied. "Well, yes! You have brought me back to this planet to do what exactly?"

"To continue and finish what we started. That's all, and then we shall leave you in peace." Said Pusa in a very commanding voice, as Pyroeis interrupted. "It will please you that your great, great, grandchildren are waiting for you on *Planet-G*. We had recreated the 5th Millennium as you remember it when you left Plant-Earth— This is what we should have done in the first place on these two planets. Instead of ending up with a mess that we can no longer intervene or take part in."

Zheng amazed at Pyroeis's response as if everything achieved in the Stella solar system was a failure as he questioned: "You haven't been back since we left 300 years ago to see your achievements then?"

"Well we have of course from a distance with help from our robots, but you're right it's our first visit. We couldn't control the superior race, so we let evolution take control and the 5th Millennium women we inseminated died giving birth to their stillborn. So we left to pursue and habitat *Planet-G* under tighter control." Said Pusa implying that their achievements elsewhere was a failure.

"But you realise that history appears to be repeating itself precisely as it did on planet earth without your hindrance. Isn't that canny and expected?" said Zheng with a convincing facial look.

"Yes, of course, we understand that; it's all written in the DNA code. However, there must be something else that we are not aware of, since although it is following a sequential logic of actions and reactions, there are certain elements where we sense a higher order of intelligence, and that is why we need you." Said Pyroeis.

"A higher order of intelligence!—What me?—I have nothing to do with what is happening." Said Zheng now confused as Pyroeis interrupted. "Yes, we know that it's not you, but we think you have already met this superior being, and we need you to meet him again—He's back on the planet, and we did not bring him here. He must have a greater knowledge of the Universe than any of us can even begin to understand, since time and space is nothing to him."

Zheng, knowing full well what they were talking about: "He's here then—at the same time, he visited the other planets? It's unreal what the hell is going on?—Are you entirely sure." as he added, "So what do you want me to do?" Thinking to himself, *hopefully not to become a disciple?*

"He met you before three hundred years ago, so he is going to be surprised when you suddenly turn up. I am entirely sure he will remember you and perhaps somehow confide in you how he can travel through time and space. If he is real, he has been around for at least 5000 years that we know of since his only visit to Planet Earth. How does he do it? So we can copy him." Said Pyroeis as if this was such a simple mission he was about to undertake.

"And what is in it for me if I do this?" Asked Zheng still doubt whether this was the same game the humanoids played on him although centuries ago on *Planet-F.*

"We shall take you to *Planet-G* where you can spend the rest of your days with your kind and live as you did on Planet Earth with the 5th Millenium race. Now established as we left Planet Earth some 500 years ago." Said Pyroeis.

"And what about my children. If they are my kids and not some clone?" Said Zheng.

"Of course, they are yours." Said Pusa as she added, "They have, however, sterilised, so they can no longer breed—for safety reasons—I'm sure you understand— Don't you?"

"We are talking about the children of Biyu only? Or are we talking about all my kids:" Said, Zheng as he looked around to make sure that Biyu was nowhere in the vicinity.

"Biyu's children are the real thing sterilised; the rest I'm afraid are clones, but they can breed naturally." Said, Pusa without a flinch on its robotic face as it added.

"We did this to benefit you, so your surroundings appeared the same and that it was not too much of a shock after hibernating for nearly 300 years."

"Well, it was a shock when I realised you put the house the wrong way round to be woken by the sun in the morning." Said, Zheng in jest as he continued. "If I'm going to do this last mission for you then I need all my gizmos back, like the amethyst stone, the laser weapon and what else you think I may need perhaps return my robots Pi and Zeta to me."

"Yes. Yes, of course, we just couldn't leave these things lying around for anybody to see and take." Said Pyroeis.

"Whatever happened apparently to the two clones we replaced. And what about Biyu's girl's where they replaced too?" Said Zheng.

"I'm afraid the clones that you and your family have replaced we had to terminate their lives." Said Pusa with that robotic look as if this was nothing and a natural thing to do to continue with this masquerade.

Realising that he was ignoring his guests suggested: "You should leave now so I can spend some time with Biyu to explain." Zheng by now had been talking for some time and as he paused added. "You were responsible for what happened at the Arena today?"

"Of course. You didn't think we were going to let a couple of cats kill you!— Did you?" Said Pusa sarcastically unrecognisable with her new appearance and unknown to anybody. Saying their farewells left with the understanding that Zheng would fulfil his mission.

Returning to the festive celebrations and Zheng circled amongst the guests whispered in the ear of Biyu as he passed, "Need to speak to you alone tonight." Before she could respond, he had walked on laughing and joking with his chariot team.

Feeling more relaxed Zheng, knowing that his robotic friends hadn't abandoned him, and what they had said about a new 5th Millennium gave him an incentive to carry on, and perhaps he thought *there was an end to what he could only describe as a nightmare.*

After the guests had departed, and the staff had cleaned away the mess, Zheng and Biyu sat outside admiring once again *Planet-F*, in all its glory, as it shone its brilliance illuminating the surrounding gardens and lawns displaying an ambience of tranquillity. Contemplating what Pusa had said, there were no longer any 5th Millennium homo-sapiens living on the planet only the DNA of the 4th Millennium. Zheng calmly explained in detail to Biyu precisely what had happened. In silence absorbing every word, with the odd sigh, disbelief, cry of astonishment and sometimes tears tumbling across her cheeks in horror on hearing that her daughters too had been cryogenically preserved for close on 300 years, only to replace clones exterminated. "So where do we go from here?" Biyu, said as she cleared her throat and wiped her eyes dry.

"I'm going to have to do what they ask, of me, and then decide to live out our lives on this planet or seek immortality on this new *Planet-G* with people that are obviously all related to us." Said Zheng with tongue in cheek.

"All related to us!—You mean they have bred a race from our embryos and the others that you inseminated!" Said Biyu as she held herself in shock and disbelief.

"That's right, a planet full of our relatives!—We are the Adam and Eve of a new civilisation." As he paused, Zheng, waited for a response, which never came, as he continued. "I'm going to meet once more Jesus of Nazareth and seek his advice, because to me, at this very moment, nothing is real anymore. I don't know whether I'm coming or going. One minute I think I know then I don't. Everything suddenly becomes meaningless, and life itself to me at this very moment has no meaning. I need to find out once and for all."

"Ok. You go, I shall stay and pray, to whom I don't know, in the belief that you at least will come back to me, because I have nobody, not even my children which I don't know them anymore, except you." She said with tears rolling down her face as she hugged and kissed him on his forehead.

CHAPTER 8

Zheng's Army.

Weeks, then months went by; there wasn't a sign or any form of communication with the robots and life gradually settled into predictability. Augustus had taken action against his daughter Julia's copious promiscuity; Iullus Antonio exposed as her prominent lover and Julia exiled to an island. Zheng never saw Julia or Iullus again after that meeting at his villa. Pinaria, Zheng's daughter never met Iullus also. After that incident with her mother Biyu accusing Iullus of being a coward and not defending Zheng which nearly caused him his death resolute never to speak to him again. Zhengs eldest boy Gaius was doing exceptionally well in the circus and was considered the best charioteer.

Years went by; life was bliss, concerned he hadn't heard anything remembered: *apparently, it's too early yet; Jesus is still a boy, and understandably, there is no reason for me to go to Jerusalem.* Augustus had brought peace to the area, food plenty, but finally, after years of waiting that day came. It had been a glorious day and the evening air cooler after a sweltering day Biyu and Zheng sat outside to enjoy the evening, observing the stars that stretched across the sky giving shape to the milky way. "I wonder if planet earth is still somewhere there." Said, Zheng as he pointed to the heavens. And, suddenly a white light slowly traversed across the sky an object reflecting the suns rays from the other side of the planet. It disappeared, not behind a cloud because suddenly became obscure from the suns rays. Zheng stood up, "That was a spacecraft." he said as he continued "They're coming!"

Zheng waited all night. Biyu had gone to bed. The sun was beginning to rise, and then he noticed in the vicinity of where he expected the spacecraft to land two images merged. He knew it had landed and camouflaged itself. He walked briskly to the area to observe the figures as they appeared to approach out of thin air. He recognised them straight away. It was Pi and Zeta. He didn't know whether to run and hug them but stopped to think "They're robots," but couldn't help himself as he grabbed Pi first, "Am I glad to see you." He said as he turned and did the same to Zeta. They stood there motionless as machines would. They had no emotion or consciousness and looked at one another as if to say "is he mad?" They hadn't changed; they looked as he left them nearly 300 hundred years ago.

They held two shepherds crooks and two sets of gemstones as they handed them over. "I believe these are yours."

"Yes. Thank you." Said Zheng with so many questions that he needed answers too. But he realised robots don't socialise, so he just asked the obvious. "When do we leave."

"Within the next hour, if you don't mind." Said Pi

"Ok, I'll just say farewell to Biyu and hand over these things that you brought." Said, Zheng, and abruptly left to find Biyu.

Biyu was fast asleep, and it seemed a shame, but he had no choice as he shook her gently.

"My love, I'm afraid it's come. I have to leave. They are here, and we are to depart immediately." Said, Zheng, as he bent down and kissed her forehead.

"Oh! No. I was hoping that they had forgotten about us." She said as she immediately rose to put on a robe. "Oh, I see they have brought back the gemstones, and that crooked shepherds hook."

"Yes, there's one set for you; I shall take the other."

They hugged and kissed and Biyu burst into tears as he left he heard Biyu shout out. "You come back to me!—Do you hear me!"

In precisely the same spot that Zheng had left the robots asked: "Do I need to take anything besides what you gave me?"

"No, we have everything, let's go!" Said Pi turned and walked directly towards the woods as a black area appeared instantly in front of him as Zeta walked through and vanished as Zheng followed him.

The spacecraft hadn't changed in all that time. It looked the same as Zheng remembered it. Very sparse inside. Seats that appeared out of nowhere as one strapped themselves in. The places seemed to be on gimbals keeping the body always upright irrespective of the craft's position, as it moved around one. There was not one button or switch inside. No lights. Just nothing but as the shuttle lifted off in complete silence one was surrounded but what could only be called a head-up display of visuals and gadgets that were touched only by telepathy as one just sat fixed in one's chair with the craft rotated around one. The acceleration was phenomenal without the exertion of any form of gravity as the planet came into complete view. It was superb. Its colours resembled that of the earth. Before Zheng could absorb everything in his magnificent sight, it was already heading back to a desert terrain as it skimmed across its surface to land in the same upright position it took off.

Zheng stood outside in the clothes asked to wear resembling that of a Jewish merchant. He stood in awe of the spacecraft as its outer shell merged into its surroundings as sand; from the rear Pi and Zeta emerged mounted on camels, followed by a third which knelt to the floor to sit finally.

"This is yours. Have you ever ridden a camel?" Said Pi

"I'll show you how to mount and dismount." Said Zeta as the camel knelt he stepped off and then back on which Zheng copied and followed.

All three set off across the desert to see in the distance an oasis a three-hour march away. The date palm trees surrounded the spring water fed from the artesian aquifer provided shade for the peach trees. As they passed through the area, Zheng noticed the abundance of apricots, dates, figs and olives as he turned to Pi. "I wondered how you were going to feed me?"

Close to the waters edge the robots set up a tent. They kept guard all night as Zheng lay there emerging himself into the starlit night wondering to himself, now this is what I call heaven. I could live here forever. It's a sanctuary. I have personal bodyguards that don't need feeding, watering or even sleeping; they are observant, alert, loyal for twenty-four hours a day. No sooner had he said those words when a caravan of just a few arrived setting up their tents to be followed by at least well over a hundred with herds of animals nearby watering. The noise erupted into something one would experience in a marketplace with the hustle and bustle of buyers and sellers bartering for goods. Zheng out of curiosity could not help himself but stroll amongst the quickly erected tents and enjoy the aroma of freshly cooked food and a pungent smell of what can only describe as an exotic perfume that he had never encountered before. It seemed to relax him as he strolled past a large tent which looked as if it were the residence of somebody of importance.

"Enter my friend." He said in Greek as he beckoned Zheng to join him and take a position close to him on the floor supported by colourful cushions.

Zheng hadn't spoken Greek for well over 300 years but hadn't forgotten the language as he replied. "Thank you, Sir,—May I ask what that wonderful aroma that seems to be everywhere?"

"My friend, you have never come across saffron. Where have you been all your life—my friend?" As he stopped and continued. "Who may I ask I am addressing."

"Zheng, Sir—And you?"

"I am Amphios from Athens a merchant dealing mainly in Saffron." He said as he added. "You, Sir speak fluent Greek but have an ancient Chinese name, I recollect."

"Yes, Sir, what you call a mixed marriage. My father Chinese but my mother, Greek—My dad too was a merchant, a silk merchant to be exact." Said, Zheng

"A silk merchant and Chinese as well, you must come from a wealthy family." Said Amphios, admiring the expensive clothes dressed in as he added. "And what may I ask are you doing here?"

"I'm on my way to Jerusalem to buy horses. Zheng said

"Horses, why travel so far to buy horses?" Said Amphios

"To race Sir. I'm a charioteer in Rome at the circus?"

Before Zheng could utter another word, Amphios stood up rushed out of his tent and shouted: "Zheng is here from Rome!" Amphios had suddenly realised who he was talking too. He recognised the face but couldn't put two and two together until he mentioned that word charioteer. The crowds flocked to the tent. Zheng was famous. Pi and Zeta rushed on hearing the disturbance as they pushed their way through the crowds to face Amphios who spoke.

"Bodyguards too. You must be a prominent and very wealthy man. Come on I invite you all to eat with me as he included Pi and Zeta."

Zheng accepted as he turned to Amphios and said. "Not my servants, we mustn't spoil them, plus they must stand guard by my tent."

"Keep the plebs down. A man of my own heart." Said Amphios as he guided Zheng to sit with him and take some wine.

That evening Zheng ate such a feast and entertained by musicians and poetry read to him as they discussed philosophy into the early hours of the morning. They also talked about a future business where Zheng would become an agent for Amphios in Rome selling saffron. A very lucrative market that would make him and his family a lot of money. Later that night, they become friends and partners in a future business selling saffron. He scribed a note for Amphios to carry to his wife with instructions to buy a certain amount of saffron that he had already agreed on a price which she would pay. That morning Zheng departed for Jerusalem leaving Amphios to stay a few more days to enjoy the oasis's ambience.

The camels were rested and well-watered as they set off that morning into the desert to make their way directly to Jerusalem. Amphios had advised Zheng the dangers he faced with robbers and villains, and as a small party of just three was inviting trouble, and must take special care at night. Amphios would never travel with such few guards as he insisted safety in numbers and offered some of his bodyguards to accompany Zheng, which he thanked but said: "We can defend whatever comes at us."

However, Zheng did take advice not to pass through the high range but to make the long journey around and always at night to ensure he slept with protection at his back. That first very day Zheng slept well after an evening of stargazing; where the stars appeared to mingle to be apart of him and felt if he was part of the evening sky himself.

The robots always stood on guard, fully alert against whatever approached, which gave him so much confidence that he didn't worry about the world and could drift into a world of his own.

The very next morning the camp was surrounded what looked like a dozen vagabonds partially dressed as they dismounted from their camels holding a variety of weapons; blades gleaming the reflected sunlight as the dawn began to break. Zheng was not particularly perturbed as the robots backed towards him in a defensive mood. Zheng realising that he could quickly kill them, take them as prisoners only for them to be crucified or perhaps keep them as his bodyguards as he cried out to Pi. "Sedate them only. Don't kill them or harm them in any way with broken limbs—I want them alive."

Zheng had had enough of slaughtering men and decided to take another line of action as the robots one by one let a series of tranquillising minute darts into each and everyone as they slumped to the floor. He walked up to them as they lay in a heap on the floor. They looked disgusting. They smelt of rotten flesh, some with their mouths open, revealing a mouthful of crooked teeth and for the majority with no dentures at all. He cut their clothing right down to their groin with his sword as their vested penis fell out showing signs of syphilis or gonorrhoea and with symptoms of shingles.

"What a mess. What a sorrow state of human flesh. It's is just too much." As he turned to the robots that looked upon them not in horror but as asking, "So what?"

"Can we clean them up?" asked Zheng as he turned to the robots which really couldn't give a toss, he thought.

"Impossible we don't have the equipment or the means to be able to do what you are asking." Said Pi.

"What would it take then?" Zheng inquired.

"We would have to take them back to the laboratory," Zeta replied.

"Ok, is it possible you can call the spacecraft here?" Said Zheng.

"Well yes, the other robots are on beck and call. They can be here within the hour." Said Pi.

"Right then this is what we are going to do. You will bring the spacecraft here. We shall all return to the oasis. The spacecraft with the other robots will take these men back to your laboratories and fix them up and bring them back when finished to the oasis where we shall all be waiting." Zheng Instructed as Pi and Zeta did what precisely said without question, and within an hour the spacecraft hovered above them. It took off with everybody on board and landed just outside the oasis where it camouflaged itself amongst the palm trees while Zheng and the robots rode out towards the palm trees and back to the sanctuary on their camels. Amphios stood there amazed as he cried out, "What happened," unaware as the spacecraft hidden from view silently left for the North Pole.

"I decided to take your advice and wait for reinforcement. It's too dangerous to cross the desert with just three of us." Said Zheng trying to catch his breath between words knowing what the next question would be.

"How do you expect to get reinforcements?—you want some of my men?" Questioned Amphios.

"No, I have sent a homing pigeon my wife will send more men." Said, Zheng, as his camel knelt and sat right in front of Amphios as he dismounted.

"Homing pigeons? I would never think, to carry such birds—well, that is great, tonight, however, you are my guest, and I have a surprise for you of extraordinary dancers that have been practising all day." Said, Amphhios, that was so happy to see Zheng, which now considered a friend as he approached him and kissed him on either side of his cheek.

Zheng bathed all day in a makeshift bath. Nobody dares enter the oasis and foul the water, especially in front of others sharing the same water. He soaked his body with saffron given to him by one of Amphios servants that massaged his back, dried him and placed oil so fragrant that made his skin tingle. His clothes were washed, dried; his hair groomed, and the stubble around his chin shaved. He felt like a king as the robots just stood there in silence.

"Would one of your manservants like to take a bath?" Said one of the girls as she dressed him.

"They're shy they like to do it in private." Said Zheng.

"What a shame and so handsome too." Said the servant as he felt her hand move to his groin, which he immediately clasped and whispered in her ear. "Perhaps later." Knowing full well, he had no intentions of bedding any women of Amphios.

The evening cool, peacefully calm and the tent of Amphios more lavish than usual with such a smell of spiced food; a goat roasted on a spit with lamb next to it, mingled with a floral and honey as the saffron aroma engulfed the atmosphere. Other guests arrived and the wine just splendid as Amphios introduced him as the famous charioteer from Rome. Rumour had already had spread about how he had faced two Bengal Tigers; killed them with his bare hands, with a look of amazement as the audience listened intensely waiting for the story to unfold. Zheng obliged and exaggerated to satisfy everybody that wanted to hear as they cried out "Oh! My! My God! Really! Oh, no!" And then to hear that he finally rode around the Arena on the horse that had killed Livia's son Drusus. "Well, would you ever." The audience gasped as he explained how the crowd had exonerated his guilt.

"Enough is enough." Said Amphios "let the man enjoy the evening."

The food in abundance laid in front; not only looked good but smelt delicious, and its taste was just out of this world thought Zheng as he poured cups of wine down his throat.

Amphios so honoured to have such a man at his table to enjoy his wine and food that he just could not wait to present the gala of the evening as he leaned across to Zheng and whispered. "Do I have something special tonight? It's a new dance that is sweeping from the Far East to Rome. It's everywhere. It is so erotic that it just wants you to fuck whatever is out there on the floor." Hysterically laughing as he laid back.

The music started playing the castanets as three beautiful girls erotically dressed entered. Their legs revealed under a garment that just covered the pubic hair but a fair few centimetres down from the belly button. The stomach bare, with a loosely held clothing that only about covered the nipples. Their movement staccato of the hips to accent the beat with the body in a continuous motion with a great deal of abdominal control and undulating the thighs and abdomen followed small, fast shimmering movements of the rib cage. Zheng stared in disbelief but had seen this before but showed so much interest which the core shapes varied combined and embellished to create an infinite variety of complex, textured movements.

"Don't you just want to fuck them all?" Cried out Amphios as he added, "Pick any one or all of them." He laughed wildly.

All three girls came to Zheng with their belly buttons so close to his face as their tummies undulated and twisting hip shimmies as Amphios slapped Zheng on the back with such excitement and enthusiasm that it pushed Zheng's head between one of the dancer's legs. They pulled back, sensing that Zheng was embarrassed as they danced towards other guests. Zheng smiled and turned to face Amphios and slurred his words "Wonderful. Beautiful. So erotic."

The following morning Amphios said his farewells as his caravan packed and left for Rome. Zheng now alone accompanied by his robots waited patiently for the spacecraft to return with the captured men. The twelve men kidnapped were taken by robots in a spaceship; heavily sedated to the laboratories at the North Polar cap, which had lain dormant for the past three hundred years after the humanoids had abandoned their mission of attempting to populate the planet with superior beings. The laboratory manned by robots had shut down except the nuclear fusion generating plant to keep equipment ready for use. As the spacecraft hovered above the hanger door, all the facilities sprung into action with robots suddenly reactivated from their quiescent state to receive the shuttle as it lowered in silence and settled onto its dock.

The men still sedated were taken to private quarters where medical and surgical equipment hidden suddenly appeared from behind disclosed panels on the floor or the walls' side. Dental surgery completed with: a full set of new teeth; damaged ears and lobes missing replaced; fingers and in some instances toes reset and repaired; hair missing or extensively damaged regrown; organs malfunctioning or failed healed or restored; scars, skin defects and facial defects made right; muscles toned to display physic fit for a warrior.

Each man required a tailored leather warriors outfit with soften leather boots and a belt ready to hold a very high-quality steel sword. They wore black leather arm shields and a hardened hat with leather flaps to protect the neck's side and back. The twelve, heavily sedated, now resembled a well-equipped small army which impressed Zheng as he patiently waited for them to come around as they slept under an already prepared tent.

It wasn't until very late that afternoon that the twelve men surfaced from their ordeal. Entirely in shock, as they carefully studied one another in disbelief as they began to recognise each other; stood in awe of the banquet of food and wine displayed on a well-prepared table as Zheng spoke in a very commanding voice.

"Men, you now belong to me. You are my servants, and you will get paid each month a gold piece. Failing to obey, I will instruct my Gods to return you dead where I found you. My Gods are stronger than anything you are ever likely to meet. I have repaired and even renewed your bodies. I am giving you all a second chance. My name is Zheng, and I am the son of the god Ares. You disobey me, and Ares will send you to Hades for him to do what he likes with you. Do you understand!"

"Yes, Zheng!" They shouted out loud as they stood to attention.

The camel's now well-fed, watered and rested after spending hours grooming and bringing the animals to a fit state are ready for the next leg of the journey as Zheng continued.

"Your camels' have been cleaned and refreshed, and tomorrow we ride to Jerusalem;" still shouting with an authoritative voice as he added. "Here in my hand are swords made by the Gods, especially for you. The swords bear the mark of Hephaestus; you raise any one of those weapons against me or my second and third in command, Hades will strike you down. Do you understand?"

"Yes, Zheng!" They shouted even louder and more convincing than before.

The robots walked amongst them, showing their authority, as no one moved an eyelid, but just stared in front as each held their head high, each was handed a new glistening sword with a distinctive mark on the handle and inscriptions down the blade.

Zheng continued. " Now, I invite you all to eat and drink and enjoy, for tomorrow we have a long journey ahead of us."

They mingled amongst themselves, admiring their swords, clothes and displaying their handsome look to one another as they ate, drank and began to laugh believing the Gods had indeed blessed them.

It was early morning just as the sun rose just above the horizon changing from crimson to a brilliant yellow, as they set off travelling East in a two by two formation, with Zheng leading the party, appeared a terrifying and a threatening sight.

As they passed by where they attacked Zheng, the twelve men still could not believe their luck as they discussed what had happened but agreed that it must have been the gods that had defeated them.

The sun now directly above as Zheng slowly drifted into a meditating state could hear his army humming a song as he swayed to and fro on his camel's back. With his head sometimes nodding off and shaking him awake as he started to think about Jerusalem. "Why would the humanoids create Jerusalem; it has been nothing but a problem? Attacked 52 times, captured and recaptured 44 times, besieged 23 times and even destroyed during its lifespan on planet earth. Why create a beginning of what is going to end up as a mess?" As he continued to drift into another trance as if he hypnotised by some unknown being; "How come the Jews realised there was only one God in this superstitious world of many a pagan god?" As he added to his thoughts. "These poor souls following me; think that I am a God. If only they knew I'm from the future acting in some enigmatic role on this planet."

That evening as they settled into a table fit for a king the twelve warriors could not understand why to go to so much trouble in concocting a banquet but never sat to eat and enjoy the food and wine with them that they had painstakingly prepared. Doron especially couldn't understand how come they never slept, always fully alert and never complained about tasks imposed upon them finally led to ask the question as Zheng approached for a simple explanation.

"My friends, I shall call you that because I believe you are my friends. These poor souls, Pi and Zeta, you refer to are not mortal beings like you and me. They are disciples of the Gods to protect us." Said, Zheng, as he could hear the astonishment and for some disbelief that they had gods within their presence as one asked. "Why do you need them and why us what is your mission?"

"Ah! A real question. We are going to meet another god that has arrived on this planet, and we are not sure if it's righteous or an evil being; and I, or should I say we, need protection if certain omens summoned from the depths of hell to attack us." Said, Zheng, as he sensed the fright amongst his army as he heard the words. "Perhaps we have to fight Hades;" whispered amongst them.

"Believe me, my friends, not Hades but other pagan Gods." Said Zheng sensing that this discussion was getting out of hand.

By now, most were seated amongst makeshift cushions around an elegant display of food, and wine. The questions came rolling in one after the other as they began to realise that Zheng not only spoke Greek, their native language but Roman, Latin, Aramaic and even Hebrew. One of the twelve suddenly realised who Zheng was a famous charioteer that he had heard about and sentenced to death in the Arena. It immediately stopped all conversation as they turned to listen with such earnest as Zheng by now decided to play on his God theory as he described the Gods who came to his aid in the Arena. They had never felt so good in their lives, dedicated to Zheng. He could do no wrong and convinced them Pi and Zeta gods sent by Ares. It's enough for everyone to believe that amidst them a God. Each one approached and kissed his feet, now eating out of the palm of his hand.

During that evening Zheng walked amongst his army, only to realise he had all nationalities, Jews, Greeks and Romans which gave him an insight into major cities such as Athens and especially Jerusalem as he asked if they had heard of Jesus of Nazareth. One particular person spoke out and said he is a Jew and knew that the high priests regarded him as a false prophet, then added: "If you declare you are God or the Son of God then you are a liar in the eyes of the Jewish religion."

"Do you know where we can find him?" Asked, Zheng.

"Well, the last I heard he was well North of Jerusalem; Heptapegon about a day marches North of Jerusalem on the banks of Lake Tiberias." Said the Jew.

"Can you take me there?" Said, Zheng

"Well, yes we can pass through Jerusalem and head direct North." Said the Jew.

The following day very late in the afternoon, they arrived at the gates of Jerusalem to be confronted by Roman guards as Zheng's army of men approached.

"Halt who goes there!" said the guard as other rallied to him with shields and spears held defensively.

Zheng handed the crest of Augustus on parchment as he spoke. "Zheng, a Roman Citizen."

The guard looked and stared with such curiosity that he suddenly recognised the face immediately turned to his guards and shouted. "It's Zheng the charioteer from Rome he's here!"

Upon hearing, the other guards let their shield and spears down as they shouted "Zheng, Zheng." Added the most senior guard. "What the hell are you doing here?" as others gathered around wanting to shake Zheng's hand.

"To buy horses—I've heard the Arabs have the best to race." Said Zheng.

"Well, yes, but they're not cheap—be careful they will steal from you." Said the guard.

"I know that's why I have an army to protect me." Said, Zheng, as he pointed to his troopers behind him.

"Very wise, this area is full of bandits and vagabonds." The guard added.

"Is there anywhere we can spend the night." Asked, Zheng.

The guard pulled Zheng closer as he whispered in his ear. "You are a fortunate man, it just so happens we have a change of guard and an empty barracks, the others haven't yet arrived, and for a small fee I'm sure I can accommodate you."

"Great!" Said, Zheng, as he handed over a small purse which the guard accepted as he turned to his subordinates. "Show these men to barracks 'B'."

That evening the barracks full of laughter, singing and jesting Zheng spoke to the Jew that he had decided would accompany him tomorrow as he sat down beside him.

"So what is your name, young man?" Said, Zheng, holding a cup of wine to take another mouthful.

"Doron, Sir!" Said, the Jew.

"Ok, Doron, you will accompany me tomorrow to Heptapegon; don't leave it too late tonight— we leave at the first light of dawn." Said, Zheng, patting Doron on the shoulder.

They rode out North towards Lake Tiberius. The day warm sunny not a cloud in the sky as they passed olive, orange and lemon trees with herdsman on the road directing herds of goats and sheep; farmers in the field furrowing the land. Zheng could not help but reflect how much civilisation had grown in what he now considered a short time of three hundred years. However, the way of life hadn't changed much; the same ragged and torn clothes; peasants and slavery everywhere; a minority vibrant whereas a majority very poor.

Appearing wealthy, tended to evoke approaching stragglers and beggars as many on the road tried to block by stretching out their arms and hands for food and money; he tugged the reins and heeled hard on the horse to gallop past the destitute leaving in the distance the city of Jerusalem. They made their way past Ephraim and reached Sychar by late afternoon where they decided to seek an inn or a place where they could rest. Tired, after a long day, Zheng lay on his bed just staring at the ceiling as his mind drifted into a deep trance, thinking: *life was now independent of any intervention from the humanoids since vacating the planet 300 years ago.*

Like many towns passed, Sychar developed, if somehow it knew that it must be an equivalent or twin town that was once on Planet Earth. Even the surrounding terrain was the same as Zheng remembered during his history lessons. It would be interesting to see; he thought, "if the Sea of Tiberius would be the same as the Sea of Galilee before it's destruction."

The following morning they set off early and cut across the land as suggested by other travels to the River Jordan to follow its path which would lead directly to Lake Tiberias. Zheng convinced himself there was something in force on this planet driving its destiny to copy Planet Earth. He was now more than ever determined to speak to Jesus of Nazareth for some answers to questions that he no longer understood.

CHAPTER 9

The Prophet

As they travelled that day, following the banks of the River closely; unbeknown to them they were already being pursued by bandits. In the evening, after catching fish and lighting a fire, they settled to cook when suddenly six armed men surrounded and confronted them. Zheng, undisturbed continued to barbeque his fish calmly spoke.“ Well, you probably think that we are very wealthy merchants with gold to steal and may I add you would not be wrong. However, we can give you just one gold coin, or otherwise, I'm sorry to say we shall have to take your lives.—Now, which is it to be?” Said Zheng very coolly without even looking at the robbers but continuing twirling his fish on the end of the stick over the fire.

“Who the fuck are you? —You little squirm—you think I will accept one miserable coin piece when I can take the fucking lot; not only that, your horses too and then I shall sit down and eat your damn fish. You fucking idiot.” Said the leader of the gang.

“Hmm! So that is your final answer.” Said, Zheng placing his fish away from the fire, stood up with the aid of his shepherd's crook, that never left his side, as he cried out, “OPEN”. A beam of light shot out high and above the robbers head.

“Are you sure that's your final answer?” Zheng asked as he swung the light beam around cutting through a tree which immediately fell, knocking the bandits to the ground. Instantly they scrambled to their feet and disappeared running into the undergrowth.

“My, God, you are a God!” Said, Doron, as he stood there in disbelief at what he had just witnessed as he listened and watched Zheng shout the words “CLOSE” to see his shepherd's crook reassembled in front of his very eyes.

“Doron, we are Gods and tomorrow we are going to meet the son of your God.” Said, Zheng, as he continued twirling his fish above the fire as he turned and calmly spoke to Pi who was still holding his rod as he asked. “Have you caught another one for the fire?”

They ate well that night, except of course for Pi, who just fished and stood guard the whole of the evening which Doron still could not understand, since Zheng a God ate, whereas Pi a God didn't.

The very next morning Zheng and Doron bathed and washed as Doron turned to Zheng pointing to Pi still in the same position from the night before said: “He doesn't need to bathe either?—or relieve himself either?”

"That's the beauty of immortality—they are not here; it's just a figure of our imagination!" Said, Zheng as he ducked his head under the water to rinse his hair.

"What do you mean he isn't here?— He's precisely here!— I can touch him, feel him; I don't understand?" Said, Doron, as he started to climb out onto the river bank.

"That's what Gods can do, deceive us. It's all a figure of our imagination." Said, Zheng as he too followed Doron out onto the river bank as he turned and asked:

"Well if you're a God, how come you do things differently to Pi; like a normal human?" Zheng just shrugged his shoulders and screwed his face into a sarcastic smile; knowing whatever he said he could never explain, stayed quiet with a broad smile on his face.

That morning they passed close by to a village and in the afternoon stopped close by Agrippina where they fished once more and decided that as there was no real hurry, chose to make camp and settle for the night. All-day Doron could not help but stare at Pi in disbelief that this so-called person was not real, He had never seen Pi take a sip of water, eat anything, pass water, and never go to sleep. Again that evening, he kept questioning Zheng. "Why is he here?— if he is not real!" As he continually starred at Pi.

"It's because the God Ayres has sent him to protect us—please accept his gift—he is here to keep you safe." Said, Zheng but sensed Doron was not satisfied as he attempted to change the subject as he asked about his family quickly.

The following day they pushed on towards the sea of Tiberius where they sought shelter in an inn. The Inn and the town were full too, with nothing but talk of Jesus of Nazareth preaching tomorrow at Heptapegon.

They didn't have to ask for directions as they set off early, just followed the crowds that gathered as they walked along the shore of Tiberius in that bright morning fresh air, passing a continuous line of small huts, observing plenty of trade and fishing by boat. The lake of pure water was colossal stretching as far as the eye could see. Zheng attempting to compare its size couldn't establish if it were the same extent used to occupy Plant Earth when suddenly he was interrupted in thought; a small boy carrying five loaves and two fish ran passed as Zheng shouted out; "are they for sale?"

"No, they're my gift to Jesus." Said the boy as he disappeared amongst the crowd pushing ahead of Zheng.

The crowds grew, but Zheng still had no idea where he would follow the moving masses only to see ahead of him a congregation gathering around a hill and a figure standing with welcoming arms wearing a white robe as the sun enhanced its brilliance.

Jesus walked towards the crowd blessing those as he approached the sick and injured as he directed people to sit down on the grass in groups of the '50s and 100's; as he came to Zheng Jesus placed his hand on his head and said. "Bless Zheng in the name of the Father, The Son and The Holy Spirit." And as he carried on to walk by turned to face Zheng and added, "When the crowd disperse late tonight seek my presence;" and carried on blessing those in front of him.

"He knew your name!—How come?" Said Doron.

"A long story!" Said, Zheng, as they sat down on the grass amidst a crowd of about fifty.

Zheng listened intently to every word Jesus preached about the love of humankind. His mind drifted into a dream thinking about Planet Earth and how for thousands of years the World had abanded all forms of religion; something regarded as superstitious and a myth after the devastation that had occurred to leave Earth destroyed, desolate and dead. But now he was witnessing something that he had read about during his ancient history lessons, which again he questioned. "Is this genuine?— or is this a holographic image the humanoids are creating?" He stopped to observe Pi sitting crossed leg meditating as he added to his thoughts, *or perhaps it is Pi creating these images before my very eyes? Jesus looks the same when I first met him 300 years ago; he must be a humanoid he hasn't changed—Come to think of it neither have I.*

The sermons continued late into the afternoon. Zheng noticed the same small boy he had met earlier handing over his five loaves and two fish as Jesus looked up to the heavens. Thanked the boy, and broke the bread into twelve baskets; fish lept out from the sea behind him as the disciples gathered and placed them in the baskets and began to disperse and distribute amongst the crowd. Zheng suddenly realised he was witnessing feeding the 5000 that on Planet Earth had gone down in history as a fantasy.

As the sunset, the crowd began to disperse and leave for home. A few went to Jesus but soon left as they said their farewells. Zheng patiently waited until he could see just a few disciples sitting by as others went about their business preparing their boats for a night of fishing.

Zheng approached alone as Jesus invited him to sit beside him.

"So, here we are again: You have travelled the stars like me, and you want some answers; If I'm not mistaken?" Said, Jesus, as he gazed into Zhengs eyes.

"Well—I just cannot believe this is happening again, the same when I met you last, some 300 hundred years ago on another planet." Said, Zheng

"God works mysteriously, but I know you don't believe and you think I am like the thing you have brought here?" Said, Jesus.

"Well no—but who is your God?—And where is He?" Said, Zheng, as he threw his arms to display the heavens and the surroundings to show doubt that somehow this stage had been set by the humanoids.

"The Kingdom of God is within you Zheng—you and the people have summoned me here—it is within all of you that brings me here to tell you what you to want to hear." Said Jesus in a peaceful and humble voice.

"What do you mean?— Are you saying that you are a figure of our imagination?—Is that what you are trying to tell me?" Said, Zheng, looked closer into his eyes to see if he could determine the same look that if he were to look into robotic eyes.

"Zheng, it is straightforward, there is only one thing I preach, the love of humankind; that's all—it's the man himself that changes what I teach and confuses the masses in the divinity of religious sectors that decree new laws. The love of humanity only happens when the masses become one. Precisely that is what happened on Planet Earth it became one. When a person prays to his so-called God, he is praying to humanity. Only you and others can help one another—nobody else—no God—no religion. That's why I say the Kingdom of God is within you and all the people."

"Are you telling me that religion should just teach the love of humanity—nothing else?— So there is no superior being it's just a figure of our imagination." Said Zheng.

"Exactly!—The force is within you and everyone, and it creates me.—I'm a life-force.—I am an essence of your imagination that you and everybody have formed within yourselves to what one considers is the right journey for humanity and want to hear and what we should all be doing.—Love humankind, but you require something more powerful to ensure the words I speak will last forever, and that is why I shall die on a cross and resurrect myself to show my immortality." Said, Jesus."I am a mortal being like you as well as a spirit" as he slightly drew a knife across the palm of his hand to show blood.

"So how can mortal beings like us, create you?—It's impossible!" Said Zheng.

Jesus looked to the stars that were now brilliant in the sky as he continued to speak with; currently, all his disciple gathered around, including Pi and Doron that had moved closer to hear what Jesus had to say.

"You have come from the stars. Your body is not a stable entity but a mass of particles that are associated with the Universe. You live not only in this Universe but other Universes too. You never die your atoms and particles that make up your body live for eternity and can reassemble in another space and time dimension. All of our soles move amongst the stars. And like farming, weeds grow, and I am the gardener which humankind beckoned and formed me as an identity of your inner souls to weed out your garden."

Zheng moved closer to Jesus as he whispered in his ear. "You know of the predicament things manipulate me." As he glanced across and acknowledged Pi in the distance to ensure his words were for Jesus ears only.

"A thing is a human-made object; it does not have an inner soul or consciousness; you control the device, and you must tell it so; you are the master. As I said before, you had told the thing a lie; now, you must tell the truth."

Zheng knew what he meant, reprogramming which he had no idea and knowledge of how to do such a function. He thanked Jesus for his private audience as he stood up to leave as Jesus spoke his final words.

"God is with you; my son."

Zheng now understood those words which meant that God is within him, and it's up to himself how to resolve the situation as he turned and question Jesus once more. "Will, I ever see you again?"

"Perhaps in another time, space and dimension, but in this Solar System, my duties finished, mankind will survive." Said, Jesus then paused and corrected himself; "Maybe one more planet?"

Zheng that evening back at the Inn, his mind again went into a trance beginning to believe that nothing is real. Everything we devise or look at we create. It's not there until we look at it. And we are here because we want to be here. The universe exists; Jesus lives; all religions exist because we want them to be. Only humankind is the saviour. "I must get to *Planet-G*, to find out what is happening with people of my kind," he said aloud, as he drifted off into a profound sleep, then thought what Jesus had said, *maybe one more planet—did he mean Planet-G*?

The following day they returned to Jerusalem; none the wiser about Jesus except that he existed and was a mortal being, not a humanoid. Zheng was even more determined to get away from this planet. Hopefully, he could meet a civilisation more advanced like himself that the humanoids had created where he could continue living without machines controlling his life. But first, he had to get to Rome and discuss with Biyu how they could leave the planet and travel to *Planet-G*.

During the return journey, Doron persisted questioning Zheng, much to his annoyance about the five loaves of bread and the two fish which feed a crowd of 5000. Zheng could explain the fish that lept out of the sea, but he had no idea about the bread except maybe it was just a figure of our imagination; but to keep Doron quiet, he answered. "Well, he is the son of your God and can perform miracles." However, it left Doron in a quandary because since his Jewish faith denounced Jesus as a liar; but witnessing what had just happened, he now had his doubts.

It took a day less than expected to arrive at Jerusalem to meet the same guard that Zheng had negotiated at the barracks for the temporary accommodation that his men had moved out to the town centre staying at a nearby Inn. Zheng thanked the guard for his hospitality and if ever he was in Rome to look him up.

However, the guard enlightened Zheng on occasion this coming weekend, knowing that Zheng was a charioteer, and chariot racing was the major event. Zheng thanked the guard and made inquiries but couldn't promise he would participate since his racing chariots were in Rome. "Oh, you can hire them at the circus." Said, the guard.

Relaxed that evening Zheng socialising with his men discussed entering two chariots into the circus this coming weekend. He needed to buy eight thoroughbreds of Arabic pedigree; much to the enthusiasm of all that agreed. The briefing entailed seeking breeders or merchants in the area who were selling. At the same time, he would inquire about hiring two chariots—accepted with enthusiasm and an incentive to participate in the newly built hippodrome that Pontius Pilot had constructed, as they split themselves into groups. It took most of the day seeking out breeders and dealers, but everything was in place by the evening. Eight horses purchased and two chariots hired. The following morning training in the arena commenced; selecting what horses were best suited to ride either inside or outside. The chosen charioteers, Pi and Zeta, had the most experience. Well over 300 hundred years. He smiled to himself, watching their performance; the prize money substantial would comfortably cover the horses and chariots' costs as he carried on with his thoughts.

A late entry considered a rank outsider; and the odds given by the bookies would allow Zheng, to make a substantial gain if he was to win. The winner would take prize money but two slave girls and an extra of the team members choosing. The girls, already selected, paraded in front of the contestants. A welcoming party was thrown that night by the organisers before the big event tomorrow. As usual not partaking, the robots explained it was best to guard the horses all night to ensure that they were not given sedatives by their competitors, or any other devious ways of slowing them down which was considered rife amongst competitors. The bookies now realised that Zheng a famous charioteer himself from Rome, although was not participating, had selected well-known riders that had competed in the circus in Rome; quickly reduced the odds, making him now one of the favourites to win. Zheng had already placed bets earlier with fixed odds and a substantial gain if he won.

The day had arrived, and it was perfect, not a cloud in the sky, and a fresh breeze kept the temperature at bay, suiting the horses not to overheat during the race. The starting lineup placed Zheng's chariots with one in the middle and the other on the far outside. Twelve chariots would start stretched in a line behind the mechanical starting gates. The games began with a procession into the Hippodrome; a herald announced the drivers and owners' name. Pontious Pilate in the imperial box dropped a handkerchief to start the race as the gates lowered. The chariot on the far outside started first, which meant Pi was first out of the gate ahead, to begin with; not considered a good position unless you held the lead for the twelve laps to avoid a collision at the first bend. Zeta started mid-position, which meant he had five chariots on his inside but behind Pi but could improve his position if he could go across the inside five before their gates opened. As Pi left his gateway, he cracked his whip so hard across the rear of the four horses and steered his chariot to get across his inside chariot before his gate fully opened. He did the same getting across each competitive barrier before it released to be the first to get the inside track. As the gate opened for Zeta, he too cracked so hard his whip that he followed behind Pi so that Pi arrived first at the bend with Zeta close behind as they did a sharp turn around the first post. With Pi in front and Zeta close behind, they could keep control of the chasing pack. Several chariots had already collided, and debris scattered across the arena made the race challenging to maintain a straight line as they swerved to miss chariots and wheels. Boxed in with a chariot on his outside and one inside Zeta could sense his wheels were under threat. He moved his body across to the outside chariot. With such force in his hand and arm grabbed the wheel of the outside chariot and stopped it dead and suddenly let go. It somersaulted in midair and came crashing down with its rider being dragged along the ground frantically trying to cut his reins tied around his waist. Steering his chariot to the inside rider, Zeta did the same, grabbed the wheel as they swept around the post; the chariot went flying.

Now in the lead Pi was oblivious to what was going on behind him except the increase in debris he confronted as he swerved to steer well clear. The other charioteers chasing Zeta witnessed his capability, much to their astonishment that he could grab a wheel with his bare hands with such force, avoided him as they tried desperately to overtake wide on the outside or the inside. But nobody could pass; he moved from the outside to the inside veering to stop anybody passing, as Pi increased his lead as Zeta held the others back. On the penultimate lap, a chariot took the outside. Zeta moved across, allowing a challenging teammate to cut through on the inside to pass, quickly caught up with Pi; swept alongside him on the last lap as they tied neck and neck on the final bend; Pi moved across and grabbed his wheel which sent the chariot crashing. Pi crossed the finish line to take first place with Zeta in a close second.

The most exciting part of the chariot race was the turn at the end of the Hippodrome at least for the spectators. It appeared to the protesters that Zeta had deliberately veered into another competitor to cause him to crash was regarded as technically illegal, and disqualified. For Pi, the authorities tried to get him disqualified too, but Zheng challenged that his chariot had the inside track on the last bend and the outside chariot trying to pass should have given his chariot room to turn so the protest failed. Zheng enthralled with his prize money and winnings decided that it was in his interest to leave Jerusalem as soon as possible before anybody realised that his robots had stopped former chariots by grabbing the wheel. His army, too with their winnings, were pleased to leave and were looking forward to what they considered was going to be a new life in Rome. Departing soon after the race and were already heading out of Jerusalem, the day drew to a close, laughing, joking, going over, again and again, the competition's details, mainly how Pi and Zeta with their bare hands were capable of stopping dead the opposition chariots. Leading the procession Zheng on his camel looked back at his party of happy men and admired his eight magnificent unscathed horses suddenly delighted, content with his life which he hadn't felt for a very long time.

Several days had passed before they had arrived at what was now considered his favourite oasis. Although they had carried a considerable amount of water they hadn't anticipated the amount the thoroughbreds consumed daily and were now running short; another day in the stifling desert would have ended up with eight dehydrated, dead horses. However, the camels took each stride as if it was a stroll in the park and were really in no hurry to drink water when they immediately arrived at the oasis, as they calmly walked towards the water's edge. In contrast, the horses held back as they tried to bolt to satisfy their thirst.

Zheng, couldn't believe when Amphios arrived the following day: "My friend, you have been busy," he said as he looked around to see Zheng's army of men and eight magnificent horses.

"Yes, we had some luck. But what about you? Did you meet my wife, Biyu? Did she pay you for the saffron?" Said Zheng.

"Yes! Yes!—What an adorable wife you have. She paid me in full— she was so happy to see me as I described our ventures." Said Amphios as his forefinger went to the side of his nose as he added. "Not the belly dancers thou!" as he burst into such a loud laugh. "But tonight we shall have another show—Your men invited too."

That day Zheng's men worked hard channelling water from the oasis so that the animals could drink; people could bathe without contaminating the bright crystal oasis. Fires lit as the evening drew in and the sky, an abundance of stars as Planets illuminated the site; the aromatic smells of food and perfume drifted amongst the crowd as they gathered around a central spot where the entertainment started. Zheng sat alongside Amphios as they ate and drank plenty, discussing their next business plan, and boasting about his winning success in the Arena with the Chariots he entered.

The entertainment carried well into the morning's early hours with much fun and laughter as Zheng's men slept well into the following day. Amphios that evening departed and said his farewells to Zheng; as he liked to navigate the desert by the stars. To ensure that his horses were well-rested after the arduous journey he had just made with temperatures in the upper 40°C, Zheng stayed a further day at the oasis relaxing and sleeping.

Biyu had patiently waited for months on Zheng's return, was amazed when he finally arrived at the villa with an army plus eight beautiful racehorses. She couldn't wait, nor could others, to hear in detail of his adventures in Jerusalem;

surprised to hear that he had competed in one of the leading events of the year in the circus to take first prize in the chariot race. She didn't ask about Zheng's meeting with Jesus, which was the real reason why he went to Jerusalem but waited until late that night when they were alone. Zheng described everything in detail about his meeting. As far as he was concerned, there was no superior being and that all the answers to the universe lay primarily within our inner consciousness and minds. Biyu had no idea what he was talking about except that he had come away with nothing that he could offer to satisfy the humanoids, and as far as she was concerned, they were back to square one.

"So what are you going to tell Pusa when she returns?" Asked Biyu with a slightly annoying tone expecting Zheng to have some explanation that would end this fiasco for them and bring some form of normality back into their lives, which they hadn't yet experienced.

"I don't know." Said Zheng. "We are going to have to cross the bridge when we come to it," as he continued but changing the subject entirely. "And what about Amphios?—Did you pay the amount that I had agreed."

"Yes, we are now partners, and we are the sole representative of saffron merchants for Rome. He will only sell to us. What I purchased I have already sold at a very handsome profit. We will receive shipments every month, not from himself, but his appointed agent. We stand to become very wealthy." She, said as she turned to show the amount of money they had already made.

"Excellent." Said, Zheng, thinking to himself. *Well, at least if we are abandoned and become marooned forever on this planet at least, we can provide for ourselves.*

Infuriated with Zheng about his relaxed attitude about Jerusalem's business, had to ask what she regarded as another unnecessary expense and worry. "And what about your new recruitments—so-called special force— what are we to do with them?" Asked Biyu

"They are our bodyguards for all the family to use."

"What as servants or playthings we can pop into bed." Responded Biyu still in an annoyed tone.

"Look, I am going to insist from now on that nobody ventures alone into Rome unless accompanied by at least two of our guards."

"Why?"

Speaking in a relaxed tone realising Biyu was becoming angry with him. "We are becoming very wealthy, our son a champion charioteer, our daughters beautiful could attract attention to robbers and especially kidnappers abducting any one of our children demanding a ransom," Zheng answered.

Biyu listened and could see the logic of his thinking. Many young girls now occupied the villa, her children, Feiyan, Chen, Niu, Yi and Guo; some cloned, she still felt a very close attachment to all and considered related since Zheng had fathered them all.

The twelve newly appointed guards and the two girl slaves settled quickly into the routine at the villa and life for Zheng and especially Biyu over time become enjoyment. Zheng had other ideas about his guards in possible matchmaking with the single girls; now that many occupied the villa. Although some were clones of his original life, he still sensed a closeness as if they were his own. In their previous lives as vestal virgins, Zheng remembered that sedated when taken; they were kept alive in the humanoid factories, producing eggs that, according to his reckoning, made close on 5000. *All that effort*, he thought, *so he can get an answer to an impossible question —What is the key to the cosmos?* Now Zheng had to face the music and decide whether or not to let the humanoids approach him, or just carry on as usual and wait. But he had forgotten about, the robots, that would have already reported to Pusa and Pyroeis.

CHAPTER 10.

Departure

Zheng didn't have to wait long for the humanoids to return from their exploits in the solar system as they expected an immediate answer to their question. "So what is the key to the Universe?" Said Pusa, as Pyroeis added, "how can we travel across vast distances of space; and what is time and space?"

Zheng had no answer, and he didn't know how Jesus of Nazareth could have returned some 300 years later to another planet. Zheng explained what Jesus had said which had nothing to do with time and space except just: "love humankind—it was that simple!" Also, he added, "that the love of humanity could never happen until all forms of discrimination, borders and barriers removed and the human race becomes a single force acting like one."

"Well, that's it!" Said Pyroeis expecting a scientific and technical explanation. "That was just mumbo jumbo as far as I'm concerned. Another false prophet, pretending to be a God preaching to the vulnerable and superstitious." He added: "But where did he come from and how did he get here?"

"No idea," replied Zheng. "I'm sorry, but I did try. I have no explanation for what happened." Trying to explain the feeding of the 5000.

Straightforward and logical said Pyroeis. "No other explanation." He added in a tone which Zheng sounded familiar of an impatient person one would expect only from a human.

"But where did he come from if he didn't come from you?" Queried, Zheng again.

"No idea! We were hoping you would tell us and for some answers before our departure to another solar system—some 1200 light-years away." Said Pusa.

"What you are leaving to go where and what never to return?—What about me?" Said Zheng concerned abandoned on a planet in a time and place that he didn't want to be.

"Well, yes, finished our job here—We have colonised three worlds—Planet G also was a failure, the infrastructure to sustain a population to give birth naturally will not work. We had underestimated the ability of the homo-sapien to continue where we left off in the 5th Millenium. The teaching is enormous to bring everybody to the knowledge that we had on Planet Earth and to be able to continue. The race will terminate as a newborn child along with its mother will die giving birth, unless they can perform a caesarean." Said Pyroeis as he added " The decree set by the Council on Planet Earth was correct only to carry 4th Millenium embryos.—We shall, nevertheless, return in 5000 years and hopefully have an answer to our question how to travel through time and space when homo-sapiens reach the level of intelligence that they once had on Planet Earth to tell us."

Zheng, disillusioned, slumped into a chair; put his head in his hands, thinking *well this is it, this is the end.* To be cryogenically preserved for 1200 years was just out of the question as far as he was concerned and the thought of staying on a planet 5000 years before his time was something he could not relish.

Pusa could sense the emotion that Zheng was going through and reassure him about what they were about to offer him. "Look, you will not be entirely alone. We have decided to leave your robots, Pi and Zeta, and the space shuttle. You will still have the laboratory at the Polar Cap with all the facilities at your disposal. You'll have your family with you and your space shuttle to reach other planets if you so desire. Again you have all the facilities here: you will become a master of this solar system, you will still be able to communicate with us at the polar caps, we have a special room for communication without any time dilation."

Beginning to think that the situation perhaps was not as bad as he first thought and possibly could sustain life with the gadgets and gizmos provided. It reminded him of his comic reading days when he was young about superman and superwoman on Planet Earth, helping others.

"Ok, so when do you depart?" Said Zheng not expecting the answer that came.

"We leave right now—We shall not return for at least another 5000 years." Said Pyroeis.

The robots showed no emotion about the humanoids departure, and Zheng, however, didn't know how to say farewell to a machine he had been with for the past 430 years. Although cryogenically preserved for the majority of the time; just gave a smile and said: "safe journey, my friends."

They departed, and Zheng saddened suddenly felt very much alone as he held back a tear that finally fell out of the corner of his eye. The robots showing no emotion turned and walked away without a word or regret that they too, were stuck on this planet. Zheng now realised he was alone; destitute to live out the rest of his life in an unfamiliar world with Biyu and his children. Somehow, it managed to bring a smile to Zheng's face when he thought of the gadgets and weapons left at his disposal; he was now master of everything, including two robots and a space shuttle.

Outside in the night on his porch contemplating, trying to see in the darkness if he could observe a space shuttle heading across the night sky of the milky way, pondered. "I wonder where they are going?"—He thought, "it's better that I keep this to my self for the time being."

"Oh, you still admiring the night sky?" he heard Biyu's voice as she came out to stand alongside him. "What is it?" you're not worried about anything?" she said, looking intently at his face in the starlight and seeing him calm and happy she smiled at him.

She understands,—he thought;—*she knows what I'm thinking about; shall I tell her or not?—Yes, I'll say to her!*" But at that moment he was about to speak, she kissed him on the cheek said "goodnight, I shall leave you with your thoughts," turned and walked in the house.

He kept his secret to himself; never explained to Biyu that they were alone. And the humanoids had departed to another solar system, some 1200 light-years away only to return when life had reached a level of intelligence, 5000 years from now.

Without the machines' interference, Zheng decided to have the implanted microchips removed entirely with his robots' help. Correct the sterilisation that the humanoids had performed on his daughters and take a risk that his loyal robots, two very well trained surgeons can perform a caesarean at childbirth.

Quickly settling into a routine and with the odd challenging question on the whereabouts of the humanoids Zheng would shrug his shoulders, "I have no idea!" It seemed to satisfy Biyu, but never mentioned that their daughters had their reproduction organs corrected and rectified to produce children once again.

His eldest son, a clone from his original boy, Ju, become very close as Zheng tried on many occasions to persuade him to abandon chariot racing in the circus and leave the competition to the robots who were now masters. But Gaius loved the attention and stardom given to him by his followers, especially when he won an event in the circus and displayed the mob's laurel crown.

His twelve faithful knights were now an elite fighting force, highly trained, well-equipped and highly motivated. One of the tenets was that Zheng forbid them from retreating in battle unless outnumbered three to one and even then only by order of his command. They were always on call to accompany Gauis to the circus as added protection against his fame and fortune. They also protected his daughters still blamed for causing disruption and the breakup of Julie the Elder and her lover Iullus Antonius and Livia's son Drusus's death. Zheng would use his knights as bodyguards since Livia, the Emperor's wife, had a contract to assassinate him after this episode in the circus with the Bengal tigers. She could never accept he was able to walk free with outside help. She always referred Zheng to Emperor Augustus as a traitor, conspiring with others to overthrow his kingdom.

Zheng hated Livia and fully conversed with the history of the Roman Empire was acutely aware of what was about to happen and contemplated on many occasion whether to intervene and change the path of history. He felt that what he was experiencing was so uncanny even without outside intervention it seemed to follow the same history path of what occurred on planet earth. The stage set by the humanoids was playing out precisely as history meant to be. Zheng was not sure what would happen if he intervened. He knew that Livia was about to be responsible for the murder of Gaius Caesar and Lucius, the grandchildren of Augustus descended from his second marriage with Scribonia, that would be in line to succeed Augustus on his deathbed. An intervention would prevent Tiberius and Caligula and perhaps even Nero becoming Emperor. He knew from history that Caligula and Nero were entirely and utterly insane a removal certainly would benefit humanity.

Gaius Caesar and Lucius, keen followers of chariot racing, followed Zheng's son in the circus and were great admirers. The children also attended martial art training at his school until Livia blocked the tuition on the pretence that the school negatively influenced their upbringing. She had mostly persuaded Augustus that Zheng being a man of power and political gain was indeed an imposter spying for the Far Eastern Empire to undermine the Roman Empire.

Augustus did not quarrel with Zheng and encouraged his grandchildren to continue. Unbeknown to Livia, Zheng had supplied two of his best knights as bodyguards to Augustus grandchildren Gaius Caesar and Lucius. He appointed Pi and Doron, one of his faithful knights to accompany Lucius to complete his military training at the front.

Zheng knowingly and aware that Livia had confided and paid well conspirators for Lucius food to be poisoned, and emphasised that Pi would be the official food taster for anything presented to Lucius mealtime. On many occasions, Pi had detected poison and had forced the culprit who supplied the food to eat it. However, Doron was surprised that Pi would sample the food since he had never seen him eat or drink before. "I thought as an immortal being you didn't eat or drink, and I don't understand how you can detect poison in the food which appears not to affect you?"

Pi looked at Doron with an expressionless facial look as he explained. "Yes, you are correct. I do not need food and drink, but my body can sense what is harmful to a mortal being without affecting me."

Doron convinced that he was amongst immortal men that others only ever talked about in stories as myths and legends. Each day he became obsessed with Pi's ability to adapt to any situation and the ability to foresee conditions and respond to what he considered unsolvable problems.

Meanwhile, Livia waited patiently back in Rome to hear Lucius's tragic and unexpected death, but as the messenger returned to report that the cook she had employed had suddenly taken ill and died was shocked. However, when the second messenger arrived some two weeks later that her other cook died as well with the same ailment as the first, she became scared—frightened what her husband might do and accuse her of trying to poison his grandchild since she supplied both cooks from her kitchen.

Zheng didn't report the incident to anyone, especially to the imperial palace's ears since he knew Livia would convince Augustus that he was involved somehow. And possibly the main instigators in the plot since Pi as the official food taster, she would inevitably ask, "how come Pi was not affected by the poison?" Zheng understood an explanation might best come from his grandson of an attempt on his life.

After the attempted poisoning of his grandson Lucius, Augustus immediately summoned his return for a full explanation. Since accused by his wife, Livia as part of the conspiracy, he also requested Zheng to attend.

At the tribunal, Lucius stood there explaining how Pi had saved his life and had detected the poison in his food by smell alone, and he didn't have to taste it, but suspected poison, and made the person who prepared the plate to sample the menu which led to their deaths.

"He knew by smell alone that the dish presented to you contained poison?" Said Augustus in disbelief as he added "Well, we shall test your theory!—I have had four different plates of food prepared, and two of them contain poison. So let's see how good your taste is?" As Augustus turned to Pi for some acknowledgement.

"Do we have to go through with this charade?" Said, Livia, as she turned to Augustus as she added and whispered in his ear, "It's obvious this is an ingenious ploy to gain your confidence for eventually treasonous treachery."

"Hmm!—We shall see?" Replied Augustus as he summoned Pi. "I believe you are the official taster. Please tell me which two plates out of the four presented here on the table is poisonous?"

"This is ridiculous!—Pi has a fifty-fifty chance of being correct." Said, Livia, as she mumbled to Augustus.

Immediately Pi sensed the two plates that contained poison as they were brought from the kitchen and laid on the table; he made no hesitation and ate from the other two. Doron looked on in shock since he had never seen him eat before. Zheng knew that irrespective poisoned or not it would not affect anyway. Livia stood flabbergasted, knowing what was in the dishes thinking *how he knew so quickly which plates contained the poison*?

After eating a sound sample from the two plates, he had selected turned to the other two and said."This one." As he smelt it and continued " Contains conium maculatum which will bring on rapid onset of nausea, salvation and vomiting, abdominal pain, headache and degrees of mental confusion. General weakness may be associated with convulsions, and death caused by progressive paralysis and respiratory failure."

Before he could finish, Livia interrupted "What is this conium maculatum?"

"I believe madam you refer to it as Hemlock what your chefs found to have in their kitchen."

Livia stood back in shock as she responded: "Well, indeed!"

Pi picked up the last and final plate "Well, this contains aconitum napellus." As he turned to Livia and added "Aconite, Monk's hood madam," continued "extremely poisonous even in small doses. Symptoms: Rapid onset of numbness and tingling in the mouth and throat. Which spreads over the rest of the body; pain and twitching of the muscles; progressing to general weakness; cold and clammy extremities; irregular heart rhythm and abnormally low blood pressure; respiratory paralysis; drowsiness (occasionally convulsions), stupor and death."

Augustus stood in silence, amazed that Pi had accurately selected the correct plates. What astounded him was the detailed account of each poison that even he was not fully aware as he questioned once more "And where did you find these toxins?"

"Well, I only found hemlock carried by your kitchen staff. The monkshood's the first time I have come across it; not served to Lucius." Said Pi as he turned to face Lucius and smile.

Livia left the room mumbling under her breath "Trickery that's what it is! Trickery! Witchcraft!"

Augustus gestured Zheng to step forward and thanked him profusely and wished for him to continue protecting Lucius since he was now acutely aware that his grandson's life was in danger. He also asked if he could provide the same service for his other grandsons Gaius Caesar and Marcus. Augustus also requested that Lucius stay at his villa until Augustus could establish the conspirators seeking his grandson's death. He also asked if Gaius Caesar when he returned and Marcus the youngest could stay with their brother Lucius at the villa.

Now acutely aware that his wife Livia was behind the conspiracy, her presumed motive was to arrange her son Tiberius' accession as heir to the empire. Meanwhile, Tiberius had retired from politics to an island and was not aware of his mother's intentions of removing succession to Emperor Augustus.

Lucius was the first to arrive at Zheng's villa and introduced to his eldest daughter Tarpeia was very much attracted towards her as he kissed her hand very gently. She also looked deep into his blue eyes and sensed to an immediate attraction towards him. As Biyu, stood alongside them, she felt a closeness as she raised her eyebrows as she glanced towards Zheng, who had a massive smile on his face. Pinaria, Tarpeia's sister, hearing all the noise of enjoyment rushed out only to stand in awe of this very young, handsome man who would stay with them for an indefinite period. And when Pinaria heard that he had two brothers that were coming too, she lept for joy there and there on the spot, as she clasped her hands and put them over her face to cover her smiling face. It was long before the youngest of the three girls Oppia arrived to join in the fun. Lucius at first had doubts about staying at

Zheng's villa, but now, after witnessing such beauty, he could see that his stay and his other brothers were to join him, was going to be an unusual period of bliss.

The three girls questioned Lucius for the rest of the day about his brothers, especially what they looked like and their pastime hobbies. They wanted to know all the details of his family, especially his grandfather Augustus and also his mother Julia, a delicate subject to discuss which they realised and avoided.

The robots were always in sight, as Lucius questioned Tarpeia, "Are they always nearby." Glancing towards Pi and Zeta standing as if they were a marble statue.

"Oh! Yes—just ignore them.—You will find they can sleep standing up." Said Tarpeia as she chuckled to herself.

Some weeks later, Gaius Caesar and Marcus arrived; bewildered why they had to stay with Zheng under close protection with his elite knights until Lucius explained that threats against his life acknowledged that they also could be in danger. Where ever they went, or whatever they did, they were never out of sight of Pi or Zeta. The boys become fascinated by Pi and Zeta, in as much as they had never seen them take time off or even go to the bathroom. Zheng realised that the boys were observing them too carefully, and though they may start to ask too many awkward questions, decided to divide their work into shift hours of 4 hours on and 4 hours off to make it a more natural role.

Gaius Caesar, the eldest, the next in line to succeed Augustus, became very fond of Tarpeia, whereas Lucius feelings tended more towards Pinaria as he got to know her more. Marcus, the youngest felt a close relationship with the youngest of the three girls Oppia wherever they went, carefully guarded, and to some extent escorted to the point that even holding hands were forbidden.

Augustus would visit Zheng regularly; alone without Livia, since it caused many arguments that she felt he was ridiculous, reaching too far over something trivial and a misunderstanding about her son Tiberius succeeding him. However, Augustus enjoyed Zheng's company and the knowledge that he and his wife appeared to have; they could discuss any subject in great depth and detail. Zheng's understanding of Greek philosophy amazed Augustus, to such an extent required knowing everything about Zheng. He couldn't believe when he told him of another great philosopher he had recently met, Jesus of Nazareth. Augustus had heard of him but never considered or associated him as a philosopher, only as a healer of the sick.

Augustus loved the villa's ambience and the way his grandsons befriended Zheng's daughters that somehow gave him peace of mind and a sense of fulfilment that his life suddenly becomes tranquil and serene. He also noticed no malicious talk or anger amongst any of his family, only a sense of peace of mind that everybody was considered equal irrespective of their position at the villa. Zheng and Biyu were unique to him, giving an aura of something that he couldn't explain at present, and he had never experienced.

However, Livia was livid with Augustus's setup and the amount of time he spent there. She was determined to disrupt somehow life at the villa and ensure her son Tiberius was the next emperor. She had already planned Augustus's death, but she needed her step-grandchildren eliminated first before she could make plans and think about getting rid of Augustus.

The boys' mother Julia now married to her estranged husband Tiberius still carried on with her promiscuous life and mistress to Iullus Antonius who Biyu had banned from stepping foot inside the villa's grounds, would come to visit also regularly. She would call when her father Augustus was not around, but she too liked the villa's calmness and ambience.

Livia had returned to the royal palace fuming that her husband Augustus had defied her plan by protecting his three grandsons which she was determined to eliminate anyway she could.

Livia remembered an up and coming recently appointed Praetorian Guard, a close colleague of her son Tiberius. He had just recently returned with her step-grandson Gaius from the front and decided to seek an audience with him and tempt him with an offer he couldn't refuse.

Lucius Aelius Sejanus, commonly known as Sejanus, was an ambitious soldier, friend and confidant of Livia's son Tiberius, had just been appointed as a prefect of the Roman imperial bodyguard, known as the Praetorian Guard.

It was a hot sunny day mid-afternoon when Sejanus arrived and escorted to the royal palace gardens where Livia was waiting:

"What I am about to discuss with you is a very grave matter." Said, Livia, as she glared into Sejanus eyes and continued as he stood to attention. "Tiberius, my son, which I know you are a friend, is in the dire position of losing his life when Augustus eventually is succeeded by his grandchildren Gaius Caesar and Lucius and perhaps even Marcus as emperor. It must never happen.—Do you understand what I mean?"

"I think so!" Said Sejanus.

"You do realise as Roman Emperor Tiberius will appoint you supreme commander of the Praetorian Guard if you succeed." Said, Livia, as she looked up at him with a grave expression on her face as she added. "If you decide to accept this mission and you fail, I will deny all knowledge of this discussion.—It never happened.—Do I make myself clear?— However, if you succeed, you and your family will be very well rewarded with a new villa of your choice in any location and enough money for you to become a very wealthy man." No more said, Livia turned away and didn't expect an answer from him but hoped he would undertake what she had requested.

Sejanus stood still to attention until Livia disappeared. He looked around to make sure that nobody overheard the conversation and slowly with his helmet under his arm left the palace and went back to his barracks. He sat that night at his usual table drinking heavily and thinking over and over again: *the wife of the Roman Emperor wants me to kill his grandchildren?—How am I going to do that?* Sejanus felt with an uneasy feeling. He knew Zheng well from his success in the arena and his elite army and trained gladiators. *It would be impossible to penetrate that villa with just a few men.* "Impossible!" He thought aloud.

"What's impossible?" Said another junior guard as he sat opposite Sejanus.

"Oh!—The wife." Said Sejanus as he supped his drink rose from the table and left.

That evening as he lay in bed staring at the ceiling he suddenly realised he had to do it away from the villa and the only place was the circus during a chariot race when Pi and Zeta would participate. He needed a plan to distract Zheng's elite guard force; It might be that he would have to wait to survey first the movement of everybody that attended a chariot race before he could make his move. He also needed to confide in other prefects of the guard to ensure that the abduction would be successful.

Sejanus's plan was not to slay the boys at the circus, but abduct them first and hand them over to Livia to do the required atrocities. Sejanus had become quite fond of Gaius Caesar when he accompanied him during his campaigns at the front and had no intentions of killing the boy.

The first Roman religious festival planned for the beginning of next month gave Sejanus plenty of time to acquire his prefects from the guard and plan in earnest how he would abduct all three boys under the scrutiny of so many guards.

On the first chariot meeting, he noticed the boys like to spend a lot of time discussing with the charioteers where they gathered the other side of the gates known as carceres. There was a lot of confusion going on, and many people milling around and discussing techniques. The boys would leave to make their way to the imperial box about fifteen minutes before the start. They wouldn't all go at once. They drifted off one by one, accompanied by only one guard. It was quite a walk and many a secluded area where the abduction could take place, he thought. Sejanus planned three zones where he could strategically put his guards where the boys would pass. He would have to make sure the accompanying security guard would need to be immobilised quickly, and a net would be ideal, thrown over him and hoisted such that his feet couldn't touch the ground. The boys would be bound and gagged and removed immediately and taken to a waiting ship in the harbour.

It was the last day of the religious festival and the chariot race's main event that the robots would compete. As usual, the boys were alongside the chariots admiring the charioteers and mingling amongst the crowds closely followed by their bodyguards. Marcus, the youngest was the first to peel off to make his way back to the imperial box followed closely by Lucius but suddenly was held up as he turned to Pi to wish him good luck. Gaius Caesar was still admiring Zeta's chariot, which was considered the favourite to win.

Now out of sight from the others, Marcus and his guard passed the first point of abduction, and the guard was immediately immobilised and knocked unconscious and hoisted up into the rafts. Marcus was bound and gagged and thrown into a sack and quickly taken out and away from the arena. Lucius was bound and silenced at the second abduction point, and his guard hoisted to the ceiling unconscious. That just left Gaius Caesar as he hurriedly left the charioteers realising that he had delayed it too late to get back to the imperial box before the start and decided to take another route that he thought would be quicker. The abductors waited and suddenly realised Gaius Caesar had gone another way. It was too late as they watched through the carceres Gaius Caesar take his seat.

"Where are they?" Said, Gaius Caesar, as he turned to Augustus and Livia.

"Where's who?" Said Livia.

"Well, Marcus and Lucius?"

"Well, aren't they with you?" said Livia as Augustus immediately turned to the guards and beckoned them to go and find Lucius and Marcus.

In the adjoining box, Zheng could see the movement and confusion in the imperial box as guards frantically left hurrying down the steps pushing those coming up out of the way.

One could hear the shouts "They've gone!— abducted!" As the cries entered Zheng's box as his guards bedraggled explained.

From the nets and ropes entangled around an unconscious guard hanging from the rafters, "evidently a planned coup," said, Zheng, as he confronted Augustus. He expected an immediate explanation of how such a thing could happen and what action to find his grandchildren.

Zheng sensed the facial smirk on Livia's face as she was apparently behind the abductions answered without hesitation and much to Livia's surprise —"I will have them back by nightfall!"

After their win, Zheng had to wait for the lap of honour as his charioteers Pi and Zeta rode around the circus. Once again much to the crowd's jubilation, as they sprang into the voice of shouting out Pizeta! Pizeta! Pizeta!

The robots were already aware of the abduction as Zheng approached with so much facial grief. Pi, spoke as he stepped from the chariot once more in that calm and monotone voice, "It's ok they're on a boat heading out of Rome heading for an island."

"How the hell do you know that?" With such a surprised voice said, Zheng.

"Didn't you think—we would microchip them?" replied Pi.

"You two are just unbelievable—So what next?" Said Zheng.

"Well, we are going for a ride in our space shuttle.—That's what we're going to do." Said, Zeta as he summoned Zheng to follow.

As they left the arena, Zheng followed closely behind as the robots walked directly towards the building opposite approaching a black door that turned out to be the entrance to the space shuttle, which had camouflaged itself. To an observer, all three had just walked into the building. As the space shuttle lifted off, the entrance door disappeared, but the space shuttle kept its camouflage as it vanished into the brilliant blue sky.

"So where are they?" Said Zheng.

"Right there!" As they looked down upon a sailing vessel that had just left the harbour.

"So what do we do?" Said Zheng.

"I suggest we take you back to the villa and we shall return to the island they are heading and retrieve Lucius and Marcus." Said Pi in such a calm and commanding voice as if there was nothing really to be concerned.

"What if they're dead." Said Zheng.

"No, impossible! Our sensors are telling us that they are fit and well."

Zheng returned to the villa only to confront complete and chaotic chaos.

"Well, where are they then?" Screamed Pinaria as Oppia burst into tears.

"They will be here tonight please be patient we know exactly where they are." Said Zheng.

"How do you know all of this?" Said, Gaius Caesar with an agitated inquisitive voice.

Carefully Zheng had to think before he responded too hastily. "We have caught some of the culprits, and we know exactly where they are, and I have sent a party to intercept them." Said Zheng with tongue in cheek.

The sailing vessel, making very little headway at one or two knots, the robots decided to help by creating an artificial breeze aft of the boat. As it camouflaged itself stern of the craft; established a funnel air on the ship sails to ensure it reached the island by nightfall.

The sailing vessel arrived at dusk, and the two boys bundled into a nearby building. The robots had embedded the microchips in their skulls monitored heartbeat and blood pressure to show that all was normal. Pi sent a signal to sedate both boys, which they immediately fell into a deep coma. The boat crew returned to their moored ship and left no visible guard at the building, which allowed the robots to enter unchallenged. Within minutes both boys were on the space shuttle heading back to the villa.

Zheng had patiently waited when he saw a ball of light streak across the sky heading his way, knowing full well that the space shuttle, camouflaged had arrived and landed in the woodland. Suddenly the robots emerged carrying Marcus and Lucius. A waiting audience shrieked with joy as Augustus leapt from his seat first to hold Lucius and then stroked Marcus's brow as both suddenly opened their eyes.

"Where are we?"Said, Lucius as he stood up in disbelief that he was now back at home.

"A long story." Said, Zheng, as he embraced Marcus that came running to him.

There was only one face that stood out with a solemn look, and that was of Livia now knowing that her coup had failed and that the chances of Tiberius her son succeeding Augustus were pretty remote.

Livia gave a kiss to each boy as she turned to Augustus and said: "Well, we better hurry on back to let everybody know of the good news."

Augustus overjoyed by such a speedy return of his grandsons could not thank Zheng enough.

"What just happened would not occur again." Said Zheng apologetically, as he slowly escorted Livia to her carriage, knowing full well that she was responsible for what had just happened that day.

The ship that took the boys slipt anchor that evening without checking on the kids. They left them asleep with some food and water thinking to themselves, well two out of three is not bad and were calculating what reduced payment they might receive. The ship arrived back at Rome harbour late the following day, and from the bow, they could see Sejanus waiting alongside the quay "I expect he's waiting to settle the payment." Explained the Captain.

The only words he could hear shouted across the harbour "You blundering idiots."

Shocked at Sejanus's welcome the Captain hurriedly leapt across to the quay before the warps were even secured as he blustered out "What do you mean by that?"

"Didn't you bother to check what was in those sacks?" Said Sejanus.

"Yes, of course, Lucius and Marcus. Why?" Said the Captain with a severe look on his face.

"Well, let me tell you now! —They're back!"

"Back!—What do you mean!—We left them on that island, I swear by the gods! "He said with a shock of disbelief as the other crew members gathered round to confirm what he had just said.

Sejanus walked up the plank to board the ship to hear what the other crew members had to say as one-handed him a charm bracelet and a knife showing the classic crest he had stolen from the boys Sejanus recognised immediately. "You say you left them on the island, but how come they are back here at their home and arrived before you? Can somebody please explain how is that possible?"

They all looked at one another, and the only explanation they could give, "This must have been the work of the Gods. They are royalty and future emperors. Perhaps they are protected, and we shouldn't have interfered." Said, one crew member.

Sejanus looked around at each individual trying to establish their facial expression if there were some form of a conspiracy among the crew members. He mumbled and muttered and suddenly threw a bag of coins on the deck; their payment and left the ship.

Livia had sent messenger after messenger for Sejanus to come to the palace immediately. He arrived late in the shadow of darkness not to be recognised as he entered Livia's chambers.

"What the hell happened. A complete and utter confusion. All three are back at the villa now under a very tight and secure guard." Said Livia with such an angry countenance as she stared into Sejanus eyes.

"Lucius and Marcus were taken to the island as planned and left with very little water and food for them to die. I saw the items that the crew members stole from them. They were genuine." Said Sejanus

"Why the hell didn't you kill them as planned?—Why leave them alive, you idiot?"

"I just couldn't kill them I'm sorrow I instructed the crew members to leave them alive." Said Sejanus as his eyes fell to the floor.

"Well, if Augustus discovers what I have done I shall drag you down with me!—You best get back to fulfilling your mission!—So we can put Tiberius as emperor, or our days numbered!" Said, Livia, as she frantically waved her arm and hand at Sejanus to leave immediately and get out of her sight.

CHAPTER 11

Tarpeia

It was a well-known fact that Livia was responsible for her grandchildren's abduction, but there was no proof only rumour and gossip.

Augustus restricted Livia's movements, especially visiting the grandchildren at Zheng's villa; even though Zheng had increased security, and assigned additional guards to protect all three boys. Meanwhile, the boys became very close to Zheng's daughters; notably, Gaius Caesar showed considerable affection towards Tarpeia. Discretely given more space to develop their relationship; Biyu, nonetheless, very fond of Gaius Caesar encouraged the love affair to someday a forthcoming marriage. Livia fuming at even the suggestion of a commoner marrying her grandson tried to explain to her step-daughter, Julie, the mother of Gaius Caesar, she should intervene. And insist that Gaius Caesar return to perform his royal duties at the frontier protecting Rome's new conquests.

Tiberius married Julie whom he loathed; who had publicly humiliated him with her promiscuous relationships with half the Senate that out of spite he insisted that Gaius Caesar, his adopted son, should accompany him at the frontier to gain experience for the sake of Rome. Augustus reluctantly agreed, but had no choice, since the Senate insisted for Gaius Caesar to gain experience and as a future emperor, join his stepfather Tiberius at the front. Zheng disapproved but offered, however, Pi and Doron as security guards. Still, Tiberius insisted that they could only become personal bodyguards if both were assigned to the Praetorian Guard and commissioned as prefects. That meant that Pi and Doron would come under the Roman army's command, which was entirely out of the question, as far as Zheng was concerned. Tiberius suggested that he alone would provide and dedicate his own two personal guards to protect his step-son.

Gaius Caesar had no intention or wished to go to the frontier to fight defending Rome's new conquests. But he couldn't refuse his grandfathers wishes, since next in line as Emperor, Augustus now insisted; persuaded by Tiberius and the Senate that it was for the good of Rome. Sejanus accompanied Gaius Caesar to the front as official protector and guardian with strict instructions by Augustus that no harm should come to him. But this command fell on deaf ears, since Livia and Tiberius had already conspired his death, and had a plan that would appear that he fell in battle.

Gaius Caesar spent the very last few days at the villa Tarperia would sneak into Gaius Caesar's quarters after dark and let him make love to her each night for nearly a week, and he promised he would marry her on his return from the frontier.

That was the last time Tarpeia spoke to or would ever see Gaius Caesar as she waved farewell, to see him ride out on horseback. She blew a kiss, watched by Zheng, who knew his death was imminent; conspired by Tiberius and Sejanus and orchestrated by Tiberius's mother, Livia. Zheng tried to warn Augustus that he was sending his grandson to his makers but no avail. Gaius Caesar's death initiated a flurry of activity in the household of Augustus but had devasting effects in the home of Zheng as he tried to explain to Tarpeia, who refused to believe that he was dead. Biyu sought to comfort her daughter, who continually declined to accept his death, now she was carrying his child.

Tarpeia did not remember how the day and nights passed; she did not sleep and did not leave her bedroom; she withdrew herself to avoid any allusion that she was pregnant. Her mother Biyu sensed that she was with child as she confided in Zheng, who had already guessed. Biyu surprised that Zheng knew because she was under the impression that the humanoids had sterilised Tarpeia to prevent pregnancy to avoid a caesarean. "How come you didn't tell me she is with child? And how did you know?" She said with a look of astonishment.

"I had the robots remove the sterilisation so that she could leave a normal life. I only thought it would be fair." Said, Zheng, as he paced the room, paused run his hands through his hair to grip the back of his head to loosen the tension in his neck and added. "Pi told me that she was pregnant.—How did he know?—I have no idea?"

"Ok, so she's pregnant!—What are we going to do?"

"Nothing!—It's up to Tarpeia to make that decision." Said, Zheng, as he tried to console Biyu.

Biyu let Tarpeia grieve alone in her room. Eventually, she knew Tarpeia would surface, she needed time to herself—come to terms with herself—perhaps confides in her younger sister, Pinaria and her boyfriend, Lucius, before she would eventually approach them and discuss the matter. It took some time: in fact, weeks before Tarpeia appeared one breakfast morning and quietly sat at the table picking at some fruit as she turned to her mother, Biyu. "I'm pregnant!"

"Well, that's excellent news.—Isn't it?" Said Biyu as she stretched her hands out first to her daughter and then to Zheng.

"Wonderful news." Said, Zheng, as he stood up and kissed Tarpeia on the forehead and added. "Congratulations, sweetheart."

"You're not angry?" Said, Tarpeia with tears streaming down her cheeks.

"It's wonderful news. I am so happy for you." Said Biyu as she wiped the tears from Tarpeia's face; and then kissed her on each side of the cheek.

"You know it's Gaius Caesar's child?" Said Tarpeia as she stared at her father, expecting an angry response.

"We know, and we welcome any child—irrespective of the Father into our house." Said, Zheng, as he continued: "May, I suggest that we keep this news to ourselves since I have a nasty suspicion that this will not be good news for some."

Tarpeia hadn't told her sister or anybody else, except her mother and father as she sat one day very quietly to explain how much she had fallen in love with Gaius Caesar. Her mother listened intensively, understanding what she had lived through and experienced, could not express in words. Biyu genuinely concerned about her daughter's welfare; besides a feeling of remoteness she showed, and a sense of estrangement from the members of her own family; even to the point of hostility, that Biyu thought, maybe—it's time she knew the truth of who she is.

Zheng liked to spend most of the evenings outside; it was quite dark now, and in the south, where he was looking, there was no clouds, just the brilliance of the Milky Way, as Biyu approached from behind and put her arms around his waist. "Thinking of home?" She said.

"No, this is our home now. I'm just trying to make sense of all of this, and wondering where the humanoids are now?" He said with a melancholy voice.

"Well, don't you know where they are?"

Zheng suddenly realised what he had just said knowing that Biyu didn't understand that they had abandoned them and are possibly by now several light-years away, as he replied: "No—I mean Yes—it's that I'm concerned we haven't heard from them?"

"Well, call them up if you're worried." She said hurriedly trying to move on to the real reason she wanted to speak to him as she continued to change the subject which gave Zheng a sigh of relief.

"Look, it's about Tarpeia—do you think we should tell her the truth?"

"The truth!— are you mad!—Firstly, she wouldn't believe us!—secondly, she'd think you were completely and insane!"

Biyu stood for a while in silence, contemplating, as she explained. "Not if we showed her the particular room and the unusual gadgets and perhaps even to take her for a space trip."

Zheng, thinking hard as Biyu added. "What if we were to explain to the robots our intentions— maybe get their advice?—What would you say about that?"

"A robot!—Do you think we will get a sensible answer from a robot? "He said in such a loud voice; and just at the moment Tarpeia approached and walked towards them and interrupted: "So about what are you two arguing?— I hope it's not about me?—Anyway, what's a robot?"

Zheng looked at Biyu, who suddenly went very quiet as she stared deep into Zheng's eyes as if to say. "Shall we tell her or not?"

"Robot?— I didn't say Robot I said, Robert! "You couldn't get a sensible answer from Robert." Said, Zheng, as Tarpeia with a wry face as she turned and walked away muttering. "Who's Robert?"

"So you're not going to tell her then?" Said Biyu with a disappointing facial expression.

"Let me think about—perhaps I'll try to get some response from the robots, either Pi or Zeta." Said, Zheng as Biyu left to let Zheng continue meditating and staring at the stars.

Zheng sat there for many an hour, just staring into the abyss of stars contemplating what he should do next—"just let life continue to my death and take my knowledge with me?" He said to himself or—"should I take this opportunity perhaps to travel back to *Planet-F,* which is now 300 years ahead of this era," he thought.—"Maybe even venture to *Planet-G* to see if anybody of the 5th Millennium that the humanoids created are still alive."—"I wonder if a space shuttle could reach those planets." He said to himself, pointing to *Planet-F*; then rose and walked toward where he could find the robots guarding Marcus and Lucius.

Pi was standing outside Lucius bedroom, standing in his usual place, down the corridor where he could see Zeta guarding Marcus's bedroom. Pi surprised to see Zheng as he asked him. "I need to speak to you and Zeta can you call him to come here?" Before the words left Zheng's mouth, he could see Zeta walking towards him along the long corridor.

"I need to ask you. Can the space shuttle make a journey to any of the planets in this solar system?" Said, Zheng as he stood patiently waiting as the telepathy transmitted between robots had finished. "Yes—of course—Why?" Said Pi.

"How long would it take to get *Planet-F*?" Said Zheng with some enthusiasm.

"We can travel about one-tenth the speed of light and take into account acceleration and deacceleration 35 hours to be exact to *Planet-F* and 72 hours to *Planet-G*." Said Pi hurriedly as Zeta agreed with his computation.

"Well, that's amazing—I didn't realise we are comparatively close" Said, Zheng, as he added, "are you telling me that I could explore the solar system?"

"Well, yes—nothing is stopping us travelling through the solar system if that's what you want?" Said Zeta as he joined in the conversation.

"Hmm, interesting." As Zheng pondered then continued. "I now have a problem Tarpeia is with a child." As he paused looked at the robots which gave him a look of, "so?"

"The father is the late Gaius Caesar's, and if it's a boy, it's next in line to be the Emperor's successor."

"Congratulations!—Why is that a problem?" Said Pi.

"Well her life is in danger and particular the coming child." Said, Zheng, as he paused; but decided instead to share his thoughts with the robots as he continued. "What if I told Tarpeia everything and persuade her to set up a new life on *Planet-F* for her safety and the newborn?"

"It wouldn't work, she would never understand, a whole new life in a different environment would be too much of a shock. She would have to be sedated, brainwashed, and new memory cells introduced." Said Zeta with such a harsh and immediate response without any hesitation. "But we can protect her here!—You don't have to go to all that trouble, all we have to do if you allow us, is to monitor her by implanting a microchip?" Said Pi.

"Well, can I at least tell her why we are here and that she must carry a microchip?" Said Zheng.

"No! You cannot do that, and we forbid you to take that risk. You and Biyu are the only two mortals that know of our existence, and we shall wait for the humanoids to return before we decide anything." Said Zeta with such a stern voice.

Zheng looked at them both, thinking to himself are they crazy as he replied in such a loud voice: "They will not be back for another 5000 years! Do you think that I am going to be here! I will be dead!" As he shook his head in disbelief at even the suggestion of still being alive.

"No!—You will be alive!—You will not die!—You and Biyu are now immortal, and we have the technology to keep you young and alive. In 5000 years you will look as you look now. You will not decay." Said Zeta as he added "You have not yet understood the meaning of time. You are now part of the stars and your lifespan like ours; it does not have to terminate; it has no sense. We are no longer part of the life cycle, like a flower, or a caterpillar changing to a butterfly which only lasts a few days. Our entropy will last as long as the stars shine. Both of you are immortal unless you want death."

Zheng sat down, stunned, unable to comprehend the robots and humanoids' logical thoughts and what could be their intent to keep him and Biyu alive for eternity. The only thing he could think of was that being the last of homo-sapiens from Planet Earth and considered their makers, the thought of losing contact with planet earth was too much for them. But that was absurd since machines don't have a conscious or an inner soul that humanity meant to have; so he has been led to believe, which has come into these worlds by revelation and doctrine teachings.

Zheng, exhausted with discussing something which he hadn't envisaged agreed, however, that it would not be a good idea to confide in Tarpeia but would allow a microchip implanted for her safety and the newborn child. He walked away from the robots and turned and spoke: "I still would like to go to the planets."

"Of course. Just let us know." Came the reply.

Zheng very tired of his ordeal with the robots didn't sleep that night as he tossed and turned in his bed rose early with the sun, took some fresh fruit and sat outside.

"Well, you're an early bird. Is something bothering you?" Said Biyu as she approached to lean across and kiss him on the cheek as she added. "Well, at least you can say good morning."

"Hmm!—Yes, of course; good morning!" Replied Zheng as he turned with an apprehensive look on his face as he gestured Biyu to sit beside him.

"Look, I have some bad news," as he paused and hesitated, "Pusa and Pyroies have left the solar system and will not return for at least another 5000 years." He said abruptly to get to the point straight away.

"Well, I'd say that's good news.—We can now live our lives normally—can't we?" Said Biyu with an interested but happy facial appearance.

"In some respects, yes—but what they have done, unbeknown to us, they have made us immortal." Said Zheng with grave concern as he continued. "What it means we shall no longer get older!— to be alive when the humanoids return in another 5000 years?"

"You must be joking!— I hope that includes everyone our sons and daughters?" said Biyu with a look of bewilderment.

"No, only us—the rest will get older and die naturally."

"You mean our children will get old in front of our very eyes as we stay young?" Said Biyu as her face showed signs of anguish as she added, "Well, I'm not going to let that happen!—I would rather die than bury my children before me!"

"Yes, yes I agree, but there is another solution—I felt the same; rather than die, we have at our disposal two robots and a spacecraft that can journey through this solar system. There is nothing to stop us from travelling to the planets to observe—we can watch our children from a distance as they getter older. We could even help—like guardian angels." Said, Zheng, as he looked deep into her eyes as if to see she had relinquished her anxiety.

Biyu with tears now flowing down her cheek turned and sobbed on his shoulder as she whispered.—"What are we going to do? —We can never live a normal life: we are always at the mercy of these machines, I don't want to become immortal, I just want to grow old and die!"

Zheng turned and walked towards the sun as Biyu dried her eyes thinking about what he had just said as she stared at Zheng's silhouette highlighted by the brilliant sun showed his handsome physique which already resembled that of a young man. She could not help but love him and could never live without him as she walked towards him and held his hand as he turned and she gently spoke: "Ok, how do we go about it?—What are we going to do and what do we tell the children?"

"There is only one solution—we have to appear as if we have died—somehow naturally or by some mysterious alignment. I'm sure that the robots can easily arrange that and we disappear by departing from the planet." He paused and gave a thought as he continued. "I suggest we return to *Planet-F* set up a new life as man and wife in a whole new environment which by my reckoning should be the year 320 AD." Said Zheng, as he lingered again to give some thought to Tarpeia and added: "Of course after the birth of our new grandchild; and all our children and grandchildren microchipped so we can monitor their lives. Remember as descents of the 5th Millenium the women cannot give birth naturally, and we shall always somehow have to be at hand."

"I see—so we can follow their progress as if we haven't left them—and we are always on hand to help." Said Biyu as she now appeared reassured that it might work as she added, "This feels like that comic book of old that we use to read about Superman and Superwoman that came to the aid of those in difficulties."

"Yes, it does feel a bit like that. That we have suddenly become those comic characters of the past on planet earth." Said Zheng with a smile on his face as he added: "Perhaps we need a costume when we appear as if we have come from the heavens."

"I like it." Said Biyu, giggling and laughing, holding him tight to whisper in his ear: "At least I have you for another 5000 years."

"What are you two laughing about?" Said Tarpeia as she came out to join them for breakfast.

"On nothing just a private joke, my dear.—And how are you this morning?" said Biyu as Tarpeia sat down at the table and picked some fruit and replied, "Just fine, thank you."

From their discussions that early morning and what the robots had said to them about immortality, it now became apparent that they were not ageing like others around them. The comments made about Biyu maintaining her youth. In contrast, Chen, the same age, looked thirty-five. They also noticed that Chu Yun, who was younger than Zheng, now seemed much older. Even, his wife Guo Wangcheng much younger than Biyu looked twice her age.

Questioned, by so many, how Biyu kept herself looking so young without a line on her face; and such a firm trim body, without sagging breasts, or a distended stomach. And after giving birth to so many that ageing had slowed down or even perhaps stopped.

Zheng had convinced himself that his and Biyu's disappearance was the best obvious option open for them; forewarned the robots that he would depart the planet at some possible point. For surveillance, especially his children, the robots were instructed to microchip everybody. A date for departure agreed depending on

Zheng's first grandchild's birth, which the robots already knew and worked towards a scheduled day sometime within the next six months.

Zheng spent a lot of time with his son Gaius preparing him to take over which he could not understand why he had to take in so much information when he didn't know or needed advice—"Well, can't I just ask you?" He said.

Zheng spent a lot of time with Doron who he had now made him commander in chief of his army and responsible for the total security of his land and property and chiefly to take care of his family. He also involved Chu Yun and most of the staff associated with chariot racing in all the business aspects as far as purchasing racehorses. Zheng tried to tie up all the loose ends, knowing the robots would not be on hand, especially for Lucius and Marcus's safety, which depended on his guards. And fully aware that the young lives were doomed; their deaths already planned it was inevitable by Livia there was nothing Zheng could do except change the course of history.

Biyu at the same time prepared her daughters and all the close women she had grown so close to: like Niu, Feiyan, Chen and Guo Wangcheng. Although clones of her previous life she still felt a very close relationship with them, especially their children.

The months flew by as Biyu and Zheng started to detach themselves from running the business and delegating more work to all those at the villa. The robots spent more and more time away, preparing for future space travel. It was still not decided how Biyu and Zheng would meet their deaths which had to appear as an accident and disappear since all bodies cremated soon after death. Also, it was still not apparent how they would go about it since Zheng and Biyu were always accompanied by their bodyguards wherever they went. The only time they were alone was on the grounds of the villa or in their private quarters. It left a dilemma with the robots since they could easily fake their deaths, but to make the bodies disappear was going to be difficult. The only solution they could think of was to replace their bodies with two identical to be found dead in their bed. The idea was to have the remains discovered as if a cobra snake had attacked them; make it look like Biyu was bitten first for Zheng to wake to find Biyu dying; to kill the snake by a sword, but bitten as he defended himself. The robots had plenty of humans at the north pole still in some form of hibernation waiting reincarnation which they could quickly change their appearance with plastic surgery. The robots knew that Zheng and Biyu would not agree to their plan to have two unknown humans killed, so the robots decided to take the initiative themselves when the time was right soon after Tarpeia gave birth.

Finally, Tarpeia gave birth by caesarian, performed by the robots, to a beautiful boy named after his father, Gaius. The whole villa celebrated and a party soon after was thrown to welcome the new baby to the Zheng household. The robots realised that now was the time; to replace Biyu and Zheng that evening, while everybody's guard was down and the replacements were already waiting in the spacecraft. The robots remained at the party well into the early hours of the morning, ensuring the majority of the guests either departed premature or kept with full glasses of wine becoming intoxicated. They had already sedated Biyu and Zheng's drinks and also most of the personal guards. They crept into Zheng's quarters to find both in a deep sleep but to make sure, sedated them once more by injection, this time to ensure they were thoroughly inebriated. When the party had finished, and in the profit of darkness, they carried both to their spacecraft: replaced both with dead bodies, already injected with venom A mortal cobra and a sword covered in blood, strategically placed in a position of attack with the snake's head removed. The stage set and copies of Biyu and Zheng laid dead, showing a snake bite that must have entered their bedroom. Zheng so intoxicated could not defend himself and Biyu.

The following morning, all turmoil erupted when the maid tried to raise them for breakfast and discovered them slumped in bed with their heads hanging towards the floor. Screams and cries heard inside, outside, and the surrounding grounds of the villa. Pi and Zeta stayed to make sure the deaths accurately recorded and attended those in a complete and utter shock. Calmed those with a potent drug which put them immediately to sleep. Gaius just could not believe that his father was dead after spending recently so much time with him. He had his suspicions that foul play was responsible for finding a cobra in their bedroom. Gaius determined that somebody in the household placed the snake in the room questioned everybody of their whereabouts, including Pi and Zeta. He began to think that Livia was responsible, knowing that she arranged Gaius Caesar's death at the frontier. Still, he had doubts since his sister had just given birth to a son fathered by Gaius Caesar that perhaps the snake was meant for Tarpeia and her newborn and somehow was put in the wrong bedroom.

Augustus arrived with his wife Livia, who couldn't believe that somebody so young could have his life taken because of a snake. He wanted to see where it happened and even inquired about the dead snake's whereabouts to see if there was possibly a clue that it was not just an accident. Livia followed her husband with her eyes scanning every part of the room as if she was looking for something thought Gaius as he waited for her to say something.

"So this is the place where it happened." Said, Augustus.

"Yes, that's correct." Said Gaius.

"Where do you think it came in?." Augustus said as Livia stood beside him looking towards the window.

"It couldn't have entered—but placed!" Said, Gaius, as he turned to stare at Livia as if she was held responsible.

Just at that moment, Tarpeia entered holding her son as Livia turned to face her and the look on her face with so much surprise as she hesitated and stuttered a few words. "Tarpeia so happy to see you—so whose baby is this?" as she gazed at the way Tarpeia was holding it so close to her bosom as if it was hers.

Gaius intervened as he took a step forward to suddenly realise Livia didn't know that his sister was with child as he interrupted while stroking the forehead of the held child before Tarpeia could respond. "Oh! That's a newcomer to the villa from Chu Wun's wife, Guo Wangcheng." As he stared into Tarpeia's eyes to say; "don't you say a word."

Livia stood looking down at the child as she inquisitively responded. "It doesn't look oriental?"

"No the child takes after his Greek grandfather, Guo Wancheng's father.

Augustus still searching for a clue in the room broke his silence as he spoke: "Seems like foul play to me. Did Zheng have many enemies?"

Livia now touching and caressing the child's cheeks spoke aloud with such uncaring voice. "Oh!—He had plenty of enemies." She paused, turned and took the arm of Augustus. "Come on we must leave these good people to mourn, in peace."

No sooner had they departed Tarpeia turned to her brother with such an angry look. "Why did you say my child was Guo Wancheng's son? I wanted to introduce a new grandson."

"My dear that was a death sentence for you and your, newborn," Gaius said with a solemn voice. "Livia does not know that the late Gaius Caesar has a son, and it's becoming apparent to me perhaps that she was not involved in our father and mother's murder. She has no reason to kill our parents. I thought maybe she was involved in plotting your murder since your son succeeds Augustus, which went wrong. But it was so obvious that she has no idea that you have just given birth."

"Oh! So you think our mother and father murdered?" Said Tarpeia with a shocked look on her face.

"Of course—this was no accident—this was conspired and plotted by someone who I shall find out who killed them. Can't you see that?"

Tarpeia clutched her son even closer to her chest, fearing for his life. Her sister's consoled her as they too were now in shock in hearing the older brother's words who was now the father figure of the family orchestrating the whole sorrow state of affairs.

Gaius brothers Aulus and Cato stood alongside to show a united force that their parent's death avenged, like Gaius, now head of the family, gave the staff instructions to prepare his father and mothers' funeral.

Mission accomplished, the robots needed an excuse to leave without raising suspicion. So they decided to replace themselves with two replica robots with the exact facial appearance. Pi left for the laboratories to fabricate two replica robots while Zeta alone at the villa could become Pi if necessary. It would appear that Pi and Zeta were both at the estate as Zeta changed appearance. It would only become evident if both required at the same time.

CHAPTER 12

Superhuman

Taken to the robotic factory at the North Pole and provided with quarters that resembled the house that Zheng and Biyu once lived in on Planet Earth, they woke to find themselves in surroundings that they did not expect. There were pictures of their stepfather, Chang, and personal items that they had left behind on the mothership all those years ago, which to them only seemed like yesterday. They were unaware; however, of the fact that the robots had proceeded without conveying to them how they planned to execute their deaths', which meant only one thing, now at the North Pole, they must be lying dead back at the villa with the family and friends stricken with grief.

During most of Zheng and Biyu's lives, they had been cryogenically preserved and had only experienced about twenty years of living themselves; now in their early thirties, they had departed from the earth more than 430 years ago. How could they explain to anybody, especially their children, the difficulty they found themselves forced to abandon their children to fend for themselves? Biyu shed a few tears as she thought *how could the machines impose such a predicament on the children mourning a false death*. Zheng tried to re-assure Biyu it was for the best. Also, he explained the boys were clones if that was some compensation, and not her real children, which she could never get to grips with since as far as she was concerned, they were still her boys, cloned or not. *Only my daughters are real, so I believe, cryogenically preserved with them when they spent all that time waiting to reach a ridiculous period in time just to satisfy the humanoids plan* she thought. *And now the machines have scheduled a return to Planet-F at another time of 320AD which I have no understanding of why we have to leapfrog centuries from one planet to the next.*

Their ordeal shattered to discover many activities with robots and humanoids running around and organising what looked like a prepared second space shuttle. There appeared so much activity around the small spacecraft that the next space flight would be in a smaller vessel and not a mothership. They returned to their quarters to relax as Zheng took up his favourite reclining chair to play with the gadgets of the 5th Millennium when a robot entered, "We have communication with Pusa and Pyroies." Said the machine.

"What now?" Said, Zheng, surprised, taken immediately to another particular room. They entered, it had highly polished black satin walls and ceilings without an edge, no reflection, but standing in front was Pusa and Pyroeis that looked somehow real. Still, Zheng soon realised it was a 3D holographic image as he circled both to face Pusa.

Pusa turning and following Zheng as he circled spoke with a smile: "Well I'm so happy that you have decided to continue in helping us to populate the stars."

"How do you do this?" Said Zheng as he threw his arms and hands to gesture the image that stood in front of him as he continued, "You must be some light-years away from us, but it's like you are here in this very room." Said Zheng still staring with astonishment.

"Yes, it's magic. We have never been able to try out our entangled room at such a distance." Said Pusa with such enthusiasm as she added: "You and I are entangled via computer imaging and audio so that we can defeat time dilation."

"I don't understand how does that work?" said Zheng

"Well in layman's terminology." As she stopped, Pusa gave it some thought and carried on "Have you ever stood between two mirrors and your image disappears into infinity, but your movements appear to be instant? Well, you and I caught between these two mirrors. I'm at one end, and you are at the other, and the mirrors wrapped around, so we meet." Said Pusa' "It's that easy; entanglement is just a reflection of the same particle, but it's a mirror image that's all.—The room you are standing in its surface mirrors entangled with the surface mirrors at which I am looking.—Except your reflection reflected my end and my reflection reflected your end across vast distances of time and space defeating time dilation."

"Amazing! I still don't understand—where are you now?" Said, Zheng with such a smile on his face reflecting that human touch when you haven't seen somebody for such a long time.

"Well, I would say we are ten light-years from you." As Pyroeis stepped forward, interrupted and continued. "Well as you know the universe is significant, and we haven't yet scratched the service, and it's going to take not thousands but millions of years to get some understanding perhaps." As he stopped not knowing what to say next or to complete what he intended to say as he continued "But I hear that you will be waiting for us when we return sometime in the next 5000 years."

"Well if we are still here!" Said Zheng.

"You will be! The robots are going to make you immortal. A Super-man and Biyu a Super-woman from the 5th Millennium." As he pointed to Biyu with a smile and added, "The Stella solar system will become your oyster of the stars. Enjoy my homo-sapiens, and we shall speak to you soon."

"What are they going to do to us to make us immortal. I thought we were already immortal." Said, Zheng, as he turned to Biyu with such a curious look on his face.

"This life of ours is getting extraordinary, indeed. I am to become a superwoman, which you and I joked about, interpreted it must have been that we wanted to become super beings." Said Biyu as she took his hand, "Come on, let's go and eat something fancy; I've had enough Roman food to last a lifetime."

Sedated and taken to the laboratory medical centre, Zheng and Biyu bodies checked to ensure they were entirely fit for the space journey. That was what they believed. However, the motor system of the brain was enhanced, especially sensory cortex. Specific areas of the brain stimulated notably in the frontal lobe area.

After the surgery, they felt no change except that they could sustain more pain than usual, which at the time were not aware of, hear and see more acutely which they had not yet experienced. Their sense of smell enhanced to such an extent; it was the same as some animals. Locomotion of the arms and legs improved to that of a superior athlete where they could jump higher run faster and throw objects further.

They had become superhuman except that they still relied on a regular blood supply to the brain, so inserted a backup miniature pump in parallel with their real heart. As long as the head remained on the body, the brain would always have a blood supply and surgery could replace any damaged part or organ as long as the mind kept intact. The robots had created the most superior human being the world had ever seen. Perfect skins, not a blemish to be seen. The hair silk and so natural. The white of the eye brilliant heightened the emerald green of Biyu's and the pale blue of Zheng's eyes. A helmet, devised by the robots, would protect their skulls and extend around their neck and across their shoulders. The material was light, but on impact would immediately inflate to absorb a blow. The helmet attached to a tunic covered their bodies to make a complete suit with fastening at the front, allowing them to step into and place the right-hand glove and stroking from the groin area to the neck. The opening would be the reverse. The shoes, gloves and knee pads had superior attractive forces that could attach to anything and sustain not only their body weight but many times more. The tunics could change colour to match its surroundings and with the facial mask pulled down across their face, they were invisible to an observer. The cover inside had a screen to give a 360-degree observation with added ultraviolet and thermal imaging.

After spending nearly a year at the North Pole and ensuring that life had settled back at the villa, they were ready to depart. Pi and Zeta had left two robots which resembled and acted like them mainly to protect the children and report any concerns or incidents which required assistance.

Two space shuttles left from the North Pole, one piloted by Pi the other by Zeta, Biyu and Zheng strapped into Pi's shuttle as they lifted off the Planet's gravity vertical to reach within minutes the outer orbit of the planet. They accelerated around the world to exert a gravity force which slung each shuttle out in the direction towards *Planet-F* 1.3 million kilometres away. Within 72 hours, reaching 10 per cent the speed of light, they would get to their destination. The visuals displayed in the head-up display the planet seemed so close as they stared in awe.

Zheng suddenly realised that his eyesight could depict every detail on the planet, which was some distance away. His hearing was acutely aware of every noise on the craft, and he could smell and distinguish the different fragrances around the cockpit as he turned and touched Biyu sitting alongside him who was dozing as her head dropped forward. "Are you experiencing what I am experiencing? My senses seem enhanced to such an extent that I can hear, smell and see much better than before." He said.

She immediately woke, rubbed her eyes as she answered. "What do you mean?"

"Look at the planet can you see every detail of the terrain." He said

"Well yes, I can—that's amazing it's like I'm wearing magnifying glasses." She said as she continually glared to pick out every aspect of the planet.

"What about hearing? And can you smell distinctive fragrances around the craft?" He said.

"Yes, I can! My hearing is identifying every noise in this craft! And yes I can smell many different aromas." She paused and took a depth breath and added. "I can detect an apple an orange and grapes that they have stored for us."

"They've enhanced our senses!" said Zheng as he stared back at the planet as they space shuttle now hurtled towards space at 300km/s.

"I wonder what else they have done?" Said Biyu too relaxed back in her recliner to enjoy the view as the oncoming planet got larger.

Zheng could sense the thrusters starting to deaccelerate the shuttle that continued for a long time he thought to reach a speed which would take the craft into a smooth orbit around the planet. As they started to traverse they got a distant view of *Planet-E* that they had just left as it surfaced on the horizon as the suns brilliance highlighted a kaleidoscope of greens, blues, yellows and many other shades of colours. It appeared so close. And then behind in the far distance, *Planet-G* emerged as Zheng pointed to it and said, "Perhaps sometime in the future that's our next port of call."

"I feel like I'm a master of the universe." Said Biyu as she immersed herself in the spectacular view.

"We are!" Said, Zheng, as he leant across and squeezed her hand.

Space shuttles one behind the other both approached the North Pole of the planet, and Zheng could see below the hanger doors open from the snow-capped terrain with both manoeuvrings in harmony and as both descended. Zheng could hear the music "The Blue Danube" by Johann Strauss II as the robots played it through the spacecraft which to Zheng was a piece of music that has now lived for thousands of years but still loved by many; including robots, put a smile on his face.

When they disembarked from the craft, the laboratory, was precisely the same layout Zheng had seen before. A thrive on the activity as robots, humanoids appeared everywhere, as if they were royalty. Zheng felt honoured and somehow proud; *I represent Planet Earth as the very last male born in the 5th Millenium, and now I have superhuman powers.* He thought.

The robots patiently waited for guidance on what to do next since he had requested a visit to the planet. "Well, I'd like to go to Changzhou or somewhere in the far east and then travel to Rome, perhaps Athens." Said Biyu admiring the quarters a replica of the quarters they had just left.

"You realise it is going to be completely different the year is 320AD." Said, Pi

"I know! Isn't it exciting! We are like time travellers, but the ironic thing is that we have created this time." Said Biyu.

"What gets me is how life is so accurately programmed. Constantine the Great should be the Roman Emperor, and Zhang Mao and Emperor Yuan Di are in power if I recall history." Said, Zheng, as he continued, "I think you're right; let's start in the far east and then work our way to Rome along the silk road. If it's still there?"

Zheng planned to return to the places he had frequented many a time before as if a holiday. But he became confused about what he could remember on what planet. Remembering the tavern; but was it this planet or the other planet? He thought.

The space shuttle landed close to a mountainous terrain hidden amongst the forestry where Zheng could set up camp. The shuttle surveyed the surrounding area, mapping out a direction and a route towards Rome. They were unsure of what to expect in this new situation and felt it best to integrate into their new environment gradually. The space shuttle made an ideal shelter while they gathered necessary basic needs. Always they carried with them horses, mules and a few farm animals to sustain living remotely and isolated until they become confident and able to live within a community without becoming conspicuous.

The year was 320 AD, and they had no idea what to expect. Zheng remembered that when he was on *Planet -E*, the Qin Dynasty constructed a wall to protect their empire against warring states. He was surprised to find the same wall continuing built even though life arranged to start in the 1st century BC by the humanoids. Zheng would often quiz Pi and Zeta on their historical knowledge during this period, when it had occurred on planet earth, knowing full well that the humanoids were repeating it here. The robots explained that powerful nomadic Mongolian tribes were waging long wars against the Chinese and other surrounding states. And that it was a dangerous place to be and they should be on their guard at all time since the spacecraft would return to the polar cap with Pi and Zeta for a prolonged maintenance repair job. The camp was now well established and would become a permanent home during the oncoming winter to stay until spring before venturing to travel West. They communicated with the robots via their blue sapphire stones which they wore permanently around their necks. The camp strategically located close to a continually running water stream and a deep pool for bathing and washing. The animals fenced off under a temporary shelter and hidden amongst the forest were protected from the rear and one side by two huge boulders that at some time had fallen from the growing mountain. The accommodation had been carved out from the rock face by laser weapons to create a very spacious area with a skylight opening to accommodate a fire in the room's centre. Trees planted to obscure the building unless one approached it from the pool area, hidden it felt secure as the robots, said their farewells to return in spring unless called upon during an emergency. It was late autumn when the space-craft disappeared that night into the abyss of stars as it headed North to the polar cap. It was the first time for a very long time that Zheng and Biyu were utterly alone except for a few wild animals that they could hear in the distance. The water cascading down the mountain gave them somehow a simple reassurance and a peace of mind as they sat on the porch gazing once more at the stars as the splashing of the water into the pool broke the evening silence.

"I feel exhausted and as if a huge burden has just lifted from my shoulders." Said, Zheng, as he leaned back in his newly constructed rocking chair as he stared into the night sky.

"I know exactly how you feel. I feel the same." Said Biyu as she too did the same rocked back and forth in her new chair.

"We should feel guilty leaving the children as we did, but somehow I am not showing any sign of remorse or regret what we did." He said as he glanced towards Biyu, expecting a facial look of guilt when she just looked and smiled and agreed that she too had no regrets.

That night they made love as they had never done before as the moans and groans of ecstasy echoed around the pool area as it amplified against the facial mountain drowning out all other animal noises.

CHAPTER 13

The threat.

Tarpeia had named her son after her father Gaius Caesar much to her brother's disapproval. Still, she wouldn't listen, impossible after her mother and father's death, had a mind of her own and was not going to take advice from anybody, especially her younger brother.

Throughout the villa and the village, Gossip reached Livia's ears that Gaius Caesar had fathered a child just before his death, and the mother was Tarpeia.

The robots (a carbon copy of Pi and Zeta) knew of the danger, but maintaining 24-hour vigilant protection was becoming difficult because of Tarpeia's stubbornness that Livia, the Emperor's wife, was involved that anybody would harm her and the newborn baby.

After hearing the plot and the threat inflicted towards his family, Zheng insisted that Tarpeia and her child come to the planet for safety. But the robots questioned his logic since he had already abandoned his family because: "He could not watch his children grow old in front of his eyes, while he stayed young."

"What do you suggest then." Said Zheng speaking through his blue sapphire stone, that hung around his neck to Pi.

"We are going to clone them and present two dead bodies." Said, Pi, as if this was the only solution available.

"Then what? How do they intend to continue and live amongst their family and friends, knowing that they are supposedly dead?" said Zheng with an angry and frustrated voice as if the robots hadn't thought this through.

"Yes, of course, we know they can't continue living the way they were; we suggest to relocate them." Said Pi

"Alone!—Live alone!—A mother and her child!—Are you crazy they will not survive!" Said Zheng very angrily.

"So, what do you suggest then?" Said Pi.

"I suggest to bring both to this planet and wipe Tarpeia's brain clean; not her son's, only her's, of all knowledge of her previous life. Make her think she is a servant that we found her in unusual circumstances—I suggest a village sacked by a vicious tribe that had slaughtered all those close to her." Said Zheng with Biyu standing by overhearing the conversation and agreeing by nodding every word Zheng said.

"Ok—if that's what you want I'll do it." Said Pi as he turned to Zeta and telepathically thought: "This conscientiousness of humans I do not understand. It's not logical thinking."

Tarpeia and her son were found dead one morning with a live cobra snake curled up in the corner of her room. Gaius immediately suspected foul play, knowing that Livia was somehow behind this. On hearing the news, Livia congratulated

Sejanus on removing the next heir to the emperor. Still, Sejanus had no idea what she was talking about but decided to take his reward and let her believe that he had organised and was responsible for the killings.

Meanwhile, in another world, time and space Zheng frantically constructed new lodgings adjacent to his own; knowing that his daughter and grandson were imminently due. Biyu so saddened on hearing what had happened felt so sorry for her other daughters what they must be going through after losing their parents and now their elder sister and nephew. But at the same time happy that Tarpeia was on her way. The day arrived when the spacecraft touched down close to the cabin with Tarpeia heavily sedated. Still, the child was kicking and smiling when handed to Biyu, who sensed immediately that the child recognised her face as it smiled and gurgled something which she could only interpret as if it was trying to say hello. Tarpeia slept as the spacecraft left the vicinity while cuddling their grandson, now wide awake was enjoying the attention. Suddenly the door threw open, and there stood Tarpeia very apologetic she had fallen asleep, and it won't happen again she promised as she picked up her son and thanked Biyu for looking after him. She had no recollection that she was standing in front of her parents but immediately prepared the daily meal with her son held under her arm.

"Please let me hold him." Said Biyu.

"Thank you, mam." Said Tarpeia as she handed her child and continued preparing the meal.

Zheng looked at Biyu with raised eyebrows as if to say, 'let sleeping dogs lie', we shall explain later at a more convenient time. Both so happy, even though their daughter had no previous knowledge of her past life and didn't recognise them, but she had survived and given birth to a beautiful boy. Biyu content with the situation knowing eventually, her daughter would understand. Tarpeia under the illusion that she had been rescued by Zheng when warring tribes had attacked her village massacred everybody and raped women and children. She was so thankful that Zheng had saved her and her child that she didn't know how to repay him except offer her naked body. "This is not necessary you are a free woman; please, we are here to help you and your son." Said Biyu as she helped her back to bed.

From that day on, Tarpeia did more than her fair share around the house; like outside attending the animals. Biyu tried to intervene, to help and take over some of the household chores, which Tarpeia could not understand. Her son spent most of the time with either Zheng or cuddled up with Biyu, which she appreciated, but couldn't reconcile why her employers had grown so attached to her son as life became routine. Now and again they could not help think about their other daughters Pinaria and Oppia and were dying to ask but had to hold back knowing full well Tarpeia wouldn't have any idea. Her mind completely wiped clean only knew of life in warring Mongolia and was led to believe that Zheng had rescued her when her village sacked and her husband slain in battle. Discovered when her child suddenly cried out by Zheng, unconscious holding her baby, hidden in an underground bunker. Tarpeia was always wary of the roaming warring tribes that would kill anybody in sight just for a handful of rice and emphasised to Zheng of the danger living the way they were and should head for the safety of a big town. Zheng explained that he intended to move west under the Roman Empire's protection but was waiting for the spring to break next year and hold up here during the winter months. It was challenging for Biyu to live so close to Tarpeia, unable to tell she was her mother and had another life with brothers and sisters in a place far away that she would not be able to understand. But Biyu was so thankful that she had at least one daughter and a grandchild with her she could accept to lie continually.

The robots had left an abundance of dried fish, salted meat, and the farm animals' milk and eggs were plentiful. However, Zheng would forage daily in the forest for edible fruit, nuts, stems, leaves, corms and tubers.

One day in the woods foraging he came across a nomadic warring tribe that had made camp alongside a stream on the high plateau above his dwellings that if they ventured to the edge of the waterfall, they would be able to see Zheng's site. As Zheng looked towards the waterfall, he could see rising smoke drifting towards him with a smell of freshly cooked fried fish. He glanced at the tribe, who were now standing with their noses in the air, could sense the same thing he had just smelt. Zheng immediately hurried back from his hiding place, slipped, fell running as fast as his legs could take him. He shouted to Biyu, "we are about to be attacked." As Zheng looked up, he could see at least six men standing at the edge of the waterfall looking down at him; but there was no way down the steep facial wall, he thought. He had counted at least twelve armoured men, which meant that six were coming to the same path he had just taken.

With their lethal weapons primed ready to attack Biyu and Zheng waited patiently and calmly. Tarpeia told to hide with the baby in the undergrowth within the nearby forest edge far away from where the villains would emerge. No sooner had Tarpeia disappeared into the brush six armed men firmly built, on horseback, came charging out of the forest with weapons drawn. It was all over in seconds as one by one the men slain as the laser beams swept over their bodies severing their heads. Zheng looked up at the waterfall at the six that stood in fright watching their comrades slaughtered took heed and ran. Zheng ran towards a dismounted horse and effortlessly leapfrogged on its back and galloped back up towards the plateau to confront the six to ensure no one escaped to raise the alarm. Within a short time, all six on the mesa lay dead; decapitated as Zheng with his weapon primed tore into them.

Tarpeia emerged from the forest clutching her son very close to her bosom covering the child's eyes to ensure that the boy could not see the decapitated bodies that lay scattered on the ground."You did this?" She, said, as Biyu approached enquiring after her and the babies health.

"No, we are fine. Thank you." She said as she just stared in horror at the headless bodies. "No wonder you are not afraid when you can defend yourselves against such animals." She added.

At that moment, she saw Zheng emerging from the forest with another six dead bodies laid across each of their horses harnessed together as he approached holding the reins.

"You did that as well as single-handed?" Said Tarpeia amazed as she held even tighter her son with both her hands now covering his face as his body suspended in a makeshift harness attached around her neck.

"We must get rid of the bodies; tidy up everywhere, so there is no sign that they ever were here or even existed." Said Zheng.

"I can do that—I can help." Said Tarpeia handing her son to Biyu, singing a lullaby rocking him walking back slowly towards the hut.

"I'll be back in a minute once he's settled." Shouted Biyu as she disappeared into the cabin with the baby now fast asleep.

It took them well into the night before the dead buried and the campsite cleaned without a trace of blood. With so many weapons, a substantial amount of money, twelve beautiful horses that Zheng had already put to graze and harnessed in such a manner that they could freely move within a confined space he felt a sense of victory.

Tarpeia slept well that night knowing she was in safe hands but somehow saddened in a way that if Zheng and Biyu had rescued her earlier; *perhaps they could have saved her late husband and the village,* so she thought.

Late autumn and winter fast approaching; the leaves had already turned sienna and umber brown to fall, to lay sodden, covering the area surrounding the newly built cabin. Zheng's enhanced senses suspected wolves and bear approaching, decided the hut needed to be added security; enclosed the compound by installing straight adjoining tree trunks to make a very tall continuous fence. The laser weapon excavated a ditch to hold the felled logs; he tied and dragged by horse into the dugout. The camp protected at the rear by a mountain face; a running stream at the forward-facing collecting into a large deep pool; meant that only two sides had to be fenced. At the same time, he created an observation platform at the main gate accessed by a ladder, to apprehend anything or anybody approaching. During Zheng's outdoor activity Biyu and Tarpeia spent time in the forest gathering nuts and fruits for storage; mainly far away from where Zheng worked; Tarpeia was not aware of the laser weapon he was using. They also spent a lot of time gathering grass for the winter feed for the animals, which suddenly had sprung up in the newly cleared areas in the forest where trees had previously felled. A long winter meant they had to make sure they had enough food; not only for themselves but for the animals as well. Although Zheng, however, was prepared to slaughter an animal to survive, he knew in an emergency, a call to the robots would bring anything he wished, but he was determined to show independence; that alone could survive without support from any intelligent machine.

Just as he finished his construction, the snow flurries started to arrive in earnest and flocks of birds headed South; Zheng knew from his experience that winter was now fast approaching. The robots, themselves, couldn't understand the mentality of Zheng, why he wanted to live the way he had chosen, whereas, he could comfortably live anywhere in a solidly constructed house built by them and guarded and protected by them. Zheng, however, insisted on his freedom far away from any artificial intelligence. He wanted his life back in some form of normality, even though he supposedly had immortality which as of yet he had his doubts; and often spoke to Biyu, "time will tell!" Biyu wanted the same as Zheng. She too had her doubts about this so-called immortality; she felt that with her daughter and grandson's arrival, believed it to be the beginning of something she had always dreamt of: an average family life. However, the robots knew their presence once again would be shattered at some period in the future as everybody around them would grow old and die.

In contrast, they would maintain youth for a glorious eternity: and not like a butterfly, just experiencing a brief moment in the history of time. Meanwhile, Zheng loved this experience of survival which the machines had initially given him when at the age of ten, they first abandoned him on an unknown planet and to live amongst unfamiliar surroundings. He had survived then; and now he considered himself back where he started, all those centuries ago, alone, nevertheless, fighting the elements of nature; and he loved it. What the machines appeared not to understand is the inquisitive nature of homo-sapiens: to climb the highest mountain; to explore unknown places; to venture into the depths of the ocean; to study the universe and to go where no man has been. Zheng laid back with his mind oblivious to everything surrounding him; rewarding himself for the achievements that he and others had made in such a short period, which gave him satisfaction and a feat of accomplishment; as he drifted into a deep sleep and another world.

The winter months came as the snow fell more massive and more substantial each day until such a point it was hard to leave the hut except to walk across to the animals were Zheng had added a roof and some facial protection against the snowdrifts, which appeared each day, growing in size. The waterfall had not yet frozen, but Zheng could see the ice collecting around the pool and icicles forming at the side of the waterfall that it wouldn't be long before wholly frozen. His laser weapon helped to melt the ice in the pool for drinking water. Hot water was easy to achieve as a few seconds of a laser beam shone down into a bucket soon made it at the right temperature to wash and even bathe. Zheng had forgotten about the pool freezing over which could give the wild animals access to cross and attack his farm animals. So he built a very thick wall out of the snow as high as the fence which blocked access to his stock. Zheng now fully protected, could sleep at night even though the howling of the wolves were at his gates burrowing in trying to penetrate the solid frozen ground and wall. However, some nights it was just unbearable, and he had no choice but go to his platform above the gate and shoot a wolf or if he was lucky a bear for the others to feed off. That would last at least a couple of nights then he'd have to do the same again.

Biyu noticed that Tarpeia living with them in the same hut was paying too much attention to Zheng. Biyu saw that she would watch him bathe with such a look that was not fatherly but as a young girl admiring a man that she was perhaps beginning to become captivated. It was something Biyu had not envisaged, or even taken into consideration as she explained to Zheng one night as he lay in bed, with Tarpeia dead to the world. "I think our daughter is falling in love with you." She whispered under the bedclothes.

"Impossible what makes you think that?" Said Zheng in a whisper.

"Haven't you noticed how she is at hand, especially when you bathe and wash with a towel; and sometimes offers to scrub your back. It's not fatherly love; She doesn't know that you are her father; You look and have the physique of a young man. I too, am beginning to look as if we are sisters and that she is older than me." Whispered Biyu as Zheng suddenly rose from where he was lying.

"Oh, my! We have a problem! We cannot tell her that I'm her father, and possibly accustomed to sharing a man like many a woman is apt to do in these parts of the woods." He said, trying to keep his voice down.

"Well, you are going to have to be on your guard. At some point, she is going to approach you, and you will have to be firm." Said Biyu as Zheng interrupted before she could finish, "Firm, what do you mean by that?"

"That you love somebody else, me of course, and that it is not in your nature or words to that effect, to share me with any other woman!" Said Biyu with a kind of protective response that Zheng had not seen or experienced before.

"Well I'll try to do the best I can; and if it just backfires! Then we shall have to cross that bridge when it happens." Said, Zheng, as he turned over, closed his eyes and went to sleep.

The following morning, nothing said, but Zheng nervous about what they had discussed the night before failed to give Tarpeia eye contact as she breastfed her infant in full view with both her breasts. Zheng had not paid attention but now realised this exposure was for his benefit so hurriedly ate his breakfast and made some excuse that one of the animals needed attending to as he stood up, excused himself and left the table.

"Is he alright?" said Tarpeia as she turned her infant to feed on the other breast and slipped the other under her robe.

"Men!—Always worried about trivial things which turn out to be unimportant in the end." Said Biyu as she stroked the infant's forehead.

"Hm!" Said Tarpeia as she paused and continued in a reticent response, "I wonder what he's worried about?"

Tarpeia put her son to sleep while Biyu went back to her sowing as she noticed Tarpeia pick up the bucket and walked towards the door, "I'll just get some ice for it to melt." She said as she went outside into the cold frozen air. It didn't take her long to rush to where Zheng was attending the animals. She calmly walked into the stable watching Zheng gathering eggs under the hens. "Did I upset you?" Said Tarpeia as she stood above him.

"Upset me? No, what makes you think I'm upset."

"I don't know—I just felt that somehow you are different today." She said as she fiddled with her robe to let one protruding leg show.

"I'm not that different than any other day.—Now come on, you will catch your death out here, you best go in," said Zheng as he checked the rest of the hens as he gathered his eggs into a basket.

"Look I just want to say I'm very grateful for what you and Biyu have done for me and if there is anything I can do, just ask. Please." Said Tarpeia as she let the robe fall entirely open to show the pubic hairs and her bare thighs.

Zheng stared in shock: "Please don't do that; betrothed to one woman and one woman only.—Do you understand?"

"Yes, I know but can't you share me with her. Most men have more than one woman." Said Tarpeia as she approached him with her robe now wholly open, showing her naked body.

"Look! Stop! Stop! Stop!" Said, Zheng, as he tried to fasten her dress and cover her naked body.

"What you don't want me—I thought you loved me?" Said Tarpeia with tears now filling her eyes as they began to fall across her cheek.

"I do love you but not in the way you think." Said Zheng with a melancholy voice.

"You love me, but you don't want to make love to me—I don't understand?"

"I love you like I am your father. Do you understand?" Said Zheng wiping the tears from her face.

"Like my father, but you're not my dad!—What do you mean?" Said Tarpeia as she wiped her face clean and straightened her robe to look more respectable as she paused then continued, "Are you trying to tell me that you are my father?"

"No!—I'm not your father." Tarpeia again burst into tears and repeatedly sobbed.

"Yes! Yes!—I'm your father." Said Zheng realising he has now just let the cat out of the bag as he continued: "Why do you think I was in the area when your village sacked. I knew you lived there. I came to save you."

"You are my father? Well, who was that man my mother married then? That left us when I was a child!"

"Me!—It was me!—I left you. I know I did wrong, but I am here to make it right." Repeated Zheng with tongue in cheek.

"Well, who is that woman in the other room." Said Tarpeia as she pointed towards the hut.

"Well, my wife." Said, Zheng, as he glanced towards the floor.

"You left my mother to die? To marry another woman!" Said Tarpeia as she pointed again towards Biyu in the hut with her hand and fingers shaking profusely.

Zheng, unsteady and quiet, giving no response to her words, went outside and tried to comprehend what had happened. "What was the meaning of it all? Was it a blessing or a great misdeed that had befallen me?" he asked himself.

Tarpeia turned to leave the animal shelter as she shouted back at him "I hate you—and as soon as this weather breaks, I shall be leaving!"

Tarpeia rushed back into the hut with such hatred on her face that she went straight to her child picked it up and hugged it as it started crying.

"My dear, what has happened?" Said Biyu

"Did you know that thing out there is my father?" Said Tarpeia pointing to the animal shelter with one hand while rocking her child back to sleep again on the other arm.

Biyu now in shock wondered what Zheng had said and was about to answer when Zheng walked in just in time for him to interrupt as he winked at Biyu and held a finger to his lips for her to keep quiet. "I'm sorry to tell you this Biyu, and I know that you will be angry with me because I know you kept asking me, why do we have to come to this village? Well, let me introduce you to my daughter."

Biyu, now realising what had just happened and the role she must play questioned immediately.

"You have a daughter?—Are you telling me that Tarpeia is your daughter?"

By now the child asleep, Tarpeia turned around surprised that Biyu supposedly didn't know as Biyu continued. "You mean you are telling me I have risked my life to fetch your daughter? You have been married before?—You have been with another woman?—You beast!—You animal— you!" Biyu walked towards Tarpeia as she quietly spoke to here. "I'm sorry my dear I didn't mean to offend you but believe me I knew nothing of this, and I couldn't understand why he dragged me here. Now I know! But where is your mother? Is she still alive?"

"After that animal left us;" Tarpeia pointing to Zheng; "she was a broken woman and died at a very young age with a broken heart. As an orphan bought up by the Buddhists." She added with tears in her eyes.

"Well!—Zheng, I have just seen another side of you that I don't like and I think its best for the both of us that you make up your bed with the farm animals and from now on sleep with them."

"What?—I'll freeze to death outside!" Said Zheng.

"Well, you have the rest of the day to fix the shelter and make it more secure and warm. Now get out of here!" Said Biyu as she turned to put her arm around Tarpeia to comfort her and the child.

From that day and event, Tarpeia and Biyu became very close indeed that they shared the same hatred, which immediately stopped the infatuation that Tarpeia had previously shown towards Zheng. Biyu playing her role felt sorrow for Zheng during those winter months but gradually started to bring Tarpeia around. Eventually, Tarpeia began to forgive what she thought her father had done. Still, it took a lot of persuasion from Biyu that he was just a typical arrogant man like many others. Biyu, however, tended to show more hatred towards Zheng than Tarpeia. Suddenly, Tarpeia began to persuade Biyu; perhaps he was not so guilty after all, especially on one particular day when Biyu showed a lot of hatred responded with the words. "Well, he is my father, you know!" That Biyu realised everything was going to be okay.

By the time spring had arrived, all was now calm and peaceful in the household with Tarpeia preoccupied teaching such words as grandpa and grandma to the baby. Life had become one big happy family after initially clearing the air that Zheng was Tarpeia's real dad, although Biyu, much to her dislike, had to keep silent about being her real mum and play along as step-mum and step-grandma to the child. Tarpeia had forgiven Zheng for his misdemeanours, although Biyu knew his innocence, was so proud of her dad that she would dump the baby in his arms with the words. "Now you play with grandpa."

As he lay in bed, contemplating, it suddenly came to him why the robots had planted into Tarpeia's mind that her father abandoned her mother at an early age, it was so obvious: *A brilliant ploy by the machines. The robots had anticipated human nature as if they were playing with pawns on a chessboard, that at some point the pressure for Biyu to keep quiet would be overwhelming and she would spill the beans and admit that Tarpeia was her daughter. For Biyu to confess, she was Tarpeia's real mum would be too difficult to explain. As far as Tarpeia was concerned, she already had a mother; since Tarpeia didn't know who her father was; if I acknowledged being her dad, then Biyu would become her step-mum.* Zheng thought as he continued; *all the robots had to do was to get me to lie that I married Tarpeia's mum, fathered her when she was a child and abandoned them soon after. For the robots that would be simple; play on Tarpeia's infatuation to make advances toward me, knowing full well that I would reject her, forcing me to admit that I was her father, for her to stop.*

Birds preparing nests, insects buzzing in the air, warmed by the sunshine. All were glad, the plants, the birds, the insects, and the abundance of mountain flowers that had unexpectedly sprung up around the cabin and in the forest meant that finally, filled with the joys of spring had arrived. The iced wall was melting fast as the icicles fell and the waterfall increased in volume from the melted snow above as the pool itself encroached upon the cabin. The freshness of the morning air in Spring enticed an early rise to enjoy the smell and the abundance of green foliage enriched in colour enhanced by morning dew somehow made the place a pictures sanctuary of beauty. As life in the forest returned, with a hive of activity, birds flocked from the South increasing noise level as mating calls vibrated and echoed as the woods suddenly became home to many an animal. Zheng loved mornings on the porch enjoying his breakfast soaking in the ambience, contemplating whether to leave such a haven. He reluctantly spent those early days preparing for the long journey, trying to complete one of his many chores in constructing a wagon to carry his belongings, farm animals and grandchild. Zheng could not help but notice how Tarpeia and Biyu looked so much alike they could quickly pass as twin sisters. They had the same emerald eyes with dark black silky hair, the same physique; the same height, as he silently thought. *At some point, Tarpeia must be curious, since others will naturally remark on their likeness, and perhaps question who the elder sister is?*

That day had finally come when they had to say goodbye to what had become home which they had grown so fond of during those past harsh wintry months. Summer had arrived, it made their departure so much harder, as Biyu took one more glance, to shed a tear, knowing that they would not return, mounted her horse, turned to look back once more as she followed Zheng into the forest to ascend their way out of the camp. The wagon was pulled by four horses, that Zheng had acquired from the nomadic tribe he had killed, with the chickens in their coup placed and secured in the back; the cow and goat tied to the rear of the wagon closely following behind. The child lay in an enclosed area made safe at the end of the cart while Tarpeia followed adjacent on horseback with two other horses tied either side to her reins. Zheng and Biyu mounted on their stallions divided what was left of the other horses tightly harnessed and tied together. A significant party as it slowly wound its way out of the forest to climb high to the plateau for a panoramic view that stretched for as far as the eye could see as they headed West towards the so-called infamous silk road.

Acutely aware of the warring tribes, the numerous tribal states close to the Chinese frontier, where nomadic peoples had overrun the Northern part. Zheng was too conscious of the imposing danger and risk he faced of being attacked, but uncertainty excited him for Zheng. *Perhaps*, he thought, *his subconscious wanted to die and that being immortal and living for another 5000 years is too much of a burden to carry on.*

By late afternoon they set up camp away from the beaten track in some location well hidden and obscure from prying eyes. Their only concern was the smoke they generated in preparing their meal and keeping warm and cosy during the night as the temperature dropped and fended off approaching wild animals. Zheng would scout the area each night after securing the camp to see if any, nomadic tribes were nearby or any other travellers were heading West that they possibly could join for safety and protection.

Late at night while Tarpeia slept Zheng would often practice putting on his dark suit to time himself to see if he could improve dressing. The fabric such that it reflected its surrounding image made it virtually invisible even though it lay in a box; always appeared empty if it weren't for the coloured identifying tags tied where the tunic joined the boot. Biyu's suit was smaller than Zheng's, so a simple solution was to match a different coloured ribbon at the heel. Pink for Biyu and Blue for Zheng. Putting on the suit was like dressing blindfolded. You could feel it, but you could not see it. For Zheng, it was like putting on a boiler suit.

Once inside and fastened, you were invisible, except for any item you carried; once the visor pulled down across your face, one had a 360-degree clear vision irrespective of pitch-black everywhere. Biyu would train with Zheng, and they turned into a competition to see who could dress the fastest. Biyu always won which irritated Zheng so much. The problem they had was any weapon they carried was visible. There laser swords disguised as shepherds crook was so evident that it would look weird and make it noticeable that something or somebody was holding a staff or a stick as they approached. A solution would be to carry two short swords under their tunics, making them invisible. The laser weapon would always be strapped in its usual position under the saddle harness to one side of the horse and used only in an extreme emergency. To an enemy, it would appear initially as a riderless horse. However, if attacked, they would have to become proficient in fighting two-handed with short swords. Each night Zheng and Biyu would practice with their two wooden small replica swords that Zheng had made in the art of close fighting. Tarpeia would watch each evening mesmerised by their martial art skills and the way they could jump so high and leapfrog one another, twist and turn in mid-air. Even the little boy would immediately stop crying or feeding or whatever he was doing as he too stared at his grandparents just doing unbelievable things.

"Where in the hell did you learn how to do such amazing acrobats and fight the way you can" Said Tarpeia one evening as they finished their training class.

In silence, Zheng glanced towards Biyu, as she went quiet too, *perhaps there was no harm in describing his youth, and his step-father Lu that had sent him and paid for martial art training in Changzhou.* He thought as he continued with his thoughts. *It would also give me a way of being able to describe how I first met Biyu in the first place; naturally not as my step-sister and on another planet, but at the martial art training class where she too was taking lessons.'*

After a great deal of consideration, Zheng described Tarpeia's life in Changzhou, not in full detail, but mainly about the martial art training and competitions that he participated. He briefly mentioned that he first met Biyu but kept on that subject just if he let it slip that there were stepbrother and sister. He then made some fictitious story that enabled him to describe how he met Tarpeia's mother and married her.

"Ah! so really you were sweethearts as teenagers?" Said Tarpeia glancing at Biyu with a broad smile as she put her child to bed as he was now fast asleep as she added. "Is that where you fell in love?"

"No, no, my dear Zheng went to war, and I didn't see him for years, and only when he returned that I fell in love." Said Biyu as she paused, had to think carefully about what they had told Tarpeia before as she added. "If I'd had known he was married though I wouldn't be standing here today." She said as she looked at Zheng as if to say change the subject quick.

"Ok it's late we have an early start tomorrow lets get some shut-eye." Said, Zheng, as he stoked the fire and added a few logs.

"Oh, I want to hear some more." Said Tarpeia as her voice saddened.

"Maybe tomorrow." Said Biyu as she kissed Tarpeia on the cheek and added "Goodnight."

It was only a matter of time before Zheng confronted with something or somebody along the silk road, that he did not expect to come across a complete massacre of a caravan with bodies strewn in ditches across dead animals hugging their young. There were well over a hundred corpses with some young females in a body posture suggesting extreme violation before death. He observed what could only describe as genocide. Biyu and Tarpeia wept at seeing the young mutilated and possible even raped. Zheng exasperated but mainly disgusted that humans could do such atrocities to one another; and for him, there was no forgiveness, as far as he was concerned; how could anybody forgive; *strewn out in front of him like disregarded manikins* he thought. Zheng had one purpose; he would kill, possibly maim to make whoever was responsible for this reckless slaughter and suffering.

Zheng stood in silence, not knowing whether to say something; perhaps a prayer, but to whom, turned away trying to comprehend why would even the humanoids or robots allow such atrocities; they had left close on 400 years ago and left the world to its destiny. However, as far as he was concerned, the machines were responsible for allowing something to happen. Zheng remembered the words spoken to him on planet earth before his departure that history would be re-run to eliminate the wrongdoings. It seemed to Zheng that nothing had changed. Violence had survived; suddenly, in that momentary instance, perhaps he could see his purpose for existence; he was going to change it.

He set up camp nearby to make sure he was upwind of the stench; knowing full well that a sacked field the culprits would not return unless something caught their attention.

Biyu started at one end while Zheng began setting light to everyone, including animals with their laser guns. Tarpeia looked on from a distance, but could not see in detail, only the flames initially. The thick smoke engulfed the caravan her visibility obscured entirely as it slowly rose upwards and drifted away downstream.

"You managed to set light to the camp?" Said Tarpeia as they approached with a blaze behind them, seen from a reasonable distance away.

"Yes, we found plenty of lanterns oil and doused each body." Said Zheng knowing full well to explain a laser beam would be impossible, so lantern oil was the first thing that came to mind.

"Don't you think that's going to bring attention to the bandits and they will return?" Said, Tarpeia, showing an intense concern that possibly that was not the best thing to do.

"Let's hope so," said Zheng

"What! —you want them to return!" Said Tarpeia with an apprehensive look on her face.

"Yes, that's correct then I'm going to kill every one of them." Said, Zheng, as Biyu nodded in agreement.

"You two are mad!—Do you think you can handle a bunch of trained killers with your wooden swords?—You must be—I'm sorry to say but mental!" Said, Tarpeia, now very frightened as she grabbed her son holding him close realising this is madness.

Zheng moved the camp further back towards a rocky area where he had previously cut a passway through a boulder with his laser gun with enough space for Tarpeia to pass who presently was out of sight with Biyu gathering their belongings and the animals. Zheng had made an entrance into a very well prepared spacious compound well protected on all sides and then covered it with foliage and broken branches to obscure the opening.

Unbeknown to Tarpeia, as she retired early that day, Zheng, had collected two dead male bodies. He then strapped one in an upright position on his horse and the other on Biyu's horse. Wearing their dark invisible suits, they mounted their horse and tied the dead bodies in an upright straight position to their chests as they sat behind them. Taking out their laser weapons, primed, waited close by away from the burning caravan that could be seen over the hills and far away, knowing full well that at some point the villains witnessing the smoke could not resist but to investigate.

As dusk fell, and the sun hovering on the horizon, fifty silhouetted riders could be spotted galloping towards the flamed caravan, expecting to find something. Realised it was the same caravan they had pillaged earlier as they raced up and down the length of the burning carnage.

From the hill above, two riders in full gallop approached fast. A reddish-orange reflected shimmering on the horses armouring as the sun rays just dipped below the horizon: the bandits turned to face with swords drawn; formed a pincer movement as Zheng, and Biyu spread out with their laser beams in full view. Zheng tore into the enemy; the rider on his right slain first, but the warrior to the left of him swung his sword and removed the head of the dead body strapped to Zheng's chest which now acted like a headless warrior continuing to fight. For Biyu, the same had happened; her corpse tied to her chest was headless. As Zheng and Biyu encircled one another in ever-increasing spirals slaying the enemy with their laser beams, it appeared from above like a catherine wheel rotating quickly; producing a display of sparks and coloured flame. The brigands suddenly became frightened of these headless warriors: fleed to escape, but to no avail, since in pursuit, Zheng and Biyu extended the laser beams to such a distance to be able to slaughter one by one. Satisfied revenge had taken and paranoid of discovered, Zheng needed to remove evidence of the fighters in case of any reprisal. He gathered the corpses: stacked them, set light to them by concentrating their laser beam on the pile, then removed the harnesses and saddles from every horse, to set them free.

Tarpeia woke from the turmoil and noise; impatient, left her hiding place and looked on from a distance to see a ball of flame and the silhouette of two headless riders which she immediately recognised as Zheng's and Biyu's stallions with a beam of light encircling the fire. Her thoughts quickly as she gasped in horror "Dead!" Frightened for herself and her son, retreated to her hiding place; secured once again the foliage to disguise the entrance as she squatted with her child in her arms expecting the worse. She waited, which to her seemed like an eternity; humming a lullaby, when suddenly removed the foliage and tree trunks she closed her eyes anticipating death.

"Is everything ok?" Said, Zheng, as he stood in front of her lifting the belt from his shoulder holding two short swords.

With a child in Tarpeia arms lept towards Zheng with tears flooding in her eyes and falling down her cheeks. "Oh!—I thought you were dead!" She said as she turned to Biyu, who entered with a smile on her face, took the child from Tarpeia and kissed it on its sleeping forehead.

"Were fine. Just a few battles. Everything is ok." Said Biyu.

"But I saw your horses, with you headless, circling that huge bonfire with such a brilliant light. What was that?" She said with such a challenging voice.

"Brilliant light?—No, you were mistaken—We were gathering all the dead bodies from the caravan and giving them a decent burial that's all." Said Zheng.

"What you were not fighting anybody then?" Said Tarpeia as she questioned, "The bandits didn't return?" Paused then inquired, "What was all that noise then?"

"No we just cleaned up that's all!" Said Biyu as she handed the child back to her mum.

"But you had no heads?"

"No—it must have been the light playing tricks with your eyes." Said Biyu. "Look we still have our heads!"Laughing aloud.

They slept that evening well into the morning to wake to a bright blue sky and the odd white fluffy cloud as they looked down at the carnage that was still smouldering as the black smoke drifted down hugging the valley across the plains to engulf a herd of fifty horses grazing nearby.

"Look at that." Said Tarpeia as she pointed to the herd of horses "Where did they come from?" She asked.

"No idea." Said, Zheng, as he shook his head, smiling at Biyu.

Tarpeia by now so challenging with a look of fright: "You don't think they are the villains' horse's somewhere in the valley?"

"Could be!—We best get on our way and leave directly." Said, Zheng, as he hurriedly gathered his belongings thinking to himself: *I just can't tell her that we killed them all last night?*

As they moved out from their hideaway, Tarpeia believing that bandits were in the area ready to strike at any time kept glancing over her shoulder all day.

They had travelled far, and were by now a reasonable distance from the massacred caravan; set up camp away from the road, close to a nearby forest with a clear view in front of the rolling grasslands when Tarpeia suddenly screamed: "They're coming!—They're coming!" Zheng stared where she pointed too; only to see in the distance the bandit's herd of horses that had followed them, and were grazing in a nearby field of lush grassland."What's that?" Asked Tarpeia.

"Looks like a herd of horses: do you want me to go and have a look?" Said Zheng.

"No, please don't!—Stay here—for goodness sake, there are bandits there!" She said.

"Look: you are not going to settle unless I go and see." As Zheng calmly spoke, Biyu brought the horses already saddled; possibly one for Tarpeia to accompany her father to overlook the herd.

Tarpeia, by now too nervous, gingerly mounted the horse, pulled the reins, cantered towards the herd, and with a terrifying look at Zheng as unexpectedly the horses' heads rose from grazing; pricked their ears, glared, only to return feeding.

As they approached now at walking speed to mingle amongst the animals only to realise they were not wild but tamed beasts.

"Looks like we have acquired a herd of horses?" Said Zheng with a smile on his face as he reassured Tarpeia, now relaxed, who also could not believe that they had just attained a herd of broken in horses. Satisfied that it appeared just tamed horses and not a bandit in sight, galloped away up the valley towards their camp only for the animals to follow.

"I see you brought our newly acquired friends." Said Biyu holding her grandchild in her arms.

Zheng had now gained an impressive herd, as he put his other horses amongst them; took on the role as a cowboy with Biyu assisting and Tarpeia currently in control of the wagon as they continued to travel West.

They left Mongolia; unhindered, decided to go North West to avoid the barren land. It would take them towards Jerusalem, where he had an excellent chance to sell his herd of horses.

In the heat of the day, as his horse slowly walked in the scorching sun, Zheng started to doze, when suddenly, aroused could smell fresh water. Biyu sensed it too: as she glanced across at Zheng and pointed in a direction. "It's over there!"

As the herd of horses started to snort and nay; bolted in the direction that Biyu looked. As they climbed the dune obstructing their view, they faced a beautiful oasis:—with date palm trees that surrounded the spring water, which fed on the artesian aquifer, that provided shade for the peach trees, loaded with an abundance of fruit. It reminded Zheng of that time when he first met his newly acquired business partner, Amphios, *but that was on another planet*, he thought: *I wonder if Amphios is still selling saffron?—And if ever made it rich?—I wonder what happened to him?* As he continued daydreaming.

The horses headed directly to a fertile patch were other animals droppings had encouraged grass to grow, which was a vast area and had become a separate watering zone. How convenient, Zheng thought, as he rounded up his herd to make sure they didn't venture into his space and contaminate the water. *It's like mother nature had deliberately made two areas; one for animals and the other for humans*, he thought to himself.

The principal aquifer fed the other at a lower level and spread over a more significant area irrigating the grassland.

Zheng always set up his camp with a panoramic view of the entire sector; enabling him to see anybody approaching from every cardinal point.

An abundance of ripe and juicy fruit made a delicious meal that evening as the heavens opened up in front of their very eyes. Zheng loved the desert where he could meditate while immersing himself amongst the stars, to stare as he laid to sink into the warm desert sand as the evening temperature dropped. He tried to locate the remnants of the earth's solar system; yet again found it hard to believe, as he gazed into the abyss of stars, that they were the only two homo-sapiens to survive the destruction of planet earth.

"Still trying to find Planet Earth." Said Biyu as she joined him, laying alongside knowing full well what was going through his mind.

"Yes—it's got to be somewhere there?" As he pointed in the direction where he thought the sun occupied planet earth solar system.

"So where are Pusa and Pyroies travelling to?" Said Biyu.

"Kepler in the constellations Cygnus and Lyra." Said, Zheng, as he pointed to the heavens to show Biyu.

"Do you think we shall still be here when they return?" Inquired Biyu

"I have no idea.—If we are—I believe that we will end up cryogenically preserved for that length of time." Replied Zheng with such a melancholy response.

They both fell asleep under the stars holding one another tight like two lost souls that were trying to come to terms with the meaning of the universe and with life itself.

Most of the time, Zheng made sure he kept himself busy, so he didn't have a chance to think whether he was happy or not. He enjoyed every minute of the day, never to look back to the past or the future. He accepted that he was stuck on a planet in the wrong era, had to make the most of it; and tried to live with minimal help from robots or machines, which sometimes he found it too difficult to do.

Zheng had travelled to Jerusalem before. Although he approached Jerusalem from another route, he did realise that it would eventually merge with a landscape that he would begin to recognise. He remembered Jerusalem when he was there some 330 years earlier when he met for the very first time Jesus of Nazareth; Augustus was Emperor and Christianity was none existent. Meanwhile, Zheng stayed at the oasis longer than anticipated without seeing any other traveller and realised it was time to move along on his way to his destination. The further North West, he ventured the greener and lush the surroundings become as he left behind the desert region. Travellers came in the opposite direction and often would exchange a horse for food and other necessary items like clothing and utensils for cooking and oil for his night lanterns. Sometimes evenings spent listening to travellers explaining what was happening in the rest of the world. People virtually wore the same clothes, lived in poverty and were still slaves to the minority few, rich and powerful. Weaponry hadn't advanced much, and wars possibly fought in the same tradition. *So far life on the planet hadn't changed much in all the time I was away.* He thought.

Hearing for the first time that the pagan gods replaced by Christianity were allowed to follow the faith without oppression, Zheng was particularly interested in the Roman Emperor Constantine and the Byzantium's new Greek city that Constantine constructed. Sunday was now a day of rest, and Christians banned from participating in state sacrifices. After listening to the travellers' stories, Zheng realised that history followed the same path on planet earth. There must be a driving force for the world to support, maybe independent of humanoids, so dominant, dictating humans' actions. He begins to wonder if religion now played a significant part in man's destiny, or was it the machines still dictating man's future?

As they approached the outskirts of Jerusalem Zheng began to recognise the terrain and its surroundings; it wasn't long before he was approached by Roman soldiers some distance away that remarked on his herd of horses. "If you are a Jew expecting to sell in Jerusalem, you might as well turn around and go back where you came from." Said the Centurian as he passed with a few of his admiring military.

"What makes you think I am a Jew?" said Zheng as he asked."And what if I am what has that got to do with it?—I'm here to sell my horses!—To whom can I ask for?"

"Well, if you're not a Jew and they let you in when you arrive at the gate ask for Cassius Chaerea and mention my name Aurelos." He replied; "and put aside two horses for me." He requested.

Zheng realised that the Centurian knew about horses and recognised the breed best known for the role as war steeds, because of their hardiness, stamina, self-sufficiency, and ability to forage independently. *But I can't understand why the Jews were being persecuted and discriminated against; perhaps it was because of Christianity*? He thought.

Zheng could see the gates of Jerusalem, and there was no way to enter with a herd of horses, so made his camp some distance in a secure spot, close to a high range with freshwater and grazing. He had no other alternative but to leave Biyu and Tarpeia alone and contact Cassius Chaerea.

Mongolian horses were rare and not often seen in that area and to have so many was just unheard. Zheng, not appreciating he had such a commodity for sale already followed and observed for some considerable time, waiting for an opportunity to steal.

If he had realised that he had been closely followed for days by local robbers and bandits, with the intent to steal the horses; take the women for themselves as slaves at the first available opportunity, he wouldn't have left the two women alone. Biyu was always aware of the danger that she and Tarpeia wherein and made sure that the shepherd's crook was nearby, mostly when they were left alone. Zheng knew the capability of Biyu; and that any attack she would be able to handle herself, but fatal to her attackers.

Zheng left that day searching for Cassius Chaerea: Biyu and Tarpeia said their farewells; prepared the evening meal and were just about to sit down close to the fire when six men approached on foot with swords and daggers in hand.

"What have we here then?" Said a tall, heavy-set man with a goaty beard and rags that barely covered his stinking body as he stooped to take a handful of rice from Tarpeia's bowl. Tarpeia instantly jumped to her feet when grabbed by two others that lifted her feet off the ground. "I think I shall fuck this one first;" as a hand slipped in between her legs.

Another had grabbed Biyu's hair from the back and pulled her to the ground. "Then I shall fuck this one." Said another as he licked her across the face with his grossly pitted tongue.

Biyu arched her back, brought her legs back and flipped to break the bond between her and her assailant; she was now standing as she cried out the words "OPEN."

The shepherd's crook that she managed to retrieve discarded it's outer sheaving as she flipped from the floor to a standing position: now held a laser beam as she pressed hard a thumbprint to activate the device; threw the bandits back to stand in awe and fright. She didn't hesitate to decapitate each one. Within seconds all six lay dead.

Tarpeia didn't see the attack since one assailant held her with her arms stretched out above her head, while the other lay between her legs and was just to about to penetrate her that they immediately rose to confront Biyu. Still, as the assailants stood up, their heads fell to the ground.

Tarpeia lay on the ground. A head rolled past with eyes wide open staring. She immediately got to her feet, screaming and in shock as she briefly turned to look to see bodies lying everywhere. Tarpeia still trembling and crying as she held her hands over her face to cover the horror rushed to her baby, who was crying profusely by now. Biyu didn't waste time in cleaning up the mess as she mounted her horse and tied the feet of each dead body to a horse and dragged them off and hid them behind a boulder. She then moved the fire closer to the waters edge away from the bloodstained ground, sought Tarpeia and the baby and washed herself first then bathed Tarpeia as she calmed down. Tarpeia still shaking as she sat on the waters edge with Biyu soaking her hair and every inch of her body cleansing the stench of the brutes that were about to rape her.

"How did you manage to kill so many?" Said Tarpeia as she pauses to count to herself, "Six of them?"

"Ah! That's where my dedication to martial training comes in!" Replied Biyu as she continued scrubbing Tarpeia's hair.

"But you removed their heads! And what was that white light that kept flashing!"

"Ah! Yes, the heads." As she paused to think and continued. "Those short swords that you once said were no good. Well—they did the job this time—Didn't they?" Said Biyu as she poured more water over Tarpeias head to wash away the soap.

"But those bright flashing lights, what were they?"

"Shock my dear; often happens when a person is traumatised. It is what is called a detached retina."

"What's a detached retina?"

"Ah! Yes, of course, its basically when the eyeball opens so much that light appears." Said Biyu realising, of course, she has never heard of a detached retina which is not the correct answer anyway and how stupid of me to even think of such an explanation.

"Look my dear it's over we are safe; now let's feed little Gaius he must be hungry." She supposed as she helped the baby to its mother's breast.

Meanwhile, Zheng had entered Jerusalem without being questioned whether he was a Jew or not, which he had expected to be asked at the main gate as he rode straight past the guards. *Perhaps it was my horse and clothes that I was accepted*, he thought, as the guards stared and nodded as he slowly walked past on his horse. Zheng remembered the Roman army's barracks, *but that was centuries ago and was it in the same place? And was it even the same planet?* He thought, as his horse continued to walk the streets to suddenly realise he had no idea of direction or even orientation of precisely where he was. He was lost. He came to an inn where he dismounted and immediately confronted a stable boy offering to take his horse's reins. "Are you staying the night?" The boy said.

"Well yes, is there room?" Said, Zheng, as he removed the shepherds crook from under his saddle.

"Just go through that door and ask for the innkeeper. You can't miss him he's fat with a white cloth strung around his waist and wears a fancy white, and an orange cloth tied around his head with a black rope." Said the boy as he took Zheng's horse to the back of the inn where the stables were.

No sooner had Zheng entered, the innkeeper's description, the boy, had given him approached immediately. "And what can I do for you, young man?" Said the fat innkeeper.

"Well:—first, a hot meal and second, a bed for the night." Said, Zheng, as he leaned heavily on his staff to emphasise the fact that he needed support to show a sign of immobility for a reason in carrying a weapon that resembled a shepherd's crook.

"Certainly, Sir, take that table over there, and I will send Aleeza to you to take your order."

Aleeza was a beautiful girl; petite with huge brown eyes and long dark satin hair that fell across her shoulders. *Her appearance is Jewish* Zheng thought, as he had seen many in his past travels throughout the city; she offered some fresh hot bread and local wine which Zheng immediately after tasting accepted as she placed it on the table.

"I can provide some goat or lamb with plenty of vegetables." She said, "Would you like a plate of fried Locusts with your wine before you start." She added.

"No, thank you; the lamb and vegetables will be okay. Thank you!" Zheng quickly replied, thinking: *Locusts; not today, thank you!* "How do you cook the lamb?" Zheng inquired.

"Today we are roasting it over an open fire since it's the meat of the Passover lamb." She said;—"and we are serving with onions and lentils." She added.

As Zheng waited for his meal, the innkeeper came over and asked if the wine was to his satisfaction. And inquired if he wanted a room to himself or to share with others.

"Thank you—I think I need a place for myself tonight I'm exhausted—and I need to make sure I'm not disturbed." Said, Zheng, as he took a mouthful of bread and washed it down with some wine.

"You're not from here?" Said the innkeeper inquiring as he cleaned and wiped the table with a cloth then added as he looked into his eyes. "Have you come far?"

"Yes—all the way from Mongolia." Said Zheng.

"My—Mongolia, what were you doing there? If you don't mind me asking." Said the innkeeper as he studied Zheng even more.

"I buy horses, and I have a herd of about fifty to sell. Perhaps you can help me. A soldier tells me that I met—Aurelos—who told me that a Centaurian by the name of Cassius Chaera is interested in buying such horses."

"Well, my friend, you are in luck, the man is sitting right over there." Said the innkeeper as he pointed to a table with about four Roman soldiers laughing and joking that looked well drunk with wine. "Let me introduce you to him." He added

"Cassius; this man is looking to sell horses." The innkeeper shouted across the room as he pointed to Zheng

"Bring him over here." Said Cassius gesturing with his arm with a slur in his voice.

Zheng got up from his table and casually walked across securely holding his staff under his armpit and introduced himself; before he could finish, Cassius interrupted and asked in a drunken voice. "So you have some horses to sell.—What are they?"

"Mongolian thoroughbreds." Said Zheng.

Cassius immediately sobered up as he spluttered out "Mongolian!—How many do you have?"

"About fifty but I have already sold two to Aurelos." Said Zheng.

"You've already sold two to Aurelos—that means they must be right. He never buys rubbish. Ok— when can I see them." Said Cassius who by now was paying attention and studying Zheng's face.

"Well whenever—may I suggest tomorrow—I'm staying at the inn tonight."

"Tomorrow it is—I shall come by in the morning." Said, Cassius; as he stood up and shouted to the innkeeper "Bring me the bill—I'm leaving, and I'll see you tomorrow." Said, Cassius, as he stood, turned to Zheng then went over and paid his bill and left; the other soldiers followed as he shouted back to Zheng:—"Hope your leg gets better by tomorrow."

Zheng went back to his table and couldn't believe what a stroke of luck he had just had.

Aleeza bought over a magnificent spread and the lamb so succulent that complimented the well-prepared onions and lentils as he wiped his bread amongst the juices and washed it down with an excellent tasting red wine. Zheng could not help and ask after Aleeza what such a young girl was doing working at the inn. She explained that her father, a Jewish priest, was banished from the city like many other Jews.—"So how come you're here?" Said, Zheng, as he interrupted and continued. "And not with your father."

"When the Romans massacred so many Jews—Gallus, the innkeeper—a very close friend of my dad took me in." She said; "and I have been here ever since." She added.

"So Gallus is—of course—not Jewish." Asked, Zheng.

"No—he is Greek a Christian—and he comes from Byzantium." She said; "and he is very kind to me and tells most people that I am his daughter— so they leave me alone."

Zheng left Aleeza, finishing her chores as he retired for the evening and slept well; dead to the world the next morning, Aleeza shouted outside the door. "Sir, Cassius Chaera is downstairs waiting for you."

Zheng had slept well into the morning and felt embarrassed as he clambered down the stairway still dressing. "I'm so sorry. I've been on the road for days herding those horses—and this has been the first night I have had a good nights sleep." Replied Zheng, straightening his clothes and tied his boots.

"No worry, my friend. I see your leg has healed. So who is looking after the herd now?" Said the Centurian.

"My wife and daughter."

"Just your wife and daughter; you know there are very dangerous bandits in the area that would kill just for a horse."Added the Centurian.

Zheng now concerned hastily mounted his horse as he slipped extra coinage to the stable boy as he shouted back—"tell the innkeeper I shall return tonight, and I need two rooms."

No sooner had he mounted he put the horse first into a canter then into a full gallop as he passed the main gates—"not so fast, my friend." Said the Centurion, with at least six soldiers on horseback following.

It wasn't long before they reached Biyu and Tarpeia patiently waiting alongside the campfire as they prepared the daytime meal.

"Are you okay?" Said Zheng with such an anguish look on his face.

"Well, yes, why?" Replied Biyu as she stirred the pot, releasing a smell of stew.

As Zheng continued talking to Biyu Cassius Chaera, his men were inspecting the herd while others explored the surroundings only to find six headless bodies. A soldier had picked up a severed head as he stabbed it with his sword to bring to the attention of Cassius Chaera. "Look what I have just found and there are others too of his gang." Said the soldier as he held the head in the air on his sharp sword.

Cassius, immediately turned to Zheng "Do you know who this is?" He said sarcastically "Well, let me tell you!—This is the most dangerous and wanted man that we have been after for years—not only him but also his notorious gang." He said, pointing to the other bodies brought out from their hiding place to lay in front under his horse's hooves.

Before Cassius could say another word, Biyu interrupted. "Yes, they attacked us last night, and I had to kill them and removed their bodies to avoid the stench the following morning."

"You killed them!—Please, you and who others?" He said with a look of amazement as he added "I'm sorry—but I just don't believe you. This bunch have massacred many and against experienced fighting men too. How come a beautiful young woman like your self can do this singlehanded—impossible!"

"Well, I am trained in martial art." Said Biyu as she showed a few movements in kickboxing.

Cassius looked on and laughed as he joked—"pull the other leg."

"Anyway, I shall buy the horses from you and give you extra because there is a large bounty on the heads of each of those villains." He added as he instructed his men to collect the bodies and round up the herd.

Zheng agreed and pointed out that two were for Aurelos when he returns.

"Don't worry, my friend, I shall see you back at the tavern tonight—he will get his horses!" As he threw a bag of coins and left with the herd and the dead bodies.

"You did that alone?" As Zheng whispered into Biyu's ear and added: "Did Tarpeia see the laser beam?"

"No—Tarpeia thinks I killed the villains with the sword."

To return to Jerusalem may not be such a good thing, Zheng thought. *The Centurian may ask. 'How is it possible a woman is capable of killing the most notorious bandit whereas others had failed?'* That Zheng decided that they should continue to head West for Rome.

Tarpeia, nevertheless, said she had been on the road for days and needed a place to rest for the babies sake; Zheng suddenly remembered Bethlehem, close by, near a lake that would make an excellent place to stop.

They travelled all day and reached the outskirts of Bethlehem later that day but decided to camp at the edge of a lake nearby. They were becoming proficient in setting up their tent utilising the wagon as support for the canopy that outstretched to make a protected area from the weather; it appeared like a Bedouin tent when you approached from the front.

Later that day wondering what to eat, Zheng noticed a fisherman dragging his boat ashore and helping laden with fish, crowds of people appeared to buy as Zheng hurriedly gathered his purchase to fill a basket full of carp and catfish. He remembered that he could dry, salt and preserve catfish for later. That evening the aroma of barbequed fish drifted around their tent and lingered during most of the night as they enjoyed a feast. Zheng loved those clear nights, close to a fire, and particularly at the edge of the lake where the lap of the water on the rocky side drifted one into a trance, and the brilliance of the milky way would send one into a fantasy dream of exploring every star and planet. As he lay back with the palm of his hands supporting his head, he began to think, what was he going to do next; set up a new life, hopefully without the assistance of the robots? They knew what he was doing—They hadn't been in contact since he arrived on this planet; they had left him to fend for himself.

Why should I worry?—Do I need them?—So I arrive at the gates of Rome, then what?—Perhaps a charioteer?—Too Dangerous—A saffron merchant?—Don't have any saffron. Zheng began to drift into a deep sleep as he could hear Biyu and Tarpeia talking and playing with the baby. *All was well,* he thought.

CHAPTER 14

The Vineyard

It is the year 320 AD, and the Roman Empire is at its peak; at heart stands the city of Rome, home to an enormous amount of monuments including the Circus Maximus, the Pantheon, the Colosseum and the Theatre of Pompey. Zheng had spent nearly a month on the road taking his time as he linked up with other travellers and merchants heading for the city. He tended to keep a low profile and not draw too much attention to interested people. He explained that he had left the warring states in the Far East to seek a new life under Rome occupancy mainly for safety and security.

"So what can you do?" Said a traveller one evening that had joined them around a campfire.

"I can produce wine—I had vineyards in the far east until destroyed and my farmhouse sacked and burnt." Said Zheng as Biyu looked at him in surprise with such a blatant lie she thought, but she kept quiet and listened.

"Ah—you have come to the right place to produce wine. The soil and terrain are perfect for vineyards." Said the traveller as he asked. "Do you have any land then?"

"No, that's the problem I need to start again—from scratch—I lost the lot." Said Zheng.

"Well, my friend, you have come to the right place. Constantine has just defeated Maxentius cavalry and pushed him, and his infantry into the Tiber river and rumoured that Maxentius body fished out decapitated." Said the traveller as he continued. "Constantine has liberated Rome from that tyrant Maxentius and people are flocking to the city and being encouraged to start a business."

"So you think I have a chance of producing wine?" Said, Zheng, as Biyu showed interest that perhaps Zheng is on to a good thing as she waited for the traveller to reply.

"My friend, I know of a farmer that would be more than happy to rent his land out—and if I'm not mistaken, he has an empty farmhouse as well."

"Well, that is certainly good news. Let me introduce my wife Biyu, my daughter Tarpeia and my grandchild Gaius. I am Zheng." Said, Zheng, as he embraced the arm of the traveller inquiring after his name.

"I am Dmetor. Pleased to meet you and your family." Said Dmetor.

"Ah—that's a Greek name. Isn't it?" Said Zheng.

"Yes I'm originally from Athens, and I have lived in Rome for many a year—but I am planning with my family to live now in the newly constructed city of Byzantium." Answered the traveller.

"Yes—I've heard of that—Isn't that city constructed by Constantine?" Said Zheng.

"That's right." Said the traveller as one of his family members approached to inform him that the evening meal was ready, turned and said: "I'll draw a map with directions and names for you to follow up—have a nice evening."

The following morning a small boy approached a map showing the farm's location and a name Gallus scribbled across the top. *Another Greek farmer*, thought Zheng as he folded the sheet and tucked it into his tunic.

The very next day, the caravan now reached the gates of Rome, and what a sight, something which Zheng had not expected, wholly rebuilt to what he had remembered when he was last here some 300 years ago. He did not recognise hardly anything, only to recall his history lessons on planet earth that Emperor Nero had burnt it down during his reign. The rebuild was magnificent, and the Colosseum was just marvellous, the Circus Maximus just breathtaking. How could anybody construct such splendid buildings with only their bare hands? Zheng gazed at each monument with impressive accomplishment as he followed the carefully drawn route described on his map. Walking the cobbled streets, he could not help but observe what he was looking at had no influence or help from robots or humanoids that abandoned the planet 300 years ago. The people of the city had constructed buildings in precisely the same manner as planet earth all those millenniums ago; *life was repeating itself: following instructions from where and whom*, he thought.

Zheng continued to follow the well-directed map, and he finally came to the farmhouse Dmetor had described and labouring in the yard a man with a grey beard and a very brown and wrinkled face who stood upright taller than Zheng as he spoke. "Sir, I'm looking for a gentleman named Gallus. Do you know where I can find him?"

"You're looking at him."

"Ah—right then. Your name was given to me by a person I met on the road, called Dmetor. He said that you might have a house and land for rent." Said Zheng with an anxious look on his face.

"Dmetor—haven't met him in months—you say on the road?—What road?" Said the old-timer Gallus rubbing his stubble beard with his forefinger and thumb.

"I met up with him along the silk road—I believe he had just come from Byzantium." Said Zheng.

"Byzantine—What's he doing there?" responded Gallus.

"I believe his moving there." Said, Zheng, as he hesitated, paused then politely added. "And rent, sir?—Any chance?"

The old-timer looked at Zheng carefully observed his wagon with Biyu and Tarpeia holding the child and the farm animals and horses. "Hm!—Rent a!—How long for?" Said, Gallus as he now walked around Zheng's possessions, scrutinising items in the wagon.

"Shall we say I pay for a year and then decide next year if I wish to extend?" Explained, Zheng.

"Hm!—For a year plus the land that will cost 150 denarii." Replied, Gallus, as he continued "I would take two payments one now and another in 6 months if it's too much for you in one go."

"No, that will be all right I will pay the full amount now.—Can you show me the farm then?" Said Zheng.

"Well, it's this one!"

"This one." Said Zheng expecting that this building was his and not the one for rent as he turned to face Gallus. "So where do you sleep then?"

"Oh—I have a small cabin close to the river Tiber."

Zheng now scanning the complete area asked: "So how big is the property?"

"Well let me see—to be quite honest—I'm not too sure myself." Said Gallus as he looked in all directions and then started to explain. "Well, let's see—the back stretches to the river as far as the eye can see—then it continues to those cluster of trees on the hillside then right around back to the river."

"Is it fenced?" Asked, Zheng.

"Oh, no—just farm as much as you want!" Said Gallus.

"Well— I want to grow grapevines for wine—What do you think?" said Zheng

"Ideal—look how the land slopes towards the river and faces South too—perfect." He said as he continued. "You going to make wine then?"

"That's right—I'm going to turn this into a vineyard." Said Zheng with a big broad smile on his face.

"Well if you're looking for a worker—just to let you know—I'm available." Said Gallus with a smile on his face.

Zheng now suspicious had his doubts about Gallus and asked: "Are you sure you own this property?" With a puzzled look as if asked—"are you the owner?"

"Yes, sir—I'm the owner—I can show you the deeds of the house and land!" Exclaimed, Gallus, as he invited Zheng, Biyu and Tarpeia into the house.

The house a quadrant with rooms that backed onto a courtyard in the middle, rundown and needed a lot of attention as Zheng carefully surveyed the building: "Well, this is large— more like a villa—so who lived here before?" Said, Zheng; not mentioning the state of the property just if he upset Gallus for negligence.

"A Centurion who went off to fight somewhere on the frontier and lost the property in a card game to another Centurion who wanted money quick—I just happened to be around with what he wanted—I paid very little for it and have since never lived in it.—It needs servants and slaves to run it—Which I don't have—I've been trying to sell it since I've had it." Gallus said as he continued showing the rooms and space available.

"So how much do you want for it then?" Said Zheng now interested in buying.

"Well let's say—100,000 denarii." Said Gallus.

"So in gold coins—aureus—I make that about 20." Said Zheng.

"Well, yes—that sounds about right."

"Ok I'll give you twenty—you give me the paper showing me the ownership." Said Zheng.

Gallus searched high and low and found the property's deeds hidden under a bench in one of the rooms. He signed the paperwork, and Zheng gave him twenty pieces of gold. Gallus so happy with the amount especially gold coins that were increasing in value each day, threw in the cabin as well, located by the river and decided to return to his native city, Athens. He had waited years to leave Roman but stuck financially with the property he couldn't sell. Hastily departed that afternoon with all his belongings in Zheng's wagon which became a part exchange of the sale, said farewell to Zheng and wished him a good fortune; now a proud owner of a vineyard.

That evening Zheng surveyed the land to find 10 hectares: *This is far too much for me to handle alone* he thought. Meanwhile, Biyu and Tarpeia checked the building to see that roof needed substantial repair and the nearby well blocked with dead animals. The inside of the facilities required a considerable amount of work, and the walls were growing fungi. The building itself was unsafe to occupy, and they had no choice but to set up camp outside. The facilities and land were just outside the inner perimeter of Rome idea for Zheng providing seclusion and most important not overlooked by prying eyes from any other property. *Access to the river and above sea level, avoiding any flash flooding adding an advantage* he thought.

As he contemplated in silence watching the sun setting due West as the river shimmered a bright crimson yellow to orange before it finally vanished, Biyu sat alongside him after she had retired Tarpeia, with the baby, for the evening, Zheng turned and quietly spoke:

"I think we have no choice but to call up the robots for help."

"I thought you would consider it's far too much work for you and me to handle. The robots, certainly, will have this place ship-shape within days." Replied Biyu.

"Ok, let's do it." Said, Zheng, holding the hand of Biyu as they slowly walked from the farmhouse to the river bank admiring the view.

After settling Tarpeia and the child, they didn't have to wait long, just a few hours as they sat by the riverbank admiring the view and gazing into the heavens when a streak of light appeared from the horizon. No sooner the space shuttle hovered above them to land nearby and merge itself into its surroundings and disappeared. A hatch door opened, showing a black void and there walking towards them their favourite robots, Pi and Zeta. Zheng always had the urge to go and hug them as well as Biyu if they were long lost friends that had suddenly returned from an extended excursion, but as always they held themselves back, and as usual, a formal greeting had. Zheng never doubted his plans and never had reason to seek advice; he assumed that Pi and Zeta would just obey his commands as he spoke:

"I have decided to settle here for the time being and have acquired this property and land." As he paused and stopped to wait for any response, the robots looked at the building and land as he continued.

"I need your help to fix this place up, and I have decided to grow vines, olives and produce wine from the grape and oil from the olives. So the area needs to be farmed. I also require machinery suitable to cultivate the land." No sooner had the words left Zheng's mouth the robots had already started to assess the requirements as he added. "Is that Ok?"

The following morning the robots had already returned with another four helpers. They were all dressed as if they were locals and to anybody slaves or servants.

"My—where did all these workers come from?" Said Tarpeia as she walked around the building holding the baby, watching two on the roof repairing the damaged slates and tiles, as she turned to Biyu following here. "How did you manage to organise this so quickly?—And where did all this material come from?" As she pointed to heaps of brickwork, mosaic tiles, frescoed walls, sand, wooden beams and panelling.

"You know your father— he will not stop until it's fixed," Biyu said.

The robots worked non-stop for 24 hours each day for several days. In weeks, the place gradually transformed itself into a great farm with vines and olive trees planted by the acre, including various white and red grapes as green and black olives. The well wholly rebuilt and aqueducts constructed to channel water to irrigate the land. The villa itself virtually restored where there were rooms for a chef and servants. There were also living quarters for the farm animals and storage rooms for oil pressed from olives, caskets of produced wine, grain, and room for anything else the farm had. Other villa places included an office, several bedrooms, a large kitchen, hypocaust-heated rooms with mosaics, and a dining area displaying frescoed walls. Above all of this had a particular place for Zheng and Biyu, which housed the 5th Millennium gadgets, weaponry, and most important their latest invisible suits. Pi and Zeta remained behind as manservants while the other robots and the space shuttle returned to the polar cap. The months went by, and the farm produced an abundance of olives and grapes when pressed made litres of oil ready for the market. The wine would take longer and would not be available until the following year.

After reaping the benefits from the harvest, it was time to sell the farm products. They set up a market stool at the Roman Forum to be confronted only by a local guard that informed the space was already occupied and told to move on. Even an exchange of money didn't help. "Nothing is available unless authorised by Jullius Vendex." Said the guard.

"Who the hell is Jullius Vendex?" Said Zheng to the guard.

"Move on now!" The guard said with an angry and irrational voice, trying to hurry them to dismantle their stool.

Zheng helped by Pi and Zeta, moved his belongings from the forum to a side street where people passed by to the marketplace. It didn't take long before he had sold all his olive oil which appeared to be in demand with local shopkeepers buying up very quickly with the price that he offered 80 denarii for a litre. Zheng hadn't noticed that he was being watched across the way until he had sold all his oil and confronted by six men described as unsavoury characters.

"By my reckoning—you owe us 2000 denarii for the amount you have just sold today." Said one of the thugs.

"I owe you nothing," said Zheng. "I will pay my tax to the authorities and not to you."

By now a crowd had entirely assembled around where Zheng and the robots were standing to see the outcome of somebody who was challenging Julius Vendex's men. Nobody ever questioned the mafia of the market and what was now becoming the main mob of Rome. A short sword is drawn immediately from the belt of what appeared to be the ringleader to Zheng's throat. "I'm telling you now for your insult—the fee is now double."

Zheng very quickly swept the legs under him as he grabbed his wrist, holding the knife and twisted his arm as the sound of a crack broke it. He lay in agony reeling on the floor as another immediately came at Zheng as he lifted a leg to punch him in the neck with the heel of his foot. He fell back, hit his head hard on the cobbled street and just lay there. Pi and Zeta immediately immobilised the other four all with either a broken arm or a leg. All six either lay unconscious or reeling in agony. The crowd went quiet as the guard they had just spoken to earlier on hearing the commotion came running around the corner to see the carnage as he shouted.

"Do you know what you have just done?—You have just signed your death warrant."

"You're dead!—You're dead!" He added as Zheng collected his belongings, harnessed the cart to the horse and left the city by the north exit.

Zheng realising he had just confronted Rome's mafia needed to watch his back and be very careful at his farm knowing that there certainly would see some form of reprisal. That evening he placed the robots on full alert knowing that at some point the mob controlling the market and from what he overheard in the streets of Rome itself would come for him. He forwarned Biyu and Tarpeia what had happened and that they were to pay particular attention to anything suspicious within the villa grounds. Days went by, and nothing happened. Nobody came to the villa, and Zheng began to realise since it was the first time he had ever been to Rome selling, that possibly nobody knew who the hell he was and where he lived. Most of the materials he had acquired himself with the help of the robots. Zheng suddenly realised the problem would be the next time at the market. He decided that he needed an upper hand in the matter, and the best solution was to find out who Jullius Vendex was and where he lived. Agreed to maintain security at the villa; Pi would disguise himself and act as a spy at the market and carefully follow anybody taking money from any of the merchants and try to establish what exactly was the setup.

Zheng appreciated that to sell his farm produce at the marketplace on the forum he needed to know what rules and regulations were in place. So he chooses to send Pi, first to investigate and observe if any organised crime was present, or was it just because some villains saw an opportunity to himself as a vulnerable newcomer. Pi casually strolled the marketplace, observing buyers' and sellers', suddenly recognised one of the villains who attacked him. Stood nearby on an adjacent stool; watched him forcibly take money from a merchant selling olive oil; overheard the villain with a threatening voice say to the merchant. "Are you a friend of that person who was selling olive oil that refused to pay me the other day?" He said as he stretched an arm out across his merchandise, grabbed and held the merchant by the scruff of his shirt.

"No!—Believe me!—Nobody had ever seen him before. I suggest you ask the guard that spoke to him." As he pointed with a frightening facial expression to the Roman soldier standing by and added in a subdued voice, "Ask him—he threw him out when he tried to set up his stool in the forum."

The villain dropped the merchant, turned and walked across to the Roman Official responsible for tradespeople selling in the market forum. The guard seeing the villain approach, realised, after witnessing the scuffle with the olive oil trader, anticipated what he was going to ask, and immediately spoke before questioned. "Never seen him before.—I did ask around—I believe from the appearance he was a trader from the Far East." Said the Soldier timidly as he tentatively added; "I imagine If you want to find him—he's somewhere along the silk road—heading back home." Said the official choosing his words carefully knowing that if he upset one of Jullius men, he could quickly end up dead in some dark alley one night. The villain satisfied with the Roman official's answer asked a few other merchants but eventually to no avail left the area disgruntled. Pi stood by and watched the unfolding events and followed him to a nearby tavern where the villain joined a group of men at a table. Whereas, Pi nonchalantly sat himself down at a nearby table close by, which the waiter immediately attended as he ordered a jug of wine when suddenly a cry came from within the tavern. "Jullius you want another drink?"

Pi looked towards the table where the villain sat to see an arm raised with a clenched fist with a protruding thumb signalling okay. *So that's Jullius, the boss*, Pi thought as he slowly swung his head around; he picked up his mug and appeared to drink his wine when unexpectedly a loud cry from whence he had been looking. "I know you don't I?" As the villain stood up, pointing a finger directly in his direction. Pi kept his head down, to obscure his whole face, knowing that the villain recognised him as one of his attackers. He knew he could easily defend himself; even kill him and all with just a fatal blow. But he thought, *now is not the time*. So he quickly with the powers and means that he had at his disposal, to alter, one side of his hidden face with signs of what appeared to many like a contagious disease, leprosy.

The villain approached, shouting and raising his fist, "I know you don't I?" and grabbed his shoulder from the back and turned Pi to face him. "Oh! My. This man is a lepra!—Get him out of here!" He yelled as he stumbled back staring at his hand that had just touched him as he turned to a jug of water, and clumsily tried to wash it. The innkeeper looked in shock, as he came running over with a broomstick. He jabbed first with the brush end, then pushed Pi away from his seat as he stood up. Held him at bay with the brush end as he directed him to the door, as others in the room lept from their positions in horror trying to avoid Pi as much as possible. Everybody rushed out and dispersed to nearby fountains to douse themselves in freshwater. Chased away from the forum by the crowd as rotten fruit and vegetables flew airborne above his head Pi hurried away from the area to vanish into an alleyway, a side street as he hurriedly changed his appearance ultimately to double back and return to the inn. Pi had picked up clothes from stalls that he had stumbled into during the commotion of the chase and was able to get back as a different person entirely unrecognisable as he mingled again with the crowd and finally stood outside the tavern waiting for Jullius to leave. The majority already went leaving the innkeeper scrubbing the tables and floors muttering under his breath "How the hell did that lepra get into this bar!"

Jullius was now holding a cloth over his mouth preventing what he thought were airborne germs as he impatiently waited for his subordinates to gather the money that had been collected for the day as he mumbled: "This place from now on is out of bounds!" As he shouted louder "Do you hear me!" Turning to those collecting his things.

"I wouldn't go in there — contaminated with leprosy!" Said Jullius as he pushed past Pi now standing at the front door that looked as if he was about to enter as he appeared to inhale in slowly, which was entirely unnecessary for a robot, to allow Jullius to pass still holding a white cloth over his mouth. Instead of entering Pi turned and discreetly followed Jullius to a house nearby. Off a sidestreet had an entrance large enough for a cart and horse to pass through which opened up into a courtyard surrounded by buildings housing two levels. The second tier spanned over the entrance to make a complete quadrangle. It appeared from the street that Jullius owned the entire property as Pi witnessed people inside, acknowledging and humbling to Jullius as he entered. There were local collection points all over Rome as bags of coinage arrived at Julius's house that evening. Pi followed Jullius and his accompanying mob late that night to a luxurious villa East of Rome. The estate heavily guarded as Jullius acknowledged the guards as his men waited outside chatting to the guards.

He's working for somebody of great importance, Pi thought aloud.

Pi left and went back to report to Zheng, who had been waiting patiently with Biyu, a complete picture of exactly what was happening. "The market itself is controlled by a mob exploiting money daily and from local businesses like taverns, inns anything that is making a profit is controlled by the mob." Said Pi, in a monotone voice with no signs of facial expression of approval or disapproval.

"So who do you think lives in that villa?—it's imperative to find out who is behind such an established setup that exploits and creates fear amongst the Roman citizens." Said Zheng.

"An easy solution would be just to walk straight in through the front door," Zheng added.

"And how the hell are you going to do that?"Said Biyu as she stared at him inquisitively.

"Don't tell me you have already forgotten?—My the dark suit, of course!" He said with a cynical smile on his face.

Agreed, Zheng would wear his dark suit and walk straight through the front door to find out who lived in that villa.

The following evening Zheng sat on the back of Pi's horse with the dark suit that made him utterly invisible to any observer. At sunset, they cantered towards the villa to approach at darkness at a strategic point that directly gave them a view into the villa's grounds.

"I think its best I climb over the wall and enter at the rear of the villa," Zheng said to Pi as he checked that the sapphire stone he had hung around his neck under his suit was still communicating, "Testing one two, three," as he then continued. "You stay here and let me find out what is going on, but keep me informed if anything unusual is happening outside."

No sooner had Zheng finished speaking Pi pointed towards the entrance gate to make Zheng aware that Jullius Vendex had just arrived. "This is my opportunity they will be too busy counting their money." Said, Zheng, as he dismounted and ran towards the villa wall at the rear. It didn't matter for Zheng how high the wall was, with his suction pads primed he could scale anything and for him the 6m barrier he climbed in seconds and slid down the other side. He stood there just to get his bearings when he could hear two dogs barking and approaching fast. *They can't see me, but they apparently can smell me* he thought. The dogs were a mastiff-type dog the most vicious with a protective type collar and mail armour. Zheng could do nothing he had not anticipated dogs and to withdraw his weapon and kill them would give the game away. Suddenly one of the dogs grabbed his leg as he tried to tear into his calf but to no avail. The other dog grabbed the other leg. Zheng just held his stance as suddenly two guards approached as one said to the other.

"I told you those dogs were mad—they think they are attacking somebody— look at them tugging as if they have hold of someone." The other soldier whistled and called both dogs as they turned; whined with their tails between their legs as if they had done something wrong just as one of the dogs cocked its leg and urinated on Zheng's leg.

If the soldiers had watched the dog peeing, they would have seen a faint outline of Zheng's calf and part of his foot, but they were too hasty to get back from where they came. Since one had urinated on Zheng's leg, they now considered Zheng a friend and followed him in silence behind where ever he went. Whatever Zheng did, he could not distract the dogs or make them stay, sit, or lay down, so he decided he might just walk through the villa's main entrance, followed by two dogs. As Zheng approached the main door and walked past the guards, he could hear one of them say: "So where do you think you're going." As he blocked the dog's entrance and shouted sit to both as they just barked continually looking down the corridor as Zheng turned the hallway casually walking towards the rear of the villa. Zheng had wandered straight into a bathing area where two men were being pampered by several naked women, as they lay in the pool discussing business. Zheng decided to enter the bath from the other end, down steps as he kept his distance, but not too remote so he couldn't hear the conversation. He had never met Jullius, but he recognised the man Pi had described earlier as he was being questioned by the other.

"So did you manage to find those culprits that beat up your men. " One said.

"It appears they had come from the Far East according to the soldier who was on guard that day." Said Jullius as he moved towards the steps getting ready to leave the pool as he added: "They'll be back. They must think to have outsmarted us and have gotten away with it; the next opportunity—I'll take everything they have—then I'll kill them.".

Sliding his body to the edge of the pool to avoid the others Zheng entered as both climbed out and were immediately wrapped in robes by loosely clad women. Noticing one held the fabric of a senator with the purple edging which he recognised instantly. He waited until they left the pool area and then followed them into what could only be called an office where two other men counted gold coins and paper money on a table.

"Quite a good talking today Volusianus." Said one of the men counting as the senator approached to observe the coinage on the table.

Hm, so his name his Volusianus. Thought Zheng as he stood in the far corner invisible to all thinking to himself, *well at least I have a name and an idea what they are doing so I might as well leave to figure out what to do next.*

Zheng walked out through the main entrance where the two dogs were still waiting patiently, now laying down, however, as they suddenly pricked their ears and stood up to follow Zheng, much to the soldiers' amazement guarding the entrance, as one turned to the other. "What's up with those dogs tonight?"

Pi knew Zheng was approaching since his sapphire stone was sending his whereabouts and exact location. "So, what now." Said Pi as Zheng removed his suit to show his physical form.

"I need to find out who this Volusianus is?—He's the ringleader." Said, Zheng, as he mounted the horse and sat behind Pi as he put his arms around his waist. Pi pulled on the rein and then heeled as the horse slowly walked, then canter and then into a full gallop as they swept past the empty streets in Rome to return to their villa where Biyu was patiently and anxiously waiting.

"How did it go?" Said Biyu

"Well, the boss goes by the name of Volusianus." Said Zheng as Zeta suddenly interrupted, who had all day been attending to other matters had joined in the conversation.

"His full name is Gaius Caeionius Rufius Volusianus."

"How the hell do you know that?" added Zheng

"We are aware of everything. We are still monitoring and keeping our databanks full of knowledge to ensure that we do not deviate from what happened on planet earth." Said Zeta.

"You telling me none is by chance most of what's happening on this planet is still being controlled by machines." Said Zheng.

"Basically yes. But there are certain incidents like this one that goes wrong, and we need to correct it." Said Zeta as he added "We don't know everything; like we were not aware that the Roman Citizens exploited to what we can only refer to as a Mafia. That was not part of our script."

"You mean all of this manipulation is still going on. I thought you abandoned the planet to leave it to its destiny?" said Zeng now completely and utterly confused as Biyu also hearing for the first time looked in shock.

"Well, I thought you knew. It is what the council on planet earth decreed to bring civilisation to the 5th Millennium." Said Zeta as added, "How do you think we do it without controlling it."

“Ok, so what do you believe we should do then to correct it?” said Zheng as he raised his arms to show Biyu his dissatisfied reaction.

“We cannot kill Volusianus we need him. But what we can do is disrupt his organisation by setting one against the other.” Said Zeta now with a programmed disillusioned human facial expression.

“And how do we do that?” said Zheng

“We steal his money.”

CHAPTER 15

The Mafia

Gaius Caeionius Rufius Volusianus was Consul of the Roman Empire. With the defeat and death of Maxentius at the hands of Constantine, Volusianus transferred his loyalty to the new emperor. He was recognised as a Companion of Emperor Constantine, making him one of the several senators who served under Maxentius and Constantine. His subsequent career under Constantine showed that the emperor was conscious of the need to win over the senatorial elite's loyalty in Rome. However, Volusianus later dismissed from office meant to be exiled by decree of the Senate due to his enemies gaining the emperor's ear, now Constantine, and bringing him into disgrace. Instead, hid East of Rome in a villa with the intent for revenge against all that plotted his downfall. Jullius, the Volusianus henchman, was a wanted criminal in Athens and Jerusalem for murder and conspiracy against the Roman Government. Volusianus, during his role as Consul of the Roman Empire, had pardoned Jullius for his crimes and set him free to live amongst free Roman citizens with one proviso that he now worked for him. Jullius began to take control of the streets then exploit every business in Rome and eventually had on his payroll influential senates that sat in the council that decreed new laws. Nobody had any inclination that Volusianus was the godfather of the complete mafia now running through Rome's streets. Zheng planned to gradually steal the funds and start to chip away and undermine Volusianus's empire. He would begin by playing one against the other to such an extent that in the end, they could no longer trust one another. That was the idea. However, Zheng's first attack plan was to steal all monies at Volusianus's villa completely. First, he had to return to find where Volusianus kept his money; secondly, a strategy how he could remove it without being seen, knowing he could easily walk in wearing his dark suit but couldn't walk out holding bags of coinage.

"A tunnel, that's the answer." Said Pi as Zeta agreed and added. "Find the room or place where the booty kept and send us a signal, and we will pinpoint your exact location."

"A tunnel? You can do that?" Said Biyu

"Of course. The excavation using a laser beam, rotating at high velocity to loosen all matter to fine dust." Said Zeta

"So what happens when you come up into the room? You can't leave a big hole for everybody to see." Said Biyu

"Yes, that's correct. We need somebody in the room, of course, to make sure its safe to cut through, then we provide a circular opening with a fine line that's invisible to the naked eye," added Zeta.

Biyu still not sure how this was going to work continued questioning the robots. "So how does one enter the room? Obviously through the opening in the floor which is supported how? And how does one open?"

"Aye, I can see you have a logical mind exploring all the pitfalls of a mission that could fail." Said Pi.

"My dear the floor opening will form the base of an elevator and held in place by a supporting frame lowered, guided and raised on magnetic beams, in the same manner as a linear motor operates. As the floor lowers into the tunnel, one will stand on the circular pad and raised into the room. To exit one will stand on the circular pad in the room and lowered into the tunnel. It's that easy." Said Zeta.

"Come on, Biyu; they know what they are doing." Said, Zheng, as he continued trying to reassure her, "Look, we've travelled to another solar system, don't you think a simple tunnel is going to defeat our robotic friends," as he faced Biyu with a broad smile on his face.

"Okay,— I know—I just don't want it to go wrong. Remember your inside this room while the tunnel built." Said Biyu with still a countenance of concern.

The robots needed to know the room's exact location or where they have to penetrate. So, Zheng went back wearing his dark suit and climbed the wall where he had scaled before only to be met by his now two friendly dogs that recognised his scent. This time he had two large bones of horse meat which they immediately took and vanished as they ran amongst the undergrowth to disappear to bury their newly acquired bones completely. Zheng very calmly walked straight past the guards at the front of the villa into the main hallway. His visual aid scanning every room as he went from place to place mapped out into a 3D image and orientated such that coordinates gave each room's exact location to the robots monitoring Zheng's movements in the space shuttle. Already agreed that it would be better to place visual aids in each room by releasing what looked like an ordinary housefly controlled remotely. Zheng opened a pocket, and about twelve flies controlled by the robots flew out to every room to land in a strategic place out of sight but giving a panoramic view at the space shuttle as it hovered high above the villa. As Zheng passed the guards at the front door, the two dogs came running as if to say thank you for the meal as one jumped up and his paws landed on Zheng's chest with his tail flapping in a circular motion.

"Look at the dog he's now dancing and look at the other one wagging his tail as if he is enjoying it. I'll tell you they are mad and we should think about getting rid of them." Said one of the guards as the other agreed but couldn't help themselves as they burst into a fit of laughter.

It was only a matter of days before Volusianus booty discovered to be located not just in one room but several places. Hidden everywhere, and so much, that perhaps even Volusianus didn't know the amount he had. A decision to excavate under the villa creating an ample space with openings to each room solved the problem. With visual aids in place, the robots had complete control of when and where to break, the elevators placed under each proposed opening. The tunnel lined with solid material and inner cased with a silicone film of light-emitting semiconductors that gave an appearance as if one was walking inside a fibre optic tunnel. The tunnel itself started well outside the grounds of the villa. It passed directly under the estate into a vast room with several elevators leading into rooms were Volusianus kept his treasure. The plan was to steal gradually, but since Volusianus didn't know how much he had and possibly wouldn't miss it, it was better to take the lot. They had to remove monies from each room and store it in the vast area created below the villa and leave it there. A day selected, and everything took, but Volusianus hadn't noticed until a couple of weeks later when Jullius visited with money he had collected from the market stools. The cries heard throughout the villa and even further afield as Volusianus went from room to room, screaming "Where is my money?" He accused Jullius that he must be involved since Jullius was the only one that had any idea of where he kept his treasure. But Jullius denied all knowledge and couldn't understand how anybody could steal so much without Volusianus or the guards not to know or hear anything that he suddenly accused Volusianus that he had taken the money himself and was planning to leave Rome with the lot. Volusianus, beginning to think a conspiracy and his guards were somehow involved, reflecting what Jullius had just said. "How could anybody steal so much money without anybody knowing," meant to Volusianus that everybody was involved, and couldn't trust anybody. Volusianus pondering went quiet for a minute as he stared at Jullius and said: "Well if it wasn't you! And it wasn't me! Then who was it?"

Jullius stared back at Volusianus thinking *this guy is lying and he is now beginning to play with me as if I'm some kind of idiot. Of course, it was him*; he felt as he replied. "I have no idea." He said as he rose from where he was sitting and looked back at Volusianus with such a facial expression accusing him of the theft.

"Where are you going?" Said Volusianus convinced he had all his money.

"Well, it's all gone!—What's left for me nothing? —I might as well leave." Said Jullius.

Volusianus weighing the situation had no choice but to see if his guards were still loyal or part of the plot shouted out. "Guard arrest this man and seize the others waiting outside." The guards obeyed Volusianus orders, and Julius's and all his men were arrested and placed behind bars in his confined jail. After the arrest, Jullius convinced Volusianus had taken the money and perhaps about to exterminate him and his men. However, Volusianus still in a quandary asked himself "How did Jullius do it without there help," as he pondered. "There is no way he could pass my guards without their help unless they intend to free him later and murder me when I am asleep." He referred.

That evening Volusianus did not sleep; he had made his bed as if he was asleep but dosed nearby with one eye open expecting one of his guards to kill him in his bed. Zheng and the robots that night entered the villa sedated Julius's and his men in jail with a doctored arrow blown from a tube, removed all men to the tunnel and took them to the space shuttle now parked and camouflaged in the nearby wood. They flew them immediately, dumped them still alive just outside Jerusalem, knowing that they were criminals wanted for crimes that they had committed in the vicinity. Volusianus curled up in a chair was awakened by a guard bursting into his room as he dosed. "They've gone!" The guard shouted at the bed, expecting Volusianus to be sleeping when he suddenly muttered from his curled up chair. "Who's gone?"

"Julius and his men." Said the guard as he stood staring at the sleeping lump in the bed when suddenly Volusianus appeared from behind as he turned in shock to hear.

"They've gone!— Gone where?" Said Volusianus

"I don't know—they have escaped." Said the guard.

Volusianus stared at the guard, thinking *how is this possible without outside help*, as he looked intently into the Guards eyes guessing this has been a well-executed plan. They let Jullius and his men escape knowing full well that they will be well rewarded; *perhaps they are going to kill me now* as he carried on thinking.

"What do you want us to do, Sir?" Said the guard.

"Search the area to see any sign and send someone to his home to find out his whereabouts, and if anybody has seen him."

The guards dispersed, and Volusianus believed that Jullius was responsible for stealing his fortune and possibly had already paid his guards to keep quiet and probably was well and truly well gone by now. Destitute with no money or control of Roman streets, he might as well go into exile as planned by the Roman courts. To ensure that Volusianus did indeed leave Rome, Zheng notified the authorities that Volusianus was still in Rome and was immediately captured the following day with his guards and deported. He also informed the urban prefect that Jullius his henchman was somewhere in the district of Jerusalem. For Zheng's reward, the money offered, but instead of receiving the payment, requested the first refusal to purchase the villa and the property confiscated Jullius owned. The Urban Prefect had no objection since a considerable amount of money was about to be handed over to the council. But couldn't understand how an unknown and a newcomer to Rome could suddenly afford such expanse until Zheng explained how he had obtained his wealth in the Far East and had to leave because of warring states. Zheng's explanation and deeds of the property exchanged meant that Zheng had a farm producing wine and olive oil; A city home in the heart close to the Colosseum and a luxurious villa on the outskirts of Rome. The money that Volusianus had acquired was substantial and now was secure under the estate. He also had an escape route to the woodlands. Zheng took up his space at the market forum and was well accepted by other traders as rumoured that Zheng was responsible for removing Jullius since he had taken over his property. Zheng decided to set up a committee responsible for the market's welfare and ensure that payment to the guards maintained for added security and protection against robbers and villains. He asked a minimal amount from every trader that they were more than happy to pay, whereas they delivered close to 50% of their profit daily. Zheng also started to return some of the money to the traders saying that he had found it at Jullius home but had kept the vast amount at his newly acquired villa just in case, which he would refer to it as; 'safeguarded for a rainy day'. Zheng kept to himself that Volusianus was the godfather and not Jullius, which everybody believed. But it was Volusianus that was deeply involved in exploiting and controlling the city's whole organised crime; nobody had any idea, not even the Senate and urban prefect.

CHAPTER 16

Citizen Zheng

Over the years' Zheng's name spoken throughout the city came to the ears of Constantine. He wished to meet him and invited Zheng and his family to a celebration function at the palace in his son Crispus's successful military operations at the front.

Attended by all essential citizens of Rome the event set in the palace grounds Zheng now regarded as a successful wine and olive oil merchant participated in the function with Biyu and Tarpeia dressed in similar silk gowns shades of yellow and blue. They both looked stunning and were the envy of all as they passed between the guests sampling Zhengs most exceptional wine given to the function as a gift. The urban prefect Valerius Maximus Basilius, commonly known as Lucius to many, had invited Zheng to meet him formally and introduced Zheng to Constantine wife Fausta, his son Crispus and Crispus's newly betrothed Helena. However, much to his betrothed Helena's annoyance, Crispus continually stared at the cleavage of Biyu's breasts firmly displayed in a low cut silk gown. Hadn't paid attention to the formal introductions, and on hearing the words wife and daughter assumed that Biyu was the daughter of Tarpeia. It wasn't until Zheng intervened between Crispus and Biyu: "And let me introduce you to my lovely daughter Tarpeia," that Crispus suddenly realised that Biyu was the mother.

"Of course—my pleasure." Said Crispus as he dropped the hand of Tarpeia to turn to Biyu.

"And this is the man that discovered Volusianus hiding in Rome." Said, Lucius, as Constantine approached.

Zheng had to think fast knowing the next question that he would ask, as he continued.

"So how did you know such an important man, exiled from Rome was living in the city?"

"I'm a wine and olive oil merchant, and I made a delivery." Said Zheng.

"I see!—Did you know the man before then?"Asked Constantine.

"Oh, know!—It just so happened that I heard his name mentioned by one of his guards and then later I happened to mention it in a conversation to another merchant that his name came up." As he paused, then continued—"Hearing of his banishment; I should immediately notify the authorities." Said Zheng.

"As simple as that—very good—nice to meet you anyway—enjoy the party." Said, Constantine, as he nodded and passed on followed by his family introduced to others.

Crispus, nonetheless, intrigued by the beauty of Biyu and Tarpeia wished to continue to talk; but he too was hurried on by Helena to meet others as they mingled with the guests. Fausta, Constantine's wife, looked envious; gazed Biyu up and down and nodded an exchange of farewell. It wasn't long before Crispus appeared again, alone, to stand with Biyu and Tarpeia, while Zheng, mingling with the guests, discussed matters with other local and influential officials.

"So how come I have never seen you two before in the city?" Inquired Crispus as he blatantly stood close to Biyu trying to gawk down her dress. Tarpeia embarrassed, tried to discourage Crispus by catching his eye and then asking about his campaign on the front. Still, his answers were short and sweet as he abruptly attempted to cease any discussion as he carried on as Biyu entirely besotted him. Biyu knew how to handle a young man, barely out of his teens, that assumed all women were his if he so desired. It wasn't until Fausta, Crispus's stepmother arrived that she was able to put Crispus in his place.

"So there you are!—Don't you think its time for you to circulate with your guests and perhaps play a little attention to Helena that appears as if she needs rescuing from that crowd of young men?" Said Fausta observing her flirting with every man in her audience.

Biyu sensed that there was more to Fausta than a so-called step-motherly love. It was as if she was a jealous woman intervening as she took complete control of Crispus; displaying annoyance of his flirtation. She watched Fausta leaving, waggling her forefinger; above what appeared to be gruntled words as if to scold Crispus as she grabbed his arm and took him to Helena.

Flavia Julia Constantia, the wife of Licinius and half-sister of Constantine, approached and introduced herself as she noticed Fausta hastily leaving. "Hope she didn't annoy you." She said, referring to Fausta as she observed her pulling Crispus away.

"Oh, no, Crispus was neglecting his guests—that's all!" Said Biyu in a very subdued and polite reply.

"What beautiful gowns both of you are wearing, and if you don't mind me mentioning," as she paused and turned to Tarpeia. "Of course—no offence to you, my dear——but you do look like sisters'; not as mother and daughter," she added; not quite remembering who the mother was.

Tarpeia didn't like to say that Biyu was her step-mother and not her real mum, but a doubt sprung to mind realising perhaps for the first time—"yes we do look alike!"

"How do you keep so young?" Said Flavia facing Biyu as she continued, "you must tell me your secret?"

"Just diet and exercise." Said Biyu as Flavia took her to one side—"you must tell me all about it." Said Flavia with an air of poise.

Tarpeia now standing alongside her father admiring the ambience of the whole party questioned: "Biyu does look like me, and younger than me?" as she turned to face him.

Zheng quickly thinking how to respond, began by laughing as he regained his thoughts and replied. "Look all women from the Far East have this unique appearance of beauty which makes them appear, especially to the Western population as if they're all related; and as far as age, you do realise that Biyu is the same age as you."

"Well, no!—I didn't realise—she has had so much more experience in life than me and has done so many more things and gone to so many places—I just can't believe she is the same age as me!" Said Tarpeia amazed that her so-called step-mother is the same age. Zheng had now planted a seed in Tarpeia's mind to avoid the explanation of why Biyu looks young and why alike sister's, but he could never tell Tarpeia her birth mother was, Biyu.

With her hand locked into her father's arm, Tarpeia introduced to every eligible bachelor at the party by Flavia as Biyu walked close behind; goggled at by every male. To hear names of people that Zheng recognised from his history studies on Planet Earth during Constantine's reign, uncanny. That everything was falling into places like a sophisticated glorified game were rules, or the plot couldn't be changed and planned so well to follow and repeat once more the life that had occurred on planet earth. It didn't bother him that men were blatantly flirting and making suggestions of intimacy to Biyu; he knew it would never happen; *it wasn't in the script* he thought. Zheng was liked and envied by everyone: he was rich, he had a famous vineyard, a magnificent villa, a property in a prime location next to the Colosseum and two beautiful women in his life. What more could a man ask for, but deep down in his subconscious none of this was real, so he thought. However, Biyu, frustrated, had lost her children except for Tarpeia. Who had no idea that her mum was Biyu, and that she had brothers and sisters living on another planet in an entirely different era? *How could she explain that? Never*—she thought.

As the party went well into the early hours of the morning more and more became inebriated, with some males bashful, blatantly taking advantage of Biyu and Tarpeia. Keeping a watchful eye, Zheng noticed that Constantine, his family and close friends were the first to leave; but observed Cripus whispering something into Biyu's ear just before being dragged off, by Fausta.

Helena, who really couldn't give a damn about her betrothed, Crispus; she was too engrossed flirting with her admirers and allowed them to kiss and grope her as she left. Finally, Zheng said his farewells, thanked Lucinius and his wife Flavia for a beautiful evening and hoped to repay the hospitality.

Lucinius had discretely made inquires to no avail about Zheng: from where had he come? How had Zheng entered into such a small fortune? How had he achieved the heart and be favoured by the citizens of Rome so quickly? Or what Lucinius always referred to as the mob. How could such a man with no family background or heritage and entirely unknown to everybody, be such a success; baffled Lucinius to such a degree that he appointed spies to keep a close watch on Zheng.

The following day, Crispus arrived at the villa on some pretence to discuss purchasing wine for Helena's forthcoming marriage. However, Zheng was not at the estate but at the vineyard explained Biyu, where customarily sampling and buying negotiated. Nevertheless, Crispus had already known that Biyu would be alone at the villa knowing Zheng had arranged with a customer that prior evening to meet at his vineyard to purchase wine. Crispus, a young man, took what he wanted as he started to advance towards Biyu. They stood alone in the garden, a distance away from the villa. At first, Crispus just gently lifted her chin and gazed into her eyes, said: "You are some woman of beauty that every man would desire," then suddenly grabbed her jaw and placed his mouth over her lips and forced his tongue down her throat. He held her tight around the waist with the other arm and ripped her robe, exposing her breasts as he tried to push her to the ground. She immediately brought her knee up with such force that he broke away in agony, holding his groin as he fell and knelt to the ground.

"What the hell do you think you are doing?" She said as she shrieked. "Get out of her you animal!"

"You scream, and you're dead." Said Crispus as he leapt to his feet, grabbed her and with a knife across her throat.

Biyu could feel the blade cutting into her skin as she laid there and didn't move. Closed her eyes expecting rape when suddenly as she gazed towards the sky, unexpectedly, Crispus was dangling from his neck as Zeta held him in such a vice that his feet could hardly touch the ground. He swung his arm around with the knife in his hand to strike; Zeta grabbed his wrist with such force that he immediately dropped it. Crispus had not come alone. He was accompanied by six armed guards that stood to wait outside the villa's main gate, heard the commotion, and began running with swords drawn.

"Take them all out and spare no lives!" Screamed Crispus as he staggered dazed from the floor after being dropped and flung to the ground with such force. The six armed men where no match against the robots, as they tore into them as they fell one by one, for all to lay unconscious in a heap on the floor. With a foot to the side of his face, Biyu stood above Crispus as he lay in agony still holding his groin spluttering "You will pay for this—you're dead!—All of you are dead!—Do you hear me!"

Glancing towards Zeta. "What are we going to do?" Biyu said with a frantic look on her face. Zeta leaned down and very quickly sedated Crispus to shut him up then replied: "They were on their way to the front to join the war when Crispus decided to stop off to pay you a visit." As he looked at Biyu, stopped, paused then walked around each body and finally spoke: " We shall sedate all; wipe their minds clean—this never happened— we'll dump them off somewhere along a road they meant to be travelling on."

"What you are going to let him get away with it?" Said Biyu.

"Don't worry, it's written; his father is going to kill him." Said Zeta as he checked if Crispus still sedated.

"For what?" Questioned Biyu

"Crispus and Fausta, Constantine's wife, have an affair and when Constantine finds out, he has both of them killed." Replied Zeta.

"I can't believe you have already planned all of this?" Said Biyu in dismay.

"Not quite." Added Pi. "This is something we hadn't planned."

The bodies removed, the horses gathered and all placed in the space shuttle and flown to the North Pole. Each mind was wiped clean of the incident as if the attempted rape at the villa had never occurred, then taken to a makeshift camp of were they meant to be travelling and to wake naturally as if the event at Zheng's mansion had never happened.

Biyu, that evening still in shock explained everything to Zheng. He carefully observed the slight blood-stained mark across Biyu's throat went berserk and wanted a full explanation if machines were always in control of the planet how could such an incident happen. Pi pointed out that not every human was under their control, and the majority left to develop physically and biologically as nature had intended without the influence of machines:

"All we are aware of is when a person must die when a newborn baby is due, and that life and death must closely follow wherever possible the same expectancy that occurred on Planet Earth. What happens in between sometimes is out of our control." Zeta explained as he clarified: "Plus, you're meant not to be part of the script or plot or in the movie." He chuckled as if he had just told a joke to give one a feeling of human response.

CHAPTER 17

The Wedding

It was some months later when an official invite arrived to attend Crispus and Helena's wedding in early January. Helena had just turned sixteen and Crispus about to attain the age of twenty-one. The wedding day arrived, and Helena wore a blue gown of silk that hugged her venus shaped body while Crispus wore the official toga embroidered with silver and purple. The ceremony, not a Christian one, was attended by family and close friends and Zheng, mainly because he would supply the wine-free wedding gift. Biyu could not help Crispus stare, expecting to catch his eye as if remembered the attempted rape. Still, when introduced after the ceremony to congratulate the newlyweds, he had to be prompted by his new wife Helena that Biyu was Zheng's wife. "Oh, thank you for such a generous gift." He said as he ultimately turned to the next guest, ignoring Biyu completely.

"My!" Biyu said as she turned to Zheng and whispered:— "It's amazing what tweaking of the brain can do. He's a different person?"

Biyu couldn't help but notice Fausta, who looked elegant, in a gown outfitting that of the bride as she stood close by to her step-son Crispus to distract his looks towards Helena who held the other side. Any observer would have difficulty in deciding who Crispus married. However, with flirting eyes, Helena exchanged glances with many a young man, and one would possibly conclude that Fausta was now Crispus new wife.

After what Pi had said to her, Biyu could sense that a love affair with Crispus and Constantine's wife Fausta was already happening; unfortunately for both, it was just a matter of time before both would meet destiny, death. Even though Biyu hated Crispus, for what he did to her, suddenly felt sorry for him, that such a young man manipulated by machines was destined to follow planet earth history and executed.

What appeared to be a tightly-knit family, Zheng and Biyu felt that they were intruding, were the first to leave and made their excuses. Biyu could not help after kissing Helena on the cheek to wish both good luck, and good fortune turned to do the same to Crispus as if to say her last farewell. As she withdrew her lips from his cheek, she glanced into his eyes and felt saddened; her eyes moist, glistened, as he too responded with such a look as if he said, sorry.

Constantine, his father, did not attend the ceremony, which must have been a great disappointment to Crispus, Biyu thought. Still, Zheng could not help see the intrigue and gossip between military men attending the wedding, considering:

Maybe there's a reason why Crispus's father did not participate in the marriage; and, remembering a particular part of his studies, while on planet earth, Lucinius went against Constantine, which eventually resulted in his death. *Perhaps I'm at the forefront witnessing history repeating itself,* as he continued thinking.

As Zheng stood outside, waiting for his transport Lucinius approached. "Ah, Zheng just a quick word before you leave—hope you enjoyed the party—look I need to discuss an essential matter with you—will you be at the villa tomorrow—let's say first thing tomorrow morning."

With a curious countenance, Zheng glanced at Biyu, expecting her to say something except she shrugged her shoulders to say okay, so Zheng responded. "Well, yes I'm free all day—see you tomorrow." As the words left Zheng's mouth, the robots arrived with the chariots as Lucinius with his wife, Constantia, who had just joined him waved farewell as she turned to Lucinius, "what was that all about?"

"I need him; he controls the mob in Rome and tomorrow I'm going to make him an offer he can't refuse." Said Lucinius with a broad smile on his face as he put his arm around his wife to return to the party.

Most of the guests by now thoroughly and genuinely inebriated, except Helena, the newly married bride, was fearful of what to expect from Crispus, who by far was thoroughly drunk, had heard from other relatives that Crispus was an experienced lover. Or what she understood they were trying to say, a persuasive lover that enjoyed violence with sex. Helena had noticed that evening, as she unintentionally flirted with other younger men as she caught Crispus staring at her with such hatred and jealousy. Confined and distanced herself from her admirers, to avoid what she thought would be repercussions in the bedroom that night. However, Helena could not help notice how Fausta, Crispus step-mother paid too much attention to him; siding him, touching him, laughing and joking as if Fausta had just married him. It annoyed Helena that she had to say something that he was making a spectacle, an exhibition of himself in front of all the other guests. Crispus, arrogant walked off in a huff grabbed Fausta by the hand as she turned to Helena with a sarcastic smile as they disappeared outside into the darkness of the night amongst the foliage undergrowth.

Out of site, Fausta stopped, pulled Crispus to face her and put her hand down between his legs, "Are you going to be able to manage it tonight?" She said jokingly and laughing as she took hold of his limp penis.

"I don't know." Said Crispus with slurred words, knowing she hated being called mum, as he put his arms on Fausta's shoulders with a broad smile kissed her patiently on her mouth and added, "so what are you going to do about it?"

"Well, let's see if I can help." She said as she pulled away, knelt on her knees gently took his limp penis and put into her mouth as it quickly erected.

Meanwhile, Helena had watched them leave the party, decided to follow as they vanished amongst the undergrowth only to discover both in a compromising position, as she brushed passed the laden branches screamed. "What do you think you are doing?" Fausta immediately jumped to her feet as she removed his fully erected penis from her mouth and gawked at Helena, "getting it ready for you my dear!" she said as she pushed passed Helena with a violent shove. Crispus grabbed Helena's arm as Fausta hurriedly left and pulled Helena around to face him as he garbled his slurred words. "Well, we might as well not waste it!" As he flung Helena to the ground and raped her there and then. Helena left sobbing with bruised arms and blood trickling down the inside of her leg as her beautiful wedding gown torn and stained with mud and blood went straight to her quarters profusely to cry as she laid face down on her bed.

Crispus returned to the party to a barrage of questions "Where's Helena?"

"She's retired." Said Crispus

"You better do your duty!" They responded, laughing.

So Crispus staggered to the marriage bedroom entirely and utterly drunk where Helena lay sobbing "What are you crying about?" He said as he tried to roll her over to face her.

"You're an animal. I should have never have married you!" She said as she turned back to bury her face into the pillar.

"I'm animal! How dare you when you flirt with every man as if you are a loose woman and a whore.—Yes, a whore!—And what do I do with whores I fuck them up the arse!" He said as he ripped her wedding dress from her back and straddled across her buttocks and inserted his penis into her anus as she shrieked and cried out in agony as he continued repeating the words, "Bitch!, Whore!—Bitch! Whore!—You fucking whore!"

She lay there silent as he raped her, again, knowing that he could easily break her neck as he grabbed her hair and pulled back to lift her chin from the pillar. She waited until he finished then slid from under him as he lay in a state of drunken unconsciousness, gathered her things and left; never to return or see him again.

The following morning Crispus left, without seeking Helena or even wanting to say farewell to join his father at the front expecting an imminent attack from some rebels who had been ravaging the land in Constantine's realm technically Licinius's territory. It was the beginning of the downfall of the relationship between Constantine and Licinius that would finally end some years later in Lucinius death.

However, Crispus did spend time with Fausta as they made passionate love that morning just before his departure. But what Crispus was unaware of was Fausta was playing with him knowing that Constantine her husband would put aside the sons she bore him for Crispus unless she could remove Crispus. She intended to accuse Crispus at the right time of attempted rape, knowing full well that Constantine would execute his son Crispus, true to his strong personality and short temper.

CHAPTER 18

Position of Proconsul

Lucinius arrived as expected with an entourage of staff including his wife Flavia Constantia half-sister of Constantine and his wife Fausta, who was curious and interested about Zheng and especially his wife and daughter sought a private audience with them. Lucinius quickly got to the point as Zheng listened in earnest as he offered a proconsul position to act on behalf of Roman citizens.

"So what would this entail?" Said Zheng.

"You would act as an administrator on behalf of the Roman citizens resolving disputes as a magistrate would—but most important of all—you would be the senates ears and eyes of any forthcoming uprising." Said Lucinius

"Like a spy." Replied Zheng.

"No! —Not as a spy—but just reporting to the Senate the wills and wishes of the citizens to direct finances appropriately—that's all. We hear nothing but praise from the citizens. What you have achieved in such a short time the council would like to appoint you as a specific mediator, and the official role given to you as proconsul; a title held by a civil governor which does not imply any military command."

It didn't take Zheng long to make a quick decision as he immediately accepted the offer and thanked Lucinius and considered it an honour singled out. Lucinius took back with such an immediate response since he thought it would be difficult and prepared to pay a substantial amount to gain Zheng's service. He didn't hesitate but pay the maximum salary for his undisputable decision.

"Wow! That's incredible 80,000 Denarii per annum.—Well, thank you." Said Zheng knowing that a Praetorian Guard earned 20,000 Denarii and regarded in society as a wealthy man. They clinched the deal with an exclusive jug of Zheng's most elegant wine as they sat to discuss in detail precisely the office Zheng would uphold as he was measured for his new toga by the imperial tailor. Lucinius could not help but observe the robots that always accompanied Zheng wherever he went and impressed what appeared to be loyalty turned to Zheng and said. "You do realise the job comes with two appointed Praetorian Guards paid by the Senate and I can't help but observe you already have your own two guards." He paused, then continued, "and if you wish we can also employ your guards," as he acknowledged the robots standing to attention as he added— "we pay 19,000 Denarii per year."

"Well! Yes—I have had these personal guards for years, and I can certainly vouch for them." Said, Zheng, as he just couldn't believe in paying for his robots.

"Well, that was easy." Said Lucinius as he turned to the tailor, "Measure these two for their outfits," as he pointed to Pi and Zeta.

Meanwhile, as Lucinius resumed discussing Zheng's new appointment, Flavia and Fausta quizzed Biyu and Tarpeia about their previous life. In what materialised to be very difficult for them to try and explain, as the subject quickly changed to the whereabouts of the new bride, Helena and the bridegroom, Crispus.

"Ah—poor Crispus he has joined his father on the front and departed early this morning." Said Fausta with a flat and snappy response.

"And what about Helena?" Said Biyu thinking *that must be hard for a new bride to lose her husband the next day.*

"She will cope. She has to. That's the price one pays to marry the next Emperor." Said Fausta with a displeased attitude that looked to say why all this unnecessary questioning.

Biyu adjourned to the kitchen to see how food preparation was progressing when she was approached by one of the kitchen staff as she whispered into her ear, "Helena was beaten and raped by Crispus lat night." She said.

"How do you know that?" Said Biyu.

"We've just heard that from the servants that Flavia brought to help."

"Was she badly beaten?" Said Biyu as she looked around to see Flavia's servants staring at her.

"Very bad mam—and he committed sodomy—she will be confined to her room for months to recover." The kitchen-maid said as she walked away to continue her chores.

Biyu couldn't believe what she had just told thinking, *what a psychopath—and I felt sorrow for him—I must have been so disillusioned—I hope he dies in the front!*

Biyu so angry returned to join her guests and blurted out "You've heard about poor Helena!" As she laid a plate of dates on the table.

Fausta looked at Biyu with a look that could kill as she hastily responded: "Yes, she had a slight mishap last night—inebriated—collapsed drunk and hit her head on the bedpost."

Biyu realising that she had touched a delicate matter, nodded and agreed as she returned to the kitchen to retrieve more food only to be approached by her kitchen-maid, which added to what she had already spoken. "Helena caught Fausta and Crispus in an embarrassing position."

"What embarrassing position?"

"She was sucking his penis!"

"Whose was sucking what?" Said Biyu

"Fausta was sucking Crispus's Penis, and Helena discovered them."

"Oh, my! Don't say another word. Keep this to yourself your life could be in danger with this information." Said Biyu as she picked up the ripening peaches to carry them back to the table.

Biyu glanced towards Fausta as she bent towards the table and placed the fruit, thinking to herself, *how could you on her wedding night?*

Biyu didn't need much persuasion to realise that Fausta was a dangerous woman and had to tread with caution and carefully chosen words to offend her. But Biyu already could sense the envy and jealousy that she and Tarpeia posed possibly as a threat to her empire. Biyu had noticed Fausta goggling at Zheng knowing precisely her full intentions and that she had no scruples about what she did and who she did it too. *The woman is a psychopath*, she thought. Unaware of the conversation going on in the kitchen, Tarpeia had sucked up to Fausta's flamboyant personality as she played with her son and had already accepted an invite to the palace the next day had some toys for young Gaius.

Later that afternoon the men joined the woman for a banquet of food arranged outside in the olive trees' shade, including a fattened goose, pheasant, lentils, boiled rice, crushed millet, fenugreek and peas served with fresh olive oil served with aged red wine. Fruit bowls containing sweet red and white grapes, dates, and very ripe peaches with pots of honey as a dip. Just as the sun was setting Lucinius and his party after what everybody considered an excellent meal, a very positive day, departed to the palace and looked forward to Zheng's inauguration at the Senate as proconsul.

Fausta had likened to Tarpeia and had invited her and her son to the palace the very next day. Tarpeia hadn't spoken to Biyu about the invite as she left early, and handed a written message to a maid, given when her mother and father woke later.

Tarpeia decided that Gaius would be best to stay at home until she checked out the palace facilities if it had the right playthings for children as suggested by Fausta. Tarpeia took a white stallion saddled it and dressed in a short tunic with her hair tied into a bun, appeared more like a young male than a girl. She put the horse into a full gallop along the dusty road as the dirt threw up, covering her legs and thighs and spoiling her tunic. When she arrived at the palace gates, she was unrecognisable. Refused entry, but had an appointment with Fausta and was about to be turned away when one of the servants that attended the banquet yesterday recognised Tarpeia and persuaded the guards to take her to Fausta.

Fausta in the bath when Tarpeia arrived. "You look as if dragged along a dirt road—you better get in here and clean up." Said Fausta as she turned to one of her maids. "And bring some fresh clothing." As she continued and asked. "Where's Gaius?"

"I left him at home—he was very sleepy." Said Tarpeia and immediately untied the bun at the back of her head as her hair fell to her back as she dropped her tunic to stand naked as she tentatively entered the pool.

"Don't be shy—come here, and I'll wash your hair."

She felt nervous and worried that she had never been affected in such a manner but at the same time felt some sort of excitement as her nipples went hard. As Fausta washed her hair with soap, Tarpeia could feel breasts touching her back. And now and again her thigh touched the inside of Fausta's leg.

"Well, it's done!—Now rinse your hair." Said Fausta as she stepped out of the pool handing a robe and then a goblet of what looked like wine. Tarpeia stayed in the pool as she continued rinsing her hair and washed the dirt from her face and body as she too stepped out to be handed a robe and a goblet of wine, which she took, but thought *it is too early to drink alcohol and placed it on a nearby table.*

"Not having a pick me up?" Said Fausta as she noted Tarpeia walk away from her drink.

"Bit too early for me."

"Hmm, what about some fruit." She said, offering a plate of dates.

She took one and immediately bit into the date which seemed overripe as the sweetened liquid spread around her mouth as she swallowed. "Very ripe," she said, wiping her mouth with the back of her hand.

"I love them—especially this time of the year." Said Fausta as she ate one too and offered another.

"No thanks—I think I'll have that wine now;" picking up her goblet to wash away the juices from the fruit.

The aphrodisiac potions placed in the wine and within the fruit, harmless enough, *are about to arouse the sexual instinct* thought Fausta as she could already feel the desires within herself: *I want to seduce Tarpeia.* Laidback on her couch, biting into another date as she allowed the front of her robe to open to display part of her pubic hair. But decided to play with Tarpeia as she took another mouthful of wine,

"Please have some more wine," As she beckoned to one of the slaves to fill Tarpeia's cup.

"Have another date." She said as she passed the plate of fruit swinging her legs down from the crouch revealing the top of her thighs as she stretched across to Tarpeia who was now laying on the adjacent couch. Tarpeia took the fruit and bit into it as she reclined on the couch to rest her head as Fausta gestured the slave to bring the ointment of saffron as Fausta commenced massaging Tarpeia's feet. The fragrance and the alcohol and delicious juices in the fruit made Tarpeia inebriated as Fausta sucked her toe while stroking the inside of her leg and pushing the front of her robe open. Fausta stood up, dismissed the slaves and leant over Tarpeia and kissed her patiently on the mouth. Tarpeia initially shocked as she opened her big wide eyes to see Fausta staring at her with a big smile. "Do you like that." As she lowered her lips and kissed again but this time put her tongue in Tarpeia's mouth.

Before Tarpeia could respond or say anything, Fausta had opened her robe entirely, and her tongue was in her vagina and sucking her clitoris. Tarpeia had never experienced such an orgasm as Fausta gently inserted her fingers into her vagina while sucking and blowing on her clitoris. The inside of her legs quivered as she arched her back; opened her legs wider for Fausta to be able to take the whole vagina in her mouth. She orgasmed again; and as her entire body shook with ecstasy, Fausta lifted her head and faced Tarpeia to kiss her mouth as she bit the bottom lip and whispered in her ear, "Now do that to me."

Her vagina was now in Tarpeia's face as she started to lick the outside of her womb when a hand from Fausta guided her tongue to her, clitoris, "Now suck here."

Fausta could sense that Tarpeia was losing her sexual inhibitions, stopped her, then swung around, so her head was under Tarpeia's vagina while she lay on top with her head towards Fausta's buttocks and said, "Now copy what I am about to do." As she grabbed her buttocks pushed open to show her anus and vagina, as she laid underneath, then inserted her tongue into her vagina. Tarpeia precisely did the same what Fausta was doing. She lifted and pushed her legs apart, with her head in between her legs they both reached orgasm after orgasm and Tarpeia absorbed the wetness of Fausta's vagina across her face. After several hours of intimacy, they both lay side by side in each other's arms utterly exhausted. Fausta had not expected such affection. She intended to sexually embarrass, exploit her guilt to an extent as to blackmail her into a submission of betrayal towards her parents, especially her father Zheng, who she was beginning to hate now that he had the ear of the Senate. However, things had changed; she suddenly felt a deep down love that she had never faced before as they lay hugging one another when unexpectedly a servant called out: "there are two guards here to collect Tarpeia."

Biyu had gone berserk when she read the note given to her that morning telling her that Tarpeia had an invite at the palace that she summoned the robots immediately to fetch her on the pretence that Gaius was screaming for his mother. They frantically dressed, rearranged themselves as Fausta shouted. "Show them in."

"Sorry to disturb you but little Gaius is distraught and his asking for his mummy." Said Pi in a very polite voice.

"You must bring him here next time." Said Fausta kissed her on the cheek to say farewell and added as she whispered in her ear. "See you soon, my love."

Biyu fuming expected an explanation instead of an angry look and told that she had no business interfering and who was she, except that she had married her dad and wasn't her real mum. Biyu tried to explain the dangers of Fausta and what she did on Helena's wedding night which as fas as Tarpeia was concerned, rumour and gossip spread by malicious servants as she pushed by and went straight to her quarters to find Gaius sound asleep. From that day on, Tarpeia had formed another opinion of her step-mother as an interfering busybody and ignored whatever she said. Her love affair with Fausta intensified over the coming months and put any spiteful talk about her new love to one side. Although Fausta had always had heterosexuality relationships, she suddenly realised that her right domain was lesbianism. She had never experienced such depth and was now devoted to Tarpeia, and her inner inhibitions unexpectedly revealed she no longer bore malice to Tarpeia's family.

Zheng never fully understood the gossip about Fausta between the women and stayed well clear just for peace of mind and was more preoccupied with his new appointment of Proconsul.

The Senate had been reduced to a municipal body since Constantine had reduced it by creating a new senate in Byzantium. Nobody wanted a magistrate's role over the mob. It was considered a dangerous occupation with many an accidental death and welcomed Zheng with open arms as somebody who could fill that position. But unbeknown to all, he had wiped out single-handed organised crime and now had the trust, protection and even security of the mob that would ensure to keep him in power.

Lucinius and other high ranking military men were preoccupied with increasing battles, leading to a confrontation between Lucinius and Constantine. It meant they spent very little time resolving civil matters that left to Zheng to decide and distance themselves from public affairs. It turned out that Zheng had become the most powerful man in Rome and for the very first time peace and tranquillity resided in Rome, with just the odd minor incidents of mainly domestic occurred that easily disputed. Years went by. The battles that raged between Lucinius and Constantine intensified and Senators in the Senate would take sides depending on the latest information. Still, Zheng kept neutral, knowing what the outcome would be civil administrator, regarded himself impartial to an opinion. As far as the robots were concerned, life should be logical, and Zheng content, that was all that mattered. Zheng was the robots prime concern, nothing else questioned, except that of Biyu. They were the seeds of the Universe and to be kept alive at whatever cost was their significant role.

In the year 324 AD Lucinius surrendered to Constantine after being defeated at a significant battle on the promise his life spared. Still, in the following year, Constantine accused Licinius of treason and plotting to overthrow him and had him hanged along with his son. As a result, it sent shivers through the Senate, ganged up against Zheng being appointed into such a dominant position by Lucinius, must have known about any conspiracy plot.

Crispus returned from the front, while Constantine remained and started to continue his relationship with Fausta. She immediately rejected, reminding him that he was married and should seek his wife Helena's welfare instead. She nonetheless had left Rome many years ago, much to his annoyance and displeasure. After a day of heavy drinking, he forced his way into Fausta's quarters late one night, beat and raped her. Crispus continued for several evenings in blackmailing and forcing Fausta for sex; otherwise, he would report to his father that she had seduced him. Fausta concerned of Crispus's violent outrages warned Tarpeia for the time being to stay away from the palace. She could not understand and would not listen as she turned up one night to see Fausta in such a state with swollen cheekbones and multiple bruises all over her body after just being violently raped again. She persuaded Fausta to leave immediately and took her to Zheng's villa under Pi and Zeta's protection until Constantine's return. Crispus, so angry that she now resided at Zheng's estate as he attempted several occasions to see her, was shown each time she was either away on business or not available for visitors. It infuriated Crispus so much that after repeatedly informed she had already left, he returned with an army and forced his way to search the premises. Zheng had smuggled her out via a tunnel into the woods were robots waited with horse and cart and took her to Zheng's vineyard where she would stay until Constantine returned.

For Fausta, the farm was a haven, and the cabin close to the river converted into a very comfortable abode where Tarpeia and her son shared. Biyu, now fully aware of her daughter's relationship with Fausta, accepted the situation and began to receive Fausta, irrespective of the bad things she had heard. Since Biyu had also experienced the violent behaviour of Crispus when he attempted to rape her, knowing that it was in the best interest of her daughter to keep Fausta well away from the palace and especially from Crispus.

After much deliberation, Fausta decided that enough was enough and left with no other option but to report Crispus to her husband when he returned from the front—knowing too exposing herself to the fact that's it —her word against her step-son. When asked the whereabouts of Fausta, Zheng would often reply, "She's visiting her daughter-in-law," knowing that Crispus would not attempt a visit since he hated his wife Helena for flirting with men on her wedding night, which humiliated him.

After many months Constantine finally returned from the front and Fausta returned to the Palace still showing the marks and scars of her Crispus' beatings. When questioned she broke down in tears and admitted that Crispus had raped her on several occasions and if it were not for Zheng and his family harbouring her she would not be here today to speak about it. Constantine immediately summoned Crispus to hear his response to the acquisitions that he denied and accused Fausta of seducing him. The thought of his son and his wife having sex was enough, and the idea that it could be an affair was too much for him to believe, trusted his wife from the marks that she bore and had Crispus arrested for rape. Helena, who had held Crispus, a son, spoke about his violent behaviour. She was raped but never mentioned that she had caught Crispus with Fausta having an intimate relationship on her wedding night. Zheng was the magistrate at the court which found Crispus guilty of raping the Emperor's wife and was sentenced to death by execution. Zheng held his position during the trial, but the Senate itself passed a judgment that Zheng acknowledged and passed according to law. Zheng already knew what the outcome would be and for him to intervene and alter history would be to no avail since *written* he thought, *but I know it is not the end, and it is only a matter of time before blame would eventually come to Fausta.*

A few months later, Constantine found out the whole truth when he discovered Fausta now pregnant that the timing didn't coincide with the rape and an affair had been going on for much longer. Finally, when Helena broke her silence and admitted what she had witnessed on her wedding night, the unforgivable sexual intimacy, convinced Constantine. And as gossip spread throughout the palace, naming Tarpeia as Fausta's lover, gave immediate doubt to Zheng's trustworthiness, who had acted throughout the trial as a magistrate, was perchance behind the conspiracy of deceit.

Constantine had decided after Fausta gave birth to a daughter to have his wife killed, who was later found dead in an overheated pool. After much pressure from the Senate, he sacked and banished Zheng with his family from Rome and the newfound city, Byzantine, that Constantine had renamed Constantinople. Zheng's life in Rome and now Constantinople, which he had never visited, had suddenly come to a bitter end.

Zheng now confused about what to do next had to think of the welfare of Tarpeia and her son Gaius. Biyu's too was in the same difficulty, but whatever the outcome Tarpeia came first she thought. It was not until Pi highlighted that the vineyard did not come under Rome's jurisdiction and was well north of the city walls' boundary.

"Well you could live in your vineyard, but you can't step within the City of Rome." Said Pi, as Zeta added, "We could make the outhouse by the river more comfortable, and you would be completely out of sight—you could live there."

"And what about the villa with all that gold under the floorboards in the tunnel?" Said Zheng.

"We keep it." Said Pi as he continued. "They didn't ban Zeta or me—we can carry on and run it for you."

"Hm!—This could work!" Said, Zheng, as he turned to Biyu. "What do you think?"

"Well, we have no choice unless we travel to the Far East completely out of Roman rule."

"Ok, we stay put for the time being and wait to see what happens." Said, Zheng, as they started to prepare to move out of the villa and head for the vineyard.

Crispus, his wife Helena and her son after the execution was never mentioned again and deleted from all official documents. Helena tried to seek help from friends and relatives. Still, they turned their back except for Zheng. He realised that Constantine's pride and shame prevented him from publicly admitting that he had made a mistake and perhaps needed more time. He decided to offer his villa for her to reside, which she accepted with gratitude. Tarpeia devastated after the death of Fausta kept herself to herself and hardly spoke to anybody, especially Biyu who let her reside with her son alone in the cabin close to the Tiber river. Helena would often visit with her son, where the two boys would play. Helena and Tarpeia became friends and never discussed Crispus or Fausta, but as time went by, Biyu, now accepted by her daughter, would often help. Zheng kept a shallow profile but left the robots running his business and maintaining access to the villa via the tunnel considered an asset as hidden unlimited gold stores were under his dwelling.

It was not until one particular day that Pi reported that on *Planet-E*, his two other daughters, Pinaria and Oppia, were in grave danger. "Explain what has happened?" Asked, Zheng.

"Caligula is in power, and for his federal payment for support, generosity and extravagance have exhausted the state's treasury." Said Pi

"So what!" Said, Zheng, as he interrupted before Pi could finish.

"Well, he has begun falsely accusing, fining and even killing individuals to seize their estate."

"And!" Said Zheng.

"Well, after your supposed death, your daughters, plus all the other girls became Christians. All Christian believers have had their property seized, including the villa you left to your children, and Caligula has decreed that all Christians shall meet their fate in the arena." Said Pi.

"Well, what am I meant to do. How can I go back?—I'm meant to be dead?" Said, Zheng

"you're now a God—Go back as a God!" Said, Pi with such a convincing reply.

"What leave everything here and go back to the other planet, which is 300 years behind my time?" Said Zheng who had now been joined by Biyu who interrupted after overhearing the conversation.

"You must go for the sake of our daughters;" encouraged Biyu.

"So are you going to accompany me or not?" said Zheng as he turned to his robots, Pi and Zeta.

"Well no—we are already there if you remember—we left two of our clones behind."

"So how do I get there?"

"By spacecraft accompanied by two other robots." Said Zeta.

"Ok! Ok!—lets set it up and let's go." Replied Zheng, impatiently, but reluctantly, since he had just got used to a routine in life, even though he had to keep a low profile; but to return to another entity and era was something he was not looking forward too. Biyu enthusiastic about Zheng's return hoped to see her children again as she gave him plenty of encouragement that everything would be alright. Zheng left that day for the North Pole in preparation for his long voyage while the robots, Pi and Zeta, remained as protection for his family. Tarpeia and the others told due to unforeseen business Zheng had to return to the Far East to set up new negotiations and a possible return to Changzhou a city which Zheng had discussed on many occasion.

CHAPTER 19

Zheng's Return to Planet-E

The North Pole factory woke to a hive of activity knowing Zheng considered the master and prime homo-sapien to travel to *Planet-E*. The machines treated him like a King and obeyed every one of his commands. However, Pusa and Pyroeis, supreme machines still had full control, even though they were several light-years away waited to be spoken to in the holographic room as Zheng entered.

"Well— back to *Planet-E*?" Said Pusa.

"Yes, it seems we have some problems." Said Zheng.

"Do you want to bring your daughters to *Planet-F*?" Said Pyroeis as he interrupted the same thoughts that Pusa had.

"Is that possible?"

"Everything is possible. Just let us know when?" Said Pusa adding. "You do realise we will have to wipe their minds clean and set up a new life for them."

"Yes, I understand—do you think it might be too difficult if children are involved?" Said Zheng in a melancholy response.

"Nothing is too difficult." Said Pusa as she sensed the sadness and despair in Zheng's reply.

"So where are you now?" Said, Zheng, as he changed the subject.

"Oh, about twenty light-years from you. Just another 1180 light-years to go." Said Pusa as she added: "Well safe journey; we shall be monitoring you-—keep in touch," as she waved goodbye and diminished along with Pyroeis to just a white dot in the room as suddenly it extinguished itself.

Zheng stood in the room in complete silence thinking aloud, "how the hell am I going to survive for close on another 2500 years before they return. If they return?"

After a few medical check-ups and what he referred to like a few tweaks here and there which somehow seemed to make him feel great was ready to return to *Planet-E*. This time he was in command assisted by four robots and all the necessary gizmos for him to fit back into the life on *Planet-E* which was now in the year AD 39. He decided that his first port of call must be to hitch up with Doron if he could find him. However, Pi and Zeta's clones should know and be fully aware of Zheng's imminent arrival. The first noticeable place was the villa. As the spacecraft touched down in the surrounding woodland stood two robots a Pi and a Zeta were waiting which seemed strange to Zheng since a few days ago he had just left the same robots on *Planet-F* took up the same conversation.

"Are they in the villa?" said Zheng

"The only people are Caligula's guards and their family." Said Pi as he continued. "The majority have been arrested as Christians and sentenced to death, including your daughters."

"What about Doron and his army.?" Said Zheng.

"Vanished somewhere in the hills outlawed by Caligula."

"Hm!. Do you think you can find Doron and his army?" Said, Zheng

"Well, yes, but do we need them?—We can just break in and quite easily take your daughters." Said Pi.

"I know, but I have a plan where I think I can get this villa back and return life to normal." Said Zheng.

Zheng had a rough idea where Doron might be, *not in the nearby hills but somewhere along the silk road.* After being forced out of Rome, perhaps converting to Christianity or staying with his Jewish beliefs, he thought *he would head for Jerusalem.*

Zheng soon after departing Rome in the spacecraft soared high above the desert plains to observe travellers' movement mainly converging on Jerusalem. And there and behold at the oasis where Zheng first encountered Amphios, the saffron merchant, camped what appeared twelve warriors—confirmed later by the visual recognition that Doron was there. The spacecraft landed nearby for Zheng and robots to leave the shuttle riding white stallions. As they approached the oasis, Doron and his men directly took a defensive attack suddenly recognised Pi and Zeta.

"My friends welcome; what the hell are you doing here?" Said, Doron, as Zheng riding behind, showed his face.

"Zheng! Is that you?" said Doron as he squinted with both eyes as his men gathered around on hearing the word Zheng.

"It's Zheng! It's Zheng!" Shouted the warriors.

"Zheng you're dead. What are you doing here?" Asked Doron as he could now see more clearly as Zheng descended from his horse to embrace Doron.

"Gods never die." Said Zheng.

"But why let us believe you had died, and your children devastated will be so jubilant of your return." Responded Doron.

"My children!— No, they must never know, do you understand!" Said Zheng as he turned and walked amongst the men and asked "Why did you abandon my family?— I left you in charge, Doron!—You meant to protect my family!" as he turned around to face Doron.

"Please!— Please forgive me my Lord, but Caligula is too powerful, and he is a madman; he thinks he is a God and has murdered so many; especially Christians and Jews. We thought it best to come away and think about how we could salvage your children before trying to attempt what could have been a fatal rescue."

"Hm. Okay —I believe you. So what is the children's fate?" Asked Zheng.

"This coming weekend in the arena with ferocious animals." Said Doron.

"This weekend!— Okay, we have to act quick—so this is what we are going to do." Replied Zheng as he discussed in detail to everybody as they listened with intrigue.

"So how do we all get into the arena without being detected?" Said, Doron, as the other warriors repeated the question, "yes, how do we enter?"

"My God will take you there—believe me!" Responded Zheng.

"Why doesn't your God just save the victims?" Said a warrior.

"Because if you're successful, which I'm sure you will be, you will become a threatening force that nobody will dare challenge, even the Praetorian Guard, they will all fear you after the event—believe me!"

"Even Galigula who he thinks he is a God?" Asked a Warrior.

"Caligula will be eating out of your hands by the time we have finished with him!" Retorted, Zheng. Laughter broke out as the warriors cheered Zheng as they turned around to respond to Pi and Zeta that had just prepared a feast beckoning all to sit and eat.

That evening Doron sat alongside Zheng and wanted to know everything, why he falsified his death and where had he been all this time. Zheng explained as a God he had duties elsewhere and other families to support but emphasised that none of his children where aware of his God activities and must always keep a secret. Doron understood but could not help ask the question. "Is Tarpeia dead?"

Zheng carefully thought about that question and what it might involve, but he had to ensure that he had God-like powers as he answered. "No, she is alive in another time and place. It was too dangerous to stay with her son Gaius, the next Emperor of Rome and Caligula would have had them both murdered."

"Wow, Zheng you must be a compelling mortal being that is capable of doing that." Said, Doron, as he listened with an incredulous sense of doubt. His apprehension's vagueness was suddenly interrupted when the sunset a caravan of travellers approached in the far distance. Zheng immediately stood up to observe the oncoming procession as he muttered the words under his breath, "it can't be Amphios?—Can it?" And before he spoke, Pi had already concurred that it was Amphios approaching and —" he thinks you're dead!"

Zheng turned to Doron, "it's Amphios—do you remember him?"

"Of course!"

"Well, he thinks I am dead, and he is going to be in shock when he sees me—do you understand?" Said Zheng in a concerned voice.

"Yes, I think so?"

"Only you know that I am immortal and a God—so please let me explain when he arrives—Ok?"

"What about my men?—They know—don't they?" said Doron with an intrusive reply.

"Yes, but it would sound like hearsay, unlikely, unbelievable that's all." Replied Zheng.

"Ok, a well-kept secret it is!" Said Doron thinking to himself *why the secrecy?*

As the caravan approached the oasis's noise level intensified as cheers of greetings rang out amongst the joining parties when suddenly a booming voice drowned all other sounds.

"Is that you, Zheng?" Echoed Amphios as his camel knelt for him to descend.

Zheng embraced Amphios, who stood speechless in shock as he uttered, "I thought you were dead?"

"Yes, a very long story; life became too dangerous for my family and me and decided in the interest of all to feign my death." Said Zheng with tongue in cheek as he added; "now I have another problem. Emperor Caligula has confiscated my property and imprisoned my family, which he has committed them all to the arena this coming weekend for being Christians."

"Oh, my!—What are you going to do?—I have come to the event mainly to sell my merchant ware because there will be crowds in Rome;— some forced to attend and witness that Caligula is now a living God I've heard." Said Amphios as he continued. "Sometimes Caligula will take people from the crowd and have them thrown into the arena during the intermission to be eaten by the wild beasts because there were no prisoners and he was bored.—That's why I will not attend the circus.—Anyway, how do you intend to release them?"

Amphios listened to what Zheng said, and very calmly replied: " Just break in and free them!"

Amphios stared in shock: "Are you mad!" was what he was about to say, but instead gave a wry smile as Doron too standing by raised his eyebrows as Amphios replied: "That might be difficult—it's well guarded you know!"

"Yes, we are aware, but we have a plan." Responded Zheng—"anyway—enough, my friend, join us for a meal and let's discuss what's been happening in the world."

Zheng and Amphios discussed all evening their exploits except Zheng had to tell a few white lies as the party carried on until the early hours next morning when most by now had crashed out drunk after a night of dancing and feasting. Amphios had agreed to keep Zheng's secret about his return just if the Imperial palace heard about it which could ruin his rescue plan. They both spent another couple of days at the oasis before Amphios departed for Rome and wished Zheng good luck and fortune on what he regarded as an impossible mission. Soon after Amphios parting Zheng's men became impatient and couldn't understand why they hadn't already left since Rome was a good few days march away. But Zheng reassured them that they would be travelling with the Gods, and their final destination would be the arena itself. The following days they spent training and what to expect in the circus and going over the rescue plan. Zheng insisted on a red cross painted on each of the warrior's tunics to represent their religious beliefs. Zheng had remembered the stories being told to him of the Templar's knights even though it was some thousand years later he had decided that he would use the same idea that they were guardians of Christianity. Doron was not too happy to wear cloth of another religion since he still maintained his Jewish faith like many other warriors. But Zheng convinced them that Caligula would be frightened of such a God has the power to send an army.

The day before the games and the army now anxious why they hadn't kept questioning Zheng, he again reassured them that their departure would be at first sunlight tomorrow. However, Zheng could hear the murmurs and mutter as they tendered their horses —"This is madness; nobody can ride to Rome in the morning!"

The morning was calm and fresh as Zheng addressed his men: "We have trained, and we now know what to expect in that arena. You will kill every living ferocious animal and gladiator insight; you will each rescue a prisoner and immediately return with them on horseback from whence you came. I will be in the Imperial box, convincing Caligula that my God is more potent than his God. What you see in that arena is not real; it will be an image to frighten the crowd and the guards. You will ignore, what will be the most frightening animal you have ever witnessed in your life;— remember it is on your side."

The twelve men now fully dressed in their armour suits and a white cloth strapped over their tunics with a red cross on their backs looked a terrible sight, still had no idea what was ordained for them, as the horses frisky and snorting stepped from one hoof to another, after such a long rest. Zheng appeared in a completely different outfit dressed in just a toga much to everyone's disbelief as he sat on his horse and turned and shouted. "Now follow me and do not ask where we're going."

Zheng heeled his horse and put it into a full gallop as the twelve followed close behind. As they left the oasis galloping towards what many could see as just open dunes; suddenly, a black opening appeared in the desert. The closer they got, it grew in size to a black rectangular shape that looked like a giant door; Zheng suddenly disappeared followed by Pi and Zeta then Doron. The twelve didn't stop they followed too, which led them to an opening of stables covered in straw and hay with buckets of water; only to observe Zheng already standing by his horse as Pi and Zeta dismounted too. The spacecraft had transformed an area into stables; the floor supported on a gimbal and held in a horizontal position as the craft lifted accelerated towards Rome in complete silence and without vibration. The men oblivious to the fact they were being transported directly into the arena continued mounted holding the reins tight in total silence wondering what next as they waited for the command from the robots behind Doron in silence facing what looked like a barn door.

Meanwhile, Zheng had changed into his dark suit: utterly invisible, preparing to leave the craft first, as it reached within the vicinity of the circus, and flew directly into the arena by controlling thruster rockets attached to his legs and arms to land near or at the imperial box.

Zheng landed in a quiet spot close to the imperial enclosure away from the guards and servants preparing the royal compound with food and wine, getting it ready for the start mid-day. Still wearing his dark suit decided to visit the cells where the prisoners kept; quickly found the girls huddled together and recognised immediately both his daughters Pinaria and Oppia along with the majority of the other girls hugging their mothers. Niu, Zheng's wife and her lover Chen with their daughters, were on knees praying and Feiyan and Yi with their children. Zheng had countered more than twelve woman and children, which meant he had underestimated the number rescued; some would have to go back or carry two on a horse. He needed to get a message to the spacecraft to make sure everybody knows there is much more to rescue than what had initially thought. Then asked himself—'what about the boys?' They were nowhere found.—'Perhaps they are with the gladiators,' he uttered quietly under his breath.

Zheng was familiar with the arena and knew precisely where the gladiators held; where spectators could admire and place bets. His mind raced with how he would manage this; mostly if his boys dressed as gladiators in the arena, perhaps even to slay his own family—*I have told my men to kill every gladiator.* He thought. And sure enough, as Zheng walked invisible amongst the crowd, there were his boys, dressed ready for the arena.—*I must get word to the robots and my men not to kill the gladiators but just capture them,* he suddenly thought.

Zheng found a spot away from the crowds and sent a message to his robots warning the numbers involved and the possibility that his sons dressed as gladiators. He also informed that he was not aware of the schedule of events, and with the numbers involved, it could stretch over several days.

Zheng now planned that they would have to overcome the guards and gain access to the dungeons to release everyone. He would also give the word and not before when the spacecraft would enter the arena and would need Pi or Zeta permanently invisible in the stadium wearing a dark suit and communicating directly.

No sooner had Zheng given instructions Pi was already in place as he kicked up some dust for Zheng to see who had now taken up his position in the imperial box. Everything set as Zheng waited patiently; invisible to all, he crouched in a corner avoiding anybody that might bump into him. Caligula was the last to enter the royal box followed by his entourage of hangers-on including his sisters,

Agrippina the Younger, Drusilla, and Livilla accompanied by men that Caligula had prostituted his sisters too. Caligula stood alone as he dropped his silk handkerchief embroidered with the royal emblem for the games to begin; sat down to an empty adjacent chair intended for special guests or a woman that he meant to bed that night. The guards stood well back. His sisters and men friends sat in a separate enclosure to frighten to approach, discuss or even voice an opinion that might displease Caligula to find themselves sent to the arena. It was Zheng's chance; he rose from his spot and very carefully went and sat unnoticed next to Caligula and spoke very quietly. "So you think you are a God?—But you're not!—you're a mortal being fit only for the sewer."

"Who said that!" As Caligula turned around and shouted at the guards and looked towards his sisters as he screamed,—"Guards whoever said that throw him into the arena!"

The guards looked at one another. Caligula so angry went from one guard to another and then to where his sisters were sitting. No one dared open their mouth as Caligula eyeballed each and accused some of the men-folk now frightened as to what had happened everyone in the royal box then went back to his seat.

"You stupid man. Today you will see what a god can do." Whispered Zheng.

Caligula stood up with such an angry face that he screamed as he turned to his guards. "I want this box emptied, and I want everybody under arrest—do you hear me!"

The Royal Box emptied, and Caligula sat alone as he said aloud to himself—"I will torture and kill anyone who said that."

"A God more powerful than any of your mediocre pagan Gods!" Said Zheng with a much louder and determined voice.

Caligula stood up and looked around to see nobody there as Zheng continued—"Sit down, be silent and listen carefully."

Caligula put his hands to his ears, thinking aloud—"demons have entered my head" as heard again the voice that said:—"Sit down and watch what my God can do."

Caligula sat down again in deep thought, thinking *I have angered the Gods I shall do what they say to appease them.* He stood up and shouted—"Guard bring everybody back."

The royal box started to fill as his entourage of followers timidly entered wondering what the hell was that all about as they took their seats daring not to utter a word as they looked at one another with raised eyebrows. A procession entered the arena followed by a small band of trumpeters playing a fanfare. Images of the gods carried in including a copy of Caligula when suddenly he heard laughter, and the following spoken words .—"You're no god—you idiot!" Caligula stood up immediately and turned to face everyone who by now dare not make eye contact as he sat down again convinced that he had angered the gods. After the beast hunts and the beast-fighters came the executions. The first was Zheng's son Gaius accused of refusal to swear lawful oaths. As a charioteer, he was welcomed by the crowd as jeers of, "Shame!—Shame!" echoed around the arena, with a finger pointing at Caligula as he stood to acknowledge what he thought were cheers of gratitude; when abruptly echoes of boos and hisses vibrated around the arena sat down immediately.— "See how the mob want to kill you." Said Zheng.

Caligula again put his hands to his ears as he bent towards his knees, asking still for these demons to leave his head.

The Bengal tigers were released as Gaius fell to his knees and started to pray as he made the sign of the crucifix across his chest. He waited as he watched the tigers running fast towards him when suddenly they whimpered, stopped and fell to the ground. The crowd now on their feet watched Gaius as he too fell forward to the ground unconscious then he just disappeared. Caligula also lept to his feet as the guards came rushing out wandering were the hell their prisoner had vanished. Pi, hidden under his dark suit, had shot sedated darts at the tigers and Gaius. He then ran fast towards Gaius as he lay on the ground and covered him with a dark blanket of the same fabric of his dark suit. He then carried him to the far distant corner in the arena where there was a minimum crowd and waited. The guards searched high and low as the Tigers suddenly gained consciousness and started to attack the guards as they frantically retreated to safety as nets thrown to gather the animals.

The crowd chanted for—"more!—More!" as Caligula beckoned for the games to continue.

Next were the Christians that included Zheng's children and friends. Tied to stakes in the middle of the arena, they waited for lionesses' pride to be released.

The spacecraft was already hovering directly above the arena disguised as it merged with the background and surrounding images reflected on its outer skin. As the spaceship lowered towards the stadium, it becomes a gigantic screen indicating pictures of one side of the other to an observer; his view appeared not to be blocked. The lionesses entered at one end, slowly walking towards the terrified women and children as they knelt and prayed to hold and protect their children. The crowd wept and screamed in horror, realising what was about to happen, when unexpectedly a black image in the centre of the arena appeared, as twelve horseback warriors came galloping out toward the animals and slaughtered them one by one. The crowd shrieked, screamed in horror and some in jubilation as they seemed to thank the heavens and their pagan gods. Caligula could not believe what was unfolding before his very eyes as he turned to face his entourage of followers with a look of disbelief asking himself,—"who the hell is responsible for this?"

Pi had already positioned himself at one end of the stadium while Zeta leaving the spacecraft in his dark suit placed himself at the end opposite. The gemstones tied around their necks; primed as the holographic images of two enormous dragons with fire in their mouths appeared. They swept around the audience showering three-dimensional holographic flames above the heads of the audience creating fright and fear as the crowd stampeded to the exits in panic as bodies fell as others trampled over crushing and causing mayhem as they tried to escape. Caligula stood in fright with his mouth dropped, as Zheng spoke in a deep and haunting voice:

"Now this is what my God can do!" As Zheng continued shouting in his ear so he could feel his breath on his face. "You interfere with my life again I shall kill you and send you to Hades—You touch any one of those in the arena Hades will visit you. Touch any one of their belongings or confiscate any one of their property Hades will visit you—Do you understand?" As he grabbed his arm to make sure Caligula could sense pain and the force of what he now considered Hades as he fell to his knees and looked towards the sky in repent and answered.

"I will free all those today in the dungeons I will return what I have confiscated please take those dragons away."

"If you lie or deceive me your horse Incitatus will feed the rats. Not until you have fulfilled my demands will your horse be returned." Said, Zheng, as he took hold of Caligula's head now buried in his hands in disbelief of what was happening in the arena to show his favourite horse galloping around the stadium to disappear into the black hole created by the spacecraft suddenly.

"Not my horse!— Please, not my horse!" Cried, Caligula as he turned around expecting to see a figure of somebody that had just grabbed and twisted his head.

The twelve warriors were unimpeded as they gathered prisoners and took them to the spacecraft. They then forced their way towards the dungeons and released others due to fighting gladiators or to be executed as the guards just stood in awe of what they were witnessing. Nobody dares to challenge what many were beginning to believe was an army that bore the crucifix sign sent by their Christian god. The dragons encircled the stadium until every prisoner was released, including gladiators and fighters to disappear into the back streets of Rome as they ran with the crowd. With Zheng's family on board, the spaceship flew to the oasis where Zheng had agreed that Amphios would guide his family to the Far East with his warriors and Doron's help to set up a new home until such a time it was safe to return to the villa.

Meanwhile, Zheng returned to Rome with Pi and Zeta to ensure that Caligula kept his part of the bargain. None of Zheng's family was aware that he was alive and he had planned the escape. Doron kept his promise and his men too as they explained the success due to prayers answered by their god.

"Does God keep dragons?" Was a question put by many?

"Only when he has to." Came the reply.

"How did we get here so quick?" Came another.

"God works in mysterious ways." Responded Doron remembering the words Jesus had said to him many years prior.

Zheng didn't have any difficulty in finding Amphios. He knew he would still be in the marketplace selling his merchandise. However, with Rome in shock, after what thousands had witnessed in the Arena, many mourning loved ones crushed to death in the stampede to exit, blamed Caligula for the madness, forced many to leave Rome, including Amphios.

A distance from Rome travelling East along the silk road Zheng caught up with Amphios; as he approached, was immediately recognised riding Caligula's horse Incitatus.

"My friend, you are dicing with death;—don't tell me that is Caligula's horse?" Said Amphios as he held the reins as Zheng dismounted.

"Well, yes, it is?—How do you know that?" Said Zheng.

"I sold it to him,"—added Amphios as he stroked the horse's head and continued, "you know he will kill you in a thousand ways for taking what he now considers his horse as a God."

"Yes, I'm fully aware. Caligula will get it back as soon as he hands back my villa." Said, Zheng, as he paused, then continued. "The real reason I am here is to let you know that my family is at the oasis waiting for you to take them to the Far East and I have gold coins for you to pay for your trouble." As he handed him a bag full of Aureus knowing full well that it was coinage established in 301AD, 250 years ahead of his time; Amphios took the bag and said that it was not necessary as he took a coin and looked at the head of an emperor which he didn't recognise. "Who is this?" pointing to the figurehead, as he added. "Is this legal tender?"

"Look, these coins are pure gold; all you have to do is melt them down into a nugget, and they will be worth a fortune," said Zheng.

"I can see that, but from where did they come? They have Roman symbols and the mark of a Roman Emperor." Queried Amphios.

"I can't explain; they are worth a fortune, please believe me and please take them." Said, Zheng, as he forced several bags to Amphios as he replied.

"Okay. There is more than enough gold to pay for my services—what do you want me to do?"

"Guide my family to a haven somewhere safe in the Far East away from Caligula and pay for a temporary residence and my men to guard them. Can you do that?"

"Well yes but for how long?"

"Until I have my villa back and can confirm that my family will be safe. It will be sometime next year. Pi or Zeta will come to fetch them." Said Zheng.

"But how will they know where to come?"

"They will know." Said, Zheng, as he shook the hand of Amphios and wished him good fortune and a safe journey as he mounted his horse turned back and shouted, "remember you haven't seen me I'm supposedly dead!" as he pulled his reins and rode back to Rome with the robots following.

They soon arrived at the outskirts of where once Zheng occupied his villa confiscated by Caligula. Only to observe that it was still being lived in by Praetorian Guards with their families and there was no sign of any movement to vacate. Zheng decided to pay Caligula another visit at night to jog his memory about what they had agreed. But first, he had an idea where one of his robots could appear as Caligula riding on his horse Incitatus and just summon everybody to leave.

A robot could quickly change its entire facial aspects to look like anybody except body height, and weight would be more difficult. However, since the robot would be on a horse, the size and weight would not be so important. A robot had built-in visual and audio storage that enabled copy and playback the same voice.

Pi took Caligula's role while Zeta became his bodyguard, which happened to look like a supreme Praetorian Guard. Zheng decided that he would become subordinate to the foremost guard, which could easily be accomplished by wearing his dark suit and portraying the Praetorian uniform on its outer skin. His helmet and visor would display a picture of one of the many guards that Pi had stored in his memory bank.

Pi rode Inciatus, with Zeta alongside, and Zheng following closely behind as they cantered towards the villa's main entrance; the sun was just about to set, casting deep shadows that obscured a clear vision to the guards that immediately stood to attention recognising who they thought was Caligula. They passed without question as they waited on horseback in the main yard as Pi shouted out in Caligula's voice. "Who's in charge here?"

It wasn't long before a hive of activity commenced with soldiers appearing still dressing in the courtyard while trying to put on their uniforms and standing to attention when suddenly what seemed to be the commanding officer shouted "Hail Ceaser!" Followed by the group now formed in a line as they too repeated "Hail Ceaser!"

"Men, I'm sorry, but this villa now required for strategic purposes, and I need you to vacate by tomorrow." Said Pi in a compelling accent of Caligula.

"Hail Ceaser!" Said a dressed army.

"Where are we to go?" Whispered the commanding officer as he looked up to Zheng with a disgruntled facial expression.

"Back to your barracks." Said, Zheng as he looked down raising his eyebrows.

"What about the wives and children they can't go?" said the officer with now a worried look on his face.

Before Zheng could answer, Pi had already turned and kicked his horse into a canter as he shouted back at Zheng. "Come on—finished here."

The guards could not believe that Caligula had come personally to kick them out of their home, confirming what was becoming a familiar sign in Rome as a madman Emperor. Zheng, now so confident that they had fooled the guards at the villa, decided to ride directly to the palace and confront Caligula himself. As they rode through the streets of Rome, people stopped, lowered their heads in recognition and respect of their Emperor as they galloped past to enter unimpeded at the palace to the central courtyard. The stable boys rushed out to take the reins of Incitatuis and surprised that Caligula had managed to retrieve his horse. Not a word said as they quickly dismounted their horse and disappeared to what appeared as if they had entered into the palace, but had sidestepped away into the gardens. Pi immediately transformed himself from Caligula into a Praetorian guard, while Zheng became invisible as he discarded his image as he handed his cloak, shield and sword to Zeta. Zheng entered utterly invisible while Pi and Zeta waited outside and out of sight, hidden in the bushes. Zheng wandered the corridors and chambers looking for Caligula when he suddenly heard screaming from a woman that leads him straight into a room where he discovered a woman, strapped to a four-poster bed, and Caligula about to mount her repeating words. "I am Hercules, and with the powers, within me, I shall inseminate you to give you a son."

The woman who lay under Caligula was his sister Agrippina the Younger, enjoying the abuse her brother was subjecting her. Zheng could not help but sit on the edge of the bed, and as he watched, then whispered in Caligula's ear "I'm next!"

"Who's that." Said, Caligula, as he jumped from the bed twirling in the room with Agrippina wrestling with her straps as she shouted out "What's wrong?"

"Did you hear that?" Said, Caligula, as he turned to his sister with such a frightened look

"Hear what?" She Said.

"It's Hades—He is here."

"Where? —I can't see him!" She said as she asked. "Please untie me?"

"No, I can't Hades want you."

As Caligula said those words, Zheng whispered in his other ear "You didn't do what I asked, now did you?—To return all the property you confiscated."

"I will!— I promise!—I will!" Said, Caligula, as he stuttered and mumbled his answer.

Unexpectedly a scream echoed through the room as Agrippina cried out. "Get off me—someone is on top of me."

Caligula watched his sister arch her back as the bed violently shook as she went into moans and groans, and her facial expression said it all that Hades had taken her. Caligula slid to the floor as Zheng pounced on him from the bed "Now summon somebody to return my property."

At that point, Claudius walked into the room and stuttered. "Is everything okay, my Lord?" As he immediately stopped and looked in horror at Agrippina laying naked on the board shouting. "Will somebody please untie me?"

Claudius immediately went across and cut her ties around her wrist as Caligula staggered towards Claudius and grabbed him by the arm as he was just about to untie the last wristband when he whispered in his ear. "Did you see him?"

"See who?"

"Hades, of course." Said Caligula bending down to look under the bed.

Claudius had experienced many times of Caligula referring himself to a God, thought nothing of it, as he played along to appease him.

"Anyway, Hades has told me that I am to return all the confiscated property that we have acquired to the rightful owners. Can you do that now—Immediately!" Said, Caligula, as he picked up a robe and threw it at her sister to cover herself.

"What now! You want me to return everything we have taken, and may I add in some cases sold, to their rightful owners?"

"Don't question my judgement; you are to do it—right now!—Do you hear me right now!" Screamed Caligula as he went into a fit of rage, just as his horse Incitatuis was brought to him washed and brushed with ribbons in his forelock and flowers attached to his ears.

"Hades has returned you!—Hades has returned you!— Because I have done what he asked." Shouted Caligula as he leapt to his feet and kissed the horse on his forehead.

Incitatuis now a God was allowed special priveledges like freedom around the Palace and would often share Caligula's quarters at night. As Caligula led his horse out, he left Claudius and Agrippina in a state of horror and shock that the Emperor was completely and utterly mad. Agrippina had no idea what had happened, but she definitely felt a body on top of her, and she observed just a large penis as it penetrated her and made her orgasm, again and again, thinking *I must somehow have dreamt that. That was not real. It couldn't have been.* She carried on thinking only to be interrupted by Claudius, "Is everything okay, my dear?"

"Yes—just that I'm still in shock and frightened of Caligula."

Zheng had deliberately raped Agrippina knowing she possibly would conceive by Caligula and give birth to Nero, another madman, who eventually would burn Rome. He was hoping that he could change history and that she would conceive his child instead and bring back some form of sanity into the Roman Empire. *Only time would tell*, Zheng thought; walked straight out of the palace unhindered to meet up with the robots. Zheng kept his dark suit on as he clung to Pi's shoulders as they rode out on horseback accompanied by Zeta to the waiting spacecraft near the villa.

Zheng returned to the North Pole to the machines' factory in preparation for his journey back to *Planet-F. Pi and Zeta would stay and arrange the villa once vacated and arrange the return of his family from the Far East,* he thought

"So you want to return to *Planet-F*?" Said Pusa as Zheng again stood in that particular entangled room that gave instant communication with the mothership some light-years away.

"Yes, the robotic clones of Pi and Zeta can complete and fulfil the mission. My presence is no longer required." Said, Zheng thinking *I hope they will not make me stay; I must get back to Biyu.*

"Okay, if that is what you want, you can return," Pusa said as she continued with what to Zheng appeared a wry and sarcastic smile. "That was naughty of you to rape Agrippina the Younger; you know she is now with your child, and we have no choice but to induce a miscarriage."

"But why?—Let's stop Nero coming!—Isn't that what we intended to do? Eradicate the misdemeanours of Planet Earth.?" Answered Zheng in a confused and agitated tone.

"No, my little homo-sapien we need Nero to burn Rome it will strengthen Roman society; remember survival of the fittest; It will weed out the week."

Zheng not expecting such a reply stood in silence as he mind raced with ideas and suddenly he had to put a question which had been bugging him for some time.

"This game of yours! What are you going to do when both these planets eyeball one another through their telescopes to realise they are not alone in the universe." Questioned Zheng.

"Exactly, you have just hit the nail on the head. Humans will begin to compete, dictate, threaten, hate, and eventually try to annihilate one another; it will rapidly increase their intelligence as they try to strive, succeed and pass a level of intelligence surpassing each other. Humans tend to stagnate without competition; they had reached a contented and saturated level on planet earth and in the end, could not resolve the meaning of life and the purpose of the universe." Said Pusa in an unexpectedly monotone and commanding voice that Zheng had never heard before as he realised the machines were manipulating life to such an extent to reach a magical goal that would explain everything. "Yes, we are not interested if they will destroy one another as they devise superior weapons of destruction as long as it leads us to fully understand and unravel the mystery of the universe, especially time and space," Pusa added.

Astounded him that humans could have programmed debauched destruction within the machines memory banks, whereas, as far as he was concerned, the intent was to kick-start life at a particular time and event and change where possible to improve not destroy. Zheng suddenly realised the evil that the machines possessed.

"The knowledge that embedded in our memory banks lead us to deem intelligent behaviour; is derived from evil, destruction. Religion plays an important part, as well as psychopathic, racist and selfish tendencies. It is what we have concluded from human behaviour." Said Pusa in that irritating and monotone sound as she continued, "that is why both planets will follow life as it was on Planet Earth. Survival will result in one being the most intelligent as it destroys the other."

Zheng suddenly grasped that the machines were reprogramming themselves to what they believed was the way forward in understanding the universe and that intelligence, from past historical events on Planet Earth, deduced mainly from evil and destruction, arrived at such a conclusion.

"So what about the superior race you started on *Planet-G*?" Said Zheng trying to comprehend the machines thinking.

"What about it?"

"Well, they are intelligent. Why not seek your answers there?" Questioned Zheng

"A mistake:—they have stagnated—they consider life utopia. They have no incentive or drive to seek answers about the universe. The race will be extinct within the next 100 years. They cannot give birth naturally and have no enticement to have children." Said Pusa as she added "A mistake."

"Can I go there?" Said Zheng thinking *I can not believe that humans would abandon the life that easy.*

"Why?—It's just a planet now full of machines and just a few humans that laze around all day." Replied Pusa with a curious look realising that Zheng, obviously scheming something.

"But you told me this solar system was my oyster a jewel in the crown, and I could do what I pleased. I would like to go." Explained Zheng.

"Okay if you want to go I have no objection." Paused Pusa as she added. "You surely will stop off at *Planet-F* before you continue to *Planet-G*."

"Well, yes. I intend to travel with Biyu."

"You love birds; that is something which us humanoids cannot understand, love." Said Pusa as the three-dimensional holographic image started to diminish to a white dot as Zheng finally heard the words of Pusa. "Farewell, my friend, the last of the male homo-sapiens." She said, continually laughing diminishing to nothing.

Zheng sometimes thought that Pusa was more human than she made out to be after her kind spoken words of departure.

Pi and Zeta's clones returned to find Zheng's family with instructions to guide them back to the Far East villa. Anticipated to take at least a year by Zheng's reckoning, would coincide with the assassination of Caligula and the inauguration of Claudius as the new Emperor, which would bring stability to Rome, perhaps allowing at long last his family to live the rest of their lives in peace. A peaceful solution knowing all was well with the family would give Biyu peace of mind and make her decision easier when Zheng suggested travelling to *Planet-G*. But that would also depend if she could leave Tarpeia and her grandchild alone to fend for herself. However, this was a problem he would attend too when he arrived at *Planet-F*; his primary concern at present was to participate in and assist in the preparations for the flight scheduled to leave within the next 24 hours. Zheng walked the factory's corridors the amount of activity, and the number of machines had increased substantially from his last visit. He could not help observing what looked like clones of Pusa and Pyroeis being assembled and programmed.

"Who the hell is in charge at this place?" He mumbled under his breath as he continued thinking to himself. "Someone must be giving orders?—They are not working for the sake of it out of boredom!—Machines don't get bored!"

Zheng had to find out as he walked into a laboratory where two humanoids were preparing what looked like Pusa and Pyroeis as he spoke: "You are creating another Pusa and Pyroeis?—May I ask why?" turning to a machine.

"It's scheduled to be built." Said the machine as he carried on punching in commands.

"But who scheduled it?" Zheng inquired.

"We don't know; just scheduled on my to-do list." Said the machine without looking but just carried on.

"A to-do list?—What is that?"

"A list of commands that I must perform to start at an explicit time and finish within a time limit." Added the machine without stopping.

Zheng is now curious that it appeared all the machines had a to-do-list, so he had to ask. "How many items on your to-do list?"

"That I don't know. There daily given what to do, and all I know, it will continue for the next 2500 years."

Zheng flambergasted suddenly realising they were mass-producing machines and many humanoids that looked like replicas of Pusa and Pyroeis; naturally to control something which could only mean this planet and perhaps all the planets in this solar system. *They didn't care what happens to humans or all forms of life in this world or any other world they just wanted an answer to their question how to travel through space and defeat time dilation*, Zheng thought. They all appeared to look up to Zheng as if he was in charge but just stopped, acknowledged him and carried on. Some machines stood utterly still in a quiescent state until Zheng approached or past and given a hello or a good day as a robot spoke.

The hour finally came when Zheng summoned to lift off, and he couldn't believe that his co-pilots again Pi and Zeta. They were mass-producing Pi's, and Zeta's so you could no longer establish if it were your favourite robot. However, Zheng knew or hopefully knew, his original Pi and Zeta were still on Planet F, which for reasons he couldn't explain he had become attached too.

CHAPTER 20

Zheng's Departure

Helena after the ordeal at her wedding night, when she experienced violent abuse by her late husband, Crispus, forcibly inseminated her to conceive and give birth to a son, it was the first and last time she had sex with any male.

After Crispus's execution, Helena and her son went into hiding. Constantine's reaction that Crispus death was not enough had Helena and her son's names deleted from all official documents, monuments and never her name ever mentioned again. That forced Helena to seek refuge, where she took up residence with Tarpeia, accused of a love affair with Fausta and banished from Rome. It had taken many months for Tarpeia to overcome the sudden death of her lover Fausta. However, living with Helena somehow helped. Fausta had something in common; both were molested and raped by Crispus. Helena and Tarpeia with the children lived in the cabin alongside the Tiber River within walking distance of the main farmhouse and the vineyard. Although the property considered outside the City of Rome jurisdiction, they tended not to venture too far and kept themselves away from prying eyes at the vineyard. Biyu, meanwhile, waited patiently for Zheng's return but carried on living in the main farmhouse. She continued as manager and responsible for maintaining the vines. The townhouse, property in the city, and the villa located the other side of town were permanently guarded and occupied by Pi and Zeta, mainly because of the gold hidden in the tunnel below. Biyu would often visit her daughter Tarpeia which she would refer to as her little girl, whereas Tarpeia still regarded her as a step-mother, forced upon her by her father's marriage. However, Helena could not help notice the uncanny appearance that they could quickly pass as twin sisters which Tarpeia detested; just the thought she hated. As the months went by, Helena became obsessed with Tarpeia, which led one night to desire and passionately make love. For the first time, Helena experienced something that she had never felt before, a pleasure most intense of such sexual excitement. From that day on, they became inseparable lovers, which hadn't gone unnoticed; somehow gave Biyu peace of mind that her daughter had finally found a partner she loved and turned a blind eye signifying to anyone approval of the close relationship.

Constantinople now considered the Roman Empire's capital city became Constantine's permanent residence; moved most of his prominent Senates out of Rome, leaving only a skeleton staff behind. And as time went by, Helena's name was forgotten and hardly mentioned in Rome. Tarpeia, which hardly anybody knew, was entirely overlooked; and the love affair with Fausta barely remembered. The only gossip that still prevailed was that of Fausta and Crispus; allowed Tarpeia and Helena to walk Rome's streets incognito. Nonetheless, Helena and Tarpeia were encouraged by Biyu to take more interest in the business and start to frequent the villa and the townhouse in the city centre near the Colosseum. Pi and Zeta employed additional bodyguards and trained them to a very high standard in a martial art, allowing themselves to move freely between properties; ensuring safeguard and security.

Biyu knew that Zheng on is return would be looking to leave the planet, which they had discussed many a time; and she had to make sure that her daughter was prepared and provided for if that day ever arrived when she had to live alone and fend for herself.

That day that Biyu had been waiting for finally came when Pi informed; Zheng was close to the planet and would be arriving soon:

"Is Pinaria and Oppia with him?" Said Biyu with such an enthusiastic voice.

"I'm afraid not. Zheng's travelling only with robots." Responded Pi.

Biyu was so optimistic that somehow she would be reunited with her girls after their ordeal. But her melancholy tone soon brightened at the thought of being reunited with her only true love Zheng that she kept herself busy that day preparing a surprise party. Tarpeia was glad too, and Helena had heard so much about him looking forward to meeting him since they briefly met just once on her disastrous wedding night.

The shuttle entered the planet's orbit; slowing down to come into the atmosphere to land just on the outskirts of the vineyard on schedule at the exact time of arrival that had already communicated. The craft hangar doors' opened to the brilliance of *Planet-E*, that suddenly illuminated the sky and its surroundings as a cloud passed, and Zheng walked towards a grass patch with the forest behind as the outline of a spacecraft silently but gracefully lifted towards the starry skies. Pi approached holding the reins of his favourite thoroughbred; hidden for the period that he had been away; quickly dressed in the clothes handed to him, composed and prepared himself, as if he had just travelled months on land from the Far East.

Biyu could hardly wait as she organised the staff to prepare the food, drinks, barbequed piglet, lamb and chickens roasting on the spit. The music was playing as Zheng rode in on his magnificent stallion that looked utterly fresh even though steaming wet snorting through its nostrils; Zheng had put it through its paces galloping fast for the past hour. The vineyard erupted into the happy festive mood as Zheng dismounted hugging everybody as he welcomed his legendary long journey from the Far East. *If only they knew.* He thought as Biyu approached to give him such a passionate kiss on the lips; to be pulled to one side as Tarpeia hugged and kissed him too as she introduced Helena; "her newfound friend." She said.

Biyu played host all night, but couldn't wait to get Zheng alone to hear about her children and precisely explain what happened. Zheng too was intrigued, how the family had coped; banished from the streets of Rome. And whether or not there had been any occurring reprisal from Roman officials. Everything seemed to be quiet; business again was thriving, and property that they had gained was still in their hands. Zheng listened in interest to Helena's story that she had entirely discarded and abandoned with her son, Emperor Constantine's grandchild. Zheng looked shocked that somebody could do such a thing to their flesh and blood, but she was now happy, and Zheng sensed that there was a more profound relationship going on between Helena and his daughter as he watched the touching and caressing all night.

"So what's it like in the Far East, and what was your line of business?" Suddenly inquired Helena.

"Well, it's certainly dangerous;—not a place for a woman!— but there are many spices to be had especially saffron, which was one of the many reasons I went to negotiate a new trade deal." Replied, Zheng, as he glanced towards Biyu indicating with such a facial look; please change the subject!

"Let me show you saffron." Interrupted Biyu as she took Helena's hand and led her towards the kitchen.

"So you went all that way just for spice?" Queried Tarpeia who was now interested as she added. "Since when have you been interested in spices?"

Zheng quickly had to think before he dug a hole that he couldn't get himself out as he answered. "Well, not only that, I needed to get away as you know I am a wanted man and even living here, I am not safe. So I went to see the possibility of moving to the Far East for all of us; safety, you know."

"Oh, yes I forgot about the banishment. I'll explain that to Helena, so she understands." Said Tarpeia as she stood up to find Helena.

It wasn't until the early hours of the morning when the guests had finally left that Biyu and Zheng were alone. Before Zheng discussed anything about his journey, they passionately made love until they both lay on the bed entirely exhausted. Biyu hen told of his exploits and that the family were safe living with Amphios; Pi and Zeta (clones), we're already about to bring the whole family back to the villa Caligula had confiscated.

"It's all so confusing; sometimes I don't know if it's this villa, that planet or this planet and even what year it is." Said Biyu as she cuddled up to him, still naked on the bed.

"I know what you mean. When I look to the skies, I sometimes have to think about what Planet am I on. When I landed, I looked at *Planet-E* so brilliant in the sky, but I had to stop and think is that E or F I have just come from."

"So you fucked Agrippina." Said Biyu, unexpectedly, raising the subject again this time however with a unique voice that sounded to Zheng like a jealous tone.

"Well, I told you why. You've heard of Nero. He burns Rome—Another madman—Why not try to stop him from coming into the world." Replied Zheng as

Biyu began stroking the back of his neck and running her hand down the end of his spine.

"So you lay on top of her while tied wearing your dark suit—How did you get your penis out—She must have seen it; if it came out from your dark clothing it must have looked odd?"

"Well!—to her all she could see was my penis; it must have looked and felt strange—although she must have certainly sensed that somebody was on top of her."

"I see!—Did she enjoy it?" Said Biyu intensely excited, just listening to Zheng as she moved her hand to his groin to hold an enormous erected penis.

"Yes, she did—I fucked her like this." As Zheng rolled on top forced opened her legs and pushed hard into Biyu's wet vagina. She arched her body and dug her fingernails into his back. Grazing the surface to slightly to draw blood as he penetrated, again and again, hearing her moans and screams intensify as she finally cried out to reach orgasm multiple times just as he pulled it out to ejaculate over her stomach.

Hugging him close as her whole body quivered and shook until her sexual excitement finished: "Okay, I don't mind who you fuck—as long as you always come back to me!" Whispered Biyu in a hesitant voice.

For the next few days, Zheng stayed at the vineyard keeping a shallow profile away from visiting buyer's of wine just in case recognised. He never mentioned to Biyu his idea of a journey to *Planet-G*, knowing that she was still preoccupied with Tarpeia's welfare and the thought of abandoning another daughter might be too much for her.

Spending a lot of time in the field harvesting the grapes Zheng often joined on many occasions with his family, including Helena, *a beautiful woman indeed*, thought Zheng. He had caught her many times as he stripped to the waist in the baking sun, picking grapes just staring at his body.

The flow of idle words that people exchange to the beauty of the day, and so forth, dried up at once: "do you fancy him?" said Tarpeia to Helena noticing how she couldn't keep her eyes from gazing at Zheng's body.

"Oh, no!—Even though he is handsome—No, I was just thinking about what you and I talked about the other evening about having a child if it was possible?" Said, Helena, as the blood rushed to her cheeks, showing a sign of embarrassment.

"A child?— Oh, yes, I remember, but we can't."

"Well, think about it. We could if your father was to inseminate me. It would be like you do it." Said Helena, now with a fully blushed face.

Tarpeia was immediately shocked what Helena suggested after her ordeal with her late husband Crispus that she would ever contemplate going with another man after being brutally abused carefully chose her words :

"My father, but Biyu would go mad—she would probably kill you. She has it in her, you know—I have seen her kill six armed men without flinching an eyelid."

"My, Oh, we better forget about it." Said Helena.

"Forget what?" As Biyu poked her head around a vine bush.

"No!—It's nothing." Said Tarpeia with that anguished look as she glanced towards Helena who by now was with a brilliant red complexion as the blood rushed to her cheeks.

Biyu had been standing hidden behind the vines and listened to the whole conversation as she suddenly uttered. "Look if Helena wants a child of Zheng's it's okay for me and I'm sure he would love to oblige."

Helena and Tarpeia were astounded as they stood in silence, not responding or saying anything. They just stared at one another, not knowing what to say:

"Well, do you want me to arrange it or not?" Asked Biyu.

Helena looked at Tarpeia as if to say well yes as Tarpeia turned to Biyu, "okay, please yes."

"Let me speak to him first— sometimes he needs a bit of persuasion." Said Biyu.

After a hard days work in the field, Zheng loved to soak in the bath and relax those aching muscles. Biyu always accompanied him to scrub his back, wash his hair and massage his sore muscles.

"Do you like Helena?" Said Biyu as she massaged the back of his neck and across his shoulders.

"Well, yes she a wonderful lady—Why?"

"You know that Tarpeia and Helena are lovers." Said Biyu as she continued to massage his back.

"Well, yes—one could not help but notice."

"Well, they want a child." She took his hand and treated his blistered fingers.

"Impossible. How do you expect to do that!" Said, Zheng, as he turned to face Biyu.

"Well, nothing in life is impossible. Tarpeia is our daughter, and she carries your genes." Said Biyu as she suddenly recognised that facial look of Zhengs as he jumped out of the bath knowing full well what she was about to ask.

"No! No! No!" Shouted Zheng as he added, "Why do you do this to me?—I'm not a stud!"

"It's for your daughter— she wants you to give Helena a child—it will be like hers, and they are in love."

"I cannot believe this is happening. You know it's dangerous; Helena will need a caesarean?"

"Yes, I know, and we have the robots to operate." Said Biyu as Zheng went quiet.

"So you'll do it?"

Zheng never answered his mind started to think about his next journey to *Planet-G* and the disruption it would cause, but then on the other hand what's a few months, and then Tarpeia would be happy with a family. "Okay, I will do it with one proviso only."

"And what's that?"

"After the birth, you and I will leave this planet for *Planet-G*."

Biyu stood in silence, knowing now what had been bugging him since his return. *He's desperate to be with his kind and come to think of it so am I*, she thought

"Okay, a done deal. Now go and fuck Helena." Said Biyu laughing at Zheng.

This plan now seemed to be Zheng's sole occupation; he could no longer give a thought to anything else. When he sought to occupy his mind with some serious business, there was always something which he would have to abandon. Still, now his heart was throbbing, knowing his mind was being enticed into excitement thinking *how beautiful Helena is and I have carte blanche to lay with her. It's a woman which I must admit I have longed for, and this moment may never come again*: "Okay as long as you join me." Said Zheng to Biyu with a wink and a big broad smile; thinking of that time they had had with Feiyan.

Zheng left Biyu in the bath contemplating as he went to dress and she started to reflect on that night they had with Feiyan, that it began to excite her; she slid her hand down between her legs; rubbed herself and placed her finger inside, quickly reached a climax and gave a sudden quiet shriek.

That evening Biyu excited and enthusiastic went to the cabin near the river and spoke to Tarpeia, alone with Helena sitting outside with the children fast asleep tucked in their beds.

"Okay, Zheng has very reluctantly agreed on one condition that he will not do it in front of you." Said Biyu as she pointed to Tarpeia: "He is too embarrassed to do it in front of his daughter." She added.

"Well, fine, I don't need to watch—as long as he makes my love, Helena, pregnant." Said Tarpeia clasping Helena's hand.

Biyu bent down to look Helena directly in the eye, "are you sure this is what you want to do?"

"Well—yes, we both have our children, but this child would be like ours together." Said, Helena, as she looked at Tarpeia with such a loving smile as she continued. "It's what we want. Isn't it?"

"Okay, then tomorrow night Helena;— Make your self-seductive, so he gets excited I know my Zheng—And plenty of perfume."

Biyu left thinking to herself: *I can't believe I just said that I'm beginning to think there is something not quite right with me and I feel like I am a madam conducting whores to satisfy men's desires.* But unbeknown to Biyu the humanoids still had influence enticing her motions to encourage Zheng to copulate with another female.

The following day Tarpeia and Helena were nowhere to be seen. Tarpeia spent the whole day preparing Helena for that night; to make it a success for her to conceive; making sure that her father would find her so attractive he'd want to seduce her. But there was more to Tarpeia's reasoning; she wanted her step-mother to feel jealous and envious of Helena and hurt like her mother experienced when her father abandoned her as a child for Biyu.

However, Zheng spent the whole day in the field grape picking and was not giving much thought to the duties he had to perform that evening. Biyu had disappeared that afternoon and was preparing herself and getting excited. Although Zheng had been joking, she could not get Helena out of her mind, mostly after suddenly feeling an intense attraction towards her.

Zheng had his usual bath, but this time he was alone and wondered why Biyu hadn't joined him until she appeared in a fabulous see-through gown which showed virtually everything as he peered from the bath looking up.

"Wow, you look gorgeous. What's happening?"

"Well get yourself ready: Helena is coming, and you have to perform your duties tonight."

"Yes I know, but why dress up?"

"Well we shall have a few drinks first to relax everybody, and then we shall see." Said Biyu handing him a towel as he stood naked. "Nothing too tight and fancy just a toga with no underwear; as she stared at his large penis hanging limply between his legs." She added.

"Am I fucking her, or are you fucking her?" Said Zheng in a sarcastic tone.

"Hm! We are both going to fuck her. She likes women, and I like women. And you are going to have the time of your life." As she resumed: "Why should you have all the fun."

"Well, you better not let your daughter see what you are up to." Said Zheng "She'd kill you," he added.

Well no sooner had Zheng dressed, Helena announced accompanied by Tarpeia as if she was offering a sacrifice or a pagan gift; which immediately sent shivers over Biyu's body as she turned to Zheng. "She's not meant to be here! Now get rid of her! Say that you will do your duty but not in front of your daughter—Now go on!"

Zheng walked into the living room and kissed his daughter on the cheek and turned to Helena, who looked stunning wearing a blue silk gown that showed a lot of cleavages and a slit at the front that she walked showing a thigh.

"Now you treat her gently do you hear me and when you've finished, you escort her back." Said Tarpeia pocking Zheng on the chest several times.

"Surely—will do! Good night sees you tomorrow." He said as he turned to Helena thinking *my what a beauty!* "Well, my dear let's have a drink to relax us;" thinking *it's me that needs the drink* as his heartbeat increased staring at Helena when suddenly Biyu walked in with a tray of drinks. "Well, there she is—And doesn't she look just absolutely gorgeous, Zheng.—Now come and sit beside me—And it's not too late if you decide to change your mind, my dear." Said Biyu, stretching across to pat Helena on the knee as she sat next to her.

Zheng felt a little embarrassed that his wife was making the first advance towards her; *it should be me*, he thought.

"Now come on Zheng sit alongside Helena and get to know her and lets toast to a successful evening." Said Biyu knowing full well that she had added an aphrodisiac portion and mixed them stronger than usual.

"That is a beautiful gown you are wearing." Said, Helena, as she took another mouthful and Biyu sensed her looking at her breasts as she answered.

"Yes, it's the finest silk from the Far East. Extremely expensive. I'm glad you like it."

"It's beautiful and may I add very revealingly." Said, Helena, as she took another mouthful which finished her cup.

"Let me get you another." As Biyu stood up allowing her dress to open at the front showing the tops of her legs as she turned to Zheng "And another for you;—you handsome brute."

Biyu came back with three cups' full, more potent than the last, as she handed each a cup and sat closer to Helena; this time allowing the front of her gown to stay permanently open as she turned to Helena and giggled. "You know I have to kick start Zheng before he can perform. You don't mind?—Do you?"

"Well, he's your husband. I feel honoured to be able to share him."

"Exactly my dear and we just have to make sure he finishes on top of you." Said Biyu as Helena put her hand to her mouth as she tried to stop giggling.

"The first thing is to get it up." She added as Helena now couldn't stop laughing; the drink was beginning to take effect.

Biyu slid around to the floor, lifted Zheng's toga to show a limp penis. Smiled at Helena as she gulped another mouthful watching Biyu take hold of his pride and joy and immediately put it in her mouth. With just one or two movements as she licked the head and sucked, it came to a full erection. Helena sat watching surprised as she quickly gulped another mouthful as Biyu stood up, opened her gown, lowered her body as she straddled across his front and guided his penis into her vagina. Turned and looked at Helena, who by now was astonished what was happening, and said.

"Let's make sure it's permanently hard." As she stroked Helena's face as she moved up and down and leant her forehead closer to Helena to touch as she moved her lips closer and gently kissed Helena on the cheek. Helena didn't move but started to breathe heavy, with her bosom heaving as Biyu carefully guided her mouth to hers and kissed her thoroughly on the mouth to take her bottom lip and suck. Biyu lifted herself from Zheng with a penis so hard and erect as she turned to Helena," And now I'm going to get you ready."

Before Helena could say a word, Zheng had now turned to face her and kiss her so passionately which took her breath away as he slid his wet fingers down across her breasts to caress her hard protruding nipples gently. Zheng took a nipple into his mouth as he carefully gently laid Helena down to put on the couch as Biyu lifted her legs, so she was utterly laying flat. Biyu didn't stop kissing sucking, touching her sensitive spot, sliding her fingers in and out until Zheng stood up ready to penetrate. Biyu lifted her head, kissed Helena on the lips. Zheng pushed hard into her as she cried out in ecstasy. Biyu swung round to lay on Helena's head; lowered herself to feel Helena kiss between her legs. Biyu held her position as she looked up to face Zheng who was pumping hard as Helena screamed out for more as Zheng passionately kissed Biyu as he reached a climax.

"Oh. No please don't stop" Shouted Helena who hadn't yet finished.

Zheng slid off and picked up his drink, seeing it was empty left to get another.

Biyu feeling that Helena still wanted more lay across so her head was now in between her legs as Helena did the same. Zheng meanwhile had come back with a drink slid on the floor to watch as both lay head to tail; gently caressing each other. The erotism of them both started to make Zheng excited, as he mounted Biyu from behind.

"Do that to me." Said, Helena, as she watched Zheng.

Helena had anal sex only once before Crispus forced it upon her on her wedding night laying her up for weeks in agony. She thought *I would never allow it again* and now excited after watching Biyu felt excited as Zheng penetrated her; cried out, only to experience an orgasm immediately. As Helena raised her head dazed with her body still shaking as Biyu grabbed her hand and said come on, let's jump in the bath as she guided her to the bathroom with Zheng following nakedly. Zheng and Helena dropped in the tub both naked while Biyu went to fix more drinks. Zheng could not help but look at the beauty of Helena as her breasts just floated as he stared down through the clear bathwater. Within seconds, Zheng could not resist but grab Helena kiss her passionately drag her on top to put it inside her once more. He held her as he lifted as she bit into his neck. Biyu walked in and just watched as they made love. She sat close to the edge and touched herself below. She watched Helena glance across, excited her even more, as Zheng come into Helena for the third time, he held her tight to make sure the sperm cells reached her ovaries. He knew she was pregnant. Biyu slid into the water, handed the drinks as all three sat in the pool with Helena in the middle. Biyu would kiss Helena on the lips slipping her tongue into her mouth as she pulled back and said. "You know that you may not have conceived tonight and we might have to do it again."

"Oh, I can't wait." Said Helena.

All three lay in the bath completely satisfied with no regrets or shame that they had revealed their animal instincts to one another.

"I best take you back as promised to the cabin." Said Zheng leaving the pool to dress, followed closely by Biyu as she held Helena's hand and kissed her on the cheek and whispered. "Goodnight my love. See you tomorrow."

Zheng took Helena's hand as they walked across the lawns towards the cabin where Tarpeia would be waiting. He didn't say anything. She didn't say a word either as they slowly strolled barefoot soaking up the dampness of the grass; felt something bonding them as she gripped Zheng's hand even tighter responded with a firm grip. Zheng couldn't help but stare at her as the bright light from *Planet-E* highlighted the loveliness realising he was in love. He looked ahead and beheld the abundance of stars, *how come this is happening to me*, he thought. As they carried on walking towards the river glistening and shimmering as the ripples of water reflected a beautiful white light with a yellow hint. *I have had enough on my plate to worry about, and now this.* He added.

Tarpeia too enjoyed the evening light sitting on the porch as Helena and Zheng approached, taking his hand away from Helena's clasp. "My that took a long time?"

"My fault I changed my mind." Said Helena; "they tried to persuade me, but I said no."

"What! All that time and you didn't do it?—What were you doing then?"

"Just talking, sorry, maybe tomorrow." Said, Helena, as she turned and smiled towards Zheng, too, with a smile on his face contorted as he heard her say. "Goodnight, Zheng. Maybe tomorrow."

Helena had fallen in love with Zheng, and they made love when and where ever they could. However, she had conceived that night when Zheng made love to her, and she experienced for the first time an orgy with his wife, Biyu. The early signs of pregnancy hadn't gone unnoticed when she suffered morning sickness, which Tarpeia confronted her over breakfast.

"Have you been with my father or not?" Said Tarpeia with a curious countenance as she added. "I think you are pregnant," as Helena sat down after a bout of throwing up.

"Yes, I didn't want to tell you I felt embarrassed, but we did one afternoon in the fields up by the vineyards." Said Helena with such rosy cheeks as she wiped a tear from her eye.

"Well, that's wonderful news—So you finally did it—So that's why you been so quiet—I thought you were beginning to hate me." Said Tarpeia as she leaned across and gave her a big kiss as Helena turned her face to her cheek.

"Well, there is no need to be bashful—You should be happy—This is what we wanted exactly." Said Tarpeia as she stood up and picked up Helena's son and continued. "you're going to have a brother or maybe a sister." Twirling the boy in her arms as Helena looked on with a wry smile on her face.

"Today, we shall celebrate." Said Tarpeia with such an enthusiastic voice.

"Well, do you think I am pregnant?" Questioned Helena as she continued sitting at the breakfast table.

"Of course you are—Look at you with those bright cheeks and those firm enlarged breasts—and that sparkle in your eyes—and don't forget the morning sickness—all the signs my dear." Tarpeia bent down to try to kiss her on her mouth as she once again turned to show the cheek.

The news spread fast through the vineyard that Helena was pregnant, and it was common knowledge that Zheng was the father. Helena had started to reject Tarpeia, putting it down to her morning sickness and tiredness which Tarpeia accepted as a regular occurrence to expect with a pregnant woman. Still, Helena had fallen deeply in love with Zheng and showed a loving affection towards Biyu who looked more and more like Tarpeia, but younger.

Tarpeia was being rejected by Helena which began to worry Biyu as she spoke to Zheng. "I believe Helena is obsessed with me, or by you, or by both of us. She is tending to push Tarpeia away from her, which could delay our journey to *Planet-G* if we have driven a wedge between them."

Zheng knew what Biyu was talking precisely about since his affair with Helena continued, and they would often meet up where ever possible to make love; he, had become infatuated and perceived to have fallen deeply in love. "No, I must say I haven't noticed anything— surely it's just your imagination." He said.

"Well, there is something odd about Helena, perhaps it is the pregnancy that's affecting her?" Said Biyu as she unexpectedly started to think about certain instances that sprung to mind; "he's in love with her!" She felt as she gazed into his eyes, knowing he was lying.

Biyu suddenly realised that she had unleashed something in Zheng that she had not expected through the fault of her own; he had fallen in love with another woman. "How stupid of me to have encouraged him! Now I have a problem, which now only he can resolve;" she muttered to herself under her breath as she continued. "I must not interfere; maybe I should encourage it—I know Zheng; he will finally come to his senses. *Planet-G* is a far bigger attraction for him than a simple love affair—I will keep mentioning our planned journey—yes, that's what I shall do."

From that day on Biyu only discussed with Zheng how she was looking forward to her next space journey and to meet up with people of the 5th Millennium and to get away from a life that she felt was too demanding. Biyu believed he was having second thoughts as his mind tendered to wonder and not to pay attention whenever she discussed the next space flight. She never questioned his long afternoons in the fields knowing that he was seeing Helena and probably making love to her. Biyu never showed any malice towards Helena always affection and even tried to be intimate but realised there was only one love in her life Zheng.

As the months went by, Biyu became more concerned that she had possibly lost Zheng for another woman. He never left the vineyard; he allowed the robots to run his business and withdrew himself to what Biyu could only think of as a lazy and depressive attitude. He spent many a night alone, if not with Helena, just staring into the abyss of stars; when approached would snap and just walk away. Suddenly a thought came to Biyu's mind; a horrible idea which she tried to put to one side, but they were living in a world built by machines; none of this was real, she thought, robots that wouldn't give a second thought to remove anything in the way. She had already experienced and witnessed manipulation and evil; this is the universe

Biyu had decided that Helena had to go; otherwise, she had lost Zheng. It even crossed her mind that perhaps Helena had to die in giving birth. Time would heal, Biyu thought, especially a Planet-G journey would take Zheng's attention away from losing Helena. She had no option to confide in the robots; they were the only ones that could help. She needed to explain, to be sure the robots would support and most important of all to keep it away from the ears of Zheng.

It was the eighth month, and Helena was huge, and she had all the signs that it would be a boy. Biyu, knowing that Helena and Zheng's affair was now severe and possibly had discussed plans after the birth, had also infuriated Tarpeia as well; Biyu, however, would comfort Tarpeia when rejected by Helena. "Don't be silly. You know, even yourself how pregnant woman can change but then after everything, it's back to normal;" which was enough to satisfy Tarpeia and give her peace of mind.

Biyu left Zheng to himself and never pressured him but offered to help. "Look, I think it's better I arrange with Pi and Zeta that everything is in place for the cesarean. To make sure it all goes to plan."

"Yes. Please, can you do that—I've got too much on my mind at the moment?" Responded Zheng with such a look of lazy rejection.

Pi and Zeta, as usual, were always around twenty-four hours a day. Nothing was too much for them as they were summoned one late night an audience with just Biyu while the rest slept.

"We have a problem. Zheng is in love with Helena." Said Biyu as the robots looked at each other as Zeta replied. "A problem—I don't understand."

"Zheng wants to stay—He just wants Helena—Zheng no longer wants me. He doesn't want even you." She glared at both robots and continued. "He doesn't want anything. He is depressed." Replied Biyu with a concerned tone of her voice.

"Why is that a problem?"

Biyu realised that robots do not understand human behaviour. *Everything is either black or white; logical or not logical; that's all they can interpret*, she thought.

"Okay, Zheng thinks he is in love with Helena, but he's not. Helena thinks she is in love with Zheng, but she not." Explained Biyu.

"So who is Zheng in love with?" Replied Pi

"Me!"

"Oh, I see. Then who is Helena in love with?"

"Tarpeia of course—She's in love with my daughter." Refuted Biyu.

By now, Biyu realised this was hopeless trying to get a human response from a robot that doesn't understand love or any feeling of compassion when unexpectedly Zeta interrupted.

"Well, we can fix that, if that's what you want?"

"How?"

"Its just hormones and testosterone level that's all."

"And how does one do that?" Said Biyu, waving her arms in the air with a feeling of hopelessness.

"We enhance certain parts of the brain for Helena to detest men and love women." Said Pi

"And what about Zheng?"

"We shall increase his testosterone level." Added Zeta.

"But surely that will make him want Helena even more?" Said Biyu with a surprised look on her face.

"Yes, but she will reject him. Remember she now likes women, not men."

"So how do we do this and when?" Questioned Biyu

"With Zheng, it's easy; it's just a potion taken daily to enhance his sexual desires which will make him angry when Helena rejects him." Replied Pi.

"And Helena?" Added Biyu

"During the operation, when she gives birth to her newborn son."

"You know already it's a boy?" Said Biyu with such an amazed and astonished look.

"Of course. We know everything. As I said, there is never a problem." Replied Zeta as he continued. "We know that she tends to love women, so we shall strengthen that part of the brain for her to reject Zheng."

Biyu suddenly feeling reassured that this might work; now much happier, acknowledged her approval as both turned and left. What meant to be a significant problem turned out to be a simple solution? *Just tweak a few buttons, and we are back to normal*, she thought, which gave her peace of mind that eventually, Zheng would come back; more vigorous than before has she started to prepare his food with what the robots had given her to increase his testosterone level.

The day arrived when the water broke as the screams heard as Tarpeia came running towards the farmhouse. Pi and Zeta had been in position weeks before as they immediately sedated Tarpeia. Biyu acted as a midwife as Helena lay on the antigravity operating table in the cabin as the cesarean performed. A healthy boy cried out as Biyu took and washed and cleaned the baby. Next with Helena's head held in a vice as a template covering her head, an injection probe inserted into a precise position as fluid passed.

Meanwhile, Zheng stayed with Tarpeia to hear a newborn cry from the adjacent room before he could stand up to see what was happening Biyu entered holding the infant. "Say hello to your son." Said Biyu as she placed the child in his arms. Zheng carried the child to his chest as he rushed in to see Helena. She was still sedated but now laying on the bed in a deep sleep looking very peaceful as Zheng bent down and kissed her on her forehead.

Tarpeia was the first to come around. "What happened?"

"You fainted my dear."

"I did. Oh, no!—How is Helena?"

"She's just fine she has a healthy boy or should I say you have a healthy boy." Said Biyu as she glanced towards Zheng still holding the child.

It was some time before Helena came to as she opened her eyes, scanning the room as Tarpeia rushed over. "What happened." Said Helena looking up to see Tarpeia.

"We have a healthy boy, Brutus, my love." Said Tarpeia taking the child from Zheng and placing it in Helena's arms.

"Oh, my what a healthy baby. Welcome, Brutus." Said, Helena, as Zheng tried to get eye contact, she only looked at the baby and Tarpeia. It was like Zheng was not there.

"Come on, Zheng. Let's leave these lovebirds." Said Biyu as she took Zheng's hand and guided him to the door.

"But—should we leave so soon?" Said, Zheng, as he tried to get Helena's attention.

Zheng waited patiently; he visited each day, but Helena thanked him for giving her such a beautiful baby and that she and Tarpeia were so happy. Her quavering voice struck Zheng; couldn't believe what he had heard; she had changed so much, and all the things they had discussed about setting up a new life somewhere as if it never happened made him angry that he demanded an explanation. Tarpeia, overhearing the conversation next door interrupted, "but Dad, you gave us what we wanted."

"But I love her." Said Zheng. "This woman loves me—after this passing weakness she will return to her former self," he said to himself.

"Dad she doesn't like men—I thought you knew that—I'm sorry if we deluded you!"

"What's this we? I love Helena!" As he tried to approach, she lay on the bed, turning her head towards the pillow.

"Dad, I think you better go and let's hear no more of this. You will make Biyu very upset if she hears what you are saying. Now go. Please."

Zheng left the cabin, trying to comprehend Helena's rejection. *Have I been taken for a ride that it was just my body she wanted; she no longer had any feelings for me at all?* He thought as he went to his usual sanctuary spot to try to think things over. The fearful misery which was driving him mad he believed that after a few months of patient effort, *I might succeed in making her love me once again.*

Biyu knew what was happening to Zheng and left him well alone and gave him plenty of space knowing he eventually would snap out of what she regarded as an adolescent love affair.

When Zheng finally was able to speak to Helena; she had no recollection of the so-called love affair and could only remember him making love to her once, which made her pregnant which she was so thankful. Zheng just couldn't understand the situation that it was only weeks ago they had made so many plans that she remembered nothing and only talked about the love she had for his daughter. Zheng felt rejected and hurt as Biyu began to bring him around to his senses each day; dressed seductively and hid her body teasing him knowing at some point in time he would not be able to refuse her advances. One evening she prepared a meal and added the aphrodisiac to his wine and wore the same dress she wore that night they both made love to Helena. She could sense his glare and the excitement in him as she deliberately let her robe fall open to show her pubic hairs as she said. "Oh, so sorry." But before she could finish, he was on top of her; Zheng was back; she moaned and screamed as if he took out his frustrations. Biyu enticed him more as he lay there; finished, she took hold of his penis and sucked it until fully erected; sat on him and fucked him as if she was spanking him for being a naughty boy, but let him ejaculate in her mouth.

The next day, Zheng returned to his usual self; talking consistently about the trip to *Planet-G.*

Zheng needed a good reason why he and Biyu were leaving the vineyard at the height of a thriving business for an undetermined period and decided to inform everyone because they were banished and exiled from Rome. It was in his interest and the family to seek a place elsewhere in a safer place away from prying eyes. Zheng felt the risk was too high living so close to Rome and continuing with a business selling wine and olive oil in the city, and it would only be a matter of time before discovered. Tarpeia, saddened by the idea of losing her father for an indefinite period, decided she wanted to come too. Still, Zheng had persuaded her that she with Helena should stay and run the business with Pi and Zeta's help. Tarpeia unaware that Pi and Zeta were robots tried to persuade Zheng that he should for protection at least allow his faithful servants, Pi and Zeta to accompany him. Still, Zheng adamant insisted on the business interest they should remain, even though he knew his favourite robots would be travelling with him.

Nonetheless, it meant that Zheng would have to arrange to have another two robots manufactured to maintain his pretence and presence. Biyu knowing Pi and Zeta would travel with them explained it was not necessary to Tarpeia and that Pi and Zeta should stay. Reminded her how she had single-handed executed six bandits that time they camped just outside Jerusalem. Tarpeia suddenly remembered and realised both, of course, we're capable of defending themselves. After much discussion, Tarpeia and Helena would finally run the business in the Western provinces, and Zheng and Biyu would set up shop in the Eastern regions. Pi and Zeta (clones) would stay to assist Tarpeia and Helena. However, later that evening, Biyu explained to Zheng there was an extreme possibility that they might never return from *Planet G* and she felt guilty that she had to lie to her daughter with no chance of an explanation in the future.

Finally, the day came when Zheng and Biyu left the vineyard alone to rendezvous the other side of the City with the space shuttle. The robotic clones exchanged allowed Pi and Zeta to meet up with Zheng and Biyu and return to the polar cap in preparation for their extended space flight.

To be continued BOOK 3.

Printed in Great Britain
by Amazon

56302248R00123